T0270368

PATTERSON HOUSE

PATTERSON HOUSE

a novel

Jane Cawthorne

INANNA poetry & fiction

Toronto, Ontario, Canada
www.inanna.ca

Copyright © 2022 Jane Cawthorne

Except for the use of short passages for review purposes, no part of this book may be reproduced, in part or in whole, or transmitted in any form or by any means, electronically or mechanically, including photocopying, recording, or any information or storage retrieval system, without prior permission in writing from the publisher or a licence from the Canadian Copyright Collective Agency (Access Copyright).

We gratefully acknowledge the support of the Canada Council for the Arts and the Ontario Arts Council for our publishing program. We also acknowledge the financial support of the Government of Canada.

Cover design: Val Fullard

Patterson House is a work of fiction. All names, characters, businesses, places, events and incidents in this book are either the product of the author's imagination or used in a fictitious manner.

All trademarks and copyrights mentioned within the work are included for literary effect only and are the property of their respective owners.

Library and Archives Canada Cataloguing in Publication

Title: Patterson House : a novel / Jane Cawthorne.
Names: Cawthorne, Jane, author.
Series: Inanna poetry & fiction series.
Description: Series statement: Inanna poetry & fiction series
Identifiers: Canadiana (print) 20220285039 | Canadiana (ebook) 20220285047
| ISBN 9781771339391 (softcover) | ISBN 9781771339407 (HTML)
| ISBN 9781771339414 (PDF)
Classification: LCC PS8605.A937 P38 2022 | DDC C813/.6—dc23

Printed and bound in Canada

Inanna Publications and Education Inc.
210 Founders College, York University
4700 Keele Street, Toronto, Ontario, Canada M3J 1P3
Telephone: (416) 736-5356 Fax: (416) 736-5765
Email: inanna.publications@inanna.ca   Website: www.inanna.ca

For Constance

CONTENTS

And, above all other prohibitions, what has been forbidden to women is anger, together with the open admission of the desire for power and control over one's life (which inevitably means accepting some degree of power and control over other lives).
—Carolyn G. Heilbrun, *Writing a Woman's Life*

PART ONE

July 16, 1873

MAUDIE HESITATES in the darkness of the narrow hall, perhaps sensing my presence. She is late tonight. A crisis in the kitchen. A mishap over the grocery order. A spilled jar of preserves. Outside the door, she reaches behind herself, presses her palms against her lower back, moves her shoulder blades together, stretches her neck from side to side as if to massage an ache, and glances back down the poorly lit stairs. Her hand rests on the tarnished doorknob. The girl is weary after a busy day and the long climb to the third-storey servants' quarters in the stifling July heat. No one hears the odd little choking sound she makes when she opens the door. She clutches her throat, as though what has felled me might be contagious. When she calls out, no one stirs. The other servants have learned to ignore any goings-on in this room.

Her eyes are slits as she regains her composure and observes the pitiful scene.

I wear my best suit, the one the tailor delivered last month. I have a good, thick head of hair; that must be said. It is the envy of many a man my age. Not that it matters anymore. The noose is tight around my neck and my tongue lolls from my open mouth. I sway slightly. My nose is bright red. There is spittle along my chin and my skin has already taken on a blue pallor. The battered Windsor chair is knocked out from under me. My last accomplishment.

I once imagined myself a great man. The great William Patterson. Now, a piss stain spreads across my trousers.

In time (how much time I cannot say), Maudie rights the chair, sits down and nibbles the edge of a tea biscuit she has secreted away in her apron pocket. Rising with a heaving breath, she spits on me. Spits. The crumb-laden globule lands on my vest and slides toward the floor.

My God, the girl is big. How could I not have noticed? Her apron is tied above a bulge and her shirtwaist buttons strain across her chest. Another bastard. The second Mrs. Patterson will be furious.

Then a hired man is with us. He unsheathes a knife to cut the body down, to cut my body down. My objections are soundless and reach no one. He employs the knife poorly, curses over its dull edge, grips me under the arms and stumbles with the sudden weight, for I am, or I was, a formidable fifteen stone. My body lands with a thud I do not feel. The hired man cannot breathe life back into me and does not try. Words are exchanged. I cannot report them because I have not listened. I am fascinated by the unnatural bend of my knee.

Maudie kicks me in the right hip. I feel nothing and should not care. The hired man grabs her and holds her back so that she cannot do it again and I am, oddly, grateful. More words are exchanged. Maudie leaves. He watches her walk down the hallway, his head bent slightly out the door, a wry smile on his face. The old rogue. Like me, he is a man who appreciates the curve of a woman's backside. He turns back to me, straightens me out and tries once, twice, three times, to close my eyes.

Damnation. Maudie has brought the second Mrs. Patterson. I had hoped to spare her this scene. My good intentions are all for naught.

I can expect no tears. I have been a terrible husband, a terrible man. The second Mrs. Patterson hardly gives me a glance. Instead, she turns to the girl, touches her belly and says, "How much longer?" To my astonishment, she is not angry at all. She already knows.

Maudie stammers, casts her eyes downward and says she is not sure.

The second Mrs. Patterson takes Maudie's hands in her own. "You may stay as long as you wish. You and the child."

And then a strange vertiginous feeling overcomes me, the feeling of time slipping, and I am ferried through the hallways and back stairwell of Patterson House, past the second-floor bedrooms and down to the kitchen, a room I have barely laid eyes upon in life. I am through the service entrance with the eyes of maids upon me. My right eye is open again, and my mouth is a rictus of repulsion. Rogers, my eldest son (but not my first), watches in horror from a spectator's distance while I am manhandled into a cart. He shifts his weight uneasily from one foot to the other, shoves his hands in his pockets, steps forward, and then, thinking better of it, turns his back, and goes inside.

Time stretches and collapses. I see everything that is ahead and behind at once. I understand. The beech trees along the eastern edge of Patterson House rustle in the wind and direct my attention to my final resting place—unmarked, unconsecrated, and indiscernible except to those with a keen eye who might note a squarish, flat stone set between the fourth and fifth trees. The initials WRP are almost worn away while the stone itself is encroached upon by thick moss and lily-of-the-valley.

Another presence wants to be known here too. The bastard.

March 8, 1916

ALDEN SLIPS THROUGH the old service entrance of Patterson House and closes the latch silently with practiced care. Snow swirls in the haggard winter dawn and her footsteps crunch along the icy stone path. Once through the gate, she looks down the street and pretends there are no other houses around, no posts, no wires, no street signs, no snow shovels leaning against fences, no abandoned sleds, no evidence of other people. She sees only what her grandfather must have seen when he built the house—trees, rocks, water. Her eyes trace the slow slope toward Lake Ontario, the rhythm of its waves as reassuring to her as her own breath. She takes a deep breath in and lets it out, watching the fog of it disappear in the wind. It must have been heaven back then.

Low, flat clouds scud across the lake. Layers upon layers of grey blur the horizon, making it impossible to know where the water gives way to the sky. Searching for definition will be hopeless today, and it is too cold to dilly-dally. More snow is coming. God willing, the inclement weather will not deter anyone from attending the march. After months of planning, nothing can go wrong. Alden refuses to allow it. Grey or not, the day will be a success. The temperance movement depends on it. Her whole future depends on it.

Her sleep had been fitful, broken by dreams of flying, and worse, of falling. Over and over, as the arc of her descent neared the ground, she started awake, damp with sweat, her fists clenched around the bedsheets. Then she would lie awake, rehearsing new rejoinders to her father, remembered phrases from Mr. Newton Wylie's explication of the merits of prohibition. Why can she never think quickly enough to find the perfect retort when she needs it? How is it that her father can still make her feel like a child? She is no child. Not anymore. She will go where she wants and do as she pleases.

When the clock in the foyer struck five and she knew any hope of more sleep was gone, she untangled her legs from the sheets and went to her bedroom window, rested her forehead against the frozen pane, and hoped the cold would clear her mind. An early start could allow Alden to be the first to arrive in the marshalling area. If so, she would be understood to be in charge, which is exactly what she wants. No matter how well-meaning the others are, they cannot be trusted to carry out her vision for the day, or rather, Mr. Wylie's vision for the day. He is depending on her and she will not let him down.

Halfway to Queen Street, she startles some house wrens from a cotoneaster hedge. A small "Oh!" escapes her and her leather-gloved hands fly to her mouth. "Buck up," she says to herself out loud, rubbing her hands together. "You can be tired tomorrow." Her stomach is as rough as the lake. Maybe she should have had breakfast. At least a piece of toast. She had been afraid that going to the kitchen would alert the household, and therefore her father, to her early departure and reveal her disobedience.

The slapdash houses she passes occupy land that used to belong to her grandfather, William Patterson. The sale of the land separated Patterson House from the lake and left it marooned like an erratic, surrounded by little boxes on a new and tidy grid pattern of streets. No one sees the grand south entryway of Patterson House anymore, the beautiful stonework carved by master masons or the oak double doors with walnut inlay and leaded panes that open onto a large foyer and grand staircase, its newel post carved in bright butternut. In William Patterson's day, the view of the lake with the doors thrown open must have been utterly magnificent. Now, visitors to Patterson House are met with a rinky-dink, makeshift porch over the former service entrance on the side of the house that faces the street. Most stop there and ring the bell, despite a small sign that invites them around to the front door. Such a shame.

The milk wagon from the Blantyre Dairy stops three doors up on the other side of the road, the scrape of its metal wheels and the clink of bottles muffled by snow. The horses fog the air in front of their lowered heads. The milkman nods to Alden in passing, refills his basket, and calls out in a friendly voice, "Off to the march are you, Miss?"

"Yes, I am," she smiles. He is a supporter.

"Too bad about the weather. Last year we were showing signs of spring by now." He offers a smile and genial salute. "Give my best to Mr. Patterson."

She nods. The wind coming off the lake gusts at her back and she pulls her scarf closer.

Last night at dinner, her father stabbed his finger against the newspaper and called Mr. Wylie "a man out of uniform, a shirker." She reddens again with the unfairness of his accusation. Mr. Wylie is no shirker. When he was a young man, barely out of school, a terrible carriage accident left him with a broken back. Her own mother, God rest her soul, died in just such an accident when Alden was an infant. If anyone should appreciate the damage a wreck like that can cause, it is her father.

Mr. Wylie was told he would never walk again, but he has proven everyone wrong. Such determination. And there is something about the unevenness of his gait that Alden likes, something about the way one leg lags slightly behind him that is somehow dignified. It is a constant reminder of his fortitude.

Now Mr. Wylie serves King and country by fighting for prohibition. He says temperance—a word he pronounces fully with three syllables—will bring a quick end to the war. He deserves her father's admiration, not his scorn.

But Alden has decided to do more than admire Mr. Wylie. She has decided to marry him.

Not that he has asked yet.

It is only a matter of time.

Alden Patterson is not the marrying kind, or so she has told herself for the past few years. What else is a twenty-two-year-old woman with no prospects supposed to tell herself? When she was sixteen with no suitors, her father redoubled his efforts to entice promising young men to marry her by offering them a stake in the family business. It was all so...so... desperate. The worst was that odious, acne-scarred Pellatt cousin who looked at Patterson House like it was second rate and looked at Alden hardly at all.

Contrary to the tripe in popular songs, not all young women are pretty. There is none of her mother in her, whose dark curls and soft features went to Alden's brothers. She is a Patterson, through and through, square-jawed, ruddy-faced, red-haired and with a long Roman nose. Her father always says that the man who marries her will want more than a pretty face, an observation that could easily defeat any woman.

Yet, she tries. A dark cloche featuring an iridescent pearl clip on its fashionable satin band covers her kinky hair. Sensible. Not too showy. It is the kind of hat a man like Mr. Wylie might appreciate if he is the kind of man to notice such things. Her charcoal coat is trimmed with Persian wool on the cuffs and collar. Instead of wearing an afternoon dress that might be more suitable for Lady Eaton's reception after the march, she chose a tweed A-line skirt with a matching tailored jacket because it feels more fitting for the solemnity of the day. An afternoon dress is simply too flippant. Besides, frippery only amplifies her lack of femininity.

After the Pellatt fiasco, there had been talk of finishing school. Instead, her father invited Mrs. Harrison, the mother of that awful Marion Harrison, who had been engaged at fifteen and was a widely acknowledged beauty, to assist Alden with her clothes and hair. It turned out, to the surprise of no one at all, that a hodgepodge of governesses and tutors and two scant years as a day student at St. Joseph's College School had been woefully insufficient to produce a "finished" version of Alden.

The very idea of being finished at sixteen seemed absurd to Alden. Men got to marry and have children and still stretch their ambitions in business or politics or whatever they wished until the day they died, often leaving legacies for others to continue. Women's ambitions ended with that same marriage and children. Alden had made a silent vow to never be "finished."

Although Mrs. Harrison arrived at Patterson House chipper and bright, seamstress and maid in tow, her spirits soon flagged. She circled Alden several times making "tsk" noises, the seamstress and maid nodding along with her. "The hair," she said. "It's not actually curly, but wiry." She said "wiry" with an exaggerated amazement. "And that colour," she added, her nose wrinkled as though she was encountering a dead raccoon on her front step. While her table manners were fine, she was too...too...something. "Do you always have such an appetite? Try not to eat as though you are hungry," Mrs. Harrison advised. Alden was well read in the classics, possessed a good grounding in philosophy, and excelled at mathematics, but none of this mattered in the business of finding a husband. "At least she doesn't read novels," Mrs. Harrison observed gravely to her father when she went in to give her report. "They can fill a girl's head with such nonsense."

For the first time in her life, Alden realized that having a mother might not be like she had thought it would. She felt a little sorry for Marion

Harrison, who must be subjected to this terrible kind of appraisal daily. Mrs. Harrison soon found excuses to break their appointments, and eventually made no excuses at all. Her father made no note of the fact.

But unlike her father or Mrs. Harrison or the execrable Pellatt cousin, Mr. Wylie appreciates Alden. As Mrs. Newton Wylie, she will not be confined to domestic duty, something she knows nothing about. She has never ironed a shirtwaist or baked a biscuit, nor does she want to. Instead, she will continue to work at Mr. Wylie's side, as she has done while planning the temperance march. With her help, he could be elected to the Legislature.

Two months ago, while they were counting the signatures on the petition for prohibition in the hall of the Bathurst Street Methodist Church, Mr. Wylie placed his hand on Alden's forearm and told her that she was essential. Essential. Her cheeks flush at the memory. His touch on her arm was light. Nevertheless, it left a damp imprint on her starched sleeve. The shirtwaist she wore that day remains unlaundered and folded carefully in a drawer. When she enters her bedroom, it has become her habit to go straight to the drawer and touch it. Why does she do this? For luck? Is that why she has worn the same shirtwaist today? It is silly and possibly superstitious. A girlish behaviour far beneath her. The stuff of novels, perhaps. Mr. Wylie would certainly not approve.

When she suggested the banner for the march, his praise was effusive. He called the group together and told them of the plan. To her shock, he said it would be a half-mile long, telling the story of the temperance movement and their steady progress toward prohibition. "It will be a focal point of the march—a visual triumph—signifying the unified purpose of our movement," he enthused. There was applause. For her. For her idea. But was it her idea? She wasn't sure anymore, and what did it matter? It was evidence that they urged each other forward. She was to have twenty volunteers for the project, and she could direct them however she thought best.

And now it is done. She cannot wait to see it.

Her stomach growls. She chides herself. Surely, Mr. Newton Wylie isn't thinking about his stomach this morning. At any rate, there will be plenty to eat at Ardwold after the march. Alden is the first Patterson invited back to the Eaton home since her grandfather's scandalous death, an event that erased all that he'd accomplished in life. Both temperance and the war have offered her unexpected opportunities to rehabilitate the Patterson name. Through volunteerism and the Woman's Christian Temperance Union, she has made a vital connection to the finest families. Even the dreaded Mrs. Harrison complimented her on her involvement, sending a note to Patterson House that read, in part, "It is good to see you taking such an active role in the great issues of our time and holding yourself so well." Unfinished indeed. In no time at all, she will be seated at the honoured guests' table, giving speeches and cutting ribbons as Mrs. Newton Wylie.

If only she could tell her father.

Two horse-drawn carriages and three automobiles pass before she can cross Queen Street. Stamping her feet to keep warm, she wonders if her boots may have been a mistake. The low heels make her feet look too large. The salesman at Eaton's told her that a higher heel would make her look more feminine. He said this while cradling her foot in his hand, turning it slightly one way and the other until she felt so uncomfortable that she jerked it away, picked up the flat boots and said, "These will be fine."

Heels. Ridiculous. They throw one off balance and make it difficult to walk. Besides, a heel would only add to her towering height. She is tall—too tall—five feet, ten inches, although she admits to only five feet, seven. Why she lies is a mystery when anyone with eyes can see the truth. She does not slouch though; so many tall girls do. One of the nuns at St. Joseph's warned her of dowager's hump and slapped her back with a ruler. "God gave you height. Use it." She has stood straight ever since. She checks her posture now and pulls her shoulders back while she scans eastward for the oncoming streetcar.

It was Mr. Wylie's idea to get extra cars running early today. He could not have known how it would benefit her. The extension of the line out to the eastern part of Queen Street has been a boon. She no longer needs a driver. No one needs to know where she is. She chuffs up her scarf around her neck, filling in the gap between collar and hat. The twitchy edge of impatience furrows her brow. Tem-per-ance. It is her new prayer and it will become her second nature, her first nature having brought too much disappointment to be allowed to flourish unabated. Temperance has given a name to the kind of life Alden wants and to everything her family lacks. Pattersons are flagrant, passionate, careless, extravagant. They are also unlucky, possibly cursed, a judgment that has stuck to them since William Patterson made his final unfortunate choice.

But the real curse on the family is a fondness for alcohol. Whenever she imagines her grandfather's last moments, there is always a bottle spilled beneath him.

Surely, one would have to be drunk.

Another woman arrives at the streetcar stop. She is bundled up with an extra scarf and wears a hat with an oversize brim. The wind catches it and the woman holds it down and nods an acknowledgement to Alden. They have never met, but everyone knows Alden Patterson, her family, Patterson House, and, of course, the way her grandfather died. What would it be like to live in a family that no one whispers about? And it is not only her grandfather who generates whispers. There is the tragedy of her mother's death. She wonders, briefly, as she does almost daily, how her life might have been different had her mother lived. She turns this speculation into a prayer.

When Alden signed the petition supporting prohibition, she used her full name, Miss Alden Lily Patterson, to honour her long-dead mother. Lily Patterson would certainly have been a prohibitionist. There is no doubt in Alden's mind about that. Perhaps they would have done this work together; her mother may have been able to persuade her father of its merit. Perhaps they would have hosted salons at Patterson House.

Poor Lily Patterson. Alden often meets family acquaintances who acknowledge her mother this way. "I knew your poor mother well," they say. Miraculously, Alden was thrown from the carriage when it flipped. She landed atop a snow-covered sumac, unharmed, still wrapped in her swaddle. Cook told Alden that when she was found, she was sleeping as soundly as if she were in her own bassinet in the nursery. Alden is not among the cursed.

She has never found a way to tell Mr. Wylie that they have both survived a carriage accident. It seems so forward and so intimate a fact to divulge. Yet it is another thing that they have in common—another sign of the rightness of their partnership.

Another woman arrives, greets her friend, and nods at Alden. "Are you going to the march, Miss Patterson?"

"Yes, I am. Will you be attending, too?"

"Oh yes." She links arms with her friend. "We're on our way early. We want to see it all." They introduce themselves and the three women shake each other's gloved hands loosely.

The second woman asks, "Mr. Patterson is a supporter, then?"

Before Alden can answer, a third woman calls out to meet them and they forget their question while they greet each other. A reprieve. Although Alden has collected more signatures for prohibition than anyone else, her own father's is not among them. Her father is right; people do make assumptions about him because of her involvement. To protect herself from his wrath, she has kept her name out of the papers. The other women of the WCTU think she does this out of a Christian desire to do good deeds anonymously. This is not so. There is nothing Alden would like more than to get the recognition she so deserves, but she cannot risk it.

The three women huddle together and chirp and chatter about the parade while Alden pretends not to eavesdrop. The woman in the broad-brimmed grey hat says, "Mr. Downey told me not to go. He said he'd have nothing to do with it, and if he didn't believe in it, neither could I." The wind threatens to take her hat again.

"He's in for a shock when prohibition goes through."

Alden appreciates their certainty in the success of the cause. The third woman says, "And what will Mr. Downey say when we get the vote?"

Their laughter is conspiratorial, and Alden stifles a smile. Some of the leading women of Toronto have promoted the nascent suffrage movement, and although she is in absolute agreement with their goals, she has not allied herself with them. She is careful not to support a cause that is likely to fail.

"He'll say I must vote the same as him or his vote is wasted. That's what Mr. Downey will say."

The second woman lowers her woebegone face and says, "My husband forbade me to come. I'm afraid I'm in for a row when I get back."

This woman is speaking Alden's own thoughts and describing the very scene that could await her at home if her father learns of her whereabouts. Luckily, he pays little attention to her.

Had she been a boy, she might have merited his notice. He might have appreciated her meticulous nature and her mathematical aptitude and groomed her to lead the family business. But he has not. To his own detriment, she thinks.

"Don't worry, dear," says the third woman. "My husband threatened me, too." She pulls up her sleeves and shows the skin of her wrists above her gloves. "See the marks where I gnawed through the ropes here?" They all laugh again. If only Alden could be so cavalier.

And what is funny about the idea of being held captive in one's own home? The unfortunate fate of all married women, as far as Alden is concerned. Well, not all. It will not be her fate. And, to be fair, it is not the fate of these defiant three. She is going to have to adjust her ideas about marriage if she is to be Mrs. Newton Wylie. After all, she could be a captive in Patterson House under her father's thumb. Marriage is not the problem. It is something else. But what?

Women reveal an alarming amount of detail about themselves in casual conversation. After Mass on Sundays, the young women halloo and wave to each other, gathering on the steps of St. Michael's. They whisper about their sweethearts overseas. Alden is not a girl who gets halloo'd to from across the street or invited to strawberry socials. And worrying about her two brothers is not the same as worrying about a sweetheart. She knows that.

Her brothers. They have not written in two months. Not that their letters were ever particularly informative. At first, they sent regular missives from a training camp in Valcartier, Quebec, and then from England. Their letters stopped abruptly once they were stationed in France. John Hunt, the gardener's helper, is also overseas and has taken to writing the Pattersons. Perhaps he has no one else, poor soul. Unlike what used to arrive from her brothers, John's letters are full of observation: the different birds, the strange thoughts he has learning to use a rifle and bayonet, the dread he feels about using them, the boys who use Quakerism to escape service, the excitement he feels about the sea voyage, and the patriotic musings he had on seeing England for the first time. She writes back and ends her letters with, "Wishing you safety and courage." This is heartfelt, although certainly nothing like how the young women on the steps of St. Michael's probably sign their mawkish letters. "More later, Dear Heart," or "Tenderly," or "With love," or "Yours forever." She shakes her head and rubs her arms for warmth. Nonsense.

Or is it? Somewhere, she has an ache. It is an old ache, like a poorly healed bone fracture that foretells bad weather. It is in her chest. Her sternum, perhaps. A tightness. No. In her stomach. An emptiness. Again, she thinks about her missed breakfast. But no amount of toast and tea will fill her up, no porridge or poached egg. A tear rolls down her cheek and she brushes it away with her gloved hand. The wind is making her eyes water.

The streetcar arrives and the women board and settle into their seats. Alden sits close enough to keep listening. A neighbour of theirs named Charlotte Lang received a telegram two days ago and yesterday, she was spotted outside without a coat on, hanging her son's clothes on the line as though it were summer. When neighbours tried to get her inside, she kept insisting he would need them for work in the morning. "Not right in the head," says one. "Lost in the grief," whispers another. "Frozen Charlotte," the other calls her, conjuring an image of the popular white porcelain doll. They all stop talking for a moment.

Alden's father has given her about two dozen Frozen Charlottes, one for every trip away. They are the kind of gifts that declare, "I don't know you." The smallest is the size of a thumb and the largest is about eighteen inches tall. None were ever unpacked, except for the thumb-sized doll, which delights Alden for reasons she cannot explain. She kept it, secretly, not wanting her father to know that any gift of his could please her. The rest went to the church and they are likely in the hands of orphans now.

Her father's ill-chosen gifts have always been poor substitutes for his attention. This she gets by being vexatious, as vexatious as Frozen Charlotte herself. The story behind the doll goes that Charlotte did not want to ruin her party dress by crushing it under a winter coat, so she went without and froze to death in her carriage. It was impossible to know if her father was using the gift to impart a message to her about the wages of disobedience or simply buying something girls were said to enjoy, but Alden suspects the former.

"Poor Charlotte," one of the women sighs. They discuss other telegrams that have arrived at other homes.

Long before these telegrams, when young men first started to leave back in 1914, Alden began going to St. Michael's every Tuesday evening to pray. At least it was something to do besides worry about her brothers.

By 1915, women of all ages knelt among the pews holding their rosaries and handkerchiefs. In the dim light of the confessional, she bared her soul to Father Moore. "How long can this go on? Everything is changing. Two funerals in one week. I hate it. I knew both of those boys. I know I'm not supposed to complain, Father, but it's too much."

"Find something to do, Alden, something to help the war effort. Try to be a part of things. Make friends. Women are working now. There's a lot to be done."

He was right. Women took up work on farms and in factories. Even munitions factories. Others wrapped bandages or knit socks. Perhaps something more managerial would suit her, something with lists to check off and rows of figures to add.

"I don't think I can work in a factory, Father." The low light and the thick screen between priest and penitent hid most of her petulance. "Is there something I can do here, at the church?"

Her confessor searched for just the right idea for her. "I hear the Woman's Christian Temperance Union needs help. Why not talk to them?" It was an odd suggestion. The Catholics did not usually have anything to do with the WCTU or any causes championed by Protestants.

And so, it began.

On the west side of the Don River, the streetcar stops with a clunk. There is no screech of metal on metal, no broken wires. It simply stops and the apologetic driver ushers everyone out into the cold. On the street, the woman in the big-brimmed hat slides out from under her heels and her friends steady her just in time. A second later, Alden's own arms reach out into space and she lands gracelessly on her backside. The women rush to her assistance and she becomes a chick among the hens.

"I'm fine. Quite fine. Don't worry about me." Alden brushes herself off, moving away from the women and their hands trying to straighten her out. "Thank you for your concern."

One of the women says, "Why not join us? We'll walk together. Hold each other up." The other two women nod in agreement.

"How generous of you to ask," she says, unsure of how to gracefully decline. "I have a bit of a role in today's proceedings, though, and I'm not going straight to the march. I'm afraid I must get to my tasks." With this, she extricates herself from their ministrations and says her goodbyes, all the while feeling a bruise bloom on her hip.

Once the women are out of sight, Alden braces herself against a wrought-iron railing. A dozen mourning doves settle on the useless streetcar cable, their long, drawn-out calls lamenting her mishap. Having given herself so much extra time for the journey, she will not be late. That is why one should always give oneself more time than one thinks one might need. By habit, she walks toward St. Michael's and, realizing her mistake, continues anyway, rationalizing that there is time yet for a quick prayer.

Inside the cathedral, she kneels at her usual spot by the shrine of Saint Jude and recites a prayer in her head. *Saint Jude, cousin of Jesus, patron saint of desperate situations and lost causes, hear me as I place my petitions before you. Help me to find temperance in all things and to use my talents wisely in the day ahead. I know you will grant my petition if it is for the greater glory of God.* She blesses herself, Father, Son, Holy Ghost and brings her right thumbnail to her lip, an affectation she recently added to the ritual before bringing her hands back together in prayer. Three or four others, all women, are already hunched in the pews.

The warmth and the lingering incense soothe her but the bruise on her hip hurts when she allows herself to lean back against the pew. Before she leaves, she lights a candle under Saint Jude. Alden loves the saints—regular people doing extraordinary things. Their exploits and adventures might have landed them in trouble in life, but in the afterlife, they are appreciated. Alden hopes she doesn't have to wait that long.

Father Moore's footfalls echo across the sanctuary. At the tabernacle, he blesses himself and then descends from the altar and walks down the centre aisle. When he sees Alden, he greets her in a whisper and walks with her down the nave to the entrance. Here, he makes the sign of the cross over her, and says, "Today is the big day."

"Yes, I'm on my way, Father."

"God is on our side." His brow creases. "Have you fallen, child?"

"How did you know?" Perhaps God really does see the fallen sparrow.

He points to her left shoulder and says, "I'm afraid you've ripped your coat."

"Oh dear." She tries to see it, cannot, and reaches around with her right hand to feel it. "Is it terribly obvious?"

"God doesn't mind," he reassures.

God may not mind, but Alden does. And what if Mr. Wylie notices?

"Any word from your brothers?"

She shakes her head.

He blesses her again, a reflex action, and lays a hand on her shoulder. "I'll have them in my prayers." He glances at his watch. "You had best be on your way."

"Will I see you there?"

"I can't. Funerals. Two today, I'm afraid."

Alden nods. They never stop.

Back outside, she adjusts her scarf to hide the tear in her coat. The snow turns to sleet and pelts her back. To stay out of the wind, she zigzags her way north and west. Three men call out from the shadow of a still-closed storefront. "Off to the march are you, sister?"

About to make a friendly greeting, she notices the bottle they pass between them. Instead, a scowl crosses her face.

One says to the other, "Told you so. Told you she was one of them."

Another yells out, "It's a waste of time. Try to tell good men fighting for their country they can't drink." He staggers from the doorway and spits on the street.

"But you're not fighting, are you? You're out of uniform. Drunk. First thing in the morning. You're a disgrace." How is it possible that there are still men spitting and drinking in doorways while her brothers are in France?

"Oh, this one's a real holy roller," says another emerging from the doorway. The third follows. The shortest of the three continues toward her, ruddy face screwed up in anger, jaw jutting forward. Probably Irish. Although she is at least six inches taller, she already knows she will be unable to intimidate an Irishman. No manners at all. Why can she never hold her tongue? Her eyes flicker, searching from side to side for a means of escape and she makes a difficult decision to turn her back on them and keep walking, straight-backed and deliberate, her pace measured. She does not want to look weak or fearful.

She hears one of the men say, "Not worth it. Let her go." They all laugh. One calls out, "Old biddy!"

Old biddy?

More laughter. At the end of the block, she quickens her pace, dodges into the next side street, and checks over her shoulder.

Mr. Wylie will be interested in this story. She will leave out the part where they call her an old biddy. The incident is added to a growing list of topics through which she can engage him in conversation at Lady Eaton's reception. So far, the list includes Lady Eaton's kind hospitality and the beauty of her home (she assumes it will indeed be beautiful), the poor weather and its impact on the march, the drunkenness of the men in the street and what can be done about such good-for-nothings and shirkers, and, of course, the success of the march itself and any other interesting anecdotes the day brings forward. She wonders again if Mrs. Johnson will come to the tea at Lady Eaton's home. She has urged her to attend. Were it not for her, the banner would never have been finished on time. Alden is careful to give her credit. She is one of many Negro women whom Alden has met through the temperance movement, most of whom attend St. James British Methodist Episcopal Church. Hard working and diligent, they are too often left out of the social occasions organized by the WCTU. Mr. Wylie says it's prejudiced, and she agrees with him. He has changed her mind on so many things.

Her unexpected route and preoccupied mind leave her slightly disoriented. Nothing looks familiar. Toronto is a city constantly under construction with streets torn up and buildings knocked down while new ones, unrecognizable ones, rise from the rubble. And the fire didn't help.

When she was a child, Toronto almost burned to the ground. The morning after the fire, her father hustled her into a carriage with her brothers, there being no one left at Patterson House to watch them, and rode far too fast to assess the damage. A grey, choking, pall hovered over the city. They picked their way along smouldering streets while the horses complained. By the time they found what was left of the Phoenix Block, her father's most recent purchase, Alden felt she could not get any air at all. The building's smoking timbers and broken masonry loomed above them. Unlike its namesake, the Phoenix Block would never rise again.

Her father yelled, cursed, and kicked at the embers. A man urged him to back away only seconds before a wall collapsed. The smell of the fire followed them all the way back to Patterson House. Her father did not speak for days. Whenever Alden is in the city, she swears she can still smell the smoke.

But today the smoke is not in her imagination. Turning around in a full circle, she realizes she is on Elizabeth Street. Dear God. She has stumbled into The Ward. A slum. Here, people will burn anything to stay warm. Ramshackle shelters line both sides of the block and garbage is piled in the middle of the street, leaving little room to get by. Through the blur of a sudden snow squall, the looming presence of the Eaton's warehouse and what might be the top of City Hall appear and show her which way to go.

A rat skitters along the edge of a slanted shack and disappears into a dark corner. Her father has talked about The Ward. He says it is full of Gypsies and Jews and immigrants. But Mr. Wylie says that while immigrants often start here, they make their way out through mutual aid and determined hard work, creating new neighbourhoods that enrich the city.

Right though Mr. Wylie may be, no one should ever live here. Something should be done. There are probably men, and their families too, living here because of drink. Women abandoned. Alden shudders and steps carefully to avoid ruining her boots. She has read that some of these "houses" have a dozen or more people in them, with more in dirt cellars accessed only from the back. Men living in little more than a cave. No sanitation. A place of destitution, disease, and moral deficiency. A few are, no doubt, hopeless cases that would be better off in the lunatic asylum. Now she sounds like her father again.

Laundry, dun-coloured against the snow, is frozen on lines that criss-cross the street. She admires the desire of these people, at least some of these people, to keep clean. She will tell Mr. Wylie of the deplorable conditions and say that having seen them first-hand, she is ever more convinced that they must win their fight for prohibition. Mr. Wylie will nod in appreciation. He might discourage her from taking such an ill-advised route again and touch her arm in a gesture of concern. She rubs her forearm with the thought.

The acrid stench of urine carried on the wind overwhelms her. Pulling her scarf over her nose, she tries to hold her breath.

There is sound coming from the pile of trash ahead. A street urchin—a little girl of about five or six with dark circles under her eyes, olive skin, and missing front teeth—sifts through debris. She stops what she is doing and stares at Alden.

"Who are you?" the child asks. Her coat is much too big for her. Its filthy hem skims the ground. Her bare wrists and chapped hands reach out from rolled up sleeves. Alden shakes her head and shoves her hands deeper into her pockets where she feels the woolly softness of the spare pair of mittens she has brought with her, just in case.

"You shouldn't play here."

The girl looks away and back to the pile. "I'm not playing." She pulls out a length of wooden crating, assesses it, lays it on the ground, steps on it near the centre and pulls up on the other end with all her might, snapping it in half. She adds it to a small pile that Alden realizes is kindling.

This is not work for a child. "There are rats here. They could bite you and give you the plague."

"What's the plague?"

Something in the garbage catches Alden's attention. A mewling.

"Is it like the diphtheria?"

"Shush. Do you hear that?"

The little girl stops, nods, and chooses a stick from her pile of kindling.

"I told you. Rats." Alden backs away.

The girl drops the stick. "It's not a rat. It's a kitten." She tosses debris aside, dismantling the pile—pulling out broken wicker, tangled wire, and a scrap of corrugated metal too small to be useful—pricks her thumb, puts it in her mouth for a second, and gets back to work.

Alden should stop her. She should take over. Instead, she only says, "Be careful. That's sharp."

The mewling becomes a squall when the child overturns a broken crate. There is a bundle underneath. A squalling bundle.

The girl's eyes widen with excitement. "It's a baby," she squeals.

Deep in Alden's mind, the truth of the girl's statement rings clear, but she does not want to believe it. "Don't be silly. Who would leave a baby in a pile of trash?"

"It's a baby." The little girl reaches down and pulls out the bundle with both hands.

Alden steps back. "Don't touch that."

The girl pays no attention and unwraps her treasure from stained linen and brown cotton twill until she comes to a ripped flannel sheet. Two bluish feet appear and then tiny calves and the backs of knees.

"Oh, good Lord." Alden's palms are on her cheeks. "Don't do it like that. You'll make it dizzy with all this twirling. It's upside down."

The girl sits on the frozen ground, deposits the bundle in her lap and unwinds the last of the flannel, revealing small buttocks and back.

"It's still upside down."

The girl turns the baby over. "It's a girl!" The tiny chest moves up and down. There is a shock of black hair, eyes squeezed shut, and a dark circle of open mouth that wails into the biting cold. The girl holds the naked baby out to her.

Frozen Charlotte. "For heaven's sake. Wrap it back up. It will freeze. Use this." She unwraps her scarf from around her neck. Cashmere. A shame. It will be ruined now. The baby sputters and cries fully awake now to the cold.

Alden scans the street. They are alone. Only half a dozen shacks have any smoke rising from them. The others must be the same temperature inside as out. And inside one is a woman who has left her baby to die.

"Where did it come from?"

"She," says the little girl. "She's a she. Like me."

"Fine. She. Where did she come from?"

The girl shrugs. "Babies come from inside their mother's tummy."

Alden has never seen a newborn before and has no way of judging how old this one is. How can one think with the crying?

"How long have you been out here?"

"Not long."

"And you didn't hear anything before?"

She shakes her head.

"And you didn't see anyone?"

"Just you."

Alden assesses the street again. There is movement at a window, the slightest shift of a curtain. They are being watched.

"Do you live here? Do you have a mother?"

"Yes, everyone has a mother." Alden is amazed at the girl's confidence in this statement.

"Where is she?"

The girl points to one of the shacks, one of the few with smoke rising from within.

Alden pushes her handbag up her arm and takes the baby from the girl. It is surprisingly heavy. "Take me to her."

The girl runs ahead and pushes through her door while Alden tries not to trip over the broken ground. She stops at the threshold of the shack, which smells of wet wool, smoke, and kerosene, and allows her eyes to adjust to the dimness. "Mama, look! A baby! Can we keep it?"

"What in hell?" The mother has her back to the door. "For the love of Christ, close the door." Alden flinches. Yes, the girl has a mother, and what a mother she is. Her hair is tied in a kerchief and she wears so many layers of clothes it is hard to tell her size. When the woman turns and sees Alden, she gives a small yelp and clutches her throat. "Oh, you scared the daylights out of me, Miss. Excuse me. I didn't know she'd brought someone in." She scowls at the girl. "Shut the door. You know better."

The girl pulls Alden away from the door by her coat sleeve and pushes the door shut by leaning her shoulder into it until it lodges in the fame. The windows are covered in newspaper and only shards of light land in the small room. Alden holds the baby out to her. "This baby. It was outside. In the street. In the garbage."

The woman recoils. "Well, it ain't mine, I can tell you that. I have enough trouble already."

"My name is Harriet," the girl says and then spells it. "H-A-R-R-I-E-T. Mama, can we keep it?"

"No."

Alden asks, "Do you know whose it could be?"

"Looks to me like whosoever's it was, they didn't much want it."

Harriet throws her giant coat on the floor and dances around her mother, her nose running. "Her. She's a she. I want her. Can we keep her? I'll look after her, I promise."

"It's not a stray cat." Harriet's mother sighs, lifts the baby from Alden's arms, unwraps it, fingers the scarf and says, "Yours?"

Alden nods. The baby's cries diminish to snuffles.

The woman lays the baby on the table. Harriet climbs up on the table and coos. "Can we keep her?"

"No, Harriet. We can't keep it."

"Her!"

The woman holds the scarf out to Alden. Alden examines it and lays it over her arm. The baby flexes and curls, throws its arms open, and lets loose a cry that seems impossible from such a small body. The woman assesses the umbilical cord with a practiced eye. "Maybe two days old," she says. "No older. Someone tried. It's been fed. It's clean. What a shame."

"*She's* been fed," says Harriet.

Another baby starts to cry. "Go settle your brother. This one will wake the dead."

For the first time, Alden notices another baby squirming on a cot in the corner.

"Your girl says she didn't see anyone."

"I told you my name is Harriet."

"Shush. For once in your life, be quiet." Harriet's mother goes to a cupboard and searches for something, comes back with a cloth, and hands it to Alden. "You'll need this." Alden holds it between her thumb and index finger and holds it up.

"For a diaper."

"Oh." She turns it over once and then again. "I'm sorry, I have never—I don't know how—"

The woman sighs and takes it back. "You'd better watch then." She folds flannel with chapped hands.

If only Alden had paid attention to where she was, she would have been at the march already. She frets about the banner. Who will manage the banner? She wanted to remind the processionists to hold the banner straight and keep a steady distance between them so that it does not droop or fold and will remain easy to read. The whole endeavour requires military precision.

The baby gears up for another squall. Alden has completely missed the diapering lesson. Harriet's mother softens and brings the baby to her shoulder. She clucks, "I guess we'd better feed you or you'll wake up my own baby and we don't want that, do we?"

Harriet's mother sits in a chair, loosens her shawl, two cardigans underneath, and unbuttons her shirtwaist, revealing a swollen, blue-veined breast with a nipple so large and dark it could not be less like Alden's. Alden has never seen or imagined such a thing. The baby moves its head from side to side and continues to cry. The woman squeezes her breast and, to Alden's astonishment, milk sprays out. She wipes some onto her finger, brushes it over the baby's lips, and then directs her nipple into the baby's mouth. The room is quiet.

"There you go," she says. A sucking sound accompanies the baby's swallows. Realizing she is staring, Alden turns away. Harriet shows Alden the little brother who has miraculously fallen back to sleep.

"Look. This is our baby, Herbert. H-E-R-B-E-R-T. I'm very good at looking after him."

"I'm sure you are," says Alden.

"And I'll be very good at looking after the new baby. I'll take the best care of her."

When the baby drifts off the breast, the woman lifts it across her shoulder and pats its back. Then she hands it to Alden, who fumbles.

"Keep it upright, up against your shoulder. Keep patting."

"Can I name her?" the little girl says. "She should be called Grace. G-R-A-C-E."

"Here." Harriet's mother hands Alden another rag. "Lay this on your shoulder in case she spits up. You wouldn't want to spoil your coat." Alden cannot tell if the women's concern is genuine but suspects it is not. How must she look to this woman? Her coat is ripped. She does not know how to hold or feed or diaper a baby. Alden tries to wrap the scarf around the baby while she is holding it in her arms and the baby whimpers.

"Do it like this." The woman lifts the baby again and holds it with one arm while spreading out Alden's scarf on the table with the other. She folds the scarf over and lays the baby down gently in the centre, wrapping her tight and leaving a flap at her head. "Pull this over her face and head, like a hat. Keep it loose though."

Once in Alden's uncertain arms, the baby opens its unfocused eyes. They are a grey deeper than the deepest part of Lake Ontario and full of inestimable need. Alden shudders and pulls the top edge of the scarf over the baby's face.

"What should we do?"

"We? All due respect, Miss, I'm not the one who found her."

"Finders keepers," says Harriet. "I want to keep her."

"It's a baby," says Alden. "It doesn't work like that."

"Why not?"

"Because it doesn't."

"How does it work, then?"

Alden has no idea.

*

No one knows how anything works. I used to think the afterlife would bring clarity. My ignorance was boundless. Apparently, it still is.

It has taken me years to understand what I can and cannot do in my purgatory. Even so, I am sometimes surprised. I spent a generation trying to "do" something. Tip a tobacco tin off a counter. Change someone's mind. Useless.

Alden is the only one I've been able to follow from the house. If only she would go to more interesting places. So much time at the damned church. But today—an adventure! And to think I had almost stopped following her at all. I almost stayed in Maudie's room, the site of my last minutes alive. I like it there. I look out the high window where I can catch a glimpse of the lake through the trees. But I digress.

Alden does not remember the day that she was found all alone in the snow. How could she? She was just a baby. But I do. And here is another baby, cold in the snow. How many can there be in one story?

Dignified as always, Alden did not cry out to be found. Well-tucked into her swaddle, warmth left her body so slowly that she barely noticed her growing discomfort. Then sleep overtook her. Another hour and she would have been frozen almost solid, her skin covered with frost, her watery blue eyes sealed shut, her little heart silent, still slightly soft at the centre, an easy feast for a wolf or coyote.

Of course, I could do nothing. This is the nature of purgatory.

I worried, even as I knew she would be found. But would she be found? What I think will happen sometimes does not happen at all. My sense of the future is as unreliable as my sense of the past.

I did not leave her side, though. Then, a neighbour, about to give up, found her before it was too late. The call rose above the rutted road and between the pines. "Over here! The baby is here! She's alive!" Another said, "Thank the Good Lord. A miracle. Look how far she was thrown." Yet another said, "God was watching out for her."

No one mentioned that God must not have been watching out for poor Lily Patterson when her buggy hit that rut with such force and overturned. No one raised the matter of the capricious nature of God's attentions, His unfathomable choices. No one except me.

*

Back on the street, Alden adjusts the baby inside her coat, raises her eyes to the heavens, and asks, "Why me, God?"

Her shoulder seam gives a little more and she feels a chill on her back.

The city is awake. More people are on the street, gathering for the march or off to work or wherever they go, heads down against the weather. Horses and cars compete for space. She will never get used to the jolt of a backfire or those infernal horns. The smell of manure is almost pleasant compared to the choking clouds of automobile exhaust if only because of its familiarity.

Everyone has a mother. The phrase rings in her ears. The child is not wrong, but so much can happen to alter the fact. Mothers disappear. They die. Her chest tightens. She does not know enough about her own mother or any of the mothers in her family. William Patterson must have had a mother. Nothing is known about either of his parents. What is known is that he boarded a ship from England at age ten, all alone, and never looked back. The first Mrs. Patterson, Agnes, died in childbirth, her son following her just a week later. "To keep her company," or so went the story. Sentimental drivel. Surely any woman would have exhorted the child to stay on this earthly plane, having gone to so much trouble to bring him into the world.

Agnes, the first Mrs. Patterson, was the cousin of Bishop Strachan. She lived in England when the marriage was arranged. Everything is known about the Strachan family because of the Bishop. The lives of men are recorded and studied. Who bothers to record the lives of mothers? The Strachan family was William Patterson's connection to the Toronto elite. Agnes was a Protestant, of course, as was William Patterson. She was to make Patterson House a place of refinement and culture, a place that others would gravitate toward. But the sense of adventure, which she assured both the Bishop and William Patterson that she wholeheartedly embodied, evaporated on the ocean voyage from England. She took ill. Frailty became Agnes's defining characteristic. When she disembarked from the Patterson Lumber and Stone ship and was deposited on the little beach, she faced a wall of mosquitos and biting black flies between the water and the still unfinished house and begged to return to London. The Bishop blamed William Patterson for her unhappiness.

How Alden knows this story, she cannot say. How does Alden know anything about her family? Did her brothers tell her? More likely the servants, with their long memories and sly opinions.

Her grandmother, the second Mrs. Patterson, Ruth, mother of Rogers Patterson, was Catholic. The marriage put William Patterson on the outs with the powers that be. No one wanted to do business with a papist. Not that he converted. But he did agree to let any children from the union be raised in the church and that was bad enough. As it turns out, Rogers, her father, does not attend church at all, although she has been told that before her mother died, he was devout.

Her devotion to Father Moore bothers her father. That's fine with her. It has become Alden's habit to talk about Mass, the happenings at St. Michael's Cathedral, and Father Moore far more than necessary.

It occurs to Alden to walk back to the cathedral and give the baby to Father Moore when she notices two policemen kitty-corner across the intersection and breaks away from the westward flow of the increasing traffic to intercept them.

The baby cries again. The scarf falls from its head. A heavy-set woman on the sidewalk catches Alden's eye, scowls, and says, "That baby's not warm enough. You shouldn't have him out on a day like this. And without a hat."

"You don't understand. It's not mine."

"What difference does that make?" She tut-tuts and walks off, shaking her head.

Alden flushes and tries to tuck the baby deeper inside her coat, pulling the scarf closer around its head, which lies like a massive goiter against her neck. The snow has slowed to a few flakes and the street is slick with icy patches and horse manure. A few shopkeepers throw down sand or sawdust outside of their doors, but for the most part, the ice is treacherous as the day warms. Pigeons squawk from the rooftops, agitated by all the activity on the street. The crowd is growing by the minute. The sooner she can get this baby to the authorities, the better.

An Eaton's delivery wagon is stuck in the intersection, surrounded by pedestrians. The driver hops down from his seat to lead the chestnut horse into an empty alley before it spooks. Alden darts in behind the wagon, seizing upon the sudden space.

The committee estimated that twenty thousand people would attend the parade. The biggest crowd Alden has ever been in before was two years ago when her brothers left for the war. About two thousand people were in Don Station to see off the 15th Battalion of the 48th Highlanders. Trains, carriages, cars, and men crowded the space and she feared she would be crushed against the steel girders of the bridge. This mob feels just as threatening. Her heart pounds. By the time she reaches the two policemen, she is panting.

"Excuse me," she says. "Can you help me please? I found a baby. I need to turn it over to the authorities." Her awkward attempt to show the baby inside her coat results in a button snapping off and falling to the ground. Carved mother of pearl with a star at the centre. The foot of a passerby kicks it. It is doomed. She will never find a match.

"We're very busy here, Ma'am."

"So am I." She stamps her foot. Any minute, the parade will start without her. She shifts the weight of the whining baby inside her coat and a stout man jostles her from behind.

"If I were you, I'd get that baby home."

"But it's not mine. I found it. I can't keep it. There has to be a procedure to follow when a baby is found."

"Found, you say? Where?"

Finally, he seems to be paying attention. "In The Ward."

"The Ward, you say?" Now she has his full attention.

The other policeman keeps his eyes further down the street and says, "We don't have time for this. Don't you see what's happening here? They've left us thin. Go to the station. They'll help you there."

The murmur of the crowd rises with a few shouts and two men run by with a barking dog. The word "coward" sails above them and a woman screams.

The police bolt toward half a dozen men, their nightsticks in the air.

Alden backs away. The police crack their batons over the backs and arms of men who appear to want nothing more than to get out of the way. The committee was so sure they would win the day. Over eight hundred thousand signatures in support of prohibition. How could there be anyone left to object?

If her father were here, he would gloat.

The very thought of it gives her courage.

Toronto General Hospital is not far up the block. Perhaps she can leave the baby there.

At the entrance, she is told to go the short distance to the Hospital for Sick Children back at the corner of Elizabeth Street. She's going in circles. It's her own fault. She should have thought of that in the first place. Meanwhile, every second spent trying to get this baby into the proper hands takes her further from the march. She has already lost the opportunity to give her final instructions to the banner bearers and missed meeting the motor cars. A place was made for her to ride the length of the parade route in an automobile donated by the Austin family for the day. She hoped one of the Austin girls would be riding in the car with her, and next year she would finally be invited to their annual garden party. None of that will happen now.

Instead of making her way through the crowd, she skirts along the edges of the buildings, sharp-eyed for any men loitering in doorways who may try to challenge her like those good-for-nothings did this morning.

In the quiet of the foyer of the children's hospital, the clerk listens patiently to her story, shakes her head at all the right times, and calls for a starched nurse in training who takes the baby from Alden's aching arms with cheerful efficiency. Finally.

"Thank you." Alden turns to leave.

The clerk says, "No, Miss Patterson, I must ask you to stay. You'll have to meet the doctor. He will have questions."

The clock on the wall strikes a quarter of ten. Patience. The cousin of temperance. Temperance in all things. What difference will a few more minutes make? She is already hopelessly late.

The nurse is probably two or three years younger than Alden and far more knowledgeable about babies. She chirps and clucks and knows exactly what to do. She leads Alden to a bright room lined with drawers and counters. Here, the nurse sponges down the baby, changes the diaper, finds a little gown, wraps her in a fresh flannel blanket, and pops a hat on her head in a matter of minutes while Alden tells the story of her day.

"It's a miracle you were there to find the baby. You saved her life, Miss Patterson."

"No—" Maybe she did. She does not think of it that way. Anyway, it was the child. Harriet. "Please don't say that." It feels like an obligation. "I am simply trying to settle this matter with the proper authorities, to do the right thing. The next person would have done the same."

"It's a good Christian deed you're doing, on the way to another good Christian deed. You're to be commended. And this little darling here," she pats the blanket, "what would have become of her? She would have frozen to death. I'm sure of it. Who knows when the next person might have come along?" She holds the baby out to Alden. "Would you like to hold her?"

Alden steps back.

"That's all right," says the nurse. "I can see it's been quite a morning. You rest. This is all very upsetting, a mother leaving a baby like that. What kind of mother would do such a thing? It's hard to imagine what would go through a woman's mind. And in the garbage! It's the devil at play. I'm afraid to say, we see it all here." The girl talks like she is ancient. "Try not to think about it. We can't know, nor should we know, such thoughts. You finding the little one is God's work. If it weren't for you, the world would have lost a little soul today."

Maybe this nurse is right. Maybe it is God's will that she found this baby. Why else would she have bothered to say a word to Harriet or stay while the girl searched through garbage looking for a rat? *It was supposed to be a rat.*

Alden leans against the door jamb. She is an imposter, receiving credit for a good deed she never wanted to do. No wonder this does not feel like God's work. The day has been unlucky from the start. Maybe it is the devil at play. The child is so dark. A Gypsy, no doubt. Those eyes. Those needy grey eyes. Maybe Alden is cursed after all. Maybe it is the baby who is cursed. Feverish, she loosens her coat.

"You're pale, Miss Patterson. You need to sit down." The nurse's efficiency is diverted from the baby and applied to Alden momentarily. A chair and a cold compress appear from out of thin air. "It really has been quite a shock, hasn't it? Don't worry. The baby is in good hands now, isn't she? She's got you to protect her."

The nurse's words curdle in Alden's stomach. Her eyes dart to the door. The room is so small and hot. Rising to leave, she waves the nurse's hand away from her forehead.

At that moment, a doctor enters, already talking. "What do we have here? A foundling, they say?" Like an actor on a stage, he gobbles up all the air in the room. Extending his hand, he says, "I'm Dr. Clement. And you are the one who found her?" He looks at his notes. "Miss Alden Patterson? Daughter of Rogers? Can it be?" He peers above his glasses. Alden tries to speak and is cut off. "Good heavens. You're the spitting image of him. Good old Rogers. We first met when this place was being built, you know. A very generous man, your father. What on earth were you doing in The Ward, my dear?"

"I was lost."

"Lost? Indeed. 'I once was lost, but now am found.' The Ward is no place for a woman like you. In the future, make sure your father's man drives you. You shouldn't be out alone on the streets getting lost, should you? You young women. Don't you all want your independence? And don't I know it? How many have I got at home? Three? Four?" He laughs. "Will they never be married? Now," he says, rubbing his hands together, "your father is a friend to this hospital and therefore a friend to me. We haven't seen him in months. How is he? Well, I assume?"

Alden nods. She has never heard such an odd way of speaking, question after question without space for a breath let alone an answer. No wonder her father hasn't seen this tiresome man in ages.

"Extend my great and warm regards to him and the regards of all of us at the hospital, will you? And won't your father be proud of your efforts today?" Alden keeps herself from wincing. "Let's have a look at this little one, shall we?" He looks at the nurse.

"Baby girl, doctor. Two days old, I would guess." She loosens the swaddle and places her on the examining table. "Umbilical cord stump still attached." The baby begins to whine and makes tiny grasping fists.

"A fighter. That's good, isn't it?" He loosens the gown and diaper, examines her mouth and ears and checks her umbilical cord. "She's got a good set of lungs, doesn't she? You've done a good job here. She's clean and dry and fit as a fiddle. This baby is as healthy as you or me, isn't she? You can take her home now." He makes a note, tucks his papers under his arm and moves to the door.

"Home?" The new pitch of the baby's cry demands attention. Alden is focused only on the doctor. The nurse picks the baby up and pats her back. "Doctor, have you forgotten? This baby has no home."

"Oh right. Of course."

"I thought I could leave it here."

"The baby's not sick, Miss Patterson. This hospital is for *sick* children." He chuckles a bit. "And we must be grateful this little one is not sick, mustn't we? May I suggest the police then, Miss Patterson? Wouldn't they be the best place to report something like this? I do applaud you for thinking of the baby's health first. Wise beyond your years, aren't you? Well done, my dear. Isn't it well done?" he asks the nurse.

The nurse nods in vigorous agreement.

Alden straightens her shoulders and buttons her coat again. The gap where her button has popped off is marked by loose threads. "I think you've lost a button there, haven't you?" he says, pointing. "Give my best to your father, will you? Tell him not to worry about the bill. It's on me." He leaves the room, still talking. "Old Rogers Patterson. I'll be darned."

Alden shuts her eyes for a moment. Temperance in all things. She holds out her arms for the baby. The nurse whips a small cloth off her shoulder, places it on Alden's, and gracefully passes the baby. Once it is in Alden's arms, it cries.

*

On University Avenue opposite the Armouries, the parade is in full swing. Alden's pace is slowed by the crowd. The baby snuffles. The motorcade has already passed. Speeches have likely begun at Queen's Park. She practically skips when she realizes she has not missed her banner. They are at the end of its half-mile length. Sadly, it is facing the other way and she cannot read the lettering. At least she got a chance to see it stretching into the distance. It is magnificent.

The men in front of her stop so abruptly that she bumps into the last one. The baby wails. Her pulse quickens. The crowd shifts and a few snowballs whiz overhead and then more. She ducks, reflexively. Behind her there are no children, only soldiers. The soldiers hurl another volley of snowballs at a group of parading University of Toronto students, and other spectators join in. Alden freezes in place and holds the baby tighter.

Someone yells, "Move!" and a rush into the parade almost pushes Alden over. Soldiers drag the university students out from behind their sign—No Booze for Us—and destroy it. Within seconds, there is an all-out brawl.

Then she sees it. Her banner. It is drooping dangerously low to the ground. Its bearers frantically scan the crowd, let go of their poles and run from their posts. The banner is trampled. Some boys run to the torn edge and jump at it, chase it in circles, rip pieces away and throw them at each other. The banner is hopelessly damaged now. A disaster.

Tears spring to Alden's eyes. Running after the banner to save what is left is out of the question. It can't be done with a baby in her arms. Mounted police move in to break up the crowd and are pelted with large pieces of ice. One policeman, bloodied by several cuts to his face, brandishes his whip to disperse the melee and finally charges straight into the fighting mob. His horse rears and dashes one of the marchers to the ground. A soldier grabs Alden by the sleeve and pulls her to the perimeter, ripping the shoulder of her coat further, and says, "Ma'am, get that baby out of here."

What must Mr. Wylie think? He will be so disappointed.

There will be no orderly march toward a better society, only chaos. People are incapable of acting in their own best interests. That much is clear. With her nose wrinkled and her lips pursed, Alden turns her back on the banner, on the students, on the soldiers, on the march itself and walks to the police station. "Idiots," she whispers to herself and the baby.

The police refuse to keep the baby for her.

"We have no facilities," says a dismissive policeman. "We have no women here to look after it. Take it to the hospital."

"The hospital sent me here." Alden's exasperation is evident. "I don't know what else to do."

"Certainly, you can keep it overnight? Just one night?"

What could she say? What kind of woman would not agree to care for an abandoned baby overnight?

By the time she gets back outside, the crowds have dispersed, and the street is filled with debris, including her own beautiful banner in pieces, broken sign posts, and empty bottles. Alcohol bottles. A few people linger. Shopkeepers sweep up their sidewalks, shovel the wreckage into trash cans, and try to bring an air of respectability back to their establishments. A man outside a barbershop with a broom sees her standing still in the street, tips his hat, and says, "Can I help you, Miss?"

She has missed the march and missed the speeches. She has missed the address from the Premier. She has missed everything except for Lady Eaton's reception. It is likely an event of commiseration now instead of celebration. Surely Mr. Wylie will have good advice. And perhaps the sight of her with a baby will jar something in him and move him to appreciate her in a new way.

She walks to him, grateful for the offer. "Yes. Do you have a telephone?"

He nods.

"Could you call for a taxi, please?"

*

I wish the ride to Ardwold was in a horse and carriage and not in one of these confounded motor cars. So noisy. One can hardly enjoy the experience.

My God the city has grown. Buildings have spread continuously to the Davenport escarpment and beyond. I remember when Avenue Road was a mere track, the trees around it home for whippoorwills and red-headed woodpeckers. And what has happened to all the chestnut trees? They're all dead or dying. Some blight or another. The forest itself is utterly changed.

Progress. I lobbied for years to improve the roads and other services east of Toronto. Patterson House could only be accessed easily by land for a few months of the year, and in the winter, when the lake froze, it could be cut off for weeks. Neither of the Mrs. Pattersons could stand the isolation. The first Mrs. Patterson, always a bit fanciful, said that the forest seemed to gobble up the road between travellers. And when the road was finally improved, the great men of Toronto did not even have the decency to rename it after me. Worse, the road allowed the rabble to come east in droves. "Ruination Road," I called it.

Everything from roads to electricity would spread to Patterson House and well beyond with or without my efforts. It was inevitable.

And now I long for the quiet of a cart track, some horses, a little dust rising behind me, the solitude that impassable roads and a frozen lake bring, the gentle glow of an oil lamp in my parlour at night.

Alden is fretful, muttering under her breath, but not to the baby. She is rehearsing. "Thank you for your kind invitation, Lady Eaton. It's an honour to be here." She verges on obsequious around these people. I can barely look at her.

But who am I to criticize? In truth, I too cared far too much about the opinions of others.

It's a curse.

I thought I could spare myself from living through their renunciation of me and their attacks on my reputation. But I couldn't, could I? I saw it all anyway, felt it all, burned with it, read every paper left lying around, until finally, the press didn't even bother mentioning me anymore. Once they had Sir John A. Macdonald in their sights, that was all that mattered. I'm not sure which was worse—being scapegoated or being forgotten.

*

The taxi driver goes slack-jawed when Ardwold comes into view. "Never been here before, Ma'am. Going to a party?"

The mansion is massive, Georgian. There must be fifty rooms. Alden's mouth is open too, and when she realizes it, she shuts it. "Yes. Yes I am." It is a minute before she notes the driver addressed her as Ma'am and not Miss. The baby. He would assume. How long would it be before her age alone made her a Ma'am?

When he stops the taxi, her door is opened, and she is ushered into a sparkling foyer. The baby is taken tenderly from her arms. "We'll keep the babe in the nursery, Ma'am," she is told, but hardly notices. Her coat is whisked away. There are flowers everywhere. Flowers. In March. She walks by an urn and touches some of the petals. She recognizes hydrangeas and roses, but the names of the rest do not come to her.

There are no flowers inside Patterson House, no William Morris prints, no marble floors. No shimmer and shine. Perhaps if her mother had lived, such niceties would have been part of the household. Instead, visitors to Patterson House are greeted with a dank smell in a dark foyer decorated with taxidermy. A pair of trophy wolves killed by Patterson while he surveyed the land stand at the front door opposite a massive ten-point buck, a reminder to all that Patterson conquered the wilderness. Stuffed birds of prey are displayed along the marble-topped radiators, presented in dioramas meant to mimic nature and covered by glass cases. Birding was a passion of her grandfather's, but the stuffed bird bodies and beady little eyes are macabre. Flowers would be so much prettier. She will mention a summer cutting garden and a greenhouse to Mr. Hunt when she answers his next letter, if there is another letter. It might be nice for him to think about the garden again.

At the door of the reception hall, the hum of women's voices rises above the din of clattering dishes and silverware. There is a pineapple in the centre of a serving table. A pineapple! She has only ever seen a picture and wants to go over and touch it. Several crystal chandeliers and a roaring fire bring light and warmth to the large room. The tables are decorated with more extravagant flower arrangements in white and ivory: roses, hyacinth, and hypericum berries with sprouts of greenery. Each has a porcelain bird with fantastical colours tucked within it, ready to spring to life. Mr. Wylie is at the head table with Lady Eaton and the other honoured guests. There are so few men, he is easy to pick out. There is no sign of Mrs. Johnson. Not a single black face.

There is a place at a table with her name card, and her chair is drawn. Her sisters in the movement welcome her warmly, coo and cluck their concern over her absence. They are dressed more stylishly than Alden. Afternoon dresses. She has made the wrong choice again. Her dark suit looks dour by comparison. Several women wear fox stoles over their shoulders while others glitter with jewellery. The woman beside her tells her how delicious the soup is and encourages her to eat. Potato and leek with three sage leaves to garnish the surface. Their cook would never imagine such a flourish.

Ravenous, Alden manages to tell the story of her day between measured and slow tastes. It is not long before a small ripple moves through the room and women at surrounding tables are turning their chairs to listen. About to describe her time in the police station and the poor, bloodied mounted policeman, she is interrupted when Lady Eaton herself approaches.

"Is it true, Miss Patterson? You have rescued a baby?" She extends her hand. Her fingers are long and tapered with well-shaped nails. Alden stands to receive her greeting. "Yes, it is," she says. "I must apologize for being so terribly late and letting everyone down."

"Oh, nonsense. No one is let down. Tell us, what happened?" Alden starts the story again, embellishing here and there in response to questions. Even those who are hearing it for the second time are absorbed in the tale. Her description of the obstreperous nature of the crowd shocks them all. It is as though they were at two different marches. Up at the front, and safe in their motor cars, they did not see the protestations that disrupted the back half of the parade.

"And where is the child?" asks Lady Eaton.

Alden hesitates. She has no idea. "A maid took her from me when I arrived."

"Good. We have a few other children with us today. You should have a good meal after your adventures." She turns and signals a butler, who receives whispered instructions and departs. "I've asked the staff to gather a little layette for you. I'm sure you are not as accustomed to babies at Patterson House as we are here at Ardwold."

"No, I'm afraid we are not." It occurs to Alden that Lady Eaton may be willing to keep the baby overnight. She is about to ask when Mr. Wylie arrives beside Lady Eaton and welcomes Alden, his hand extended.

"We were worried. Indeed, we were. I hear that God gave you a different mission today." The other women murmur their approval of his interpretation of events.

Alden blushes deeply. "I'm sure anyone would have done the same."

Mr. Wylie nods. She imagines he approves of her modesty. He reaches out and touches her arm. She feels weak. "Miss Patterson, your planning helped the day go flawlessly."

Lady Eaton nods. "I'm sure you know the march was a great success. We're all sorry you weren't there to share in the triumph. The Premier himself pledged to bring in prohibition. We have won."

Alden could not be more surprised to hear it. Maybe the day is not a disaster after all. "It is such a shame about the hooligans."

Mr. Wylie's wiry brows knit together. "Hooligans?"

"Yes, the violence at the end of the march. And the banner torn to pieces. It was terrible to see." Women look to each other and Lady Eaton cocks her head to the side. They do not know. "Yes, that is why the police were unable to help me. Too many other concerns today."

"A few bad apples," Mr. Wylie says, changing the subject. Their triumph is not to be marred. "And how is the child?"

"The doctor said she appears healthy, and if her cries are any indication, her lungs are perfectly fine." Alden smiles and a few of the women chuckle knowingly. In this moment, she is one of them. Although this is not how she anticipated the day would go, she has found herself exactly where she hoped to be: in Lady Eaton's home, basking in the light of Mr. Wylie's admiration.

Mr. Wylie looks behind him and says, "Oh, there you are, my dear." He steps aside and brings forward a plump woman in an ill-fitting blue tweed suit whom Alden has never seen before. Greying hair and crow's feet betray her age. "May I present Mrs. Wylie. Mrs. Wylie, this is Miss Patterson."

Alden extends her hand, but her mind goes entirely blank. Time stops. The next thing she knows, she is being lowered into a chair by the women next to her. Lady Eaton says, "Oh dear. She must be exhausted." Mrs. Wylie takes charge and asks for water and smelling salts. For the third time today, Alden is being ministered to by other women. First the women on the streetcar, then the nurse at the hospital, and now Mrs. Wiley. Again, she brushes off the smothering attentions.

"Please, I'm fine," she says, hands waving, attempting to stand.

Mr. Wylie holds the arm of his wife, his concern matching hers.

How could she not have known? Woozy again, she can hear only blood rushing in her ears.

Someone passes her a handkerchief and there is a hand on her shoulder.

"There, there, dear. It's been quite a day, hasn't it?" The attention is too much. She gathers her strength and rises unsteadily, her hip still sore from the morning fall.

Lady Eaton signals a maid. "Take Miss Patterson to lie down."

She has made a scene. What can be worse? "I think it is best if I go back to Patterson House. Thank you for your kindness, Lady Eaton."

"Of course, dear. Whatever you wish." Lady Eaton herself accompanies Alden to the foyer. Her coat appears as mysteriously as it went away, the shoulder mended, and the button replaced with a plain mother of pearl. This is what it is like to be rich.

Alden is grateful that everyone assumes her lapse is the result of a difficult day, grateful she has told no one of her feelings for Mr. Wylie. Her humiliation is known only to herself. When a maid hands her the baby, Alden is surprised. How could she have forgotten?

Lady Eaton says, "Good luck to you, my dear. So charitable. You are an inspiration."

Of course, Lady Eaton will not keep the child for her. What was she thinking? She bundles the baby in her arms and says, "I'm sorry. I'll need a cab."

"Nonsense. My man will drive you."

Alden is whisked into a waiting carriage with a bassinet full of baby things, and the baby in her arms.

*

Rogers Patterson bellows when Alden comes in the door. The stale air of Patterson House is more apparent than ever. Tobacco. Smoke from the fireplace. Dust. Age.

Alden can barely breathe. The maid looks at the baby in Alden's arms with bewilderment. Alden whispers, "Find a place for the baby to sleep tonight, please. Not where it will disturb Mr. Patterson. See about some food for it." She struggles with her coat. "There must be something. Milk. Whatever babies have. Ask Cook." The maid is about to speak but Alden raises a finger to her lips and indicates she is going in to see her father in the blue parlour, so named for the blue silk damask that lines the walls.

The room is Renaissance Revival, outdated now, but it speaks of old money and so it is kept intact. It also reflects the first Mrs. Patterson's taste for Orientalism with several pieces of Chinese porcelain on the mantel. It is the finest room in the house, the room in which important guests are entertained. Bishop Strachan once sat in this room.

Her father is at his usual place, whisky in hand, standing beside his favourite chair and facing the portrait of William Patterson above the mantel. The air is thick with pipe smoke. Alden takes her usual place in front of the fire. This is not a room in which she sits.

"There was a message from the Eaton household that they were sending you home in their carriage."

Damn the telephone. The newspapers and telephone have destroyed any semblance of privacy anyone could hope to have.

The fire roars and a spark lands on the runner along the hearth. Alden stamps it out and pulls the grate over and lets it drop too loudly. An ugly black burn marks the carpet. Like the black mark on a sinner's soul.

"Leave that," her father snaps.

"Would you prefer I let the carpet catch fire and burn the house down?" She is picking a fight, trying to delay the inevitable. She stands before him, chin forward, back straight.

"How dare you go to that infernal march? How dare you defy me?" He slams his glass of whisky onto the console table beside him for emphasis and launches into a lengthy tirade that finishes predictably. "You are almost twenty-three years old. You should be married by now, running your own household and tending to children, not running around with every pious zealot in the province and embarrassing me."

The baby starts to wail from another part of the house. "What in hell?"

"It seems you have your wish. I have brought a baby home."

He is momentarily speechless, mouth open.

"I found a baby today. I saved it from freezing to death." She does not know what she is expecting. More praise perhaps.

He says nothing.

"I'll turn it over to the authorities tomorrow. I tried to get it into the proper hands today. It was not possible. The police have asked me to keep it for now."

"Keep it?"

"Just until they find a place for it."

A sly smile spreads across his face. "Indeed. Maybe you will learn something useful from the exercise. Go tend to it. Keep it away from me."

Dismissed, she enters the foyer to find the maid, Della, the one she likes, waiting. "We're not sure what you want us to do, Miss." Another maid, the one that met her at the door, is on the second floor, looking down from behind the railing, the baby in her arms.

Alden sighs and goes upstairs where she empties the supplies Lady Eaton sent over in the layette and studies them. "Lay these blankets out in the bassinet and leave one or two for a cover." An unpleasant stench catches her nose. She holds up a few squares of thick flannel that must be for diapers. "Let's get her diaper changed and get her ready for bed."

"I'll do that," says the youngest maid "I've got younger brothers and sisters," she says, by way of explanation. She handles diapering with the same efficiency as Harriet's mother.

Alden looks to Della. "I don't know when the baby was last fed. Have you talked to Cook yet?"

Della shakes her head. Must she do everything herself?

"Go ask Cook what to feed her. Maybe she can find a wet nurse."

Cook comes upstairs with a bottle full of warmed milk and the two maids hover as she fits on a spout. Not much milk makes it into the baby's mouth. Alden looks on from behind them, watching rather than helping. The younger maid coos and clucks and volunteers to keep the baby in her room with her, and Alden is grateful. Of course, it can't be left alone all night in a room by itself. Why had she not thought of that?

*

The next morning, Alden wakes and imagines her surroundings before she even opens her eyes. She has a three-quarter-size bed and sleeps diagonally so her feet don't touch the oak footboard. The mattress is lumpy, but the groove created by her body is so perfect that she will never ask for it to be changed. She burrows a bit deeper under her quilt and coverlet and opens one eye. Her tall dresser is in the corner, a picture of her mother upon it in a silver frame. On the opposite wall are framed drawings of Patterson House from different perspectives. Her favourite illustrates the winding path that led to the lake before the land was sold. She has spent many a morning imagining herself sauntering down that path to the small beach that used to be there. Beyond the beach, a ship belonging to her grandfather's company is making its way to port, an homage to the family business. Across from her and beside the window is a vanity she uses as a writing desk with a short stack of correspondence tied with string. She must write to her brothers again, even if she has no idea if they receive her letters.

She is about to turn on the light at her bedside table when she realizes her room is already bright. She did not close her curtains the night before. Nor did she hang up her clothes. They are draped over the back of her chair. She pushes herself up on her elbow and all the events from the day before come rushing back to her. Then she hears it—the baby.

Della knocks at her door and opens it a crack before entering. "Good morning, Miss." She bustles around and hangs Alden's clothes in the closet as Alden pulls herself to sitting. "Sorry to wake you."

When she reaches for the shirtwaist, Alden says, "Leave that, please."

"Does it need mending?"

"No, just leave it."

Della looks skeptical. She folds it and sets it on the vanity. "We've found a nanny. She's a girl I know from home. She has six younger brothers and sisters."

"What time is it?"

"Quarter past eight."

"Is my father still here?"

"Yes, Miss. At breakfast. Everyone had a late start today."

She dresses quickly so that she and her father will cross paths over breakfast, something she usually avoids.

On her way to the dining room, Alden stops in the kitchen with the shirtwaist she wore to the march, the same shirtwaist that Mr. Wylie anointed with his damp hand, and throws it into the kitchen fire. Cook looks up at her, back to the fire, back to her, and says, "Eggs?"

"Two please."

In the dining room, Alden nods to her father, who is behind a newspaper, and realizes she hardly ate a thing yesterday. She serves herself three sausages and two pieces of toast from the platter Cook has left at the table. Once at her place, she lays a napkin on her lap and butters her toast. The scraping sound irritates her father enough that he looks over the edge of his paper and shakes his head. "You eat as much as your brothers."

The casual mention of her brothers adds tension to the room.

"No mail yet?" she asks.

He ignores her and returns to his paper.

Cook enters and serves her two fried eggs from a plate and leaves again. Her father lowers his paper and shakes his head.

Alden ignores him and swallows several bites. She pours her tea before she brings up the nanny.

"The maid has found a nanny. For the baby."

"So now this orphan of yours is going to cost me money? Give me one good reason why you can't care for it?"

She is more frank with him than she has ever been and sets her knife and fork down on the edges of her plate before looking him in the eye. "You can't expect the baby to suffer because you want to punish me."

One of his bushy eyebrows rises and he nods, sets the paper down beside him, and brings his hands and fingers together like a steeple in front of him. He cannot resist his opportunity to berate her. "How will you ever make a decent wife and mother when you can't look after an orphan for a few days?"

"I have no interest in looking after children. This is not what I want."

"Not what you want? What do you mean?" For an instant, he seems genuinely interested.

What can she possibly say? He waits. She cannot meet his eye. "I want more than that."

He makes a sound, dismisses her with a wave. "It's no wonder we can't find a husband for you." He stands, drops his napkin on the table, and leaves the room in disgust.

Alden's appetite is ruined. She returns to the kitchen to tell Cook the nanny can be hired. "Just for a day or two, until the authorities find a place for the baby. Make sure she knows this is a temporary position—a very temporary position."

Cook nods. "The baby had a good night, I hear. No surprise after the day before. Poor wee thing was probably worn right out."

Everyone seems to have a sympathetic heart for the "poor wee thing" with none to spare for Alden. But only she knows that she needs any sympathy. She'll have to give it to herself.

"You'll manage?" Alden wraps her arms around herself, as if cold.

Cook nods again.

Alden does her best to look determined. "Right. I'm out for the morning."

But once she is in the foyer, Alden stops, unsure what to do and where to go. She cannot return to the WCTU. She cannot bear to see Mr. Wylie. Nor can she stay at Patterson House to be bullied by her father.

When she was little, Alden used to count all the eyes she could see in various rooms of Patterson House. The foyer has the most eyes—thirty-two—and she feels them all upon her, waiting to see what she will do. Four belong to the wolves, two to the buck, sixteen to different glass-covered birds, and ten to the subjects of five portraits: the first Mrs. Patterson, the second Mrs. Patterson (who, for some reason, did not remove the portrait of the first Mrs. Patterson), Rogers Patterson, and her two brothers. There is no portrait of her, although her father once commissioned one as part of his ongoing efforts to find her a husband. The photographer sat her on a stool and had her look over her shoulder. The pose emphasized the length of her nose and her hair appeared as a fuzzy halo. Alden has no idea where the framed version is—her father probably burned it—but a smaller version is in one of the family photo albums in the small parlour, the one that used to be called the "ladies' parlour," at a time when the Mrs. Pattersons had guests.

Of all the eyes upon her, the cormorant's eyes are the most demanding. She looks away. It seems to dare her to do something. But what?

Father Moore will know what to do.

Just yesterday, full of ambition, she made the same journey, if unintentionally, to St. Michael's. Today, she is utterly defeated and in charge of a baby. She walks to the streetcar, but not seeing it in the distance, she begins to walk and does not stop even when the streetcar approaches her and then passes her at Coxwell Avenue. As she walks, she retraces every facet of every encounter she has ever had with Mr. Newton Wylie.

How could she have got it so wrong? How could she have permitted herself such a sentimental daydream? Mr. Wylie was not interested in her at all. He did not lead her on. Every word he said to her was entirely proper and related to the movement. She made it all up, imagined it, like a foolish schoolgirl.

Wind gusts across the bridge over the Don River and she avoids looking down into the water. There is a break in the cloud over the lake, and on the other side of the bridge, she swears she can smell the earth again after months of winter. But the promise of sun and spring brings her no joy. The drunken man's voice rings in her ears. Old biddy.

She is at as great a loss about what to do with herself as she was before she found the WCTU and Mr. Wylie.

Approaching St. Michael's, her feet are tired. She has walked for more than two hours. Inside, she blesses herself with the holy water from the marble font. In the pew, she stares into the shrine of Saint Jude but cannot think of a ready prayer.

She is not a lost cause. There will be something for her.

If this is to be her life, it is best to get on top of it, to be in control of her own story. She tells herself that she wants to be alone, that Mr. Newton Wylie was nothing to her. Nothing at all. She imagines herself in the future saying, "I cannot remember the man's name. What was it again?" She is better off without him. A man out of uniform.

She does not believe herself.

Tears rise. A revision like this takes time. Like the Pellatt cousin.

Father Moore is in the confessional and there are only three people waiting. When her turn comes, she slips inside and the screen between them slides open. "Bless me, Father, for I have sinned." Today's confession is serious. She has indulged in self-pity. She has failed to honour her father. She has lied. She has coveted another woman's husband, but she did not know he was married. She cannot bear to speak it and will take this sin—if it is a sin—to her grave. She explains about the baby. Father Moore, often ponderous, pauses before speaking.

"You're too hard on yourself. I confess I did not realize the advice I offered to help out with the WCTU was against your father's wishes. Had I known he objected to prohibition, I would have directed your efforts elsewhere." He pauses. "I put you in a difficult position. I take responsibility. You can hardly be blamed for following my guidance." Through the mesh, she sees him rest his chin on his hands. She wonders if he kneels on his side or sits on a low stool. "And now you have been brought together with this baby. If the child's mother does not come forward, the child will need care. Consider the many gifts you have to offer such a child. God seems to have spoken quite loudly to you.

Perhaps this child is your calling. For Matthew 25 tells us the story of the talents. Remember the last servant who hid his talent instead of making something of it to honour his master? This is what God wants us to do with our gifts, dear child, not hide our light under a bushel. God has given you a task. How will you answer?"

She barely remembers the rest of the priest's words. He gives her no penance and says she needs no absolution. Back in her pew, Alden drops down to the kneeler and rests her elbows on the back of the pew ahead. Think of her many gifts? Her talents? If she were a man, she would be free to use them. Is it her fault that God gave her talents that do not belong with the weaker sex? And what does the baby have to do with her talents? Father Moore assumes she can be good with a child simply because she is a woman.

Perhaps her father is right. She has been a fool to think that she could be a different kind of woman. For a woman, all roads lead to the same place.

She whispers, "Dear God. Find the baby's mother."

*

That evening, Alden and her father sit in their usual places at opposite ends of the polished walnut table. He does not inquire after the child. Instead, he rises and slaps a folded newspaper down beside her as though he is killing a fly. The headline he points to is below the fold and one of several stories about the march and the ensuing riots. It reads, "Abandoned Baby Found in The Ward."

Alden reads, afraid of what it will say, while her father practically marches back to his chair. It describes the march and identifies her as an organizer and stalwart of the WCTU. No wonder her father is livid. The article quotes both Dr. Clement and Lady Eaton, who said the Patterson family has agreed to care for the child while the search for the mother continues.

Her father booms, "An organizer? A stalwart? How long have you been deceiving me?"

Alden flinches as he bangs his fist on the table hard enough to make the silverware jump.

Her stomach flips. "I don't know where they got this information. I can't imagine." Indeed, she very well can imagine any of the dozens of the women at Lady Eaton's home speaking to the press.

"It was probably that blowhard Clement. Trying to look like a hero." Her father fumes. "Now what am I supposed to do?"

"What do you mean?"

"You better pray the child's mother shows up."

She has done nothing but.

For the next two days, Alden checks in with the nanny between trips to the police station. The nanny's competence highlights Alden's incompetence and the result is she is officious with the girl. The police have no sense of urgency and tell her there is no word on the mother at all. Nothing. It is as though the woman never existed. Alden considers returning to The Ward herself and knocking on doors but simply can't bring herself to go back.

The child has been with them for three days when her father lays another newspaper article by her place at the breakfast table. He sits at his end, already finished with his slab of ham and three eggs. He dabs at the crumbs in his beard with a white napkin. As Alden approaches her place, he folds his arms and says, "Read. Out loud."

Alden reads, "Daughter of Lumber Magnate Mr. Rogers Patterson Praised in the Legislature."

"Continue," her father commands.

"Premier William Hearst has issued special praise to the daughter of Toronto lumber magnate, Mr. Rogers Patterson of Patterson and Sons Lumber and Stone, for her actions during the Temperance March that saved the life of an abandoned infant. Miss Patterson discovered the baby while on her way to attend the March in support of Prohibition. In his remarks, Premier Hearst said, 'I have heard of this terrible situation and the good deed performed by Miss Patterson, who is a woman of exemplary values and charity and a role model to all women in the Province of Ontario.' Premier Hearst allowed that, 'This dire situation may indeed be even more proof of the immediate need to implement prohibition, which this government is united in its determination to pass. Long have we known the evils of drink and the preponderance of the use of alcohol, particularly in The Ward. Let us pray that such a sad and potentially tragic event as this is never repeated as we end Ontario's chapter with alcohol.'"

"It appears you and your ilk have won the day."

Alden bows her head and stays silent.

"It matters not. In the end, it will be good for business." He gives one last swipe at his beard with his napkin and lays it on the table.

"I don't understand."

How could she? He has never shared his business with her. "It's Patterson and Sons," he has said in the past, "not Patterson and Daughters."

Her father says, "We've taken the foundling in, apparently."

"The mother might still come forward."

Her father's eyes roll. "It's been three days. It's been in the papers. If she were going to return, she would have by now." He rises and brushes his hands over his hard, round stomach. "I have said it is time for you to settle down and look after children, and so you will. The police called last night. There is no one available to take the baby. It's wartime. The orphanages are full. The churches are at their limit. What can we expect? They've asked us to do our part, and we will. She is all yours."

"You can't be serious."

"Never more. You may not be able to find a husband, but the child is yours."

Alden is too stunned to object.

"Her name shall be Constance. Constance Patterson. Let her be a constant reminder to you of your duty."

The future stretches ahead of Alden, and it is too bleak to contemplate. Her breakfast untouched, she lets the newspaper fall to the floor. Fleeing the dining room, she runs through the kitchen, past Cook, and out the back door without a coat. In the frozen garden where the lily-of-the-valley will grow in the spring, she sits on a stone bench in the cold and weeps, the tears turning to ice on her cheeks.

*

Alden is in the garden without a coat. She is a small thing from up here, yet I can see the tremble in her shoulders. The girl's crying is disturbing. It's only a baby—a small thing.

It's a pity she is so unattractive. It was hard enough to find a husband before. Now, with a baby in tow, even if the reasons are completely admirable, it will be near impossible. I wouldn't have taken such a situation on; that I know.

When I drum my fingers on the windowsill, there is a simultaneous belch in the furnace. I like to think this is no coincidence, but I have learned that kind of fancy is ill-advised. Instead, I'm minding my own business. Not that I have any anymore.

I won't bother the girl. I will remain a passive observer. (What else can I do?) It's best not to get involved. Besides, none of us is obliged to reveal our deepest thoughts or motivations to anyone. When I decided to leave this mortal coil, people whispered about a note. They wanted an explanation, a reason. A note would not have made a jot of difference. No matter how hard I might have tried to explicate the seemingly inexplicable, to bring cohesion to the inchoate, my words would have been subject to endless scrutiny and interpretation. Or should I say "misinterpretation." Even if I told the truth, even if I managed to capture the ghastly contradictions of my own motivations, I still might not have been believed. They would have determined I was only concerned with myself. With so much potential for misunderstanding, a note hardly seemed worth the effort. So be it.

I have no regrets. Not one.

The furnace belches again as if in rebuke.

Yes, I lie to myself. Suicide was a mistake. I realize that now. It freed me from nothing.

But how could I have known?

Thankfully, Alden's religiosity banishes any thought of suicide from her mind before it emerges. She will not follow in my footsteps, no matter what the setback.

And there will be setbacks. In only a week's time, her world will be turned upside down again. Just as Rogers softens in his resolve that Alden keep the foundling, just as its presence begins to frustrate and disturb him, just as he realizes that keeping a foundling as a way of punishing his daughter is untenable and that he can ill afford the additional staff, not one, but two telegrams will arrive. My grandsons will be dead. To Rogers, nothing else will matter.

November 15, 1918

B ONE-ACHING FATIGUE drives Rogers Patterson to his bed four days after the armistice. He longs for the unconsciousness that sweeps over him in waves to settle upon him for good.

His wife, Lily, has been dead twenty-five years. His sons are also dead, their bodies lost in the French mud, their graves mere markers. No peace will bring them back. Was it yesterday that the telegrams arrived? No, that was more than two years ago.

His eyelids are dark bruises. They weigh heavily, as though pennies have already been placed upon them. His skin is clammy and mauve, darkening to deep purple and brown at his hands. Alden, a scarf pulled over her nose and mouth, sits by his bedside and ministers with a cool cloth to his forehead.

He has been far too hard on her. He wants to say thank you to this defiant, impossible girl. He wants to say, "You've been a good daughter." These are the kind of words that should be said in the hours—or is it minutes—before one's death, but there will be few words anymore. He cannot manage them. His voice emerges as a wet gurgle.

A scowling William Patterson perches on the arm of a wing chair opposite Rogers's bed, his bushy brows furrowed together. He wears the same suit he wore the day he died, but it is clean and pressed. His beard is trim, and his eyes shine with a vigour that Rogers does not remember in them.

This must be a hallucination. Rogers's mind is playing tricks on him again, like it does when he is near the bottom of a whisky bottle and he shares confidences with his dear Lily until the blackness takes over. He tries to summon an image of her, but it will not come.

The priest has been here to rub oil on his brow. Alden sent for him. It felt good to listen to him, to be the subject of his ministrations, to be told that God cared. He has confessed. All of it. It is such a relief. He is ready. *Domine, non sum dignus.*

William Patterson sneers. "Not worthy." He spits the words. "Worthy of what? It makes no difference, you know. It's a bit hypocritical to find piety now. Desperate. At least I had the courage to face my death alone."

"You left your family behind. Your wife." He pauses. "Your son. Face it. *You're* the coward." He cannot tell if he is thinking these words or saying them aloud. What does it matter?

William Patterson shrugs. "I left you the business. Where's your gratitude? And now you've ruined everything."

Rogers nods. He has. With his sons dead, what does it matter? Even the name of the business, *Patterson and Sons,* grieves him.

"You forget. You still have a daughter."

Rogers's heart contracts. Yes, he does. He always meant to make provisions for her. He was so sure she would marry, so sure that she would not be his problem.

"You've left her with nothing," says William Patterson. "At least I left you with something."

She has the house.

"The house? Look around you, man. An albatross."

Rogers does not want to spend his last moments arguing with his dead father. He is tired. His skin weighs heavily on him. He does not want to listen to William Patterson recite his failings. He has already been absolved.

Rogers whispers, "Leave."

Alden leaves the room, shoulders slumped, head bowed.

He tries to rise, to say, "No! That is not what I meant," but it is too late; the girl is gone.

*

After the funeral, Alden returns to Patterson House and stands in the centre of the foyer, a lone gull over a vast lake. She is the last Patterson. How odd. What is the last Patterson supposed to do?

Her father's last word, "Leave," echoes. Even in death, her father did not want her.

The service was poorly attended. The epidemic has made everyone wary of crowds. Alden could not miss her own father's funeral, though.

The cold November rain turned to sleet at the cemetery. Her coat drips on the floor. She grips the umbrella in her hand, her fist tight around it.

Yesterday, she met with the lawyers. How could it have been only yesterday? There were three of them, all patronizing vultures. Three against one. They did not waste any time getting the meat from the carcass. They talk about business like it is a mystery that only they can solve—no—that only *men* can solve.

It's not difficult to understand. The forests and quarries are spent. There are no new leases. The ships and equipment need repair and cost a fortune to operate. And her father spent more than he earned. The business is done.

But there was something else, something kept in a separate ledger, something she did not know about. He converted the mills. Liquor is much more profitable than lumber, they said.

No wonder her father was so angry with her. Everything made sense now. In the end, he'd realized that prohibition was profitable. But he didn't want to be seen as a hypocrite. No. Having taken a position, he would never change his mind, especially not with her.

The ignominy of it. She slams the metal end of her umbrella against the floor and water sprays in a circle around it.

And the lawyers had the nerve to advise her to keep the liquor flowing. "Get rid of it," she said.

They proffered dire warnings. They told her the liquor business was the only thing keeping her afloat. Stubbornly, she insisted. "I will not live off the avails of alcohol." She might not go to WCTU meetings anymore, but she is still a believer.

They closed their files and left.

She still has the house. Barely. There are taxes. She is going to have to learn about taxes. She could mortgage it. She is going to have to learn about mortgages.

She looks up, as though answers might be found above. The crystal chandelier, nestled perfectly into the curve of the stairs, makes her feel slightly dizzy. The chandelier must be worth something. The house is full of things that have got to be worth something. She could sell it all. She could sell the house too.

Her father's last word sounds endlessly in her head. "Leave." Maybe her father was telling her what to do. Leave Patterson House.

But the thought of it makes her feel blown off course. She is a bird lost during migration, her instincts failing. She moves to the banister and grips the newel post to steady herself. She imagines people in the house, auctioneers, bargaining over Patterson history—her history—and the dregs left to the rag and bone man. It is too awful to contemplate.

And who would she be without Patterson House?

Her grandfather's trophy wolves stare at her from the doorway. Their yellow sightless eyes have no answers for her.

How could it be that two years have passed since her brothers died? What has she done with herself? Nothing. Her life was consumed by keeping her drunken father out of the public eye where he would humiliate her and send the family reputation back decades. She caused countless tirades by draining his liquor down the sink. But he would always get more. She could never figure out who brought it to him or where it came from. It had to be the servants. A conspiracy. To the servants, he was easier to handle while drunk. Or he simply paid them enough that any scruples they had disappeared and instructions from her did not matter. But now he is gone, and it is only her instructions that matter.

To supervise a house is a task so dull yet so necessary. She still cannot understand how it can eat up every available moment. Just when one thinks there might be a lull, one maid complains about another, the ice man needs to be paid, a pipe freezes and bursts, or her father fires everyone again. It's always something.

And she has Constance. Her penance, according to her father. Her calling according to Father Moore. Perhaps they are both right. But her penance for what? For her defiance? For wanting more than marriage to some podge of a man who is not her equal? For not being able to pretend that marriage is enough?

Alden slumps on the lowest step, still in her wet coat, still holding her umbrella. It's not that she sees no value in marriage and motherhood. Of course, she does. But it is probably easier if it is something one wants. Thrust into the role unwillingly, she has made an effort. She does not like to be bad at things. But motherhood? She rests her elbows on her knees and her head in her hands.

The child inevitably cries whenever Alden attempts to bathe or dress her. The nanny does everything so much more efficiently. Alden once dressed Constance so clumsily that later, when she took the child on her lap, the diaper leaked everywhere. She could have tried again. But the nanny was so anxious to take over. It was the nanny's job, after all. It made more sense for Alden's role to be supervisory. Distance and dispassion were, after all, assets in a guardian. She consulted with Cook about proper food so that Constance would be robust. She instructed the nanny about proper intellectual stimulation so that Constance would be curious. The day-to-day details, the diapering and spit up, were best left to others.

The tight pang in her chest when she sees the nanny rocking Constance to sleep or clucking and cooing while she ties the ribbons of her bonnet unsettles Alden. Nanny showed her many times how to hold the child so that her head was supported. But it was a worry. What if she made a mistake? Babies are so fragile, especially the little soft spot on their heads where the pulse beats up and down, up and down.

She sits up straight and tries to think. With the nanny, she could manage. Now, with no money to pay staff, she would bear the full responsibility of Constance herself. The possibility of failure looms large.

There are options. The child could go to an orphanage. With the war over, there must be room somewhere. But what would people think? What would Father Moore think? The one charitable act for which she is known would be forever soured. Yet, that is not what really stops her from sending Constance away. What stops her is a small bird rattling within her chest, fluttering against the cage of her ribs. She imagines the bird is fear, fear of what others will think, and then knows it is not. It is love. Alden loves Constance and that love is deep and fierce and frightening. God help her. If there is one thing Alden seems to have always known, it is that love and loss are the same.

"Leave." Her father's voice echoes like the rain pounding against the windows. She hoists herself up from the step with a grunt.

The foyer is airless. She tugs her scarf from around her neck and throws it to the floor, drops the umbrella, struggles out of her coat, pulls the sleeves through to the inside, and whips the coat to the floor too. Her breath comes too fast. Sweat beads on her forehead. She rips open the top buttons of her shirtwaist, gasping for air.

Around the foyer, all thirty-two eyes are upon her. What do they want from her? The birds. The damned birds. Why do they stare like that?

The osprey accuses. The northern harrier chastises. The peregrine falcon is poised to tear at her flesh. The cormorant, that damned cormorant, gloats. She takes up the umbrella again, raises it over her head, and brings it down upon the birds one by one, smashing their cases and sweeping the glass from the marble radiator covers. She stabs at the inert bird bodies with the end of the umbrella, piercing a corvid with the metal tip again and again until it leaks sawdust. The echo of her destruction rings against the walls. She pauses, sees a shiny raven eye still looking at her, and kicks it. With the umbrella in midair, she turns her fury on the wolves, glass grinding under her feet, and holds the weapon above her right shoulder like a spear before she throws it at them. It bounces off the back of the wolf closest to her and slides across the floor. The wolves seem to avert their eyes.

Wise, she thinks. Look away.

Above, she hears a gasp. The maid and the nanny huddle behind the second-floor railing aghast. Cook is frozen in the pass-through door between the dining room and the kitchen, wringing her apron. She might be crying. Alden picks up the umbrella, slams it into its home in the stand, crunches back across the floor, and picks up her coat. Glass tinkles to the floor, glinting in the reflected light of the chandelier.

The maid, Della, the one she likes, steps tentatively down the stairs and approaches Alden as though she is a wild animal. Gently, she takes her coat from her, places it over the newel post and whispers, "I'll take care of all of this, Miss. Why don't you go lie down? Cook will bring you some tea."

The nanny, still on the second floor, scurries away.

"I don't need any tea." Alden stifles a sob and shakes off the attentions of the maid. Her legs ache on the stairs. Nausea grips her.

Maybe she has the flu.

No. She will not be so lucky.

At the top of the stairs, she does not look back down at the destruction she has wrought. Instead, she focuses on the bedroom at the end of the hall where the nanny is in hiding with Constance. Collecting herself, she corrects her posture and walks through the door as though nothing has happened.

To her credit, the nanny has made the child's room a place of comfort. The drapes are drawn against the storm outside. Three small books of nursery rhymes sit on a table beside a low rocking chair which has a quilt of green and pink florals laid over the crest rail. The light from the lamp envelops the spot in a bright circle. How many hours have they sat there together?

It should be Alden reading to the child.

The nanny is bent over the crib, laying the babbling Constance down for her nap. No sooner is she down than she stands back up, hands gripping the side bars. She laughs at their funny game.

This is how affection blooms, in the day-to-day details and the physicality of care. Maybe it's not too late for them. Alden interrupts. "I'm here now. You can go."

The nanny, a look of confusion on her face, stammers, "Miss, you must be tired."

"We'll be fine. Please ask the staff to assemble in the blue parlour in half an hour."

The nanny scurries out the door and down the hall.

There is no point in looking away from what must happen next. Alden picks up Constance and raises her to eye level in extended arms. Constance cocks her head, perhaps amused at the novelty of being held by Alden, opens her mouth, and says, "Ma."

Alden flinches. "No. I am not your mother. But I will look after you. You will be safe with me. I promise. I am Alden. Say Alden." The child's eyes have become deep brown, her lips pink, her skin smooth and unfreckled, her hair dark and thick. She could not be less of a Patterson.

Alden sets her back down in the crib and tucks a blanket around her. The child does not reach for her.

"It's going to be just the two of us now. Try not to be too much trouble."

PART TWO

February 12, 1894

L ILY PATTERSON is sprawled in the snow. Black tree branches reach into the grey sky far above her. Dancing skeletons. Someone is groaning. Not someone. Something. A horse. Poor thing. It will have to be shot. All her fault. Rogers will be so upset with her. She is not supposed to go out with the buggy when the roads are bad, especially not on her own.

Looking around, she sees the wisdom in his caution. But it could have happened to anyone. That's what she'll tell Rogers. This road. If you can call it that. Ruination Road indeed.

Have her skirts ridden up? She could be exposed to the elements—or worse. But she cannot lift her head to check herself. Oh dear.

William Patterson is kneeling over her, his head cocked to one side, as if curious, his moustache just as bushy and beguiling as it is in his portrait in the blue room. She sees now how Rogers takes after him. If only she could pull her skirts down.

"Dear Lily, such a shame," he says.

Dear God. She had the baby with her. Her eyes widen and dart around and her heart beats frantically. "Where's the baby?" Why can she not move? "Help me! Help me find the baby."

He puts his hand on her arm but she cannot feel it. "Don't worry about that. Someone will come for her."

Why will he not help her? "Please, I beg you, find her and bring her to me."

He shrugs. "I cannot."

"Help me get up."

He shakes his head. "That is impossible."

A crow lands above and caws. The facts of the matter dawn on her. "You're dead," she says. That sounded rude. She tries again. "This isn't possible." Just as bad. There is an awful taste in her mouth. It's blood.

"Am I dead?"

"No."

Lily scans the scene again, the section of it that her position will allow her to see. "Do you know where the baby is?"

He points beyond her, to a place she cannot see.

"Is she alive?"

"Yes, she is alive. You don't need to worry about her."

"What's that sound?"

He listens. "Just the wind."

"Are you a ghost?"

"I don't think so." He searches the distance. "Someone is coming."

Her teeth chatter.

"Why did you go out on a day like this? What was so urgent?"

"I'm not sure. I haven't been myself since the baby." He is gone. The wind shifts the branches above her, but she does not feel it on her skin. Oaks. One tree is reaching out to the other, offering a graceful bow as the music starts. Oh, what she wouldn't give to dance again. Rogers is a fine dancer, but they haven't danced in ages. From the corner of her eye, she sees a cedar waxwing perched on a shrubbery with something in his beak, possibly a winterberry. The bright red of the berry and the little tuft of feathers on its head—what a distinguished little fellow. She wants to show it to the children. Oh dear. The boys. The baby. What has she done?

She looks skyward again. William Patterson is sitting in a tree branch, his legs dangling.

"Where were you going?" he asks.

"The city." She stifles a little sob.

"Were you going to come back?"

She would turn her head away if she could. Of course she was. She brought no cases with her. Just the baby.

In an effort to console her, William Patterson says, "Don't worry, it won't be long now."

"Long until what?" When he doesn't answer, Lily starts to cry in earnest. "I'm going to die, aren't I?"

He does not respond.

"Is it because of what I said? Is that why this happened? Is God punishing me?"

"I'm sure it's not because of anything you said or didn't say. It doesn't work like that." He hesitates and then can't help himself. "Why? What did you say?"

"I didn't say it. Truly. I never said it," she shudders. "I thought it. I thought, 'I'd rather die than stay in this house another minute.'"

Her eyes lose their light. She is gone.

He goes to the baby and asks, "Who can understand women? You provide, give them a house, a position, children, all the modern conveniences. Running water for heaven's sakes. That cost a pretty penny. And still they are unhappy."

August 11, 1930

CONSTANCE WAKES to a fantastical mechanical racket outside. It's a new sound that sets dogs barking and makes the windowpanes vibrate. It is as though Patterson House itself is alarmed. She fumbles with her robe, runs downstairs to the second floor in the dark, flies around the corner at the landing, and bangs on Mr. Hunt's door halfway down the hall. "It's here! It's here!" The R-100, a dirigible, the biggest airship ever, is making its Toronto debut, right now, in the middle of the night.

Alden appears at her bedroom door at the other end of the hall and scolds, "For heaven's sake, Constance, don't run around like a savage. And fix your robe."

Constance closes the robe, searches for the ends of the sash, and struggles to tie it.

"Dear God. What have you done to your legs?"

Her knees are scabbed and there are at least six bruises on her shins in varying shades of yellow and purple.

Constance is too excited to answer and knows no answer is really expected.

Alden is, of course, fully dressed. After twelve years of having boarders in Patterson House, she would never unlock her bedroom door without being dressed. The fact that the last boarder disappeared in May—still owing a week—makes no difference to Alden's sense of decorum. Constance imagines she sleeps in her clothes.

"Leave Mr. Hunt be. He needs his sleep." But Constance knows that Mr. Hunt is almost as excited about the airship as she is. They have been poring over the newspapers together for days marvelling at the details. Mr. Hunt likes reading about its twelve Rolls-Royce engines and the amount of fuel it carries, while Constance reads everything she can about the pilots. Her best friend Gwen wants to marry a pilot. Constance wants to be one.

To be excited about the airship is to be patriotic and patriotism is running high in Patterson House. Mr. Hunt rustles from the other side of his door and calls out, "It's all right. I'm awake." Constance claps her hands and practically jumps up and down. Opening his door, Mr. Hunt yawns, covers his mouth where his lips should be, and rubs his stubby fingers across his scarred face and through his patchy hair. Constance is so accustomed to Mr. Hunt's appearance, his missing ear, his snub of a nose, that to her, he looks sweet in his half-awake state, like a boy.

"Who could sleep through that?" Mr. Hunt turns to Constance, "Well, young lady, let's go outside and get a look at it." The awful smell of his homemade camphor plaster envelops Constance as she takes his hand and pulls him toward the stairs. It helps him breathe at night. His lungs are knackered. Mustard gas. Mr. Hunt was at Ypres.

"Slow down. Be careful," says Alden. They hurry down the stairs and through the foyer, past the wolves that guard the door, and out to the garden. As her eyes adjust to the night sky, Constance gapes slack-jawed at the future. The dark mass of it blots out the view of the stars beyond.

Alden stays at the door, arms crossed. "Constance, you'll get your slippers wet. John, are you warm enough?"

The dew is already soaking Constance's feet and Mr. Hunt is shivering. But who cares?

Mr. Hunt calls back to Alden, "Come on out and join us!" and she takes a few tentative steps onto the grass.

"I'm going around to the street to get a better view," yells Constance over the droning hum.

"You certainly are not. Pattersons do not go in the street in their night clothes."

Constance pouts, but only for a minute.

"It's very low," whispers Mr. Hunt to Constance.

The thrum reverberates in her chest. Lights blink along the bottom and in some of the windows.

Constance clutches Mr. Hunt's hand in hers and steps closer to him.

"What's the matter?" he asks.

She can't say. Her heart pounds. "How does it stay up there?"

"You're worried it won't? There's nothing to be afraid of." He squeezes her hand a little tighter.

"Just think. There are people in there. I wonder what they're doing."

"Sleeping," says Alden flatly, tiptoeing through the wet grass, "like we should be."

Constance says, "I wish I was in it."

Alden laughs. "Don't be ridiculous."

Mr. Hunt says, "Why not? Times are changing. These days, our Constance could be a pilot."

"Don't fill the child's head with impossibilities, Mr. Hunt." Alden looks to the sky again and shakes her head.

Constance shivers. "What about Amelia Earhart?"

Mr. Hunt nudges her as if to say, "Not now."

"You are *not* Amelia Earhart," scoffs Alden.

"You could be if you wanted to be," whispers Mr. Hunt so that Alden will not hear. Constance gives his hand a squeeze and is comforted by the smoothness of his palms.

It's not that Constance wants to fly. What she wants is to have a purpose. A destiny. Earhart is famous everywhere, but particularly in Toronto. It was here that she caught the flying bug while she was working as a nurse at the Spadina Military Hospital. She used to help men like Mr. Hunt, men who were injured in the war. Constance knows everything about her. She's a modern girl, just like Constance. Or just like Constance would be if Alden would let her.

"You know, Alden, Amelia Earhart is a teetotaler," says Mr. Hunt. This fact alone should win Alden over, but she dismisses it with a wave of her hand.

They all watch in silence, necks strained, faces upwards, as the ship disappears to the west of them, the thrum of the engine rumbling into the distance. A few bursts of applause break out in the yards around them and Constance joins in with the clapping.

Alden crosses her arms over her chest. "Mark my words; that thing is dangerous. I don't want anything to do with it."

Mr. Hunt's chuckle turns into a gasping cough. When he recovers, he says, "Then it's a good thing for you that no one has asked you to have anything to do with it."

Alden raises an eyebrow as she ushers the other two back inside. "There was a time, as you know, Mr. Hunt, when the Pattersons would have been in the thick of it. And I still wouldn't have set foot in that thing, not if they asked me to cut the ribbon with a pair of golden scissors."

Who would not want to go on the airship? Constance elbows Mr. Hunt and says, "You mean you wouldn't want to ride in it and look through the portholes at the insides of clouds or look down at the Atlantic Ocean? You wouldn't want to climb the grand staircase or walk on the promenade deck or sleep in the sleeping cabins or eat in the fancy dining room? They say it's fit for royalty."

"There's nothing in the airship that we don't have safe on the ground in Patterson House. And this house has welcomed royalty in the past."

"It has?" This is news to Constance, who is certain she knows the entire history of the Pattersons from front to back and back to front. Mr. Hunt also looks skeptical, the right side of his forehead stretching slightly upward.

"Not the King, of course. An earl," says Alden.

"Which earl was that?" asks Mr. Hunt.

"The brother of the Earl of Buckinghamshire. Still the peerage," she sniffs. Alden waves Mr. Hunt's half smile away and says, "Stop splitting hairs. My point is that Patterson House has all the finery anyone might need."

However, the harsh incandescent light of a rickety floor lamp set behind one of the wolves inside the front door reveals a house King George might find a little down at the heel. The anaglypta is coming up at the seams, ruining the illusion of leather-clad walls. The hardwood floors, although clean and polished, are terribly scratched and water marked, and the stair runner is threadbare at the edges of the risers. The chandelier hanging from the second-floor ceiling within the curve of the staircase is covered in dust and has not been lit in two years. Too many of its bulbs need to be replaced and they are expensive.

Constance whispers to Mr. Hunt, "I can't wait to see the airship in the daylight."

"I beg your pardon?" Alden turns to face them.

"Tomorrow. It's coming back across Toronto. I'm going to go downtown to see it. There's going to be a huge crowd."

Alden bristles. "Under no circumstances will I have you running around downtown in a crowd by yourself. Anything can happen in a crowd."

Constance has been in this argument before. Alden hates going downtown, hates crowds, and even hates the streetcar. Constance, on the other hand, loves all three of these things. She knows how to convince Alden to let her go.

"I won't be by myself. Gwen is coming."

Alden rolls her eyes. "Running around with that Gwen might be worse than running around alone."

Constance is about to argue when Mr. Hunt touches her shoulder and shakes his head ever so slightly. He always says, "Pick your battles." Apparently, this is not one to pick. She looks at him in disbelief and tugs on his arm, her lips pursed together. He pulls away and pats her back. He has something in mind.

Alden turns away and runs her hand along a marble radiator cover. "Where does all the dust come from?" She doesn't expect an answer to this question, nor is she criticizing Constance's work. And Constance doesn't take comments like that personally. Instead, she makes a mental note to give the foyer the once-over before the week is out. The clock strikes the quarter hour and Alden looks tired. "I'll never get to sleep again. Does anyone else want tea?"

Mr. Hunt yawns and declines, gives Constance's shoulder another pat, and says, "I'll be heading up."

"Me too," says Constance.

"Good. You can help Mr. Hunt up the stairs."

"I'm not an invalid," Mr. Hunt says. He wobbles a bit at the first stair and Constance stays a short distance behind, prepared to steady him if he falters. Mr. Hunt slides his hand up the oak railing and raises each foot deliberately, like an old man.

When Constance was a child, Mr. Hunt's room was on the third floor beside hers. It made sense; with the two of them housed in the old servants' quarters, the better bedrooms on the second floor were left available to rent. When Mr. Hunt started having more trouble breathing, Alden sacrificed some income so he would have fewer stairs to climb. Since then, Constance has been alone on the third floor.

At first, she was lonely. Accustomed to hearing Mr. Hunt's wheezing through the paper-thin walls, she missed it. Now she almost revels in her isolation up there. The rooms are full of the weirdest things: shoe stretchers and sock darning eggs, a sewing dummy she used to dress up in old hoop skirts, riding outfits, and all manner of suits and hats tucked away in the closets. She has found three hunting rifles (none of which are loaded), and a variety of furs, which she sometimes uses on her bed in the winter. She imagines living in a cave, huddled under the fur of a woolly mammoth. There is also plenty of taxidermy stored on the third floor: a fox, a weasel, a horrid looking badger, a beaver, and a raccoon. When she was smaller, she used to dress these up too, name them after boarders, and set them around a pretend dining table. There is even a train set in a box in the last room on the left. She thinks it must have belonged to one of Alden's brothers.

Local legend claims that the ghost of William Patterson roams from room to room with a green glow emanating from him that can be seen from the street. Excluded from God's grace because of his last, fatal choice, he will never rest. Children make up rhymes about his suicide and pass the house with their fingers crossed inside their pockets. *Old Man Patterson hangs from a rafter. Run by fast or he'll chase after.* Nonsense. Constance has never seen a glow drift from room to room, greenish or otherwise, and she's certainly never heard any moaning, except from the odd boarder below her.

The rumours linger, though.

Mr. Hunt stumbles a bit on a step and Constance says, "All right?"

"Yes, yes, I'm fine," and he continues his slow march upwards.

Alden's silence on the topic of her grandfather's death is total. She only speaks about him as a great man, a great businessman, a philanthropist, and one of the founders of the Beach.

Last year, with All Souls' Day approaching, Constance asked Mr. Hunt about the suicide while he was raking up leaves in the garden. Poor Mr. Hunt checked over his shoulder and shushed her.

"Why on earth are you asking about that?"

"The kids say Patterson House is haunted."

"Malarkey," said Mr. Hunt dismissively. "Fetch another rake and help me here."

Constance wasn't ready to let Mr. Hunt off the hook. "Did he really kill himself?" She whispered the question in deference to Mr. Hunt's obvious discomfort.

"It was well before my time. Before Alden's too."

"But what happened? Do you know?"

Mr. Hunt stopped his raking and checked over his shoulder again. "It's not something to talk about. Promise me, you'll never ask Alden about it."

"Why not?"

"It's upsetting to her."

"If it was so long ago, why does it matter?"

Mr. Hunt lowered his voice even more. "It's a taint."

"A taint?"

He nudged her over to a pile of leaves between the fourth and fifth tree, cleared a spot, and exposed a square stone with WRP engraved on it.

Constance's eyes grew wide. "It's him?"

Mr. Hunt nodded. "William Rogers Patterson himself."

"Does Alden know he's here?"

Mr. Hunt shrugged. "As I said, we never speak of it. I assume so, but I don't know for sure. I never see her come out here."

Maybe he would tell her more about it tonight. At the top of the stairs, Mr. Hunt recovers his breath before walking down the hall to his room. When they get to his door, Constance can hear wheezing deep in his chest. She won't ask. He needs to sleep.

"Do you need any help?"

Mr. Hunt shakes his head. "I'll be fine, dear. It's the humidity. Try and get back to sleep. Don't worry about tomorrow. You and Gwen will get to see the airship. I promise."

"Thanks." Constance hesitates.

He leans against the door jamb. "Anything the matter?"

Constance sucks on the palm of her hand where there is a red puncture wound. Mr. Hunt takes her hand and studies it. "What happened here?"

"Nothing."

He waits, knowing the truth will come out in a minute. "I slapped Mary Atkinson. Yesterday. In the playground."

"You what?"

"I slapped her. I cut my hand on her hairpin."

"Why on earth would you do such a thing?"

"She called me a name."

"Oh, for heaven's sakes. You must rise above it. You know that. Gypsy. Orphan. They're just names. What do I always say? The best answer is always kindness."

"I know."

"You'll apologize to her."

Constance nods, but does not meet his eyes. She is not truly contrite and is afraid that Mr. Hunt will know. She feels no kindness whatsoever toward Mary Atkinson or any of her other tormentors.

Mr. Hunt turns the palm of her hand up and kisses it. "Take care of that. It looks red."

She is about to leave him when she turns around and hugs him with such force she almost knocks him over.

"What's this?" he asks, laughing and hugging her back.

"I don't know. Good night."

Mary Atkinson did not call her a Gypsy or an orphan. She called her something else. A bastard. It's not as though Constance has never heard the word before, yet for Mary Atkinson to say it right to her face shocked her. On her way up the stairs to her room, she brings her hand up to her mouth and sucks on the wound again. Stupid hairpins. Stupid Mary Atkinson.

Will she ever know the truth about herself? She awaits a comprehensive explanation of her origins, but none is forthcoming. Mr. Hunt swears he has told her everything he knows, but she doesn't believe it. He must know something else. All Alden says is that she found her on the steps of St. Michael's Cathedral and brought her home. One story Gwen told her, a story she heard from her mother, is that Constance is not a foundling at all. A young Alden Patterson was seduced by a wealthy man, a cousin of the Pellatt family, who left her unmarried and in the family way when he died in the war. It's a common enough story, a woman tarnished by a soldier, but it is still scandalous. In another version, Alden was in love with a tradesman, and since it was an unsuitable match, their affair remained clandestine. In this story, it was he who left her in the family way. It would be too good to be true if Mr. Hunt were the tradesman. After all, he was the gardener at Patterson House before the war.

At the top of the stairs to the third floor, Constance recites, "Rapunzel, Rapunzel, let down your hair," and stops to think. If Mr. Hunt were her father, wonderful as that would be, it would also mean that Alden was her real mother, and that is something Constance is far less keen to imagine. Easier to think there is someone else out there, someone less… less…Alden.

Once in her room, she takes her robe off, throws it across the old Windsor chair, and flops down on her bed. It's too hot. She turns her pillow over to the cool side, switches on her bedside lamp, and looks for her book, *The Hound of the Baskervilles*. It's from the public library at Queen and Kew Gardens. Alden told her that the old library was just a little storefront at Hambly. Alden's always telling her how things used to be. Back then, Patterson House would send books to the library. Now, the public library has more books than Patterson House could ever hold. There are books of all kinds, not just dusty old classics. Mysteries. Westerns. Travel books. Gwen likes romances and could just as easily read *Pride and Prejudice* over and over for the rest of her life. Gwen's crush on Mr. Darcy is her only fault.

Constance opens to her bookmark, a long black feather that Mr. Hunt says is from a hawk and Alden says is filthy. Holmes and Watson could surely find out who her mother was. She chews the end of the feather, sets the book aside, wraps her arms around her knees, and rocks back and forth on her bed, making the springs squeak.

Maybe she should have shared some tea with Alden after all. She's too wound up to sleep.

Constance could sell tickets to Patterson House. She imagines leading the kids from school on a tour of the attic and capping it off by showing them William Patterson's grave. It would be better than the haunted houses they slap together at Sunnyside Amusement Park or the ones they used to have at Hanlan's Point. It would have the force of history and the half-truths of well-established gossip to give it credence. The part of the rhyme about Patterson hanging from the rafters was entirely believable. Constance shudders. What if he did the dastardly deed in this very room? She looks up. No rafters. Just the light fixture.

Not being a real Patterson frees her from being tainted by anything William Patterson did, but it does create other problems. For one thing, her origins are always suspect. She could have any number of other terrible taints upon her. She gets up from her bed, pulls the old Windsor chair to the small, high window, stands on it, and looks at her reflection in the glass. Olive skin, dark and deep-set eyes, thick black hair. And she does little to help her own case. When one of the more uppity girls at school gets on her nerves, she pulls the lower lid of her right eye down with her index finger and stares at her, pretending to give the evil eye. Whenever she does this, Gwen howls with laughter, even the time she scared Mary Ellen Brennan so bad she wet herself. Constance felt bad about that, though. She gave Mary Ellen her sweater to tie around herself so she could get to the bathroom.

From up here, she can see Gwen's house. She rests her chin on the shallow sill. So many lights are on—everyone else must have been up to look at the airship too. She watches as a few lights go out here and there. Gwen's lights are all off. How could Gwen have slept through the whole thing?

No one understands her like Gwen does. Gwen is different too. Gwen had polio when she was only three years old and although she doesn't have to wear those horrible metal leg braces, she walks with a limp. This alone would be cause for relentless bullying by the other children at school, but on top of that, she is two years older than everyone in their grade, the result of having started school late on account of the sickness. The meanest children pretend she has been kept back, but Gwen is smarter than all of them tied together.

If anyone dares yell out "Gimpy Gwen" when Constance is around, she belts them. Last week, she decked Jimmy Slater and he ran away with a bloody nose. He'll never tell. No boy wants to admit being beaten up by a girl.

Mr. Hunt says you can't blame people for making up stories, and Patterson House is the kind of place that invites them. It sits atop the slope, a raven among the chickadees. It is old, as big as some of the apartment blocks on Queen Street, and has always been full of alarming looking men. Well, not always. In her lifetime. Most of the boarders (that is, back when there were boarders) were war veterans. They might be missing a limb or wearing an eye patch or using a hook for a hand. Constance doesn't even blink when a prosthetic leg is left leaning against a bedroom wall or an arm is left on a dresser. There was a boarder who regularly forgot his glass eye on the edge of the bathroom wash basin. If she found it in the morning when she cleaned, she would wrap it in a handkerchief and drop it off on his dresser. He would apologize and once explained that although he tried to use it, some days it felt very heavy in the socket and he preferred his patch. This made Constance wonder how much a regular eye weighed and why the people who made glass eyes couldn't make them weigh the same as a real eye. These are the kinds of questions Alden tells her not to ask the boarders. None of her business. Mr. Hunt says her questions show a curious mind.

Her breath creates a little circle on the window, even in the heat.

There is so much that is none of her business. Her own life is none of her business. She gets down from the chair and goes back to her bed, throws the coverlet off to the side, and leaves herself with only a sheet.

Alden says the comings and goings of Patterson House's variously maimed boarders remind neighbours of a time everyone would rather forget. "They should be ashamed to turn away. Each one of them should come over and introduce themselves to every new man and thank him for his service." Alden is at her best when she is taking umbrage.

Mr. Hunt is a different case entirely. He has been at Patterson House so long that it would be impossible for the neighbours not to acknowledge him, although some remain nervous around him. He worked for the Pattersons before the war, and when it was over, he had nowhere to go so Alden took him in. It's what her father would have done, she said. Her father, Rogers Patterson, admired the Eaton family for taking care of their employees while they were overseas. They sent extra provisions—tea and coffee and chocolate among other things—to their boys and rehired those who came back ready and able to work. Mr. Hunt is no longer an employee, and although he still enjoys the garden, the heavy work must be done by a hired man.

She stifles a yawn and covers her mouth even though she is alone and in her own narrow little bed. She can hear Alden's voice in her head. "Good manners never rest."

Mr. Hunt's problem is that hardly anyone outside of Patterson House has ever seen him without his balaclava. He wears it because he doesn't want to startle anyone, but what he doesn't understand is that by leaving his ruined face to their imaginations, he invites others to invent a visage far worse than the one he actually has.

"That's the man in the mask," people say when Mr. Hunt passes by, although they know his name.

About her, they say, "That's the foundling," even though they know her name too.

Alden's demeanour doesn't help keep the gossip about Patterson House at bay, either. While the house is clearly past its prime and Alden cleans and cooks for boarders, Constance believes that the very fact of the house, its size and the history of the family, reminds the neighbours that they are not of the same ilk. Most think of Alden as a taciturn old spinster sitting on piles of money. She speaks cordially but tersely to her fellow parishioners, to Mrs. Schiffley, the butcher's wife, and to other local shopkeepers with whom she does business. Father Moore was their only regular dinner guest until his gout got the better of him. Now the dining room is empty seven days a week.

Just as well. The dining room is, to Constance's mind, the most depressing room in Patterson House. It is the most formal, even more formal than the blue parlour. An interior room, it is without windows. Its dark wood-panelled walls make it feel small despite its size. She is always afraid she will mark the table somehow, leave a ring from a cup, or drop a piece of cutlery and scratch it. She has polished it so many times that she knows its surface like she knows her own face. The sideboard is weighed down with three sets of china that they never use. Alden moved the silver upstairs a long time ago when she started having boarders. Then there are the paintings. Unidentified landscapes, always trees and rolling hills or flowers. Boring.

To compound their isolation in Patterson House, Alden has also managed to alienate herself from a good number of neighbouring Catholics in recent years because she refuses to attend Mass at the newly built Corpus Christi Church. It's so different from St. Michael's. The interior archways of alternating blue and pink stone are so cheerful. But Alden insists on continuing to go to the gloomy cathedral. This is a matter of loyalty to Father Moore, but it has added fodder to her snooty reputation as a real Bluenose. The new little church isn't good enough for her, people say.

Constance always begs Alden to go to Corpus Christi. A few months ago, she whined, "It's so much closer. We could walk there."

Alden decided to teach her a lesson. "We can walk to St. Michael's."

Constance could see where this was going. "But it would take all day. If we went to Corpus Christi, we wouldn't even have to take the streetcar. You always say you don't like the streetcar."

What Constance hadn't counted on was that Alden likes to walk more than anything. "The walk will do us good," Alden had said. And much to

Constance's dismay, they walked all the way to St. Michael's three Sundays in a row. Finally, even Alden agreed it took too much time from the day.

Mr. Hunt is Presbyterian, whatever that means. She has never known him to go to church at all.

Constance turns over and closes her eyes. She likes to fall asleep imagining her mother. Her real mother is fun and modern, like Gwen's mother. She is beautiful too, like Mary Pickford. Or Lillian Gish. She and her mother would do things together, like go and see the airship, go to Sunnyside and catch the ferry to Hanlan's Point and picnic on the beach. Her real mother would go with her to the Canadian National Exhibition at the end of every summer and let her eat cotton candy and red hots. Mostly, her real mother would never make her clean the house.

She and Mr. Hunt once saw *The Kid*, and she has never been able to get the image of the woman leaving her baby inside a stranger's car out of her mind. "The woman—whose sin was motherhood," the title card said. She shudders to think of it. In the movie, thieves steal the car without realizing there is a baby in the back. Reckless as they are, when they discover the baby, they leave the poor thing in the street alone. Charlie Chaplin discovers it and he doesn't know what to do with it either. He tries to leave it in a woman's pram with her real baby and she catches him and hits him over the head with her umbrella. That is probably one of her favourite parts. At one point, Charlie Chaplin thinks about dropping the baby in a sewer grate. The audience gasped and some yelled, "No, don't do it!" The very idea shook Constance to her core. Mr. Hunt wrapped his arm around her shoulders and whispered, "Don't worry, dear. The baby will be fine." The baby becomes a child and Charlie Chaplin teaches him how to steal. Just think what kind of person Constance would be if someone like that had found her?

Constance imagines her mother again and how she carefully left her at the steps of St. Michael's. She waits across the street, hidden in the bushes until someone, until Alden, finds her and carries her inside. Constance is never in any danger. Her mother makes sure of that. She leaves her, full of regret, but consoled with the knowledge that she is safe.

She gets out of bed again and stands back up on the chair to see if all the lights are out now. There are still a few lights on, but not many. There is something white in the yard. It is Alden, her shawl and light-coloured skirt almost glowing in the moonlight. She is holding a cup of tea in her hand and staring into the night sky. Constance turns off her light and goes back to the window to watch her.

*

Alden sips her tea and looks at the sky. Her shoes are wet with the dew, yet she does not move. There are so many stars. When was the last time she was out in the middle of the night like this? An owl hoots from a pine tree in the neighbour's yard across the alley. "It's just me," she whispers in response. She must ask John if he has noticed it.

Constance's light goes out. Since she moved John downstairs, Alden has worried that Constance feels cast out on the third floor. She has such an imagination and reads too many novels. Just in case, Alden tucked away the copy of *Jane Eyre*, moving it from the small parlour to her own bedroom, so that Constance would not find it and imagine herself as the madwoman in the attic. The girl has such a vivid imagination.

Alden doesn't go up to the third floor enough, and she hasn't done enough to make the girl's room comfortable. She's always so busy. Constance still has the pink and green quilt with flowers she has had since she was a baby. It's probably threadbare. Now that there are no boarders, she could move her to the second floor. It wouldn't be as hot.

Or not.

Why can't she decide anything lately? She used to be a person of action. Now she dwells. Ruminates. Hesitates. But when options are limited, it is more important to make the right choice. There is less room for error.

She will leave Constance where she is. When men come back, the girl would just have to move again.

And if men don't come back, all of them will be moving soon enough.

Constance's skirts are getting short. She'll need new school clothes. Maybe they'll find something upstairs to alter. She has outgrown her shoes and is almost as tall as John. Her legs are a disgrace. Are they ever without scabs and scars? And that nail biting has got to stop. She shows no signs of womanhood, but it will come, suddenly and inevitably, and she'll need new clothes again. She remembers that dreadful Mrs. Harrison, Marion's mother. So critical. Is this what she has become? She must try to focus on Constance's positive traits.

Alden has still not talked to her about menstruation. She dreads it. Tomorrow will be the day. She can put it off no longer. She sips her tea again and places the cup back in the saucer with a tiny clink that seems far too loud in the darkness. The world smells so different at night. She can practically taste the soil. Now that the infernal racket of the dirigible has passed, she would like to walk down to the lake. But it is the middle of the night. What would people think?

And why had she not joined them on the lawn right away to watch the dirigible pass? Why had she held back and stayed at the threshold of the house? What is it in her that keeps her from joining in? John is so close to the girl. But someone must be the disciplinarian. Someone must ensure she grows up to be respectable. Again, Mrs. Harrison comes to her mind. Horrible woman. Surely, she can do better than Mrs. Harrison. Even Marion, her perfect daughter, ended up being abandoned by that fellow she was engaged to at fifteen. A scandal. It can happen to anyone. Alden sighs and turns the rest of her tea out onto the garden. She dislikes it when she is annoyed with John. But she is. He fills the girl's head with nonsense. She wants Constance to have goals and ambition. But he must realize that she cannot be anything she wants to be. No woman can. Has her own experience taught him nothing?

There are voices across the alley. The Williams family. They are a good family. How they manage with all those boys is beyond her. He recently lost his job. She's taking in mending and came over to ask if Alden needed anything. Alden truly regretted she could not offer the poor woman work. She does her own mending now. She hears the boys talking loudly to one another, makes out the words, "Wanna bet? Race you!" and hears their mother telling them to quiet down and get inside. Sensible. A very sensible woman.

The airship has everyone worked up. That is reason enough to dislike it.

In the alley, she hears shuffling, and the lifting of the lids of bins. The hobos are everywhere, scavenging. The fence seems a paltry barrier between herself and a strange man. Her mind goes to the carriage house door. Is it locked? Can he get in there? A hobo was found living in the Leuty Lighthouse recently. That's too close to home.

It's not that she doesn't feel for these men. She does. But men worry her. All men. Any men. Rich or poor. Housed or not. They're so unpredictable. They always have something to prove, no matter what their station in life. They lash out. Even though she is worried sick about money, she must admit that it has been a relief to have no men in the house for a while. Except John, of course. But he is different.

The hobo is right outside the gate, looking in their bin. He won't find much. She slips soundlessly into the house, locking the door behind her and checking the latch. Taking off her shoes, she sets them on the mat to dry, slides on slippers, and checks the lock on the door to the garden from the kitchen and then locks the main doors before she goes upstairs to bed.

*

In the morning, Constance wakes early, stretches, and looks up at her window from her bed. She imagines her room as a nun's cell. Being a nun is an option for her. It is natural for the girls to think about becoming a nun, what with all the nuns at school. Even the girls with good prospects talk about it at one time or another. Even that awful Mary Atkinson has talked about becoming a nun. If Mary Atkinson became a nun, she would be one of those mean nuns that hits your hands with a ruler. Constance giggles.

But still. It's so romantic. Marrying Christ. They have all seen *The White Sister* with Lillian Gish, who is far too pretty to be a nun. While that film was dramatic, and she and Gwen re-enacted scenes for weeks after they saw it, the lives of the nuns they know seem dull. Trying to imagine Sister Mary Agnes with a secret love is impossible. If *The White Sister* taught her anything, it's that becoming a nun is the kind of thing a woman only does when her life is a wreck.

Dressing quickly, she bounces down the back stairs in her bare feet and through the kitchen to the service entrance where the milkman leaves his delivery. This door is about as far as it is possible to be from the icebox. Alden hates having groceries carried through what she calls the "public" parts of the house, so Constance walks outside along the stone path that leads to the front entrance, past the big double doors, and along the narrower path that leads to the east side of the house, the garden, and the kitchen door. If Alden saw her walking outside barefoot, she would tell her she is going to get worms.

When she tries the kitchen door, she is surprised to find it locked. She sets down the milk and eggs on the stone stoop and retraces her path back to the service entrance and makes her way to the kitchen again via the inside of the house through the foyer and the small parlour and back to the kitchen. She unlocks the door to the garden, looks around, shrugs, and carries everything to the icebox, which sits alone in a little alcove that used to be a second stove.

The kitchen is so old it still has a huge fireplace that was once used for cooking. There is a cast iron contraption set into the mortar from which pots used to hang. Alden says the chimney isn't safe anymore. It's been sealed for years, but last week Constance heard something fluttering in there and told Alden. Alden rolled her eyes and shook her head. "Birds," she said.

Opening the icebox, Constance catches a whiff of the ice. It stinks. They've started getting ice from Lake Ontario instead of Lake Simcoe because it is cheaper. No wonder. Next, she starts porridge on the stove, slices a few plums she picked yesterday from the tree by the carriage house, and prepares the tea. It is a beautiful day outside, and she lifts the windows wide open and breathes in the freshness of the morning. Already, the bees are humming around the garden.

On the work table in the kitchen, a hamper full of clean sheets wrapped in damp towels await the iron. She sets two irons on the stove and pulls the ironing board from the broom closet. Usually, she would balk at ironing sheets. A pointless task. Like drying dishes. Why put the effort into drying dishes when they will dry anyway if you just let them be? Why iron sheets when they wrinkle the minute you lie down? But this morning, if she does everything Alden likes without being asked, maybe Alden will let her go downtown with Gwen.

Besides, there is no winning this kind of argument with Alden. She dries the dishes and puts them away. She irons the sheets. To fail to dry dishes or iron sheets would be to invite barbarism. Everyone must do their duty. And Constance's duty is to do what Alden tells her to do, even when it doesn't make any sense. She wets her hand under the tap and flicks some water onto the iron. No sizzle. Not ready yet.

Duty is why Alden makes a point of renting rooms to veterans. Whoever they are and whatever their origins, they have done their duty and that makes them admirable, even if nothing else in their background does. Constance, in her more uncharitable moments, moments she should probably confess to Father Moore, suspects it is all bunk and that Alden would like nothing more than to be able to close the doors on boarders forever. But that choice isn't available to her. Alden is broke.

The boarders rarely stay long. They sense the falseness of Alden's hospitality. Although they can't complain about the meals or the housekeeping, many don't stay more than a few weeks. The more tactful of the men say Alden is "formidable." Others are far less complimentary. It would help if she didn't do things like correct their table manners, but she can't seem to help herself. It's no wonder they say she puts on airs. Mr. Hunt's geniality goes a long way with most of them. They figure he's related to Alden and no one corrects them. Alden says it's safer that way.

Few boarders have ever come back to visit Patterson House after leaving. Occasionally, one comes to see Mr. Hunt. Just a few weeks ago, Mr. Jenkins came to the door. Alden was gracious, hoping that perhaps he needed a room again. "No Ma'am," he said. "I'm here to see John. I've been given two tickets to the ball game and wondered if he might like to come." He and Mr. Hunt sometimes went to the Toronto Maple Leafs baseball games at Hanlan's Point, and this would be Mr. Hunt's first time at the new stadium at the base of Bathurst Street. Constance was jealous.

"And who is this?" He appraised Constance from head to toe.

"You remember Constance," Alden said.

"My goodness. You were just a child when I saw you last. I didn't recognize you."

Something in the way he assessed her made her want to curl into herself. She crossed her arms.

Alden stepped forward, creating a barrier between them, and sent Constance away to find Mr. Hunt.

After Mr. Jenkins and Mr. Hunt left for the ball game, Alden said, "I never liked that one. I caught him in the back stairway once."

"Why would anyone be in the back stairway?" asked Constance, mystified. All the boarders know that the east side of the house, the kitchen, the small parlour, and the third floor are for family only. It's one of the rules.

Alden didn't answer.

"The men," as Alden refers to them, are always a source of concern.

As for Alden's other rules, every man in Patterson House must, first and foremost, be employed. "A man with nothing to do is a dangerous man," Alden often says. Equally important is Alden's rule that no alcohol is permitted on the premises. She once threw a boarder out simply for having alcohol on his breath. Constance watched from the window in the small parlour while Alden dumped his things on the porch. "Let this be a lesson to the others," she said.

But no one at Patterson House has more rules to live by than Constance. She can't slouch, sit with her knees apart, chew with her mouth open, talk too loudly, bite her fingernails (which she does anyway), wear her long hair loose, or do anything that might reflect poorly upon the Patterson name. She must use her knife and fork properly, read one book each week, set the table, be polite to the elderly, give up her seat on the streetcar to anyone who needs it, attend Mass every Sunday and on all the holy days, and go to confession every Saturday. She must pray every night and help out at the churches (both St. Michael's and Corpus Christi) whenever asked. Most importantly, Constance must keep herself and Patterson House "presentable." The definition of "presentable" changes all the time.

When Alden comes downstairs, Constance is checking the iron again.

"Good morning. Getting an early start, I see. Nicely done." Alden lowers the open window six inches, touches a few things on the table making slight rearrangements; and then she frowns, removes the sugar bowl from the centre of the table, and tucks it back in the cupboard. "We're running a little low."

Constance loves sugar. It's the only reason she drinks tea. "Can I have honey instead?"

Alden frowns. "I'm sure you can."

Constance takes the hint. "May I have honey instead?"

No answer.

"May I *please* have honey instead?"

"Yes, you may."

Although there are no boarders, Alden has found plenty for Constance to do this summer. The last part of July was dedicated to cleaning the second-floor boarders' bedrooms. Constance had already cleaned each room as boarders vacated, but that was not good enough. Mattresses were flipped, beds made up again, every drawer was cleaned, every rug beaten, and every floor polished. On a breezy day, she opened all the windows to "keep the fug out," as Alden said. They look as good as they can look. She can do nothing about worn carpets or the chipped enamel on the wash basins. There are two rooms in which she can only shake out the curtains. Alden is afraid that if they are washed, they may disintegrate.

As a make-work project, the second floor was not nearly as onerous as Alden's blitz of the first floor, which took up the first part of July. Constance thought she might keel over in a haze of linseed oil. Every rug was hung outside and beaten, every shelf dusted, every knick-knack and doodad and gewgaw washed, every bit of silver polished. Constance has done this work even though it appears unlikely that a new man will move in anytime soon. In this desperate summer of 1930, the newspapers are full of tales of the unemployed riding the rails and lining up at soup kitchens. No one can afford seven dollars and fifty cents a week to board at Patterson House. Lowering the cost will only bring a lower kind of man, Alden says. And Mr. Hunt says that even if they did reduce the price, it would not do any good. The cheapest rooming houses are going empty. Men sleep rough now on the outskirts of the city, in camps in the Don River Valley, in the Rosedale ravine, and near the railroad yards.

Constance suggested that Alden try renting rooms to women. It made perfect sense. Women were coming into the city to find work and they certainly could not sleep outside. Besides, she said, they might be tidier, and they eat less. Alden scoffed. "People would think I was running a house of ill repute," and that was the end of that. Whatever dangers men posed, they were, apparently, less a threat than the dangers posed by women.

The only people who come to the door anymore are hobos. Alden refuses to give them anything. "My charity is done through the church," she says. "I have nothing against them," she is careful to make clear. "Poor souls. It's not that I don't feel for them. I know many are decent men in bad circumstances. But they have a code they use to communicate with each other. If I gave one something, the next thing you know, every unemployed man between Saskatoon and Halifax would be at my door and I can't cope with that. Look what happened to Mrs. Offhill."

Mrs. Offhill's good nature left her so inundated by hobos she eventually closed her curtains and stopped answering the door. "A virtual prisoner in her own home," said Alden. Instead, Constance gathers the fallen fruit from the trees and sets it in a basket in the alley. So far, Alden hasn't noticed, and the fruit always disappears.

Alden places a pot of honey on the table. "I looked in at the rooms yesterday. You're doing a good job. We're almost ready."

"Ready for what?"

Alden turns her back, walks to the icebox, opens it, takes nothing out, and closes it again. "For the next boarders. I'm sure it's only a matter of time."

Mr. Hunt joins them. He is dressed to putter in the garden, his straw hat under his arm. He sets it on the windowsill, opens the window six inches higher, and clears his throat. "Good morning." He stands back from the table and appreciates it for a moment. "Isn't this lovely? Honey. That's a nice change." He rubs his chin and settles into his chair.

Alden joins him at the kitchen table and says to Constance, "We'll do the ironing after. Sit down and have breakfast." Alden's use of the word "we" is not literal. "We" means "Constance." Alden pours tea into all three cups and adds a dash of milk into her own. Constance takes a spoonful of honey and is about to have a second when Alden reaches out and stops her. "One is enough."

Mr. Hunt clears his throat and sends a meaningful glance over to Constance before he starts his speech. "Alden, I know how you feel about crowds, but I think you could allow Constance to go downtown today with Gwen. It's a big event. Not just for the girls. For the city. For the Empire. They'll be talking about this for years, and I'd hate for Constance to miss it. The ironing has waited since yesterday. I'm sure it can wait until this afternoon."

Alden purses her thin lips. "I'll have to dampen it again."

Constance is practically bursting to beg and grips the edges of her chair so that she can hold herself still. Alden looks from one to the other and says, "Fine. You may go with Gwen. You must be back by two o'clock. Not a minute later."

The deadline is completely arbitrary. Constance knows this but doesn't argue. Instead she claps her hands together and says, "Thank you."

"Wonderful," says Mr. Hunt. He reaches into his pocket and pushes two nickels into Constance's palm. Streetcar fare.

"You're spoiling her." Alden reaches for the sliced plums. "Constance, eat your breakfast."

Constance slips the nickels into her skirt pocket. For as long as she can remember, Mr. Hunt has been pushing nickels into her palm. Between Mr. Hunt and what she has earned for mending and doing errands for the boarders over the years, Constance has a nice little nest egg saved—twenty-two dollars and sixty-five cents. It's stashed away in a Winchester tobacco tin which, in turn, is nestled inside an old hat box at the back of her closet.

"Tomorrow we'll start cleaning the third floor."

"What?" Constance can hardly believe it.

"Don't say 'what.' Say 'pardon.'"

"Why do we need to clean the third floor? No one goes there but me."

Mr. Hunt taps the table with his fingertips and says, "What do you have planned?"

Alden reaches over to the sideboard and searches out a napkin. Mr. Hunt points to the napkin at her place and she says, "Oh," and places it on her lap. "I thought we'd try to help out in the parish clothing drive. There are plenty of things upstairs that might be useful in these times." Mr. Hunt and Constance exchange glances. Who needs fancy gowns, hoop skirts, and riding outfits? There is something Alden isn't saying.

"There might be something useful in the men's clothes," Alden continues as if sensing their skepticism. "I expect we'll find ourselves with a fair amount of mending to do. Perhaps there are outfits that could be altered to be suitable for today's uses. We might salvage enough fabric for a new skirt for you," she says to Constance, as though this is any kind of enticement. Her interest in clothes is non-existent. "And there's some furniture we could part with too. Some things might need minor repair. Do you think you could lend a hand with that, John?"

He chuckles. "I think I might be able to do that. I'm still pretty handy with a hammer."

Constance swallows the last bite of her oatmeal and asks to be excused. She might as well have fun while she can.

"It's a little early to call on Gwen."

"Don't worry," says Constance. "They're all up. Mr. Hughes goes to work at four in the morning. May I be excused, please?"

Alden inspects her, checks her fingernails, and frowns. "Change your clothes first. You're not going downtown like that. Get a fresh shirt and wear that skirt with the stripes."

"It's got a big tear in it."

Alden bites her lower lip. "Can it be mended?"

Constance shakes her head.

"Bring it to me and I'll find something useful to do with it. I don't know what you do to ruin so many clothes."

"Can I wear the blue one instead?" She likes it. Alden sewed a yellow ribbon along the bottom to hide the fade line where she lowered the hem.

"Yes, you can, and you may."

Constance stacks her dishes in the enamel sink and says, "Do I need to stay to wash them? They say the R-100 is going to fly over by nine this morning."

Alden checks her watch and waves her off. "Don't get into any trouble."

Constance practically flies up the stairs to change her clothes and runs back down and out the door without passing Alden for further inspection. There is no time to lose. Closing the gate behind her, she runs down the sidewalk to Gwen's home, grateful to be free and outside. Her socks fall around her ankles.

Sun glints off Lake Ontario. The sky is cloudless. It could not be a better day to see the airship.

At Gwen's door, she gives a quick knock. Gwen's whole house could fit into the blue parlour and the foyer of Patterson House. It's one of the smaller cottages built on Patterson land, a little square with a covered porch that was originally screened in and meant only for summer but is now part of the house. Gwen still has a biffy out back, even though they got hooked up to city water already and have a new indoor toilet and cold running water in the kitchen. She and Gwen have been friends since Constance was seven and Gwen's family moved to the street. Only a few months later, Gwen's father died. Cholera. Constance doesn't remember him, but she pretends she does when Gwen talks about him. It's the least she can do.

Gwen's mother is the opposite of Alden. She takes Constance along on their outings to Sunnyside Amusement Park and to the Islands. They go on the rides and swim and play games of chance. She has seen bearded ladies and Siamese twins and the world's biggest baby, which was actually a dwarf in a diaper acting like a baby, but what did she care? Gwen's mother lets them run around alone when she goes to see the fortune teller. Alden would have a fit if she knew.

Fascinated by the palm readers, Constance once found a book called *The Fortunate Hand* in a cramped junk store on Dundas, bought it for five cents (quite a bargain, the storekeeper assured her), and studied it, careful to keep it hidden in her room and away from Alden's eyes. She loves to read Gwen's palm, to hold Gwen's hand in her own, and trace the lines. The lines on Gwen's hands tell a story she wants to know. Gwen's heart line is particularly deep, while her life line doesn't even reach halfway along the mound of Venus. The book explains that the length of the life line isn't important and that its other qualities matter more, but Constance can't help checking it often to see if it has changed.

When Gwen's mother got remarried last year, Constance was jealous. "Call me Gwen Hughes now," Gwen told everyone. It was as if Gwen herself was the one who was married. What really wasn't fair was that Constance never had one father and Gwen got to have two. But soon enough, it was clear that Gwen wasn't too happy about Gerald Hughes. "He thinks he's the boss," she said one day.

"He *is* the father."

"Stepfather," she corrected, "and we used to do just fine without one."

Constance knocks on Gwen's door and Gwen opens it with flair and says, "Ta da!"

Her hair is bobbed. Constance can hardly believe it. "Wow."

"What do you think? Mum did it last night." She twirls and fluffs up the back.

"You look great." Constance feels like she has swallowed a peach pit. Her own hair is the bane of her existence. Thick, always tangled, and so hot, it sticks to her neck and seems to wilfully eject bobby pins. Alden won't hear of her getting it bobbed. "It's not decent. There are no flappers in Patterson House."

Mrs. Hughes is firmly in the grasp of the twentieth century. Even expecting, she is fashionable and taps her feet to jazz on the phonograph while she works in the kitchen. Alden's wardrobe hasn't changed since before the war. She still wears a corset to church. She hates jazz. She won't let boarders play it on the radio. Another one of her rules. She once heard one of the boarders joke that Alden probably took the roar right out of the twenties. Mr. Hunt laughs her old-fashioned ways off and says there was a time when Alden was dead set against the radio, too, but now you can't drag her away from the Canadian National Railways Radio program when they play the symphony. She's practically in a trance. Constance likes the radio plays, but more often than not, Alden switches them off. "Melodramatic drivel," she says.

When Mrs. Hughes navigates around the corner from her bedroom holding the walls of the hall for support, Constance is shocked by how swollen she is. She is due in a couple of weeks. She curls a lock of hair around Gwen's ear and says, "She looks sweet, doesn't she? I wish I could go with you girls, but I might get mistaken for the blimp."

Gwen hugs her and says, "No. You look swell."

"That's the sweetest lie I'll hear all day." Mrs. Hughes hugs Gwen back and reluctantly lets her go. "Gerald has been calling me the R-100."

That's pretty mean, thinks Constance, but she keeps it to herself. Gwen's low opinion of Gerald is influencing how she feels about him too.

"Oh, don't listen to him," says Gwen.

Mrs. Hughes laughs. "Now, don't start." Reaching out, she appraises Gwen's hair again and tucks another curl behind her ear. "I might do my hair, too. It's been so hot."

"You can cut your own hair?" Constance is amazed.

"Sure. It's not that hard. I might need Gwen to clean up the back for me though."

"Wait till I get home, then," says Gwen.

"Bye, Mrs. Hughes."

"Constance, how many times have I asked you to call me Frances?"

Constance shakes her head. "I can't do it, Mrs. Hughes. Alden would have my head."

Mrs. Hughes laughs and says, "Get going you two. Have fun."

Gwen kisses her mother goodbye and Constance feels a little twinge. She waits, hoping Mrs. Hughes will give her a hug too, but she doesn't.

Once they are at the sidewalk and Mrs. Hughes is out of sight, Gwen asks, "So, did you get in trouble yesterday?"

"For what?"

"For smacking Mary Atkinson! Why, what else did you do?"

"Oh, no. Mary would have to admit she used a bad word, so she never told. I've got two nickels for the streetcar from Mr. Hunt. Do you want to take it there or back?"

"Back."

"You look just like Mary Pickford."

Gwen glows with the compliment. When she was only eight and Gwen was ten, Mr. Hunt took both girls downtown to see Mary Pickford and Douglas Fairbanks Jr. in person. Mary Pickford walked along the crowd of admirers accepting flowers and shaking hands. Of course, that was before she bobbed her hair for her role in *Coquette*. After *Coquette*, the papers said that Canada's sweetheart had gone bad, but Constance and Gwen know the truth. Mary Pickford is A-okay. When Mary Pickford saw Mr. Hunt in his balaclava and took his damaged hand, her face didn't change at all. Not for a second. Her smile never wavered, never became false or stiff. She looked him in the eye, smiled at him, asked him if he had been in the war, and thanked him for his courage.

"Let's catch a ride." Constance hesitates for a second, knowing Alden wouldn't approve.

"Alden will never know." It's like Gwen can read her mind. They stick out their thumbs on Queen Street.

Sure enough, they wait only a minute or two before a family offers them a ride in the back of their truck. They're going to see the airship too. They drive them all the way to Front Street where she and Gwen say their thanks and are carried into the buoyant crowd on a wave of optimism. Shopkeepers stand on their stoops and look up at the sky, shading their eyes against the bright sun. A group of nuns move rosaries through their fingers and keep their eyes above. On every patch of grass, families sit on blankets and wait. Mothers are dressed in their best with infants in prams. Toddlers hang from the sides and young ones run in circles around them and jump with excitement. Gwen nudges Constance and points, not quite discreetly enough, at a family of Negroes sitting together and looking up, like everyone else. They don't see many people like that in the Beach. They keep walking and find a spot with a clear view of the lake and wait.

Gwen says, "Look!" and pulls two Winchester cigarettes from her skirt pocket.

"Wow. Ready-mades. Where did you get them?"

"Nicked them from Gerald."

"Won't he notice?"

Gwen shrugs.

They have been learning to smoke for a month now. Constance has a Zippo lighter that she found on the floor of a closet behind a luggage rack after Mr. Jesperson left. It's not a good one, not silver or anything. She doesn't feel that bad about keeping it, although she is supposed to give anything she finds to Alden. Gwen says Constance doesn't have a disobedient bone in her body, but she does. The lighter proves it. She flips the lid open, runs her thumb over the flint, and holds the flame out for Gwen, lights her own cigarette, and snaps it shut.

"Why thank you, sir," jokes Gwen. "You're getting really smooth at that."

Constance takes a drag of her cigarette, coughs, and grimaces. "I'm never going to get the hang of this."

An older lady in a jacket far too heavy for the day frowns and shakes her head in their direction. Constance looks away and feels the heat rise in her cheeks. Alden would die of shame if she knew Constance smoked—and in public too. This is definitely not the sort of thing that is becoming to a Patterson. Constance stubs the cigarette out, careful not to break it. "Here, you keep this. Save it for later."

"Just don't breathe in so deep. Look what else I've got." Gwen dips back into her pocket and pulls out lipstick.

"Where'd you find that?"

"Borrowed it from my mum. She hasn't been getting too dolled up lately." Gwen slides up the tube of colour, fishes a compact out of her pocket, and applies the lipstick like an expert. It's red, but not too bright.

"It's the bee's knees."

Gwen takes another drag of her cigarette, leaving lip marks on the end. Constance has a sudden urge to match her lips to the print that Gwen's have made.

"You try," says Gwen, and she offers Constance the tube.

"Alden would send me over Niagara Falls in a barrel."

"So, wipe it off before you go home."

"I don't know how to do it."

"I'll do it." Gwen touches Constance's chin and turns it toward her. "Open your lips a bit." She draws the colour on, intent, a crease across her brow. Gwen's breath is warm and sweet, like the plums from the tree. Constance realizes she is staring at Gwen and makes a dramatic face, pursing her lips.

"How do I look?"

"See for yourself." Gwen hands her the compact.

Lipstick doesn't make Constance look like a grown woman. It makes her look even more like a child. A child playing dress-up. "It's better on you." She licks her lips, hoping it will wear off. The texture is waxy and dry. It tastes odd, not like food and not like candy. "Give me a handkerchief."

"Use your own!"

"I can't have a big lipstick mark on my handkerchief. What if Alden finds it?" Gwen hands Constance her handkerchief with an exaggerated eye roll and Constance smears colour across it. "Thanks."

"Sure, more washing for me. That's all I need." But Constance knows Gwen isn't mad.

Then, in the distance, a smudge in the endless blue over the lake appears. The crowd becomes alert as it gets larger. For the next half hour all eyes look upwards and a hush falls over the crowd. Traffic slows to a standstill. Then, Constance and Gwen are in the massive shadow of the thing and Constance's stomach lurches. She grips Gwen's hand tighter. The air cools slightly. The blimp is so big, so impossible.

"It's not going to fall," she says, remembering Mr. Hunt's words.

"Why would it?" asks Gwen, looking sideways at her. She feels ready to flee and quashes the urge by reminding herself she is right where she wants to be—in the thick of it—with Gwen. Next to seeing Mary Pickford, this might be the most exciting day of their lives.

Maybe Gwen and Mr. Hunt have more faith than she does. Not the kind of faith that Father Moore is always on about. They have faith that everything works out for the best while she lets her imagination run wild imagining the worst. She probably gets that from Alden.

It doesn't take long for the airship to pass. As it shrinks in the northern sky, they lie back on the grass together, holding hands, not talking at all, while the crowd chatters around them. Men talk loudly about the mechanics of the thing, trying to outdo each other with their knowledge.

If only she and Gwen could stay on the grass holding hands forever. Strangely, after all the anticipation, she doesn't even really care about the airship anymore. Being here with Gwen is what is important.

What would she do without Gwen?

She is gripped with the sudden urge to say so but stops herself. Gwen would laugh it off anyway. She doesn't like anyone to be too serious. Instead, she squeezes Gwen's hand, which Gwen takes as a signal to sit up. She shields her eyes from the sun and squints north into the distance.

"I guess we'd better get going."

"Already? Alden said I didn't have to be back till two."

"It's all over. And I've got to get home."

"Rats. I was hoping we could sneak into a movie. *City Girl* is playing." Constance stands, grasps Gwen's hands and pulls her up.

"What's it about?"

"A city girl named Kate who falls in love with a farmer and goes to live on his farm, but his family doesn't like her."

"Oh." Gwen's lack of interest is disappointing. She's usually enthusiastic about anything that smacks of a difficult romance.

"I like the name 'Kate.' It's so snazzy. One syllable, like yours."

"Why don't we call you 'Con'? That's snazzy too."

Con. It feels right. "I like it."

"Okay, Con it is then!" Gwen touches the heel of her hand to Constance's forehead. "I baptize thee."

"That is not how baptism works. There has to be water."

"And God too, I imagine," laughs Gwen.

Gwen brushes the grass off her skirt and is twisting around to check the back. "Am I all right?"

"You look great."

Gwen turns Constance around. "Uh oh. Looks like you sat in something. Maybe it's just wet."

Constance shrugs and tugs her skirt around to see. "It's not so bad." She rubs at the stain for a second and then twists it around to the back again. "No one will notice. Hey, the Marx Brothers have a new movie coming out in a couple of weeks. *Animal Crackers*. Maybe we could go to that." They haven't been to a movie together in months.

"I can't. No money."

"That's never stopped us before."

"I'm getting too old to go sneaking into the movies."

There's nothing Constance hates more than having their age difference pointed out. She makes a face.

"It's one thing if you're a kid and get caught. They just throw you out. If you're a grown-up, they might call the police."

This could be true. Constance has no idea. "Maybe Mr. Hunt would take us both. He likes the Marx Brothers."

"Let's get the streetcar."

While they wait, they play the clapping game to the tune of "A Sailor Went to Sea, Sea, Sea," but Constance can tell Gwen isn't paying attention. She keeps missing the beat. On the streetcar home, Gwen stares into the distance out the window. It's strange considering it is such a good day.

"Are you mad at me?"

"No. Why would I be mad at you?"

"I don't know." Constance waits. "Are you going to tell me what's wrong?"

"There's nothing."

"All right. If you say so." There's a soup line snaking down Sackville Street from Queen. It's probably run by St. Paul's. There are hardly ever any women in the soup lines. Always men. Aren't women hungry too? She sneaks a peek at Gwen and decides not to ask.

If Constance is quiet, Gwen will eventually tell her what's on her mind, but after a few more blocks, her patience runs out. "Hey, did I tell you Alden is making me clean the third floor now? She wants to go through the closets and donate clothes to the church's drive for the poor."

Gwen looks interested. "Clothes?"

Constance nods. "Lots, but old stuff. I mean really old. Nothing great. Unless you want a hoop skirt or an old corset." They both laugh. "I don't think Alden knows there are moths up there. Everything is full of holes."

"Save me anything good."

Constance nods. Even the prospect of new clothes does not lighten Gwen's mood for long. They ride in silence, and when they get off and walk down the street toward their houses, Gwen stops in front of the LeBlanc's four-room house with its jumble of sweet peas climbing the fence. The walkway to the door is made of two-by-six boards pushed together. This is the kind of rinky-dink stuff that drives Alden crazy.

"I have to tell you something," says Gwen. "It's Gerald. He says I can't go to secretarial school next year. He says they need the money for the new baby."

"No!"

Gwen nods.

"But the money is already saved."

"It doesn't matter."

"What did your mum say?"

"What can she say? She says he's looking after everyone. He's in charge of the money now. Once you're married, everything belongs to the husband. And he's got the final say."

"But she saved that money before she was married. She saved it for you."

"That's marriage."

"It's not fair." She imagines her savings, hidden away in the back of her closet. "I'm never getting married."

"Me either, at least not to anyone like Gerald." Gwen scuffs the toe of her shoe on the ground. "He told me to start looking for a job. He says I have to start pulling my weight. I have to go this afternoon to some place he saw in the paper."

"But what about school?"

"That's all over for me."

"Aren't you going back?"

"Between looking after the baby and working, I don't know how I can."

This changes everything. School will be unbearable without Gwen. She'll be left without an ally against girls like Mary Atkinson. But how can she think of herself at a time like this? Gwen is looking anywhere but right at Constance. Her lower lip is trembling and she brings a hand to the corner of her eye to wipe away a tear that hasn't spilled yet.

"I'll leave too. We can find work together."

"You're too young."

"Am not."

"Yes, you are. And besides," Gwen says and stiffens, "you don't *have* to get a job."

Everyone assumes that Alden has money. If they stopped to think about it for a minute, they would realize that anyone who takes in boarders is not well off. But Alden says that it is impolite to talk about money, whether you have it or whether you don't, so Constance says nothing. Not even to Gwen.

Gwen links arms with Constance and forces a smile. "I'm sorry. I haven't wanted to tell you. You know I'll miss you like crazy. But you go to school. Tell me everything you learn."

Constance has been jealous of Gwen's plan to go to secretarial school after next year, but not because she wants to be a secretary. Typing and sitting at a desk all day while truckling to a boss doesn't appeal to her at all. If she's going to do that, she might as well keep cleaning Patterson House for Alden. She's jealous because Mrs. Hughes thinks about what Gwen might do in the future. Constance's own future looms before her like Lake Ontario in a winter fog: mysterious and vaguely threatening. And Alden hasn't said a word about it.

On the sidewalk by Patterson House, Mr. Hunt is paying the knife grinder. He rides by with his horse and cart on a schedule that only he knows. Alden complains about him; either the knives are not sharp enough or he has kept his foot to the pedal too long and taken too much of the blade. Mr. Hunt pets the knife grinder's horse and waves goodbye, but not before taking an apple from his pocket and cutting it in half for the horse with one of the newly sharpened knives. He wraps a canvas around them and sets them down inside the gate. "Girls! You're home early. How was it?"

Gwen smiles and says, "It was gigantic." She flings her arms wide. "I wish you could have seen it."

"Oh, I got a good look last night."

"It's not the same at night."

Mr. Hunt hands her half of a bunch of freshly cut hydrangeas. "For your mother. How is she feeling?"

"Well, thank you. I'll tell her you asked after her."

Mr. Hunt gets a quick hug for his kindness and Constance can tell he is blushing.

Alden, watching from the service door with arms crossed over her chest, waves Constance in.

"I'd better go," she says.

"Bye, Con!"

Mr. Hunt smiles. "Con. A nickname. I like it." He hands her the knives and says, "Here, take these. Be careful."

Constance takes three steps, stubs her toe, and staggers. "Whoops."

"Oh, for heaven's sake. Pass me those knives before we have a tragedy," says Alden. "You look like a ragamuffin."

Constance tries to tuck her shirt in and pull her skirt around so the seams are on the side again.

"What is that on the back of your skirt?"

"Gwen can't go to secretarial school anymore. Because of the baby."

"That's a pity," says Alden, walking through the hall to the kitchen and setting the knives down on the work table. Examining them, she frowns.

"Do you think I should go to secretarial school?"

Alden regards her as though she has proposed a trip to China.

"I'm just wondering what I'm supposed to do. When school is finished."

"Let's worry about that when the time comes." Alden gazes up as though beseeching the heavens, like the nuns did before the dirigible arrived. She points up. "Look."

The paint on the ceiling of the kitchen is peeling.

"This house is going to be the death of me."

*

The death of her! The expressions people use! I can't help but chuckle.

Patterson House is a shell of its former self, just like me. It is so much worse than paint peeling. Most of the land is gone—even the lakefront and the little beach are gone. So is the pretty path I built to get there, made into a gravel alley, and straightened for convenience. No one notices the fine stone edifice at the front of the house anymore. Instead, they see only that wretched makeshift porch over the side service door facing the street. It is a blight on the house. If I could smite it down, I would. The fence is a scandal. Shingles slide off the north side of the house in every storm. The rockery and the flower gardens have been turned into vegetable beds. Not that I ever cared much about the gardens, but to have turnips growing within sight of the house is not what I imagined.

English ivy, its vines as thick as axe handles, loosens the mortar and works its way into cracks and crevices, breaking them wide open. That gardener fellow should know how damaging ivy is. But his loyalty is to the plants, not the house.

Worst of all, the portico was torn down when the land was sold. Not enough room. There was nothing I liked more than standing under the portico when it rained and looking to the lake. Magnificent.

This house was such a triumph when I built it. A gem of civilization perched in the wilderness.

Maybe its current state is my comeuppance.

I have owned to the fact I was not a good man. The stone for the house was, how shall I say, *diverted* from the shipment intended for the Provincial Lunatic Asylum. John Howard, that show-off, was building a palace for lunatics that was fit for a king, as though they cared where they lived, and he expected the rest of us to pay for it. "To heal them," he said. Pah! Enormous windows, gardens, running water. The expense! It was doomed to fail. And it did. Nevertheless, I sold him the stone. What else could I do? So what if I held a bit back. No one ever knew. And no one ever noticed the similarities between the stone used to build Patterson House and the stone used to build the asylum, not even Howard. Now the asylum is a monument to overreach and neglect. And Howard had the nerve to call my home "Patterson's Folly." Too far east, he said. Too prone to flooding. Well, who was the fool in the end?

*

"Come with me." Alden's demeanour is stiff, even for Alden.

"What about the ironing?"

"It's done."

"You did it?"

Alden stops short and turns to glance back at Constance. "'Thank you,' would be a more appropriate response."

"Sorry. I didn't mean anything. Thank you."

Alden leaves her apron on a peg by the door in the kitchen and leads Constance into the dark service hallway where she climbs the narrow stairs to the third floor. Constance decides Alden is simply anxious to start sorting the closets, but then she stops at Constance's bedroom door. "I've been thinking about your room."

Constance has a moment of panic wondering if she made her bed this morning. She turns the corner and is relieved to see it is done and her room is reasonably tidy.

"I brought you a few things from other parts of the house." There is a rag rug on the floor made of brightly coloured scraps. Two small, framed pictures have been added to her dresser top. Surprisingly, one is of a dog.

"I don't know that dog, but I thought it was a friendly enough looking thing and you might enjoy the picture."

Over the back of the Windsor chair is a fresh quilt with a rose edge and flowers. On the bed is a fresh set of pink sheets. "The quilt is a little fresher than the one you have now. I'm also going to make up a new curtain for your window."

Her window is so high, Constance never bothers to close the one she has. But it is nice of Alden to think of it.

"You might find other things up here that appeal to you. If you see something you would like, ask. You may even decide you would like a bigger dresser. You are getting older and you might need a little more room for your clothes."

She clears her throat. "I have also purchased a few items for you that I think you will need soon." Alden picks up a bag inside the doorway and sets out the contents on the bed. There is a rubberized apron, a large garter-like thing, a packet of safety pins, and a tidy pile of small white cloths, not new, but clean and sewn around the edges. They are like dusters, but different.

Constance sits on the bed and the stack of cloths falls over beside her. Alden winces. She clasps her hands together in front of her, lets them go, and clasps them again, interlacing her fingers together in front of her chest as though in prayer.

"Soon, you will need these things. You are going to menstruate."

Constance has never seen Alden so uncomfortable and has no idea what she is talking about.

"What this means is that you will bleed. The blood comes from between your legs. This happens to every woman. It lasts for a few days, about once a month."

Constance cannot fathom what Alden is talking about.

"It's best to be prepared, I believe." Alden forges on with her speech, pacing the width of the room. "Many girls don't learn about menstruation until it happens. As you know, my mother died when I was an infant. Unfortunately, no one thought to tell me about it and when it happened to me, I was, well, I was surprised. Unprepared. Cook had to explain it to me. You will be prepared." Alden sits briefly on the battered Windsor chair under Constance's window and then rises again. "It is perfectly normal but, like everything else, it requires management." She peers beyond Constance and to the door, as though she is desperate to escape.

"What?"

"Don't say 'what.' Ask for clarification properly, or say 'pardon.'" Alden continues. "It is not a sickness. You will find you develop your own schedule although it is said that many women find they menstruate around the time of the full moon or just after. I don't know if that is true. It could be an old wives' tale, for all I know. I cannot tell you with any certainty when this will start. When you see this blood, do not be alarmed. It is normal. You are not dying. It will last about a week. It is something all women have, unless they are with child, and then it stops until the child is born."

Constance picks up the apron. "Every month?"

Alden nods.

"For the rest of my life?"

"Well, until you are about forty-five or fifty. It's part of being an adult. An adult woman." A bit of perspiration is forming on Alden's brow and the bun in her hair is getting fuzzy with little tendrils of hair curling out of it.

"Does it happen to you?"

"Of course." Alden's brow creases. "I'm hardly fifty," she says curtly.

Constance rarely even thinks about how old Alden is or that it might be something that matters to her. She cocks her head and sees her in an entirely new light.

Alden takes the apron from Constance's hand. "You wear this backwards, under your skirt, to protect your clothes from being stained." She demonstrates outside of her clothes, tying it at the front.

"Isn't it hot?"

"Yes, it is. You get used to it. You'll learn what you need to know in this pamphlet."

The pamphlet is called "Marjorie May's Twelfth Birthday." Apparently, twelve-year-olds know about this.

"The druggist suggested the pamphlet. It is about proper hygiene." She coughs. It is a made-up cough.

Alden breaks eye contact and looks at the floor. "Menstrual hygiene."

Alden has discussed this with Mr. Baxter? Unthinkable.

Alden lifts her head again and looks directly at Constance. "Do you have any questions?"

Constance is too flabbergasted to think of any. She turns the pamphlet over in her hands.

"You are a late bloomer, Constance. There is nothing wrong with that. I was a late bloomer, too. Many of the girls you know might have already begun to menstruate. But we don't talk about this with others. It is impolite."

"Not even Gwen?"

"Not even Gwen," says Alden.

Unlike the other girls at school, or Gwen, Constance has not been anxious to see her body change. She has not been anxious to have a boy pay attention to her. While the other girls have become curvy, she is still flat-chested and straight-hipped, and she likes it that way. The way the boys look at the girls differently when their chests develop makes her feel uncomfortable. Noticing a slight change in her own chest, she has begun wrapping a thick ribbon of cloth around herself to stay flat.

Events seem to rearrange themselves in her mind. She recalls some of the girls at school behaving as though they were better than her. Not better. Older. As if they knew something she did not. Now Constance understands. Menstruation.

There is absolutely no way this has happened to Gwen already. She could not have kept such a big secret. No matter what Alden says, she'll talk about this with Gwen the very next time she sees her.

Alden interrupts her thoughts and says, "Read what I've left for you and find a private time to speak to me if you have any questions." Alden turns and leaves Constance alone in her room with her pamphlet and everything else. Constance listens to her footfalls echo down the stairs.

The room feels airless and she lies back on the bed.

Pushing herself up again, she looks at every item, turns the cloths over, unfolds them and refolds them and pulls at the garter. The pamphlet is too short. On the question of where the blood comes from, Marjorie May's mother isn't specific.

Constance feels a little ill thinking of the blood, tucks everything away in her lowest drawer, looks at it again, covers it with a sweater, and goes downstairs. In the kitchen, Mr. Hunt trims hydrangeas and arranges them in a vase on the sideboard. "For Alden," he says. "She's a bit out of sorts today."

"Uh-huh."

"Where is she?"

Constance points up, indicating the second floor.

"Try to stay out of her way," he says in a low voice. "She has a lot on her mind. Sit down for a minute so I can talk to you about something."

Not again. Constance sits in her chair at the kitchen table, dreading what Mr. Hunt might say. If he talks about menstruation with her, she fears she will die. She can imagine her obituary: "Constance Patterson, also known as 'the foundling,' dies of embarrassment at the age of fourteen."

Mr. Hunt glances around conspiratorially. "Alden is worried about money."

Constance's relief is instant. She already knows that. Alden never speaks of it directly, but Constance observes her studying the prices in the grocery and revising her lists repeatedly.

Mr. Hunt motions for Constance to come in closer and in a softer voice says, "I talked to her while you were out this morning. She's trying to sell some things. That's what this blitz of the third floor is about." Constance's eyes widen. Mr. Hunt nods. "She has asked me to go through the garage and set aside anything that might be worth something. Tools and so on. Ones we don't use anymore. I thought I should tell you, but don't let on that you know. But I've been thinking about it and I don't want you to be taken by surprise."

This is the second time in under an hour that Constance would rather have been left in the dark. Becoming an adult seems to involve learning about things you would rather not know and then keeping quiet about them.

"The car, too."

Constance's eyes widen. The car, a 1912 Lozier Landaulet has been an object of fascination her whole life. She has spent hours sitting in the carriage house pretending to drive. She knows that car almost as well as she knows her own room.

Mr. Hunt nods. "No one has driven it since Alden's father died. Alden doesn't even know how."

"Do you?" Constance has never seen Mr. Hunt drive.

"Learned in the war," he says tapping his right temple with his index finger. "I think I can remember. Like riding a bike."

"I've never seen you ride a bike."

Mr. Hunt laughs. "You know what? I don't know how!"

Alden once said that her father was so enamoured with the car that he invested in the company. To hear Alden tell the story, his investment was the curse that doomed Lozier to bankruptcy a few years later. She always says her father lacked business acumen and ruined everything her grandfather built.

Mr. Hunt rubs his chin. "We'll be lucky if we can give it away, to be honest."

Constance figures the same is true for much of the Patterson finery. No one can afford fine china or silver serving dishes. Imagining the Patterson furniture out on the lawn is not possible, although there have been several sales like this recently throughout the Beach. Alden refuses to glance in their direction. "It's like gawking at an accident. It's undignified. Let the poor people be."

Mr. Hunt says, "I'm encouraging her to hold off until people have money again, but she says she's out of options." He raps the table lightly with his knuckle and purses his mouth. "She might sell the house."

Constance can hardly believe what she has heard.

Mr. Hunt nods. "I think that may be what she's getting ready for, but she hasn't said so. Meanwhile, pray for a new boarder. A little income would take the pressure off."

They hear Alden's footsteps upstairs and Mr. Hunt makes a slicing motion across his neck.

"But—"

Mr. Hunt points upstairs and shakes his head. "Later," he says.

A small, shrill steam whistle blows up the street.

"The peanut man and the knife grinder on the same day!" Mr. Hunt reaches in his pocket and pushes another nickel into Constance's palm. "Go get yourself a treat. I'm going to lie down. Our adventure in the middle of the night has left me tuckered out."

Constance saunters to the peanut man and stands back while the younger children swarm his cart. Mary Atkinson is waiting her turn and glares at her. She pretends not to notice but feels all the anger of the day before rise again inside her. Was it only yesterday? She rubs the puncture wound from Mary's hairpin on her hand. It looks a little less red today. There is no sign of Gwen. She waits until everyone else has their peanuts, sticks her tongue out at Mary Atkinson behind her back, and gets her own bag. Mr. Hunt's voice is in her head. How can she answer someone like Mary Atkinson with kindness? Impossible. She would have to be a saint. She puts her nose in the peanut bag and breathes deeply. The peanut man continues up the street and the youngest children go back to their shady spots to play while a group of boys with a makeshift bat and ball head toward the lake for a game of rounders. Two of the boys point at her and call out "Gypsy!" and the others laugh. She sticks her tongue out at them too.

Back inside the gate of Patterson House, she shelters beneath one of the beech trees for respite from the sultry mid-afternoon heat. The strange whirring song of cicadas rises and falls. Cracking peanuts open, she tosses the contents into her mouth and lets the shells fall around her. Two squirrels steal whatever she drops, and she leaves them two full peanuts for their trouble. The squirrels squabble. One squirrel takes both peanuts, which doesn't seem fair. When it runs away triumphant, she drops two more peanuts, her last, for the other. "There you go, little fella. Don't let that bully get the better of you." She imagines the squirrel bowing slightly and saying, "Thank you," like it might if it were in a storybook.

Unlike the house, the garden is comfortably unkempt. Last year's leaf litter still clings to the bases of the perennials. While the house feels stifling, the garden seems full of possibility. Bees come and go every minute or two in a line that runs southeast from the main trunk of the tree she leans against and over the fence to parts unknown. It is ridiculous to envy a bee, but Constance does. Bees know what they are doing. They have purpose.

Two starlings trill back and forth from the tallest branches. "Good thing Mr. Hunt isn't here," she says, wagging her finger at them. Mr. Hunt will tolerate almost anything in the garden, so attached to life he is. He doesn't even like pulling up weeds. But, if he sees a starling, he will scare it away. His aim with a stone is remarkably accurate. He knocks starling nests down in the spring, climbing up on rickety ladders and risking his own life and limb to do it. "Don't be fooled by starlings," Mr. Hunt says. "Starlings are the carpetbaggers of the avian world. They take over the nests of the songbirds and eat the eggs. They are invaders, like the Germans." The discovery of a broken blue eggshell is a grim occasion that leaves him searching the branches for starlings. The starlings answer Constance by fluttering to the lower branches. "Sure, you're brave now," Constance says and picks up a stone and hurls it at them. They don't flinch.

Constance leans back on her elbows and looks around. This is her world. The beech trees, the perennial beds, the path, the vegetable garden, the hedge that hides the fence, the carriage house, even the crumbling foundations of the old ice house and privy. What would it be like to leave it? If Alden sells, maybe she will encourage her to get a job and she can join Gwen walking to the streetcar every day and doing whatever it is that working girls do. Plenty of their schoolmates—and now Gwen—have not waited to finish school before going to work. Not that there's much work anywhere. The jobs are often part time or temporary, but all work is honest work. At least that's what Alden says. She plucks a stem of wild mint and chews it.

Constance and Gwen could go live together in an apartment downtown. There's a place called Midmaples. It is for independent working girls, the kind of girls she admires in the pages of *Hush*, the ones who wear trousers and smoke cigarettes. Alden hates that magazine. She only reads *Mayfair* and *Canadian Home Journal*.

She stops chewing and is completely still. What on earth would happen to Mr. Hunt? Where would he live if Alden didn't have Patterson House?

It is too much to think about.

She swallows the mint and pushes herself up with her hands, brushing leaves from her skirt. As Alden would say, it's been a long day.

Anticipating Alden's dinner instructions, Constance opens the gate to the vegetable garden and finds three ripe tomatoes, picks a stalk of dill wilting in the afternoon heat and a long cucumber, checks the beans and decides they need a few more days in the sun. She will consult with Mr. Hunt, and together, they will decide what day to harvest. There are so many beans Alden will be able to put some up for the winter. She dips a bucket into the rain barrel and gives them a little water before going inside to the kitchen.

The kitchen is cool compared to outside and she sets the vegetables on the drainboard. In the icebox, there are boiled potatoes and Alden has already made the leftover chicken into a salad on a bed of lettuce. Alden can really stretch a meal. This is the third day for the chicken. With some dill and vinegar, sliced cucumbers will add a fresh tang to the meal. The tomatoes will be better if sliced at the last minute. She washes them and leaves them on the drainboard, thinks better of it, listens to make sure no one is stirring, and eats a tomato like an apple over the sink. She missed lunch completely and the peanuts and mint only whetted her appetite. Red juice drips from her chin onto the porcelain and some seeds rest by a big black chip near the drain. A careful rinse hides her tracks. In the icebox, she finds a hard-boiled egg, bangs the shell against the counter, peels it, salts it, and eats it in two bites. This is how she would eat if she lived at Midmaples. No dishes.

Constance swallows the rest of her egg and wipes her mouth with the back of her hand. Footsteps echo through the sultry silence of the afternoon heat and approach the house from the street. Whoever it is does not stop at the makeshift porch over the service entrance to knock. He knows to come all the way around to the front door that faces the lake. It must be Father Moore.

Constance goes to the small parlour to peek through the lace curtain. An enormous man with a suitcase struggles toward the door. A boarder.

Mr. Hunt will be happy, and Alden too, but she feels disappointment. Now there will be no big changes, no chance of her getting a job with Gwen. Alden will need her. There will be more laundry and she will have to clean the second-floor bathroom every day. It is one thing to clean the bathrooms for the "family." No one minds if she gets to it every other day or every three days. But she despises cleaning up after strange men.

They leave their whiskers in the sink. They are incapable of hanging a towel straight. She cannot contemplate what happens in a man's bowels to create such a mess.

She waits for the man to knock and then opens the door. His silhouette blocks the sunlight behind him. He is not as wide as he is tall, but it is something someone might say by way of making a point about him. The size of a blimp. Constance almost giggles. But it was a mean joke when Mr. Hughes said it about Mrs. Hughes, so it is a mean joke now. Kindness, she tells herself. He breathes heavily and dabs at his forehead with a white handkerchief.

Removing his boater, he gives a slight bow. A sheen of sweat beads down his pink face and dampens his high shirt collar. Nevertheless, his tie is still smartly tightened, shoring up his loose jowls. He sets down his suitcase with a long exhale. A watch chain stretches across his capacious girth. His shoes are perfectly shined and his suit, a loud, wide check, is a bit too tight and damp with sweat.

"Hello. May I help you?"

"Yes, I'm sure you can." He dabs his handkerchief across his forehead. "It's powerfully hot today. Powerfully hot. I've come to see Mrs. Patterson. My name is Grant, Mr. Carling Grant." The words puff out of him in laboured breaths.

Constance ushers him in. "Please wait here."

"I must sit down." There is no chair in the foyer. He looks toward the blue parlour. Constance feels she has little choice and indicates he should go in. He pats the head of the trophy wolf on the right distractedly, as though they are old friends and says, "Yes, yes." He selects a low, wide ladies' chair, meant to accommodate a hoop skirt, and eases into it, filling its whole width. He takes out his pocket watch, flips it open, looks at it, shuts it, and slides it back into his vest. "A glass of water. I'll need a glass of water."

Constance goes to the kitchen and returns with a glass of water to find Mr. Carling Grant standing with his back to her, examining a figurine of a Victorian woman holding an umbrella and wearing a long dress, which he has removed from the étagère. Constance coughs, imagining he will be embarrassed. Instead, he turns the figurine over and studies the backstamp. He does this right in front of her, without any hesitation, and then sets it down. "A good Germanic bisque. Lovely piece, this one. Shame about the break."

Constance's face reddens. Ever since she knocked the figurine off its perch nine long years ago, she has dreaded this discovery. Mr. Hunt mended it so well that the break remained undetected. Until now. Constance assumed it would be Alden who would find it. "Break?" Constance says, feigning surprise. The figure of the woman seems to be pointing her umbrella directly at Constance as if to say, "You always knew this day would come."

"Here, see?" He shows her the figure's wrist and assesses her with flat brown eyes. "But you already knew that."

Constance hates him.

He sets the figurine down and takes the glass of water from Constance. Water dribbles down his chin and he catches it awkwardly with the palm of his hand, his handkerchief having disappeared somewhere in his pockets. He pats himself down in search of it. There is a lot of ground to cover. "Never mind. It only matters if it's for sale. Sentimental value," he almost sneers with the phrase, "is often increased with such damage." He runs his hands along the arms of the lady's chair when he sits back down and says, "A fine piece. Jacques & Hay, I see. A good manufacturer." He makes a show of appreciating the room. "This is a charming parlour. So well preserved. It speaks of stability. I shall do well here."

Even Constance knows what "stability" means. It means "money." Mr. Grant has the cold eye of an auctioneer. There is an air of the carnival about him, a whiff of candy corn and red hots. He has the vocal tenor of a barker. He might break open his suitcase and offer to show her an octopus in formaldehyde in exchange for one of her nickels.

Alden will not take him.

"I'm still waiting to speak to Mrs. Patterson."

Constance corrects him. "Miss Patterson."

"Miss?" He betrays a split second of consternation and then recovers. "Of course." He looks at her again. "And you are?"

"Miss Constance Patterson."

"Related how?"

Constance has never been asked this question so bluntly before and she flounders for a minute. She knows the question is incredibly rude.

But if there is one thing she has learned, it is that she cannot explain her place in Patterson House with ease and it is better not to try. In her silence, his eyes become sharper. He lets the question go.

"I was not expecting a house with children. Are there others?"

"No." She feels compelled to defend herself. "In fact, there are none. I am fourteen. Almost fifteen." She straightens her posture. This is a lie. She will not be fifteen for another seven months.

"Indeed. A young woman then. Forgive me," he says without a hint of apology in his voice.

Constance is distracted for a second by a glint of light. She looks toward the window. It is nothing. William Patterson remains inscrutable inside his frame above the mantel. Mr. Grant follows her eye.

"A fine figure," he says.

"William Patterson," says Constance. "Miss Patterson's grandfather."

Mr. Grant nods, picks up another piece of china from a lower shelf of the étagère, this one a hunting dog with a pheasant in its mouth. Again, he turns it upside down and checks the backstamp. "English," he announces. He checks his watch, flips it shut, and looks up expectantly. "And Miss Patterson?"

"Oh, yes. I'll get her."

*

Upstairs, Alden tries unsuccessfully to rest on her bed with her right arm over her eyes. The peanut man's steam whistle caught her just as she might have dropped off and any chance of sleep has been lost. The curtains are drawn to block the heat and they rustle with a rare breeze.

Last night after the dirigible rumbled over Patterson House, Alden said she would not get back to sleep and she was right, unfortunately. Wracked with worry, she wonders if she will ever sleep again.

What has she done with the last twelve years of her life?

Nothing. A description of one day could serve as a description of a year and a description of a year could serve as a description of a decade. She is lost, drifting through her life without purpose. The world has moved on, and she has not. She feels disoriented in this new world, disrupted by the new sounds, the motors, the inability to find silence anywhere.

Toronto is built and rebuilt every year it seems, and whole blocks that were familiar disappear. It's disorienting. Alden prefers to stay close to home, except for her visits to St. Michael's and Father Moore.

Constance runs to the chaos, loves the city, the noise, Sunnyside, and worst of all, the Canadian National Exhibition. John has promised to take her this year, though where he will get the money, she does not know. Alden cannot trust Constance with Gwen's mother anymore. She suspects Mrs. Hughes lets the girls run around by themselves at Hanlan's Point.

The only place Alden feels truly safe is inside Patterson House. It wasn't always like this. There was a time she longed to break free of it. She remembers those first few weeks after her father died as a time of sharp terror. She spent the night hours inventing scenarios of doom, checked the fireplaces and stove obsessively until finally she built no more fires and would not use the stove. Insomnia plagued her. She took note of each noise the house made—the creaks that sounded like footsteps and the way the wind battered the south side. Imaginary burglars paralyzed her with fear in her bed or kept her roaming the first floor, checking windows and doors. She took to bringing the child with her into her bedroom at night and barring the door behind them. Then, she became afraid to leave the house, afraid of what would happen if she did, afraid of coming back to find an intruder or find it had burned to the ground, just like the Phoenix Block in her childhood.

Finally, Father Moore came because Alden missed Sunday Mass two weeks in a row. Embarrassed at the state of the house, she pretended illness. Of course, he sent his own housekeeper over who refused to be turned away, gained entry to the house, and brought her to the kitchen where she made Alden a cup of tea, took care of a pile of unwashed dishes, freed the surfaces from crumbs, prepared a soup that would last four days, and told her she would have to get a hold of herself. Alden begged her not to tell the priest of her foolishness.

"You need to get out, Miss, see your friends."

How could she explain that she didn't have any? What kind of woman has no friends? The only people she spoke to regularly were the grocer, the butcher, and the fishmonger.

"You don't need a big house like this," the pragmatic rectory housekeeper told her. "It's a burden." When Alden made no reply, she snapped and said, "And if you're going to stay here, you'll need help."

Alden asked, "But how will I pay for it?"

"Sell something," the good woman said.

"Like what?"

She held up a spoon she was drying. "Sell the silver." And Alden did, shocked at how easy it was and how little it was worth. Counting the money, she knew that selling Patterson possessions was a temporary solution. She needed a better plan.

When John showed up at the door, he was terribly frail and hideously damaged. Constance was crying on her hip. He held out his arms and took the child from her. The weight could have knocked him over. Constance tugged at his balaclava and he pulled it off. It was all Alden could do not to gasp. The child, however, did not avert her eyes from the raw, red scars. She patted his skin with her tiny fingers, explored the places where it was raised and angry and the grafts where it was stretched thin and smooth as glass, and laughed.

While Alden feared John's arrival would be yet another burden for her to bear, it turned out to be the answer to her prayers. He was a natural with the child. On a rainy day, he could sit on the floor with her for hours and pretend. Despite everything that happened to him, he could still find ease and delight. His demeanour, so calm and reassuring, reminded her of temperance.

Given his condition, there was never a whiff of impropriety about their arrangement. Alden was understood to be his caregiver, his former employer and current landlady, and nothing more. In time, precise memory faltered. People came to assume John Hunt and Alden Patterson were related somehow. A cousin perhaps.

With John in Patterson House, she was safe again.

And if she could give John a place to live, why not others? They discussed converting Patterson House into a boarding house. His advice was eminently practical. But it was his simple presence that made the plan possible. The men who lodged with her saw that she was not alone. She would not become prey.

There have been sixty-three boarders now. Sixty-three. Man after man after man. All different, all the same.

Alden shifts from her back to her side and then to her back again and sighs. For twelve years she has held on, and now, this afternoon, in the stultifying heat, she must face the truth. She will lose the house. She will be left with nothing. Experience has bent her toward pessimism. Low expectations are a good hedge against disappointment, and today her expectations are particularly low.

In New York, men jumped out of buildings when they lost it all. William Patterson hung himself in a servant's room upstairs. All Alden knows is that she will not come to such an ignoble end. She is too angry for that. The poor and the soon-to-be-poorer, like her, have been sold a bill of goods, encouraged to live on credit and do the Charleston while the dance hall burns. They waste their time at Sunnyside and throw away their money on the midway. All this "amusement" is designed to distract, and it does. Time and again, she watches people act against their own interests. When women began to vote, she had been glad to cast her ballot, hoping women might make a difference. She has been disappointed. Women vote as their husbands do. Nothing changes.

There is an inevitability to all the bankruptcies. The Home Bank's failure in 1923 was ample warning of what was to come. Even the church lost its money. Bank directors, men of high standing, were arrested. Their arrests gave the people the impression that justice would prevail, but there is no justice. At best it is meted out sporadically and by the teaspoon. The farce of watching those scoundrels have their convictions overturned demonstrated with impeccable clarity that the system was rigged. She would never invest, never trust a bank.

Instead, she hid what little money was left, keeping some in the clever cabinet built into the back of her closet, some in one or two uninteresting books placed high on the shelves in the small parlour, and some in the cold storage room in the basement beneath the wooden slats that cover the dirt floor and in sand-filled crates used to store vegetables. No one would find anything there.

And now the money is all but gone.

Her next descent will not mean the difference between being in high society and taking in boarders. It might mean the difference between taking in boarders and being a boarder. This is what Alden has spent the last three months learning to face; this is why she is on her bed in the middle of the day, head pounding, her arm over her eyes.

When she mortgaged the house for a second time, she knew she was doomed, but she has let another five years slip by and done nothing to brace for the fall. She should have sold Patterson House then. Maybe she should have sold it when her father died. But she didn't have the nerve.

She was a fool. Is a fool. Alden Patterson, the fool.

Although Alden understands all the ways she does not fit in with the working class, she knows she is of them and her sympathy is with them. Her manners and education aside, she cooks and cleans all day. Poverty is poverty, no matter how genteel and well-mannered it might be. She has read about the communists. They believe in dignity for the working class, as does she. "From each according to his ability; to each according to his needs." Christ himself could have said that, and she has tried her best to live it. Now it is she who has needs. Who will meet them?

Constance answers the door downstairs. A man's voice. Probably a door-to-door salesman. In this heat. People are desperate.

The girl is strong and reasonably level-headed. She will always be able to work. She can cook and clean. Alden has taught her that. She hasn't raised her expectations. Why disappoint? When times get better, she will find a place as a domestic. Meanwhile, Alden will try her best to support her. Even if she loses the house, she will find a way. No one could possibly say she hasn't done her duty.

Alden Patterson, the dutiful fool.

And as for John, maybe he will decide to leave of his own accord once she explains the situation to him. She could not possibly be expected to live with him in a small apartment. That would be unseemly. Yet, she cannot imagine her life without him.

Alden studies her hands. Her knuckles have become red and thick, the palms calloused. Several raised scars on the inside of her right forearm attest to her difficult relationship with the oven. A cook. A housekeeper.

Self-pity must be a sin.

*

I give Alden credit for finding a way through the mess Rogers made.

Even I, I who am vilified, made plans for my wife and family before I left this world. I protected them from the worst of it. No one can accuse me of failing to provide.

Alden has played the only hand she has. It never occurred to her to get another deck of cards. She has let her circumstances dictate her actions. She appears to believe it is her duty to maintain what I built, not to use it for her best benefit. How she got this foolish notion into her head, I have no idea.

Perhaps it was the house itself that did it. It is imposing. Grand. Even surrounded by squatters, the house speaks volumes. It demands appreciation. It demands fealty. Perhaps this is a fanciful notion. But it is, indeed, what I built it to say. It is a shame that only my granddaughter heeds its call.

Her belief in temperance has limited her, too. In her soul, temperance has become synonymous with compromise. It has become pragmatism. Alden has often said that if there were more talk of frugality and less of flappers, everyone would be better off. She is probably correct, but she would be better off if she let her true nature out. She is no martyr to a cause. She is no shrinking violet. She should not have tied herself to a life of penury.

Occasionally, when money is particularly tight, she sells something. When she does, I am happy for her even though I feel the loss. Such contradictions. The Oriental urns were favourites of the first Mrs. Patterson. Dear Agnes. The rug in my bedroom is gone. It was hand-knotted in India. I liked to tell people I brought it back with me. I was never in India. I was always such a liar. I used to tell people I shot those two wolves at the front door when I was clearing the land for Patterson House. The truth is, I won them in a card game from the foreman in one of my lumber camps in the Ottawa Valley. There was nothing I liked more than winning back wages, and my foreman got in a bit too deep one night and threw the wolves into the pot. But I digress. Again. It is what I do.

Alden and I are the only ones who see the few places on the silk damask walls of the blue parlour where the outline of a missing painting can be discerned. We are the only ones who feel the void left behind by a small sculpture removed from the surface of a chiffonier or the emptiness where the piano used to be. Only we know that there once was an ivory chess set in a small gaming table by the window. These tiny losses are like termites that eat away at the foundation of Patterson House. On a day like today, I can hear them chewing.

But while the house elevated me, it enslaves Alden. Everything she does is in service to it. The income she earns is never enough for her to do anything but placate it. Fix a roof. Fix a window. Fix a broken step. The banister on the stairway is loose. The fireplace is caked with soot. The foundation in the southeast corner will crack. Not immediately, but soon. Then the house will sink just a bit and the roof will sag and the structure will lose its integrity. Corners, once perfectly square, will twist. Everything twists.

Perhaps I am wrong. Perhaps this is not purgatory; perhaps this is hell.

*

Constance taps at Alden's door and whispers her name.

Alden is at the door in an instant. "What is it?"

"A man is here. His name is Mr. Carling Grant. He wants a room."

Alden opens the door, smooths her skirt over her hips, checks her fingernails, sweeps up stray hair and re-pins it, all without consulting a mirror. "I hope you haven't kept him waiting."

Constance whispers, "He's very rude. He came right in without being invited. And he's enormous. He's picking things up and looking at them, turning the china upside down and checking the backstamps." She is whispering and looks behind her, over the railing, and down the stairs.

"If the man can pay his rent, I don't care how big he is or what he looks at." She brushes past Constance and goes down the stairs, stops in the foyer, takes a deep breath, and crosses into the parlour while extending her hand to Mr. Carling Grant.

Constance watches the entire exchange from the doorway and is aghast to realize that Alden will accept this preening blowhard into the house.

When Mr. Grant hands Alden six months' room and board in advance, she shows him to the largest room, the one in the southeast corner where he will get the morning sun. "It has a lovely view of the garden," she says and gestures out the window where the vegetables are at their peak. She tells him that the room used to belong to her oldest brother, who died in the war. This is new information for Constance, and she studies the room as if for the first time and wonders which room belonged to the youngest brother, or to Alden for that matter.

Constance waits for Alden's usual explication of the rules of the house, but it never arrives. Alden does not say, "This is a genteel home, a respectable residence." She does not tell him there is no tolerance for alcohol. She does not offer her usual warnings against jazz music on the phonograph in the parlour. There is no sarcastic reference to Al Jolson with his nonsense words or how his red, red robins can keep bob, bob bobbin' along. Al Jolson himself can perform in the blue parlour if that is what Mr. Carling Grant wants.

"And the staff?" he asks. "You have given them the day off to see the airship?"

Alden sets her face in a frown. "Impossible to keep these days, I'm afraid."

Impossible to pay is more to the point, thinks Constance.

"We keep a simple household," Alden says, "and get by with occasional staff."

"And they rob one blind, don't they?" he replies.

Her sideways glance at Constance confirms that she is uncomfortable with the comment. Alden would never stoop to suggest anyone is dishonest by virtue of their station in life or their profession. Except lawyers. She never trusts lawyers.

Alden shows Mr. Grant back down the stairs. "Constance, please find Mr. Hunt and ask him to come meet Mr. Grant."

For the second time in twenty-four hours, Constance is at Mr. Hunt's door. How he could have slept through all that is beyond her. When there is no answer, she opens the door a crack and realizes he is not there. She runs down the back stairs, out the kitchen door to the garden, and looks around. The door to the carriage house is open and Mr. Hunt has his head and shoulders under the car.

"When did you come outside? I didn't even see you."

"Turns out I couldn't sleep after all," he says, pulling himself out from under the car.

"You have to come," she says.

"What's happened?"

"There's a new boarder. He's awful."

Mr. Hunt frowns. "That's not very nice, Constance."

"Just wait till you meet him."

He rubs his hands clean on a rag and follows her inside.

When Alden presents Mr. Hunt to Mr. Grant, Mr. Hunt extends his hand with a smile, but Mr. Grant is so startled by his appearance and the state of his hands that any manners he has pretended to have fail him. Mr. Hunt's hand drops, unshaken. "I was out working on the car," he says, as though the problem with his hands might be some black grease from the engine. "You'll be joining us, I understand?" asks Mr. Hunt, trying to move past the moment.

Constance rolls her eyes slightly so that only Mr. Hunt can see. He sends her back a cautionary frown, but there is something in his eyes. Disappointment, maybe.

Mr. Grant nods, attempting to recover himself.

Mr. Hunt continues, unfazed. "And what is it that you do for a living, Mr. Grant?"

"I'm in Toronto with the British Airship Scheme."

Constance practically gasps. A thousand questions pop into her mind. She might have to like this man after all.

"We are considering a passenger service to all points in the British Empire, and Toronto is under consideration as a possible point of embarkation. Because Toronto is a hub of the booming aviation industry, it is thought to be an excellent choice."

Mr. Hunt nods his head slightly and says, "Is that so? Did you hear that, Alden? Mr. Grant is with the BAS. Isn't that wonderful?"

"Yes, isn't it?"

Few people besides Alden and Constance would be able to recognize that the expression on Mr. Hunt's face is one of mirth. There is a slight tightening on the right side, the lift of that edge of his mouth. Alden will have something to do with the airship after all.

*

An hour later, in the basement, Alden clutches Mr. Carling Grant's money and whispers, "Thank God." Perhaps the world is not such a malign place after all. She says a quick prayer and makes the sign of the cross over herself before she counts the notes three times onto the sandy surface of the carrot crate. Then she counts it into three piles, one on the potatoes, one on the turnips and one on the carrots, thinks and sorts, rethinks and recounts. It is not quite enough. But if she can delay the bank, it will see them through to Christmas.

The bad times are over. More boarders will arrive.

She wraps two piles of money into separate handkerchiefs and buries them deep in the sand of the turnip bin. The third she slides inside her shirtwaist.

The pantry shelves along the back wall are still half full. She cannot afford to make more preserves this year. They have the fruit—the trees are doing well—but not the sugar. A dilemma. There are still two hundred and sixty-three jars of preserves, jams and jellies, chow chow, relish, chutney, chili sauce, tomatoes, peaches, cherries, and various pickles, although some are a little older than she would like. The gherkins have some bubbles in them, and there are six jars of strawberry jam that have gone mouldy. Bad seals, no doubt. She reorganizes the oldest jars to the front and loads the mouldy ones into her apron. There may be enough salvageable to make a trifle.

Off to one side are several of John's concoctions: various teas, camphor, and a lily-of-the-valley salve that he applies to his skin. He swears its healing qualities saved his life in France, and although Alden understands his desire to try to replicate it, it is a waste of perfectly good mason jars. But she appreciates his dried herbs: mint, sage, savory, oregano, thyme, lemon myrtle, and rosemary. These are useful. There are more than enough sacks of flour and there is still a small supply of sugar. God knows that man has made his way through enough bowls of sugar. There is tea, proper tea that is, and lots of it. No coffee. She will say she believes coffee to be unhealthy and that will be the end of it. There are still root vegetables and apples from last year. And the vegetable garden is a veritable jungle. She will redirect Constance's efforts to the garden.

Last week, she offered a set of fine china—the Spode she has packed away in the sideboard in the dining room—and a tea service to Mrs. Schiffley, the butcher's wife. Mrs. Schiffley fretted over the decision for a long time. It is a sad state of affairs when the butcher has more money than the Pattersons. Mrs. Schiffley suggested a trade instead and offered credit at the shop. Alden declined. Now, she will take her up on it. This will keep them with a steady supply of beef for a while. Maybe she can make another trade later. But she won't need to. Everything will be better in 1931.

And if it's not, another plan is forming deep within her, still too deep to assign it words. Even if she were to find the words, she would deny them the moment she did. The scheme is too devious, too awful. Unholy really. But a man who can pay six months in advance....She runs her fingers along her face, feels the furrows between her eyes and the crow's feet at the outer corners, pinches her cheeks and brings some colour to them, runs the palm of her hand under her jaw and down her neck, which is still lean and long.

*

Sitting at his desk in his room that night with his crossword puzzle from the *Telegram*, John hears the new boarder lumber down the hall to the bathroom, humming something modern. He can't carry a tune, so it is hard to tell. It could be "West End Blues." Hunt shrugs and hums the real tune himself, tapping along on his desk with the pencil.

Dinner was a treat, although it was a bit heavy for such a sweltering evening. A light salad, or maybe the end of the chicken would have been nice. But instead, Alden sent Constance off to Schiffley's for a slab of roast beef. They haven't enjoyed roast beef since Mr. Garner left. Alden ran poor Constance off her feet to get a full supper ready on such short notice.

Now that they have a new boarder, he regrets worrying the child today with his talk of Alden selling the house. When he finds her alone next, he will tell her to forget the whole thing.

There was even dessert. A strawberry trifle. Mr. Grant should not have said it tasted off. Alden looked aghast. John and Constance both praised it. Mr. Grant did not appear at all chided.

Seven down. Fleece. Seven letters. Starts with "s." Fifth letter is "d." He taps the blunt end of his pencil on the desk and his mind wanders back to the new man. He will not hold his failure to shake hands against him. Mr. Hunt knows exactly what he looks like. Best to look beyond people's small failings and to try to see the good. That's the better way to live. But Carling Grant certainly likes to hear himself talk.

He rubs his eyes and yawns, sets the crossword down and readies himself for bed, applying lily-of-the-valley salve gently to his face, arms, and the scars on his torso and legs, finally rubbing it into the tops of his scarred hands, between his fingers, and into his palms. When he lies down, he brings his palms together in front of his nose and breathes deeply, enjoying the floral, spring-like scent.

*

From the dining room, Constance hears Mr. Grant go down the hall to the washroom upstairs. He runs the bath. A man of that size, in this heat. Her stomach turns with the thought. After dinner, he told her he would leave his shoes outside his door for her to shine. She could not think of a word to say, but her panicked face was not lost on Alden. "This is not a hotel, Mr. Grant, and Constance is not a servant. You take care of your personal items yourself." Constance was grateful.

Her last task of the night is to set the table in the dining room for breakfast. No more informal meals in the kitchen. The jam smells a little off. She sets it in front of Mr. Grant's place.

A few minutes later, in her room on the third floor, she checks her undergarments to see if she has started to bleed.

Nothing.

She still needs to talk to Gwen. There is a lot to talk about. She stands on the chair in her room and looks out her little window to see if Gwen's lights are on. They are. She can't see Gwen's bedroom window from here, but if the rest of the house is still up, Gwen probably is too. She would like to sneak out of Patterson House and run over there. She's done it before. Lots of times. They whisper to each other through Gwen's window. Once, Gwen's mother opened the door and Constance ducked fast.

"Who are you talking to?" She could hear Mrs. Hughes's voice from outside. Gwen said she was praying. That was quick thinking.

But the day has been long. Constance is too tired. The new sheets and quilt Alden brought her today are still folded on her bed and she pushes them aside. She doesn't have the energy to strip her bed and change sheets now. It was awfully nice of Alden to try to do something nice for her, but it doesn't much matter to her if her sheets are new or old. Changing out of her clothes, she realizes she has been wearing her stained skirt all day. She tosses it into the corner.

So much has happened. With fingers interlaced together behind her head, she studies the damp spot on her ceiling. It is almost dry tonight. If only she could talk to Gwen. Gwen would help her sort through it all. Good old Gwen. What would she do without her?

The last thing she hears before she falls asleep is Mr. Grant returning to his room beneath hers, whistling out of tune.

PART THREE

July 17, 1930

MAUDIE GRANT smiles weakly. Her devoted son, head bowed, takes her hand in his. He is teary. A life-long bachelor, Carling has always been too devoted to her. A mama's boy. A bit of a dandy. A constant worry. Her heart quickens for a beat, skips two or three, and then beats again. He lost his savings in the crash, and hers too. She doesn't blame him. Everyone is in the same boat. The *Titanic*.

It hasn't been easy for him.

Such a big man. His weight on the side of the bed makes the mattress slant downwards. Her body slides into his. She lacks the strength to dig her heels in and stop herself. The covers pull against her legs. She is trussed like a Christmas goose.

"Get off. Please." It is too much effort to explain.

The look on his face—an infant with the breast pulled away—reminds her of someone. Who is it? It is so hard to remember. Oh yes, William Patterson.

She does not want to think about William Patterson. But Mrs. Patterson—now there was a saint. A real saint. No one else would have kept her on. The other servants thought she had gone a bit barmy. They all called her "the second Mrs. Patterson," which, Mrs. Patterson confided to her, made her feel like an intruder in her own home. Maudie was always careful simply to say "Mrs. Patterson." After all, she was the only Mrs. Patterson alive and therefore the only one that mattered. In return for her kindness, Maudie vowed that Mrs. Patterson would never have a more faithful maid.

The last few years with him were difficult. Mrs. Patterson may have been grateful to leave that part of her wifely duties to another. Stranger things have happened. He was, by the end, so unpleasant, so drunk and careless, and his breath was so foul.

Maudie and her son stayed on at Patterson House for nine years until Mrs. Patterson died. Maudie laid her out in her finest clothes, the pleated silk frock that she liked so much with the self-covered buttons and three-quarter sleeves, and rested her atop a fresh coverlet. She took particular care to arrange her hair the way she liked best, parted at the side and wound around the top of her head with a few loose strands framing her face. She still looked so very young.

Rogers Patterson couldn't be blamed for their departure. There was a good severance. The man could hardly be expected to keep his mother's maid on, could he? And besides, there was talk he would sell. He did, but not all of it. Only the land. He kept the house, the last she knew.

Poor little Carling was distraught when they left Patterson House. He never understood. After all, it was the only home he had ever known. How was he to understand that it was not actually his?

A tear falls from the corner of her eye and slides to her ear. She wants to wipe it away, but cannot muster the strength.

As hard as it is to let the scraps of one's history scatter in the wind, wet-eyed sentimentality is always a mistake. With the severance from Rogers and the money Mrs. Patterson left her, Maudie moved to Newmarket with her son, eager to start fresh. She pretended to be a widow and married Mr. Davis Grant, a tannery worker, who died after only two years, leaving her with a new name, a decent three-room home by the tracks, and a year's worth of stacked firewood. Not a lot, but enough. She made her way, provided for her boy.

Another tear falls. She is wet-eyed. Sentimental.

A boy should know who his father is.

October 3, 1930

CONSTANCE AND GWEN are deep in the Glen Stewart ravine sitting in their favourite oak tree. The autumn air smells of leaf mould and pine, and the ground is slick with wet yellow leaves. All kinds of people would think Gwen wouldn't be able to climb a tree, what with the limp and all, but she can. Gwen can do anything. Their route up the tree is so well worn that the bark is slippery smooth. Each girl is perched on her preferred branch, but with the leaves already falling, they are not hidden as well as they are in the summer. Anyone who bothered to look up would see them there, two girls high in an oak tree, not children anymore and far too big for such a pursuit.

Gwen's got the sulks. They both do. Constance tugs at her fingernails with her teeth and stops herself. For a second, she almost loses her balance on the limb.

"Whoa! Be careful," calls Gwen.

"I'm okay." Constance resettles herself onto her branch.

Gwen's half-sister is four weeks old already. It is Gwen who gets up in the night. Gwen brings the baby to her mother for night feedings. It's wearing her out. But her poor mother can barely get out of bed. She isn't the same. That's an understatement. The spark is gone. She never laughs anymore. Most days, she doesn't even make dinner. Meanwhile, Gwen is rejected for job after job and trying to do everything her mother used to do. Gerald is furious with her, but it's not Gwen's fault.

The boys find work, but for the girls, there is nothing. Even domestic jobs are scarce. The big houses on the Davenport escarpment are not hiring. Today, Gwen applied to stock shelves, a job she found on the men's side of the help wanted page, and when she asked about it, the man at the door laughed at her. She breaks a twig off the tree and slaps it against her branch. "I'm perfectly capable of stocking shelves," she says. "There are twice as many jobs in the men's section of the classifieds. Three times as many. Maybe even four! It's not fair. Mum worked in a factory during the war making some kind of cylinder. She says lots of the women did heavy lifting. Sometimes I can't tell if I don't get work because I'm a girl or because of my limp."

It is undoubtedly both, but Constance keeps her mouth shut. That's what friends do. A breeze comes through the trees and the dry leaves whisper to each other.

"I wish I were still in school."

"No, you don't. We don't do anything, and Sister Mary Agnes has a sore tooth and she's in a terrible mood and is always holding the side of her face." Constance carries on with her Mr. Grant diatribe. "Did I tell you he told me to call him 'Uncle Carling'? Ugh! I could hardly believe it."

"What did Alden say?"

"You should have seen her face. But all she said was, 'I don't think that's appropriate, Mr. Grant.'"

They both laugh. It's not really that funny, though. The suggestion was somehow sneaky. It certainly did not stem from any sort of avuncular affection. He is trying to establish a new pecking order in the household.

Constance plays with Mr. Jesperson's lighter, running her finger along the wheel and listening to the rasp of the flint. Gwen has no cigarettes today, and it's just as well. Smoking still makes her feel sick to her stomach.

Gwen snaps, "Cut it out with that," gesturing at the lighter. "You're driving me crazy."

A little hurt, Constance slips the lighter back into her skirt pocket.

"Carling Grant wants to be my uncle and you want to be Alden." They are not often so short with each other.

"Sorry. It's not you," says Gwen, and Constance knows she means it.

Several minutes of silence pass. "Did I tell you about how he told me to take my coats out of the front closet so that there would be more room for his?"

Gwen nods. Even though Constance knows Gwen has heard it all before, she keeps talking.

"It's like he owns the place. Everything revolves around him. I don't understand why Alden lets him get away with it."

Mr. Grant keeps a meticulous schedule and Patterson House's usual rhythms have changed to accommodate it. He arrives each night at a quarter past five, pats the head of the mounted wolf to the right of the door, takes off his coat and hangs it up, and then he retires to the parlour to read the evening papers until supper. At his request, supper has been moved to six thirty. He who pays the piper calls the tune, and since

Mr. Grant is the only one paying the piper, the tune is entirely his. They have stopped eating rabbit, a more economical choice in these lean times, because he doesn't like it. He says soup is not a meal. Alden is going through her credit with Mrs. Schiffley entirely too fast.

Mr. Grant cleans his suit every night with a horsehair brush, shines his shoes every Tuesday and Saturday, and insists that his tea steep for precisely four and a half minutes. He would have preferred his tea poured by Alden, but he has learned not to try her too much. He times the tea with his pocket watch. It is his habit to punctuate his remarks by flipping the watch open, raising it to his ear, winding it, and flipping it shut again, as though he is giving his dear listeners time to digest his wisdom.

He claims expertise in limitless areas. Constance embarks on her ever-improving impersonation of him. "It is best not to use shortened language or any sort of abbreviation in public speaking and to keep slang out of polite conversation." She imitates his actions with the watch: open, listen, wind, shut. "When you remove a book from the shelf, grip it by both sides of the spine and pull evenly rather than tug it by the top." Open, listen, wind, shut. Gwen's mood lightens, and she starts to laugh as Constance drones in the low and sombre voice of a politician. "It is right," she says, pointing into the air for emphasis, "that the grocer on the corner of Lee and Queen turned in that ragged thief. It does not matter if the man is hungry. One must work for what one receives. On this point, I agree heartily with Prime Minister Bennett, a man of flawless thinking." Open, listen, wind, shut. "It is wrong of Mrs. Hutchins to hang her family's personal items on her clothesline in plain view of my bedroom window. She should, at the very least, screen them between bed sheets." Open, listen, wind, shut.

This one gets Gwen laughing. "He didn't really say that, did he?"

Constance nods. "He did. It was all I could do to keep from bursting. He even criticizes Father Moore's sermons." She mimics his voice again. "Too much First Corinthians, not enough Gospel of John." She rolls her eyes. "And he always finds fault with me. I swear, he stays up at night thinking of new ways to pick on me."

A gloomy silence descends again, broken only when a garrulous evening grosbeak lands on a branch above them. Gwen looks up at it and says, "What do *you* want?" and the bird squawks back. Everyone is quarrelsome today.

Constance slides down her branch, swings her leg over it, and climbs to the ground. Gwen follows. They brush themselves off.

"Presentable?" asks Gwen.

Constance nods. "Bee's knees."

"He's just another boarder. He won't be here forever. Not like Gerald." Gwen picks a leaf off the back of Constance's sweater and flicks it into the wind.

Constance isn't so sure. He has moved furniture in the blue parlour to accommodate his desire to sit in the biggest chair by the window. He has recategorized books on the shelves. Constance has noticed that a picture with William Patterson and the second Mrs. Patterson in a silver frame is missing from a console table. She suspects Mr. Grant has taken it.

They walk single file on a rough path out of the ravine, snaking their way back up the hill to Queen Street.

"He's still asking questions," says Constance from behind Gwen.

"Who?"

"Carling Grant! Who else? It's like he's some sort of spy."

"Questions about what?"

"About the Pattersons. About the house."

Alden is delighted to have an audience for her old stories and enjoys taking him from photograph to photograph to introduce him to the dead Pattersons. During his first week at Patterson House, his interest was so keen that Alden asked Constance to go into a cupboard in the small parlour to find another album of photographs. She spread it out on the coffee table, and they sat side by side on one end of the blue jacquard chesterfield, their bodies only inches apart. Constance watched from across the room and imagined Mr. Grant's weight pushing down his end of the chesterfield like a teeter-totter and Alden sliding into him.

Alden turned the pages, each separated by a stiff interleaf, with the care of an archivist. She showed him a photograph of William Patterson and his second wife with Mr. James Austin at a garden party the Austins held to celebrate their new home, Spadina House, in 1866. "The house is still there, on the Davenport escarpment, beside that hideous Casa Loma. The Austin family sold their golf course off in lots. Their intention was that many smaller houses might be built, much like what happened here. Instead, Mr. Henry Pellatt bought every lot and built his monstrosity. Of course, the Austin family was shocked. Everyone was." Alden said this as though she were there. "But in the end, one pays a price for that kind of ostentatious show. Pellatt went broke in twenty-three." Alden looked like the Cheshire cat and Mr. Grant nodded. She showed him a photograph of William Patterson with Timothy Eaton at the opening of his dry goods store in 1869. "We helped him get started," she explained confidentially, leaning ever so slightly toward him.

At first Constance found it fascinating to see Alden like this, setting out her pedigree. "This is Grandfather Patterson at the Toronto Hunt. The Hunt Club was already here when he built Patterson House. He hoped it would be a stopping point for those travelling between the city and the club. Agnes, his first wife, needed the company of society, but he loved the wilderness and was a big believer in the healthful qualities of the outdoors, having spent so many years in the great white pine forests of the Ottawa Valley. For a few years, Grandfather Patterson scared away poachers, if you can imagine. He shot the wolves that now stand at the front door while he was surveying the land."

Mr. Grant chuckled. "Magnificent specimens."

"Agnes, the first Mrs. Patterson, found it hard here, though." Alden told the story of Ruination Road, which made travel back and forth from Patterson House easier but also made it possible for the hoi polloi to travel to this part of the lake. The rabble set up camps with tents along the lake in the summer. "It was a shambles," she said.

"All progress comes at a cost." Another Carling Grant aphorism. "He was not the first here, though, was he?"

Alden bristled slightly. "Certainly, some settlement had taken place nearby. The village of Norway was to the north, named for the Norway pine that was harvested there. The Ashbridge family had their farm and the Thompsons and Simcoes were already ensconced. But they had ignored this stretch of shoreline completely. They declared it hopeless. They did not see the possibilities. My grandfather, on the other hand, had a vision. He puzzled it out, crisscrossed the marsh and devised a culvert system. He used the Patterson Lumber and Stone ships to bring in fill. A monumental undertaking. He bought it for a song and made something from nothing."

"Truly a visionary," Mr. Grant agreed. Alden turned the pages until she reached one of herself at sixteen, a professional photograph, staged. In it, Alden is in profile and looking over her shoulder.

"And who is that charming young woman?" he asked, as if it were not obvious it was Alden. Alden actually blushed. He slanted the album on the table toward himself and studied it a little too intently. "Why, this is a photograph that should be framed and displayed."

Alden pulled the book back and said, "Oh, I don't think so," but she was smiling.

Constance doesn't tell Gwen about the time she found Mr. Grant in the small parlour. He said he was searching for more photographs. She picks up a pine cone and tosses it against a tree and then tosses another. A squirrel drops its acorn and scurries into the underbrush, and two nuthatches flutter to a higher, safer branch.

Constance hesitates and finally speaks again. "Sometimes I wonder if Alden is going to marry him."

Gwen is suddenly sharp-eyed. "What do you mean? Why would she do that?"

"I don't know. I've been trying to figure it out. I think she's flirting sometimes."

"Alden? You're all wet."

"I'm not."

"You're serious?"

Constance nods her head vigorously.

"Well, you can't let that happen."

"What can I do about it?"

"Point out his flaws. Complain about him. Get her thinking about how annoying he is."

"Alden won't like that."

"Trust me."

"Is Gerald that terrible?"

Gwen nods almost indiscernibly. "It was so much better when it was just Mum and me. I wish she never got married." Tears well in her eyes, but she brushes them away and gives a broad, fake smile. "But it's Alden we're talking about. Let's not be a couple of dumb Doras. I can see what's in it for the old geezer. Alden's rich and has got the house. Any man would be interested in that. But what's in it for her?"

Constance considers telling her that Alden is broke, but still can't bring herself to say it. Gwen wouldn't believe it, anyway. She's not sure she believes it. How can it be true when they live in that big house?

"Maybe Alden is lonely," says Gwen.

"She's got Mr. Hunt." As Constance says the words, she knows that's not what Gwen really means. Gwen looks at her sideways. "I know. I know. But that can't be it. Even if she was, she thinks he's ridiculous. I see the expression on her face sometimes when he talks. It's all she can do to keep from putting him in his place. I don't have to convince Alden how annoying he is."

"I thought you said she was flirting."

"She is! I don't know. I don't get it."

"Why doesn't she set him to rights, then?"

"This is what I'm asking. Why doesn't she?"

They walk in silence together. Just before they get back onto Queen Street, Constance finally says, "He's always watching me." Constance says this gravely and Gwen stops walking, turns back to her, and nods.

"Gerald watches me too."

Constance wants to explain how Mr. Grant appraises her like she's another piece of china and not one worth keeping, she figures. Unfortunately, no matter how many books she reads or how good her table manners are or how much family history she learns (and she has learned all of it, she is sure), she will never be a true Patterson. As soon as she walks outside Patterson House she is "the foundling." And now, even inside the house, she is "the foundling" thanks to Mr. Grant. Somehow, he has learned of her origin and never ceases to remind her of it. And who would have told him? It could have been anyone. A neighbourhood gossip, perhaps. It would not have been Alden. Or would it?

Lately, Alden's admonishments are different. She sounds more and more like Mr. Grant every day.

Gwen interrupts Constance's thoughts and reaches out to clutch her hand. "Keep your door locked."

Constance is taken aback by this advice. "Why?"

"You said he's watching you."

"Not like *that*."

"How do you know?"

"You think so?"

"I know so." The air between them is heavy with everything they have not said.

"Oh. So, he—" She does not know how to finish the sentence. She crosses her arms over her chest. "Do you lock your door?" she asks, almost afraid to hear the answer.

"I wish. I can't because of the baby."

Constance whispers, "Do you need to?" The question fills her throat and almost chokes her.

Gwen doesn't answer, but instead, she releases Constance's hands and her face hardens. "I'm telling you, the day I get a job, I'm leaving. I don't want a single cent of my pay to go to Gerald. He's not going to get it like he got my money for secretarial school."

"You're leaving?" Panic rises in Constance.

"Have to," says Gwen, giving Constance's shoulder a squeeze. "I have no choice."

"But your mother—"

"I can't think about that now. I'll figure it out later. Don't tell anyone, for God's sake. Don't tell Alden. Or even Mr. Hunt."

"I won't. I promise. Where are you going to go?"

"I don't know yet." Gwen's shoulders droop.

"I read about this place called Midmaples. All girls. Six dollars a week." Gwen whistles. "Six dollars."

"It's a lot." Constance hesitates. "Maybe we could share a room and do it together." She can hardly believe she has said the words out loud.

"You said that about getting a job too."

"I mean it. You're my best friend. And what is there at Patterson House for me? More cleaning?"

"On the level? You'd come? You'd leave Alden and Mr. Hunt?"

Constance hesitates. "Cross my heart. I would."

Gwen's face is suddenly bright, almost feverish. "Do you think we really could?"

Constance takes a long time to answer. She cannot imagine how, and then thinks of Amelia Earhart. If Amelia Earhart can fly planes upside down, Constance can get a job and work and move into an apartment with Gwen. "Midmaples is for modern girls. We're modern girls. Modern girls make their own way." The words are right out of *Hush*. They sound so sure, but in her heart, Constance knows she is bluffing.

"It's decided then," says Gwen, happy for the first time in ages. "Now all we have to do is get jobs. You'll start looking, too?"

Constance nods.

They start to walk along Queen and Gwen asks, "How do I look? I have one more stop to make today. Would you give me a job? Do I need a little colour?" she asks, fishing her lipstick out of her pocket.

"You look great." Constance laughs. "Hey, maybe instead of wearing lipstick to get a job, you should dress up like a boy."

Gwen stops walking. "That's not a bad idea. It might be the best idea you've ever had."

"I was kidding."

"Do you still have clothes in the closets upstairs?"

Constance nods, understanding.

"See what you can find that looks like it might fit me."

"You're crazy," says Constance.

"Crazy like a fox," Gwen says, touching her index finger to her temple.

*

When Constance arrives home, Alden is at the door and ready to shuffle her out again. "You're late."

"I ran into Gwen."

"I don't like it when I don't know where you are."

There is no use in arguing with Alden. "I'm sorry. I should have come straight home."

"Dinner is prepared. There's still time. Let's go."

"Where?"

"Eaton's."

"Why?" This is highly unusual. Trips to Eaton's usually only happen twice a year to purchase utter necessities like new school shoes at the end of August and a new Sunday dress before Easter. Constance awaits an explanation.

"I've noticed you need a brassiere."

Constance unconsciously crosses her arms across her chest. It's her own fault. At home, she has not always wrapped her chest.

Alden is impatient. "Oh, good heavens. No one is here. There is nothing to be embarrassed about," but Alden's own brusqueness belies the statement. "The girls don't wear corsets anymore. And a brassiere," she hesitates, "it's not something I can get for you. You need to be fitted. Now, let's go. We need to get back in time for dinner. You know how Mr. Grant hates for dinner to be late."

Alden is all business. Unlike trips downtown with Gwen or Mrs. Hughes or Mr. Hunt, going downtown with Alden means receiving a constant stream of instructions and things to watch out for. Watch the step into the streetcar. Watch that your legs are crossed properly. Give your seat to the woman boarding. Let others off first. Look both ways before you cross the street. Don't touch anything in the store. Alden takes the stairs instead of the escalator. "That contraption is dangerous," she says.

In the ladies' department, the clerk, a stout woman with a slight moustache and grey hair in a tight bun, brings three different styles, and Constance hides in a fitting room believing she will be left alone to decide. No such luck. The woman knocks and, without awaiting an answer, bustles in and runs her hands along the straps and checks the fit. Constance must assume this is normal and submits to her adjustments while blushing from head to toe.

The clerk says, "Let me get your mother," and calls out to Alden, who is sitting in a chair in the waiting area, "Do you want to check?"

"No, I'm sure it's fine if you both are satisfied."

Small mercies. The clerk purses her lips and says, "We should try one more. This one really doesn't do a thing for you." She looks among the possibilities and says, "This one."

When Constance doesn't move, she takes the hint and says, "Oh, I'll just wait out here then."

Constance barely has herself covered when there is a knock and the clerk barges in again. She shrugs and stands back appraising Constance's chest. "I think this is the best for now. A little extra padding helps. Don't worry. You'll fill out. Soon the boys will notice." The clerk winks and Constance wants to be invisible, like the man in the H.G. Wells novel. Perhaps she should write a book. *The Invisible Woman*. "This one is fine," she says. Constance would agree to anything to get herself out of this store and away from this woman's hands.

At the sales desk, the clerk writes up the bill and addresses Alden. "Are you sure you don't need anything for yourself? We have a few new designs that might interest you. The new foundation garments are so much lighter."

Alden looks as though she could squash this woman like an errant potato bug, and Constance must turn away to keep from laughing.

"No. I don't need anything new."

The clerk looks chastened and tries to recover her good relationship with her customer. "Your daughter is a fine young woman. Good manners. You must be proud."

Typically, Alden corrects strangers when they call Constance her daughter, but this time, she does not. Instead, she smiles at Constance and says, "Yes, I am."

Surprisingly, they buy two brassieres. "So one is always clean," says Alden.

In the streetcar on the way home, they are silent. Constance realizes that she should say thank you.

"Thank you, Alden. I, um—"

"It's no trouble." Alden reaches her hand out and pats Constance's knee. She hesitates and looking straight ahead says, "I'm not very good at these things. I know that."

"Neither am I," says Constance. Alden glances at her and raises an eyebrow. For a minute, for a second, Constance feels they understand each other. It has been weeks since Constance felt this way.

Then the streetcar screeches, grinding metal wheels on metal tracks, and they both wince. The moment is over.

*

The next night at supper, the table is laid with a good linen tablecloth, but not their finest. Mr. Grant tends to leave stains behind, and more than one cloth has been ruined. Alden is fed up with it. He holds forth, describing his time in the Boer War and the infamous Battle of Paardeberg. Constance is barely listening. Her new brassiere is itchy under her shift and she struggles not to pull at it.

In her raid of the other rooms on the third floor, Constance has found a pair of tweed trousers and jacket, a shirt, a good collar, suspenders, a pair of shoes, which are likely too big, and a cap in which Gwen can hide her hair. Then she can tackle the men's side of the help wanted ads.

Mr. Grant goes into his most sombre oratorical tone when he begins to describe Bloody Sunday. Kitchener, the Imperial Commander, ordered an ill-considered straight charge into the Boer trenches down a thousand-yard slope without cover. "It was a massacre. We all knew it would be. Somehow, I survived."

Alden listens intently, but Constance notices Mr. Hunt tense. He says little for the remainder of the main course and leaves the table, claiming a need for rest when Constance clears the plates.

Constance brings in the cake and asks if she can bring a plate up to Mr. Hunt. Usually, no one eats outside of the dining room. It is Mr. Grant who answers, as though he has the authority to make such a decision.

"Of course. Take the poor man his cake. Make sure he is comfortable."

Constance waits a minute to see if Alden will say anything. "Yes," she says. "Do make sure he's comfortable," and turns her attention back to Mr. Grant, who turns his attention to his cake.

At Mr. Hunt's door, she taps and whispers, "It's me."

"Come in, dear."

She is welcomed by the light scent of camphor, which is almost covered by mint and rosemary. Mr. Hunt's room is comfortable in the lamplight, haphazardly kept, and chock-a-block with bits of the garden. He keeps several bowls on his chiffonier, one with interesting rocks and fossils, another with arrowheads, and another with chestnuts and acorns that he has polished to a high shine. Several mason jars hold various iterations of the burn salves he concocts. He has herbs hung to dry from the ceiling light and curtain rod, in neatly tied bundles. They come from pots along his windowsill that he overwinters inside. The quilt on his bed is a masculine log cabin pattern in browns and greys with splashes of orange and red. He is the only person in Patterson House who still uses the wash basin in his room instead of going to the washroom, and his comb and toothbrush are set up along the edge of the stand. On his bedside table is a stack of Zane Grey novels, several dog-eared seed catalogues, and a half-dozen dried roses in a vase. At his feet, under his desk, he keeps his most cherished dahlia bulbs, which he will plant again in the spring.

"I brought you some cake."

Mr. Hunt is at his desk, his hands fidgeting, the crossword from the newspaper folded and ready, but otherwise untouched. "I don't think so. But thank you."

Constance sets the plate and fork down. "Do you mind if I do?"

He laughs. "No. You go ahead."

The cake is made with ginger and molasses and has a white cream icing. It is one of Constance's favourites. She talks with her mouth full. "I'm still hungry. He ate almost all the chicken. All I got was carrots and onions and the gravy. I know you've told me to give him a chance, but it's been two months! I don't like him." Cake crumbs spray from her mouth and she covers it with her hand. "Sorry."

Mr. Hunt nods. "I don't think you need to give him a chance anymore."

"What?"

"That man was not at Paardeberg."

Constance drops her fork on the plate with a clatter. "How do you know?"

"I know. He talks about Paardeberg like he read it in a book."

"What do you mean?"

"It's hard to explain. It's a feeling. Have you ever heard any of the boarders talk about a battle they were in, about the overview, the objectives?"

Constance shakes her head. "No. They don't talk about those things at all."

"Right. Maybe they'll mention a funny thing that happened to them with the other lads, a little anecdote about finding a bottle of wine or meeting a girl."

Constance nods.

"It's like he was giving a lecture about it. Anyone who was there, anyone who survived, would not be able to be so," he hesitates, "thorough."

"You think he's lying?"

"I do."

"Why?"

"I don't know yet."

Constance decides to drop the bombshell. "He drinks, you know. In his room."

Now it is Mr. Hunt's turn to be incredulous. "How do you know?"

"I clean, remember? I know everything."

Mr. Hunt looks uncomfortable for a moment. "You shouldn't snoop."

"I don't."

Mr. Hunt rolls his eyes.

"This is different. He's up to something. Anyway, he's got a quarter-full bottle of gin and a third of brandy. He keeps them on the top shelf of his closet, at the back."

"It does no good knowing. You'd have to explain to Alden how you know, and you can't do that."

"I could spill it or something."

Mr. Hunt shakes his head and stares out the window at the failing sunlight while Constance takes another bite of cake.

"You want to know something else?" Crumbs spray from her mouth again and she covers it. Mr. Hunt nods. "I don't think he works for the British Airship Scheme. I don't think he works at all."

"What would make you say a thing like that? Where does the man go every day if he doesn't go to work? Where does he get his money?"

That is exactly what Constance has been wondering. She has wanted to follow him, but she must clean in the morning and get to school. And now she has to look for work, too.

"It's like you said. A feeling. There's nothing in his room about it except four Waterford pens in commemorative boxes, the same ones he gave to us the day after he moved in, remember? Anyone can get those. There's not a letter, a file, a cheque stub, nothing."

"And nothing in his valise?"

With this question, Mr. Hunt has become her accomplice.

"Locked."

Mr. Hunt drums his fingers on the desk. "This is bedevilling." He picks up the commemorative Waterford pen from his desk and looks at it with fresh eyes, like Sherlock Holmes might.

"What I don't like is that he takes a number of liberties. For one thing, have you noticed he's started calling Alden by her first name?"

"Alden told him to."

Mr. Hunt lays his pen down. "No."

"It's true. I was there. I caught him snooping in the little parlour."

Alden, Mr. Hunt, and Constance usually spend their evenings in the little parlour, the least formal room downstairs besides the kitchen, listening to the radio on low, away from the boarders. "He was on his knees and looking through the cupboards behind Alden's chair." It's a relief to finally tell him all of this. "When I asked him what he was doing, he said he was looking for more photos. I told him the little parlour was just for the family. He walked out but I knew he was angry. Then later, I waited until he and Alden were together in the hallway and I mentioned that Mr. Grant was in there looking for photos. I said it like I was trying to help, but I was really trying to tell Alden he was snooping around. I was sure she would tell him that the little parlour is private, but instead she asked him what he was trying to find. Can you imagine?"

"What did he say?"

"He said he was wondering if there were any pictures of Patterson House in its heyday, with the staff."

"Odd. Why would he want to see that?"

"And then Alden invited him in and found one for him. I couldn't believe it. All these people lined up outside the front door when there was still a portico. He studied it for a long time. Then he said something about those being the days, and she agreed, and that was that. Then he called her Miss Patterson and she said, 'Please, it's time you call me Alden.'"

Mr. Hunt tilts his head to the side slightly and purses his lips.

"That's what happened. Every time I think I've caught him at something, it doesn't stick to him. I don't know how he does it. What bothers me more is he calls you 'Hunt' without the mister, or even John. It's rude."

"It's confidence," Mr. Hunt says with a sigh.

Constance wonders if that's why they call grifters "confidence men."

She eats the last bite of the cake, licks the fork front and back, and rests it on the plate. "That's not the only time he's been snooping." She licks her index finger and uses it to pick up crumbs.

Mr. Hunt faces her, giving her his full attention again.

"Remember how he asked Alden if he could have another room?"

"Yes. That was strange. He's got excellent light in his room and it's the largest one."

"You mean, next to Alden's." She hesitates. But she's come this far, so there's no point in holding back. "I think he did it so he could see everything else. He looked in every closet, I mean, really looked. He ran his hands along shelves, looked in empty dressers. It was weird. And then he decided to stay where he was."

"What's he looking for?"

"I don't know. He even tried to come into your room, but I wouldn't let him."

"Into my room?" Mr. Hunt looks around, startled. "What would he want in here?"

"I don't know. I told him you would not be moving rooms, so there was no point." Alden keeps her own room locked, so she is probably safe. Even Constance doesn't go into it—not to clean, not for anything.

"He's been in my room too."

At this, Mr. Hunt stands. "What?"

"He's such a lug that he bumps into things without realizing. He left my lampshade tilted." She does not tell him that when she checked her drawers, she noticed subtle shifts in the contents. To her horror, her undergarments, her sanitary belt, the rubber apron, and the cloths that Alden gave her had been touched. The sweater that covered them had been knocked to one side. She took everything to the laundry in the basement and used the hottest water her hands could stand to wash it. She blushes with mortification at the memory.

Mr. Hunt notices. He has trouble asking the next question. "Does he bother you?"

Constance hesitates. She can't meet his eyes. "Not like that."

The words hang between them. With her words, she has inadvertently revealed her knowledge of what men and women do. She cannot make eye contact. How can she explain how he bothers her, how his appraisal of her reduces her?

Mr. Hunt takes her hand and they sit together for a few more minutes. One thing about Mr. Hunt is he knows when to be quiet.

Finally, Constance says, "Yes, he bothers me. He bothers me all the time. He bothers me by being here."

Constance hesitates and then asks, "Do you think they're flirting?"

"Who?"

"Mr. Grant and Alden."

Mr. Hunt drops her hand and his whole body stiffens. "No." The force of his response startles her. This conversation is over. But his certainty does nothing to ease her mind.

*

After washing up from dinner and setting the table for Sunday lunch after Mass, Constance returns to the third floor, folds up clothes she has found for Gwen, wraps them in brown paper, and takes them over to Gwen's house. She knows she won't be allowed in with Gerald home, and she doesn't want to give Gwen's plan away, so she slips around the side and taps on Gwen's bedroom window. Gwen slides the window up and whispers, "What?" She does not appear happy to see her and is scowling.

"I brought these for you." She passes her the package and Gwen looks inside and smiles. "There's even a cap. You can tuck your hair into it. Are you really going to try this?"

"You bet." Her smile is sudden and bright. "Thanks." She looks back toward her door and shoos Constance away. "Get out of here before he hears you."

Constance slinks though the backyard, over the fence, and into the alleyway leading to Patterson House. The back gate squeaks and clanks shut behind her as she walks past the carriage house and along the line of beech trees, past Alden's favourite bench, and enters the back door by the kitchen.

Mr. Grant is waiting for her in the back hallway, arms crossed. "Where have you been?"

Constance is indignant. "I don't need to explain myself to you." He shouldn't be in the back hallway.

"To Alden, then." He calls out to Alden, who comes rushing from the small parlour, a volume of William Blake's *Songs of Innocence and Experience* still in her hands.

"Why, Mr. Grant. What are you doing back here?"

"I've just caught Constance coming in through the back gate. I saw her leave earlier and was concerned. It is inappropriate for a young girl to go sneaking out alone at night." He licks his lips.

Alden looks annoyed. But instead of being annoyed at Constance, she turns on Mr. Grant. "Mr. Grant. It is not your place. Constance was out with my permission. The comings and goings of Constance and the day-to-day tasks of the household are none of your business. And please, this area of the house is not for guests."

Surprised beyond measure, Constance watches Mr. Grant return to the main hallway. If he is chastened, he does not show it. Once he is out of sight, she faces Alden waiting for her own chastisement to begin.

"What is the meaning of this? Where on earth were you?"

"I went to Gwen's house to give her some clothes. She's been having trouble finding a job and thought something a little fresher might help." It's only half a lie.

"You should have told me."

"I'm sorry. I wasn't sure you would approve of me lending her clothes."

Alden shakes her head. "Don't sneak around. There's no reason for it."

"I wasn't sneaking. Really. And I didn't think I needed permission to run down to Gwen's after dinner. I'm fourteen."

Alden is out of sorts. "You didn't think you needed permission, or you didn't want me to know you were lending your clothes? Which is it?"

Constance can't meet Alden's eyes. "Both."

Alden crosses her arms over her chest. "I don't think your dresses would fit Gwen." The observation stings more than it would have before yesterday's outing to Eaton's.

"I offered her some things I found in the upstairs closets. You were going to get rid of them anyway." Technically, she still has not lied.

"You still should have checked. But, yes, it is fine." She sits heavily in the kitchen chair and drums her fingers on the table. "Mr. Grant has very particular ideas about right and wrong."

"I don't have to answer to him," she says, and then adds, "do I?"

"No, you don't. But please. Don't cause me any trouble."

If Constance had a nickel for every time Alden said that to her, she could afford six months at Midmaples.

*

The sound of that man's voice calling her from the back stairway sent a chill through Alden. She draws the drapes closed in her bedroom, brushes her hand down the length of one panel, and shakes her head. They need a good cleaning, but the fabric won't hold. She turns down her bed, folding the edge of the sheet under itself so that the bed looks tidy and inviting. Then, she goes back to her door and checks again that it is locked. She has come up to her room early to escape him. Can there not be a moment of the day when Carling Grant is not prattling on about something?

The nerve of him. In questioning Constance, he is questioning her. It is not his business to monitor the comings and goings of her charge. The man can find myriad ways to irritate.

They goad each other, Mr. Grant and Constance. It's a problem. She goes into the washroom and applies tooth cream to her toothbrush and cleans her teeth without looking in the mirror. She spits, rinses the sink, and washes her face with cool water. It's too early to go to bed. She sits in the slipper chair beside the dresser and turns on the light, opens Blake again, and lets the book drop to her lap.

*

The bastard moves his glass in a small circle, watching the wave of liquor move within, and smiles, self-satisfied. He looks ridiculous, sitting there in his chair, his sock feet up on the edge of his bed, his jacket and tie off, his shirt unbuttoned. This is the true nature of the man; slovenly, lazy, gluttonous. He has a piece of cake stowed away in a napkin in his jacket pocket. Alden will count the napkins, six, seven times, when they come out of the laundry and wonder what happened to it.

He reaches behind him and sets the glass down on his dresser and opens one of the drawers to get the picture of myself and the first Mrs. Patterson, dear Agnes, that he took from the blue parlour. He studies it, studies my face, and stands to look in the mirror over his wash basin. He moves his head from side to side, checks his profile, and holds back his thick jowls as though that might help him see a jawline that is like my own.

He hides the photograph back in the drawer and finds his piece of cake. As he eats, crumbs land on his chest. Alden does not see what he steals, preoccupied as she is. The girl is right to watch him so carefully. She is right about everything.

*

Monday after school, Constance spends her time with Mr. Hunt, who is doing some plumbing repairs. His head is under the kitchen sink repairing the clogged drain. Alden has blamed Constance for the trouble. She lets too many food scraps go down.

"I'm sorry," she says. "I'll scrape the plates better before I wash them. I promise." What she is really sorry about is that she is breaking her promise to Gwen. She is not out looking for a job. She doesn't know where to start.

Mr. Hunt has been busy lately repairing one thing after another. If he would teach her how to fix things, he wouldn't have to work so hard. "Men's work," he says. Relegated to handing him tools, she harrumphs loudly every time he asks for something new. He ignores her. "Small pipe wrench please. The one with the red handle."

"I know what the small pipe wrench is," she says, practically slapping it into his hand. "Who decided what was men's work and women's work? Gwen is trying to find a job and the only work out there that pays is for men. It's not fair."

Mr. Hunt pulls his head out from under the sink and looks her square in the eye. "If you want to do men's work, prove you can do it. Don't give up, for goodness' sake."

"How can I prove it if no one will let me do it? Let me fix the sink. Teach me. There is plenty I can do around here."

"You're right. Okay, get under here." The sink is attached to the wall at the back and has two legs at the front to make it look like a table. It has draining boards on either side, which make it wide enough for the two of them to fit easily between the legs. Patterson House has always had running water, even before there were sewers and city water hookups. It was built with a cistern on the roof. Modern conveniences made it easier to attract and keep good help. But the kitchen has fallen behind again. There are gas stoves now that work with ease and refrigerators that are electric.

While they both lie on their backs, Mr. Hunt describes what to do. "You might want to be careful what you ask for, though. There's no glamour in plumbing, I'll tell you. That leaky tap yesterday in the boarder's bath was an all-day job in the end." The dripping noise was annoying Mr. Grant, but Constance suspects that what he really wanted was to order Mr. Hunt around like he does her. Mr. Hunt describes how he replaced a washer but then the fitting broke, requiring another trip to the hardware store on Queen Street. The delay annoyed Mr. Grant, who was forced to use the small powder room on the first floor for the duration. It would be awkward for a man of his size to turn around in the tiny space.

"Tighten it up now. See it?"

"Which way?"

"Right tight. Left loose." He chuckles. "At lunch, Mr. Grant suggested that he use the bathroom adjoining Alden's bedroom."

"That must have gone over like a lead balloon."

"Alden pretended not to hear him." He laughs.

"It was probably just an excuse to do some more snooping around."

"Shhh." Mr. Hunt looks around conspiratorially. "Not here."

"Even I'm not allowed in Alden's room."

"You used to sleep there."

"I did?" Constance has no memory of it.

"Yes, when I first came back to Patterson House. She kept a crib in her room for you."

Constance can hardly imagine. "When did I get my own room?"

"Well, you went up to the third floor with me once Alden started taking in boarders." She passes the wrench to Mr. Hunt, who checks to make sure there is no give. "Good work."

Constance pulls herself out from under the sink, settles her skirt back around her, and sits on the floor examining the tools in the box, turning over hammers and fitting the pieces of a socket set together. She likes the weight of the tools, their solidity. It doesn't matter to her that she doesn't know what the purpose of each tool is—at least not yet. The idea that they each have purpose is reassuring enough.

Mr. Hunt runs the water and it goes down the drain easily. "That's got it."

"She should sell it. Sell the house."

"I beg your pardon?"

"It's falling apart. Every day there's something else. A bird in the chimney. A leak here, a broken step there. The step outside the kitchen door is crumbling. Someone is going to hurt themselves. You said she was thinking about it before. Remember?"

Mr. Hunt is in a mood for philosophizing. "You know, an old house like this is a lot like a person. When a person is young, you can take the body for granted, take health for granted. But when it's older, it needs a little more attention. Just because something is a little older, it doesn't mean we should get rid of it."

"Wouldn't it be better to just let it go? I mean, at some point, aren't you throwing bad money after good?"

"You mean good money after bad."

"Throwing money away. You know what I mean."

Mr. Hunt picks up the toolbox with considerable effort. "I'm as creaky as the house," he says. "Will you sell me when I'm old and sick?"

"Of course not. And it's not the same thing and you know it. But this house…" Constance never completes her thought. What she wants to say is that it is because of the house that they are beholden to Mr. Grant. Instead, she says, "If Alden sold, we wouldn't have boarders anymore."

"Ah. No more Mr. Carling Grant. Yes, that's true. But then Alden wouldn't have her house anymore, either. I admit, it's a dilemma."

They hear movement by the service entrance and know that Alden is back. Constance has not worn her new brassiere. Itchy, uncomfortable thing. That clerk was crazy to think she would want padding to emphasize her chest. She has wrapped herself again. With luck, Alden won't notice.

"The sink is as good as new," says Mr. Hunt to Alden, rubbing his hands together.

"I helped," says Constance and Mr. Hunt pats her shoulder.

But Alden is distracted. Her coat is still on and she lays her brown paper package from the butcher on the drainboard and does not stop to store it in the icebox.

"What's happened?"

"I'm not sure. Turn the radio on."

Mr. Hunt looks at his grimy fingers and tilts his head at Constance to do it. In the small parlour, Constance moves the dial until she finds the news. Alden is at her side, her hand covering her mouth, and Mr. Hunt washes up in the newly unplugged kitchen sink. He is still holding a hand towel when the news draws him into the parlour. The R-101, the R-100's sister ship, has crashed in France.

"So, it's true," says Alden. "Oh dear."

The three of them listen in shocked silence.

Alden takes off her coat and sinks into her reading chair. Constance and Mr. Hunt remain standing by the radio, listening to the announcer describe the tragedy through hiss and crackle. So many are dead. This may be the end of the British Airship Scheme, the announcer speculates. Constance must turn to the window because she can't stop smiling. It will be the end of Mr. Carling Grant, too.

"Turn it off." Alden rises with effort and returns to the kitchen. Both Constance and Mr. Hunt follow. She hangs her coat over the back of a chair and unwraps the brisket she brought home. She slides the slab of beef onto a cutting board, folds the bloody brown paper into itself, puts it in the burn box, and washes her hands. She makes no comment about how well the sink is draining again. "We'll have an old-fashioned boiled dinner tonight. Mr. Grant will need cheering." She points to another bag of groceries and says, "Constance, get all this put away."

"Terrible news indeed. All right then," Mr. Hunt says, rubbing his hands together. Addressing Alden, he says, "I'm off to the carriage house. I've got a good collection of tools cleaned and ready to sell. And I have a lead on the car if you're still interested in selling it."

"Really?" Alden's eyes light up. "Some good news. Yes, please pursue the buyer with vigour, Mr. Hunt. I trust you will negotiate the best possible price. It hasn't been started in years. Perhaps getting it going will help."

"I'm working on it."

Constance is grateful to be able to hide for a moment longer, arranging items in cupboards, lining up the Bon Ami, Murphy's Oil Soap, and other cleaners.

There is Empire and there is Mr. Grant, and if Empire must be sacrificed to get rid of him, so be it. And get rid of him they will.

When Mr. Abernathy, a boarder from two years ago, lost his job after he got his arm crushed in the press room at the *Telegram*, Alden gave him an extra week's notice. When he left, he could barely drag his suitcase down the path with his good arm. Constance watched from the window in the dining room, uneasy. Surely, he could have stayed another week. Then he yelled, "There's not a drop of the milk of human kindness in you, you old cow." The neighbours tittered from their porches.

Then there was Mr. Putnam. He pretended to go to work for a whole week after he was let go from Lever Brothers. Alden was so furious when she learned of his deception that she said he'd had his week's notice already and cast him out.

It won't be long before Mr. Grant is out the door too. She finishes organizing the new cleaning supplies in the broom closet. She turns a giggle into a cough.

"Cover your mouth," says Alden. "There's something going around. We don't want it running through the house. Get started on the vegetables."

Constance reaches in the bins for carrots, a turnip, and onions and looks over her shoulder. Alden sets out six potatoes beside her. They both turn toward the carriage house at the sound of the Lozier's engine trying to start.

"Scrub. Don't peel. There's nothing wrong with the skins. Think of the Armenians." According to the newspaper, the Armenians are starving. It has something to do with Turkey, the country, not the animal. All Constance knows for certain is that to waste food is to be complicit in the tragedy.

Constance wants to keep Alden talking about the airships and see if she can turn the conversation around to Mr. Grant. "What do you think will happen with the airships?"

"I don't know. Maybe Father Moore will dedicate a prayer to the dead on Sunday. If not, we'll do so ourselves. Silently."

"And for the Armenians," Constance adds, trying to sound sincere.

"Yes, and for the Armenians." Alden picks up a stack of ironed and folded tea towels from the work table and puts them in a cupboard beside the sink.

Constance slices the tip of her finger with the knife and yelps. That's what she gets for mocking the Armenians.

"For goodness' sake, don't be so clumsy. You'll get blood on the potatoes."

Under the cool tap water, the bright red dilutes to dull streaks of rust. Alden ties a scrap of cheesecloth around Constance's finger to stem the flow.

"Pay attention."

"I wonder why it blew up," asks Constance.

"Hubris."

"I beg your pardon?"

Alden turns to Constance. "Of course, that's not what they said, but that's the cause. Hubris. Pride. Any other reason is a symptom of that." Alden really is beginning to sound more and more like Mr. Grant. Any minute she could launch into a sermon.

Pride is a mortal sin, one of the seven deadly sins, and the source of all the venial sins, according to Alden's personal theology. Alden has her own slant on Catholicism. When her thoughts conflict with those of the Church, Constance knows enough to agree with Alden. Even though pride is a mortal sin, Alden urges Constance to take pride in herself. To be a Patterson is to be a cut above the rest, and to Constance, the statement sounds an awful lot like pride. It's also a lie. They are above no one. What do either she or Alden do besides cook and clean for boarders?

She's not even a real Patterson.

Mr. Grant is always ready to remind her just how low she is. Last Saturday, he instructed her in her cleaning, and Alden, without realizing it, added insult to injury. He pointed accusingly at a cobweb running from the ceiling to a bookshelf and looked at her as though she, herself, had put it there. "What is *that*?" he asked, as if pointing at a nest of flies.

"A cobweb," she said.

"Don't be impertinent. What is it doing there?"

"What do you mean?" she said, hands folded across her chest.

"Get it down," Mr. Grant said. "Or would you like me to tell Alden you are shirking?"

Alden passed by at that moment and came in to see what they were looking up at. "Oh dear," she said, shaking her head. "Constance, get the library ladder and take care of that, would you?"

Mr. Grant could not have looked more smug. "Exactly as I was suggesting, Alden. The girl needs to attend to her duties with greater vigour." Alden, already on her way from the room, either did not notice the comment or worse, agreed with it and made no objection. Constance was stung. She wishes Alden had told him to mind his knitting, and then she reminds herself, her issue is not with Alden but with Mr. Grant.

Flattery is never Constance's first choice with Alden, but with her back turned, she cuts the potatoes into quarters, and says, "I guess you were right about the airships all along. You said they were dangerous from the start."

Alden replies, "This is no time for I-told-you-sos," but Constance can tell she is pleased. Constance tries to sound casual. "I wonder what will happen to Mr. Grant?"

"That's not your business." Alden's brow furrows as she slips the brisket into a pot of water and lights the stove. "When you're finished, set the table, and go see if the *Telegram* has arrived."

Usually, Constance is supposed to deliver the paper to the blue parlour for the boarders to read first, and she, Alden, and Mr. Hunt read the crumpled version later. But tonight the three of them spread the fresh paper on the kitchen work table and study it. Above the fold, the photograph of the R-100 flying above the Canadian Imperial Bank of Commerce skyscraper on that beautiful sunny day last summer is set beside a photo of its destroyed sister ship, still smouldering on a farmer's field in France. The accompanying articles include memories from those who watched the triumphant summertime flight. A Mr. Frank Williams of East York says, "It's the end of a dream."

Mr. Hunt clucks his tongue now and then and mutters, "Just like the *Titanic*."

Alden nods.

Constance shivers, remembering what it was like to be in the shadow of the thing. Imagine. What if it had crashed then? She and Gwen and all the people watching would be dead.

"Refold that now. Smooth it out. Carefully." God forbid Carling Grant should get a wrinkled paper.

At supper, conversation revolves around the crash of the R-101. Mr. Hunt asks, "How do you think it happened? Have you heard anything from the home office?" He leans in for the answer, with a quick glance at Constance.

"The papers know as much as I do." It amazes Constance how the man can lie without actually lying.

Mr. Hunt asks, "Do you know what it will mean for you and the Toronto office?" This time it is Alden who leans in.

"I do not know yet what it means for us here," he says, pointing his meaty index finger to the sky. "To predict the end of the BAS, the end of the whole scheme, is likely premature. Alarmist, I think. I await my instructions. The home office has other priorities at the moment, contacting the families of the deceased and so on. My own fate is of little consequence by comparison." He slips his watch out, flips it open, winds it, listens, and snaps it shut again.

The question cannot be asked again without making them appear even more callous. The man's cunning is a marvel.

*

At Mass the next Sunday, Constance sits in the pew on one side of Alden while Mr. Grant sits on the other. He goes to Mass with them now. This means they finally attend Corpus Christi instead of going all the way to St. Michael's because Alden can't expect him to go that far. Too fat. She hears Alden's voice in her head, "Be careful what you wish for."

Constance uses the time during the sermon to assess the choices she has in front of her, careful to keep an attentive look on her face. Although she has promised Gwen they will live together and she will find work, a whole week has passed and she has no time to look. The only time is during school, and if she skips school, the nuns are bound to alert Alden.

Alden elbows her. Her expression must have slipped.

As a foundling, Constance is a potential heathen. Who knows what evil lurks in her? For all she knows, she could be Jewish. Her baptism saved her. Unlike those who are Catholic at birth, she is held to a higher standard. Whereas others might be able to get away with forgetting to make the sign of the cross or failing to genuflect toward the tabernacle when leaving the pew or visibly swallowing the host, Constance cannot. She is careful to ensure the kneeler does not clunk too loudly when she flips it over. She waits until the host dissolves before she dares to swallow. She is never the first to rise from the kneeler, never the first to raise her eyes. But it is important not to be last either. Too much piety is as bad as too little. In the algebra of her life, attention always equals trouble.

When she joins the line for Communion, she wonders if everyone can see her lack of faith. She has been hoping that faith would find her, eventually. It would not crash upon her like a fiery airship; it would be more like when Douglas Fairbanks Jr. kisses Mary Pickford. It would make her feel full and wise and kind. She would be a better person with faith. Until it came, she would do the best she could. She goes back to her pew, kneels and blesses herself, and waits for Alden while a new black mark denoting her continued faithlessness finds a place on her soul.

On the way home, Constance gestures toward a help wanted sign in Yong's Chinese laundry.

"Look."

"Not many of those these days. But people always need their laundry done," says Alden.

"I should tell Gwen," says Constance.

"Don't be ridiculous," says Mr. Grant, only too willing to insert his opinion. "They hire their own."

"Then why would they have a sign?"

Constance goes to the window and peers in through the glass, wondering if Mr. Yong is there. He sees her and waves her away, pointing at the closed sign. "Sunday," he says loudly.

"Just a second," she says to Alden. "Mr. Yong is inside. I'm going to ask about it."

Mr. Grant taps his foot and crosses his arms over his chest above his stomach, ensuring all around know that he is inconvenienced. "Are you going to let the girl defy you?"

"It's hardly defiance, Mr. Grant," says Alden dismissively.

"I hope that you do not frequent such an establishment," he says.

"Mr. Yong runs a fine business."

Mr. Grant's eyebrows arch.

"But, as it happens, we do our own laundry at Patterson House." This seems to satisfy him. Constance remembers how Alden helped Mr. Yong when he first opened. Her patronage of the establishment helped them find success. Yong's was the first Chinese business outside of downtown. The sensational case of the mad Chinaman who killed a young girl a few years before coupled with rumours of opium kept many away from

Chinese businesses. But Alden said that there was nothing wrong with a Chinese laundry, went to inspect the place herself, and deemed it clean and less expensive than the other laundries nearby. She made a point of using it when she needed extra help, that is, while she could afford extra help. Others followed her example. If it was good enough for Alden Patterson, it would be good enough for them. But with only Mr. Grant boarding now, it is true that they do all the laundry themselves.

Although Alden does business with Mr. Yong, she would never bring a Chinaman in as a boarder. This goes without saying. Not that any Chinamen have ever shown up at the door. They have their own places to live. Many of Alden's boarders are referred to her by Father Moore. Constance remembers Irish, both Catholic and Protestant. If Protestants and Catholics could get along in her own family, Alden said, they could get along anywhere. Nevertheless, to prevent unpleasantness, she made it clear that religion or the political concerns of Orangemen were not topics to be discussed over the Patterson House dinner table. A few years ago, there were two Polish men, brothers with broad foreheads and muscular shoulders, who shared a room. Constance doesn't remember any other time when men shared a room. But another long-term boarder brought them to Patterson House from his work at Lever Brothers and begged Alden to let them in. They had nowhere to turn, he said.

Alden's consternation was obvious to Constance whenever they arrived at the table. Although they were polite in their looming silence, over the dishes one night, Alden said that she could tell they did not like her cooking and this troubled her. She surprised everyone when she went into the city and sought out sauerkraut and sausages. The Polish brothers were delighted and thanked her profusely, but the meal left a stink in Patterson House that lasted for days.

Alden even took in a Jew once and while she did so accidentally (neither his name nor his looks alerted her), she did not turn him away when she found out. But a Chinaman is different. Her business would be ruined. Apparently, it's one thing for a Chinaman to wash the sheets but quite another for him to sleep on them. This makes no sense to Constance but less and less of Alden's world makes any sense to her anymore.

Constance points at the help wanted sign and Mr. Yong raises his hand to her in a silent greeting. He comes to the door and opens it but does not let her in. "Closed today."

"I was wondering about the position." She points to the sign hanging on the door. "What is it?"

"Delivery."

"Would you hire a girl?"

He looks her up and down like her clothes are on inside out and glances at Alden and bows his head to her. Alden returns the gesture with a nod.

Constance says, "No, I'm not asking for myself. For a friend."

He shakes his head. "Boy for delivery."

Constance thanks him and he closes the door and locks it again.

"Well?" Alden asks.

"They want a boy."

"Sensible," says Mr. Grant. Constance is about to talk, but Alden gives her a stern warning glare.

Why on earth could a girl not deliver laundry? Wait till she tells Gwen. It's time for them to test their theory.

*

After Mr. Grant's enormous appetite is once again sated by Sunday lunch, Constance runs to Gwen's house. Gwen opens the door wide and gives her a hug, just like she used to before Gerald arrived. "Mum and Gerald are out visiting Gerald's brother this afternoon to show off the baby. I wasn't invited." She makes a face. "Not that I'd want to go anyway. Come in."

Constance doesn't wait to cross the threshold before she blurts, "There's a job."

"Where?"

"At Yong's laundry. Sign just went up. It's probably still there."

Gwen's interest dims. "I don't know."

Constance rolls her eyes and Gwen flushes.

"Chinese?"

"Their money is as good as anyone else's."

"What's the job?"

"Delivery boy. We've got to try the clothes. Mr. Yong doesn't know you. You could get away with it. Where did you hide them?"

Gwen pulls the bundle out from beneath her bed.

It takes over an hour to hem the pants and get the shirt tucked so everything sort of fits, but even then, Gwen does not look passable. "It's the hair," Gwen decides. With the addition of a cap and about a hundred bobby pins and some of Gerald's pomade, they are forced to admit it's not the hair.

"This is hopeless," says Gwen, sinking onto her bed. The bulkiest men's clothes couldn't hide Gwen's curves or the roundness of her cheeks, her heart-shaped face or her thick, soft lips. There is not a masculine thing about her. "It was a crazy idea anyway. How could I deliver things in my own neighbourhood dressed like a boy? Someone was bound to recognize me."

Constance doesn't want to admit defeat. But there's the limp too. Gwen's limp is unmistakable.

A mischievous smile replaces Gwen's frown and she slips off the jacket and tosses it at Constance. "You try."

"Me? No. Mr. Yong knows me."

"Forget about that. Just try them on."

"I'll never get away with it."

"It was your idea."

"I was making a joke," says Constance. "You're the one who took it too far."

"Just try it."

Constance doesn't want to undress in front of Gwen and hesitates. "Wait outside."

"What?"

"Please."

"Aren't we modest?" says Gwen, but she does as she's asked.

Constance can pull the pants over her straight hips without unbuttoning them. "I'll need a belt," she calls out. The shirt, which Gwen could barely button over her chest, buttons easily for Constance and is a little big through the shoulders.

Gwen pops her head around the corner with her hands over her eyes and says, "Ready?"

"Yes, I guess so."

Gwen enters and is unusually silent. She adds a tie and a jacket. "Your hair," she says, frowning.

A single French braid is easily hidden away in the cap with four bobby pins. The disguise complete, Gwen stares, a look of confusion crossing her face.

"Is it that bad?"

"No. It's that good. You look like a boy. Really. Go in the bathroom and check the mirror." She follows her across the hall. "And not just any boy. A handsome boy."

Doubtful, Constance looks at herself in the mirror as though she is meeting a stranger. She barely recognizes herself. Gwen is right. She looks good. Even more strange, she feels good. She stretches her arms ahead of her, tugs at the waistband of her pants and bends at the knee and comes back up. Gwen appears behind her in the mirror. Turning, she checks herself in profile, straightens her shoulders inside the jacket the way she's seen boarders do thousands of times and adopts a serious expression. She has never looked better. Her heart quickens and her face flushes. Gwen is staring at her, her mouth open.

"I don't like this." She pulls off the hat.

Gwen takes her by the shoulders. "Don't. I swear, you could be a leading man."

"I don't think so." Constance is perversely desperate to get out of the clothes.

"I mean it. You look good. Really good." Gwen starts to laugh. "Just my type. Maybe you'll ask me out."

"Stop it." Constance pulls the jacket off and throws it over the towel rack. She tugs at the tie and Gwen stops her.

"Here, let me do it. You'll tear it." Loosening it, Gwen looks up into her eyes. For a second, Constance imagines she is going to kiss her, but her eyes turn pleading. "You could do it. Get a job. As a man. Think of how much more money you could make."

Constance scoffs.

"You could! Look at you! If you asked me out, I'd swoon."

Constance looks at herself again in the mirror. "Don't be ridiculous."

"What are you saying?" Gwen laughs. "You wouldn't ask me out?"

"Stop it."

Gwen laughs. "I've made you blush."

"I'm not blushing," she says, but Constance can feel the heat in her face.

Gwen sits heavily on the edge of the bathtub. "I'm sorry. I'm desperate to get away from here." She fidgets with her hands, picks up the comb, and sets it down again. "I shouldn't make this into your problem, but," she hesitates again. "Do you think I could borrow some money? Maybe from Mr. Hunt or maybe Alden? A few dollars to get started?"

"Definitely not Alden. And for goodness' sake don't let on I'm leaving. I haven't told them yet."

"You're going to do it, aren't you?"

"I said I would." But she's still uncertain. She has never felt their two-year age difference more acutely than now. Gwen is ready. Really ready. Constance is finding it hard to imagine leaving, no matter how mad she gets at Alden or how much Mr. Grant gets on her nerves. She also hasn't told Gwen about her savings that she has stashed in a tin at the back of her closet and feels guilty. "I'll get out of these clothes."

Gwen stays in the bathroom to get her hair back to normal while Constance changes in the bedroom. With the clothes folded and stacked, she meets Gwen in the kitchen. "I'll say one thing: pants are a lot more comfortable than a skirt. I wish I could wear pants all the time." She's trying to lighten the mood, but it's not working.

A knock at the front door startles them both.

"Am I all right?" asks Constance.

Gwen gives her the once-over and nods.

"Me?"

"Yes, all back to normal."

At the door, Constance could not be more surprised to hear Alden's voice. She must have forgotten to do something. Or maybe there is a new boarder. Constance checks her hair and realizes the braid is still in. There is no time to do anything about that.

Constance is at the door in a second. "Is everything all right?"

"Everything is fine. I have come to see Gwen." She redirects her attention. "Gwen, Eaton's hires a few extra girls in the catalogue department to handle the Christmas rush and I thought of you. Why don't you try there? Try Simpson's too. If one does it, so does the other. And don't be discouraged. Patience and persistence pay off. I realize Christmas is still weeks away, but you might get your name in early." Her gaze moves to Constance. "Your hair."

"Gwen did it."

"Hmm. It's fine. Tidy. Don't be much longer, please." And with that, Alden turns and walks back toward Patterson House.

They close the door, wait a few seconds, and burst out laughing. "Can you imagine if I were still in those clothes?"

They sit back down at the kitchen table. "Gee, that was swell of Alden to tell me."

Constance wraps her feet around the chair legs, unwraps them, and sighs.

"What's the matter with you?" asks Gwen.

Constance won't say. A part of her wishes Alden told her about the job and not Gwen. "Nothing. I'd better go."

Constance walks home by way of the alley, the men's clothes in a bundle in her hands. She doesn't want to get caught with them and decides to stash them in the loft of the carriage house. No one ever goes up there. It used to be the place where the chauffeur slept, back when there was a chauffeur. Inside the carriage house is the fruit of Mr. Hunt's recent labours: unneeded tools are cleaned and separated from the rest and the Lozier is polished to gleaming.

On her way into the house, she notices Mr. Grant's curtain move. She waves, an act of defiance. Let him think she has nothing to hide.

In the kitchen, Alden is gathering ingredients for supper. Constance says, "It was nice of you to think of Gwen."

"I don't like the thought of her so desperate for work that she'll apply anywhere."

By that, Alden means Mr. Yong's laundry. "You always say there's nothing wrong with Mr. Yong." Constance flops into a kitchen chair.

"Oh, for the love of—" Alden wipes her hands on her apron and faces Constance. "What's the matter?"

"Everything is changing."

"What do you mean?"

"Half my class has left and gone to work. I miss Gwen at school. I'm not learning anything. Alden, can I apply for one of those jobs at Eaton's?"

"You're only fourteen."

"Other girls my age are working."

"So far we haven't had to resort to *that*."

Constance feels offended somehow. "I could work. If Gwen can work, I can work. You do expect me to get a job someday, don't you?"

"Of course. Eventually. And Gwen is older than you. It's the children from the poorest families who leave school early. It's bad enough you're not going to be able to go on past sixteen, but there's no need to cut off your education earlier than we must. We are not poor. At least, we are not that poor."

Constance realizes that, for Alden, keeping her in school is a point of pride.

"You will continue your schooling." She seems to sense Constance's disappointment. "Besides, I still need you here and Eaton's doesn't hire Catholics."

"They don't?"

"Of course not."

"Why would anyone let on that they're Catholic then?"

"What are you saying?" Alden is aghast. "You would deny your faith?"

"If I needed work."

Alden drops the knife she is using to slice the stewing beef, rinses her hands under the tap, and says, "That's it. Off to Father Moore with you. Get your coat."

"You're not really sending me to Father Moore, are you?"

"Don't make matters worse."

Alden hasn't marched her off to Father Moore like this since she was a child and she told everyone, including the nuns at school, that her real parents were coming to get her, and she would be leaving Patterson House to go live in Boston, Massachusetts. Constance really liked saying the word "Massachusetts."

"I wasn't serious."

"I'm not so sure," says Alden, studying her face before picking up her apron again. "You'll add this to your sins at confession next Saturday, and until then, you'll say an extra Hail Mary every night. Get the potatoes ready."

While she's quartering potatoes, she remembers Gwen calling her handsome and blushes. She looked good. She looked right. Correct. Like herself. She has an urge to go back out to the carriage house and try everything on again.

*

At dinner, Alden spoons a stroganoff heavy on the cream and notably light on beef from the chafing dish to Mr. Grant's plate. There are, at most, one or two small cubes of beef left for the rest of them while Mr. Grant has at least seven.

Constance narrows her eyes at him and his full plate. "Mr. Grant, I notice there has been nothing in the papers about the BAS in the past few days. Have you heard anything?"

He looks at her peripherally and chews without answering. But Alden seconds the question, adding, "Yes, I too have been wondering."

He swallows and dabs delicately at his lips with his napkin. "No, nothing yet. The funerals are still not finished. I understand there are a few that have been delayed what with the need to transport the bodies home and so forth. A sad business." Mr. Hunt seems about to ask another question and is pre-empted by Mr. Grant, who says, "My apologies. That was not appropriate for dinner conversation." He casts his eyes downward and lays his napkin back on his lap. The topic is closed again.

"Is there any more gravy?" he asks.

Constance wants to throw the dish at him. Alden glares at her. She passes the dish to Mr. Grant, a fake smile pasted on her face.

*

By the time the trees have lost their leaves and the backyard bonfires have gone cold, Gwen has given up hope that she will ever find work and Constance has given up hope that Mr. Carling Grant will ever leave Patterson House.

Then, more than a month after the crash of the R-101, on a day pregnant with a looming blizzard, Mr. Grant himself introduces the topic over dinner. It is Friday, and he has eaten his first serving of fried perch with alarming rapidity. The idea of a fast is lost on him. His first helping is usually gone in half the time it takes the rest of them to eat and he has already asked for more. "You have been so kind as to inquire about my position with the British Airship Scheme. Sadly, it has come to a close."

Constance drops her knife and Alden scowls at her.

"Do be careful," Mr. Grant admonishes. "There is nothing more important than good table manners for a young woman."

Constance wants to stab him with her fork.

Mr. Hunt steps in. "You're doing just fine, dear."

Constance shoots him a grateful look and Mr. Hunt's lips twitch into a lopsided grin.

A settlement has been made, he explains, as though he is speaking to toddlers. He is certain that he will find employment again if he wishes. He says this while piling potatoes onto a fork already full of fish, which he then raises to mid-air while he speaks. "But I am disinclined to look for work again. After all," he says, swallowing once more and bringing his napkin to his mouth to stifle a small burp, "I came out of retirement for the British Airship Scheme. Yes, I felt that strongly about it. When one is asked to serve, one doesn't say no. Isn't that right, Hunt?" Mr. Hunt has no time to reply.

Alden nods approvingly.

"Leaving the job is not a blow to me, as much as I fear the closure of the enterprise is a blow to the Empire. My own destiny is unimportant. It is the halt in progress over which I am concerned. For me, this is a return to the status quo, a return to the quiet life I imagined awaited me when I first retired." He loads the contents of his fork into his mouth, chews, swallows, and says, "Could you pass the potatoes, please?"

Constance knows the three scoops of potatoes left in the bowl are the last. She offers them to Mr. Hunt first, who declines. She passes the remainder to Mr. Grant, who scrapes the bowl clean. Alden passes him the butter without being asked. They all know he will slather on at least three pats and let them melt all over his potatoes, creating little yellow reservoirs, which he will sop up with bread. "Is there any more bread?" He looks around expectantly.

"No, I'm afraid we've eaten the last slice, Mr. Grant." Alden does not offer to get more, something she would have done in the first weeks of his stay. His jowls sway as he chews. Constance has come to hate the sound of him eating, the smack of his lips, the clink of his knife and fork, the expectant expression on his face as he waits to be informed of dessert, and the inevitable appearance of his tongue as he licks his lips in anticipation.

"When do you plan to return to your home?" asks Constance. All eyes at the table turn to her.

Alden snaps at her. "Constance. Please."

"I only thought," she continues, ignoring Alden's warning, "now that his work has ended, Mr. Grant would be going back to his home. I was wondering where that will be." She looks back at him. "It's Gravenhurst, isn't it? Or is it Newmarket?"

Mr. Hunt coughs and sips his water.

Alden lays her napkin on the table with a deliberateness that is a warning. "This really isn't your concern, Constance."

Constance feels the opportunity to get rid of Mr. Grant is somehow sliding away from her. "But you always say the boarders have to be employed."

"Constance!" Alden is embarrassed.

Mr. Grant rests his knife and fork for a moment on the edges of his plate, baffled. He looks as though he has lost a match by some technicality that he knew nothing about.

She has come this far so she continues, doggedly ignoring Alden's stiffening posture. "You said you didn't want men in the house without employment or purpose and that an unemployed man is a dangerous man."

Alden is fully red now, right to the roots of her hair. "I don't recall saying anything of the sort!"

Mr. Grant gestures to Mr. Hunt. "I don't see how that can be. Hunt here is not employed."

"That's different." Both Constance and Alden have said the words at the same time and look at each other. Constance withers under Alden's exasperation.

"Constance, that's enough. Being retired is quite different from being unemployed. Mr. Grant is welcome to continue his time here at Patterson House if he so chooses. Go to your room until your manners and good sense have returned to you."

Mr. Grant looks from person to person at the table, smiles slightly, picks up his knife and fork again, and eats his last bite of mashed potatoes.

If Alden can change the rules on a whim, so can she.

"I'm not a child. You cannot send me to my room." She pushes back from the table and walks with deliberateness to the foyer. She will not bolt. She is an adult. Adults do not run. From the foyer, she hears Alden apologize for her behaviour and call her name. Constance yanks a coat from the closet and goes out the door, which catches the wind and slams behind her. She winces. This was not her intention. But, so be it.

Underdressed and without a hat or mittens, she runs to stay warm and to let out the anger that is bursting within her. When she arrives at the lake, she catches her breath by a bench in front of the Balmy Beach clubhouse, the cold air searing her lungs. The full force of the wind from the lake blows through her and leaves her shivering. Lake Ontario is a dark expanse, the sliver of the crescent moon an empty cradle above. She sits on the frosty bench, pulls her knees up to her chest and inside her skirt, tucks it around her ankles, and digs her Zippo lighter from her shift pocket, flicking it open and shut repeatedly, watching the sparks unable to catch in the wind.

Her head is jammed full of Mr. Grant and his rotten lies. "What is he up to?" she says aloud. She thinks of his eyes on her, of his whisky, of his enormous hard round belly. It is more than she can stand.

Maybe it doesn't matter what he is up to.

Her tangled thoughts separate one from the other and a single idea persists: it is time to leave Patterson House. She thinks of Amelia Earhart and finds courage. With or without a job, she will leave. She will leave with Gwen. The sooner the better.

Mr. Hunt approaches from behind the clubhouse, his cane tapping the sidewalk. He coughs as if to let her know he is there. He is slower than usual and a bit shaky.

Constance stands and gathers him toward her. "What are you doing? You shouldn't have walked all this way. It's too cold."

He pulls his balaclava off and his face and hair are damp despite the freezing night. The walk has been too much of an effort for him.

"Sit for a minute and then let me walk you back."

"Running out of the house wasn't a good idea." His knees crack as he sits heavily on the bench.

"I know." She holds his hand, grateful that he has come after her. How can she ever dream of leaving Mr. Hunt?

They look out over the black lake. Ice has begun to form near the shore, creating a layer of slush that is continually broken by the action of the waves.

"Carling is putting all kinds of ideas into Alden's head about you." He wheezes slightly. "I tell him he is speaking out of turn and that you are a good girl, but I'm not there for all of his pernicious tête-à-têtes."

It is good to know Mr. Hunt is as bothered by Mr. Grant as she is.

"He's bedevilling. I know. Nevertheless, you should come home now. Don't give him any reason to criticize you. Try to be more tractable."

"He'll always find something."

Mr. Hunt does not coax her back to herself like she wants him to.

"Yes, I know it's been trying. But don't antagonize Alden." He wrings his balaclava in his hands, twists it, flattens it out on his knee, and then wrings it again. His lips are taut and his forehead slants as it does when he is concerned. "You only push her away. Your attitude around Mr. Grant is terrible. It's as though you are trying to get the man's goat. You're going to have to learn to rein yourself in to keep the peace."

Constance jumps from the bench, flinging her arms out. "You just admitted he's got it in for me. Why aren't you on my side?"

"I'm always on your side."

"Then why are you telling *me* to behave instead of talking to Alden about *him*? Why doesn't *she* see it? He's wheedling his way into the house, putting his books in the blue parlour, acting like he's Patterson himself, like he's entitled to be there."

"He *is* entitled to be there. He's paid for his room."

"For his room—not for the whole house."

The wind picks up over the lake and the force of it temporarily halts their conversation. When it abates, Mr. Hunt says, "You don't need to be dramatic." He coughs, and his cough gets the better of him for a minute. He brings his balaclava over his mouth like a handkerchief and Constance sits beside him again and pats his back. Her stomach feels awful, like it is full of stagnant water. Mr. Hunt rests his arm around her shoulder. She leans into him as she has done so many times before and breathes in his earthy scent.

"Remember when I pulled you from the water?" he asks. "You gave me such a scare."

She does. She cuddles in closer to him and he hugs his arm tighter around her shoulder. When Constance was three years old, she and Mr. Hunt used to sit on this very bench together. One beautiful day, he dozed off in the sunshine with Constance playing at his feet. She thinks this is her first memory. The sun was hot on her hair. Her little shoes were tucked beside Mr. Hunt on the bench with her socks folded neatly inside. She pulled the shoes off the bench and filled them with sand and then poured sand on the tops of Mr. Hunt's shoes. Then she became entranced with a pattern of seagull tracks and she followed them a few yards. A duck paddled by the water's edge and she toddled toward it, the soles of her feet hot on the sand. The duck kept ahead of her until it found safety in deeper water, but Constance kept up her pursuit. She took one step into the water and then another and laughed. The water soothed the hot soles of her feet and she waded in after the duck, the glint of the sun on the water blinding her, the gull playing a game of peekaboo, bobbing up and down in the low waves. Then the ground dropped out from under her and she was under water, gulping. Looking up, she could see the yellow circle of the sun through the water above and the duck's feet spinning underneath its body. She laughed again, but the water filled her lungs. She was not frightened; she did not have enough time to be frightened. In an instant, Mr. Hunt's hands were pulling her into the air and she was coughing and could smell the sick on herself and wondered where it came from. Mr. Hunt held her to his chest, a gaggle of strangers around them. It was their panicked faces that told her she should be frightened.

As though reading her mind, he says, "You're growing up. I won't always be here to protect you." Constance can hardly bear the thought even as she understands its truth.

They sit in silence until Mr. Hunt says, "It's cold. We should go." They rise together, Constance steadying him. "Don't let Mr. Grant get between you two."

Constance almost laughs. "It's not that hard to get between me and Alden." Mr. Hunt looks genuinely mystified. "It's not as though she's my mother."

Mr. Hunt strikes her. The slap knocks the wind out of her, not with its force, because it has little, but with the fact of it. The echo is eaten by the darkness and swept away in the wind.

Constance touches her hand to her cheek. Her mouth is open and soundless. The anger in Mr. Hunt's eyes evaporates instantly and changes to regret, but he does not apologize.

"Don't you ever say that again." He turns away. "I'll get back on my own." He pulls his balaclava on and leans heavily on his cane as he walks over the frozen grass and to the street.

Constance wants to run to him and apologize but her body feels leaden and she cannot move. Now she knows. If sides are to be chosen, Mr. Hunt is on Alden's. It is not the two of them against the world after all; she is alone. She is a foundling, as Mr. Grant never fails to remind her.

Two women passing on the boardwalk stop and ask her if she needs help and she realizes she is crying. They are older, matronly, on their way home from work, carrying their buckets and cleaning supplies with them. She shakes her head, dries her tears, and says, "Just having a bad day."

One woman pats her back and says, "We all have them, dear. Why don't you go home? The snow's starting. You're not dressed for it."

By the time she makes her way across the park and back to the street, it must be almost ten o'clock. She is cold to her core and she cannot feel the tips of her fingers. She pulls both her arms inside her coat, tucks her hands under her armpits, and walks as though in a straitjacket. Lights are going out in the houses around her. The snow swirls in the wind and gathers along the edges of lawns and fences. Patterson House looms midway up the block. It is the last place she wants to be. Gwen's bedroom light is on and she wiggles her arms back into her coat sleeves and creeps through the Hughes's gate and around to the side of the house, afraid her steps crunching along the frozen ground will give her away. All the other windows are dark except for Gwen's. She brings her face up to a break in the curtains and realizes that Gerald Hughes is there too. He is sitting on Gwen's bed. The baby is asleep in the crib. Gwen is standing in front of him, her dress unzipped at the back, and he is pulling it from her shoulders. Gwen is like a statue, unmoving. When Gerald's hands reach for Gwen's breasts, Constance lets out a yelp. Both Gwen and Gerald startle and look to the window. The baby cries. Constance ducks down under the sill, her hands across her mouth and waits to be discovered in her crouch, but nothing happens except more cries from the baby.

She waits for what feels like hours, certain that she will be discovered. When the baby stops crying, she listens carefully. No one else is nearby. Gerald has not come outside. The light turns off, leaving the shrubbery in front of her in darkness. She inches her way up to look in the window again. Gwen is holding the baby; her dress is back up and Gerald is nowhere to be seen. She hears the front door open and close, ducks down and curls up even smaller. She tries to hold her breath so the fog of it does not reveal her. But he does not come around the side of the house to look for the source of the noise. Instead, he goes down the walk and toward Queen Street. A gust of wind brings the first big snowflakes.

She taps the glass, and Gwen deciphers Constance in the dark and drops her eyes to the floor. Constance's palm is on the glass. She beckons her to open the window, but Gwen does not. Instead, she shakes her head and, even in the darkness, Constance can see tears glisten on her cheeks. Gwen turns her back, tucks the baby in the crib, and gets into her bed, her dress still on and her back turned to Constance. Her shoulders are shaking. Gwen is crying. Constance taps the glass one more time and then lets her hand fall, its outline held in the frost.

Nothing will be done about this tonight. She tramps through the yard and over the fence, oblivious to the noise she is making. She wants to scream into the night and stomps her way up the alley, heat rising in her despite the cold outside.

Gerald Hughes is a monster.

Poor, dear Gwen. No wonder she has been so desperate to get work and get away. Constance has been so obsessed with her own problems and the machinations of Mr. Grant that she has failed Gwen in her hour of need. She stops short in the alley just before the gate to Patterson House and chastises herself mercilessly, kicking at the fence and the ground. A terrible friend. Self-involved. She will make this right tomorrow.

The back gate to Patterson House squeaks and she doesn't care. She flings it shut and lets the latch crash. Mr. Grant peers in the yard from between his curtains. A great blackness sweeps over her and she is blind with anger. She looks directly at him, defiant, daring him to come downstairs and say something to her. He moves away from the curtain and it drops back into place. She picks up a stone and hurls it at his window, but it falls at least fifteen feet short and the frustration of the failed effort makes her even more angry.

When she enters through the kitchen door, no one is waiting to scold her. She is almost sorry, itching for a fight. With her coat still on, she pounds up the stairs two at a time to the third floor and slams her bedroom door behind her. Shivering, she removes her freezing clothes and pulls her flannel nightdress over her head. In bed, she tugs the covers up to her chin. Thinking better of it, she gets up again, picks up the old, beat-up Windsor chair, and shoves it under the door handle. No one is coming into her room. No one.

With the covers up around her neck again, her heart thuds in her chest. She needs to think like Holmes. Orderly. Logical. Cold. Keep her emotions out of it. But how? Unlike Holmes, she cannot determine which points in this mystery are essential and which are immaterial.

The familiar sounds of Patterson House are joined by strengthening wind gusts and snow hitting the window like needles. She listens until she hears a light rapping. At first, she believes it is her own rapping on Gwen's window, a kind of dream she must be having. She must have fallen asleep. But she gets her bearings when Mr. Hunt whispers her name. It is morning. How did that happen?

Mr. Hunt tries the door and is unable to open it. Constance gets up, moves the chair aside and opens the door for him. They hesitate, standing across the threshold from each other like it is a great divide.

Mr. Hunt looks askance at the chair. "Do you feel that's necessary?"

Constance goes back to her bed and pulls her blankets around her. "Yes, as a matter of fact, I do." She gestures to him to enter and he brings the chair to the side of her bed. What does it matter if she impugns Carling Grant's character? Gwen's silence has not protected her. Oh, Gwen! Her dear Gwen. Just thinking of her brings tears to Constance's eyes. Mr. Hunt probably assumes the tears are about their falling out the night before.

It takes him several minutes to work up to whatever he has to say. It always does. She is willing to wait. He gathers himself.

"I've forgotten how cold it gets up here." He looks up at the frost gathered on her window and runs his hands up and down his arms. And then, for the first time, Constance understands with a split-second of clarity why Alden has given her a room in the servant's quarters. The realization lifts her from time and space. Pieces of Alden's strange management of Patterson House fall together. The lock on the door from the second floor to the servant's stairwell cannot be opened from the boarder's side. It is a one-way door meant to keep her safe. Moving her upstairs was about more than merely making more money by freeing up another second-floor room. It was an effort to keep her safe, out of sight and out of mind from the attentions of men.

Mr. Hunt coughs, bows his head. "I apologize. I'm ashamed of myself."

Constance can't help but bring her hand to her face where Mr. Hunt slapped her. "I'm sorry, too." She hesitates before speaking. "I understand now. I didn't before. I know Alden has done her best by me. I know she has protected me. That you both have. I've been ungrateful and I'm sorry. I am only just beginning to understand everything she has done for me." She is surprised to find she means every word.

If only she could tell Mr. Hunt what she saw last night, but if she speaks the words, they will change everything. They will demand action, not just of her but of Mr. Hunt as well. She doesn't want to burden him with it the way she is burdened. Soon enough, she will get Gwen out of harm's way.

Mr. Hunt wheezes a bit. There is a catch in his breath that Constance doesn't like. He sounds full of fluid. "I think it's time I told you something about Alden and me." Mr. Hunt shifts in the chair, leans forward, and rests his hands on his cane. "You see, it was the war. You can't know what it was like. And you shouldn't know. It's over now. Everyone wants to forget, including me.

"Of course, you know that I was employed here before the war started. I wasn't regular staff, just an extra hand hired by the gardener. I lived with an old uncle on Kingston Road. I'd send my wages back to my parents on the farm, and what I didn't send there, he'd keep and spend at the racetrack. It wasn't a good life for me. I was the seventh of eleven children, and the youngest boy, and there just wasn't a place for me. Even some of us with big families don't much benefit from them. Uncle Reggie, well, he needed looking after and my mother didn't want to send one of the girls." Mr. Hunt fidgets in his chair.

Constance nods. "You don't have to explain." Constance understands all too well the dangers facing a young woman.

Mr. Hunt's forehead furrows slightly, his discomfort revealed in the tightness of his skin wrinkling over his left eye.

"How old were you?"

"Oh, just a gaffer. About ten."

It is almost worse than being abandoned as a baby.

"Patterson House was like a dream to me. It was the most beautiful place I had ever seen. Sure, there were grander houses in Toronto— Chorley Park for certain—and those up on the escarpment and whatnot, but I had never been to any of those. I thought I'd work my way up, one day be the head gardener and live in the loft over the garage. The gardener was a fine fellow with a wealth of knowledge. He taught me that you can't belong to a place if you don't know its flora and fauna. And he's right.

"The first time I saw Alden, she was home from school and outside with her brothers. She took my breath away, so tall, her red hair ablaze in the sunlight. Her brothers were tossing chestnuts at her and she was screeching and throwing them back. It was all in fun. I was under the impression that Patterson House was a happy place. Maybe it was back then. But now I know that was a rare moment. Alden's father was trying to marry her off. It wasn't going well.

"She was being presented here and there and everywhere, but there were never any takers, which I found astonishing. The staff gossiped about it. One day I found her crying under the beech trees, sitting in the lily-of-the-valley. She tried to compose herself but could not. I found a handkerchief to offer her. A gentleman should always have a handkerchief. My Uncle Reggie told me that."

Mr. Hunt coughs, brings his handkerchief to his mouth. "My dirty thumbprint was on the handkerchief. She thanked me and said it didn't matter. She told me that while all the other girls received offers, the only men who wanted her were those who thought that an alliance with the Pattersons might add to their own coffers. They wanted the association, the connections, not her. I told her any man who got to marry her would be the luckiest man in the world."

Constance makes a face and pulls the bedclothes tighter around her.

"I know. It is terribly corny, but I was just a boy and I wanted to make her feel better. But I wasn't simply being polite. I meant it with all my heart." Constance thinks Mr. Hunt might be blushing. "She said she never wanted to get married, ever, and that the Pellatt cousin was the last straw."

"The Pellatt cousin?"

"I don't know the details, except that her father pushed for the match. In the end, the boy turned it down."

"She was jilted?"

"No, I don't think so. It didn't get that far. But she did say she had been turned down. Well, you know Alden doesn't like a scene. I promised her I would keep her confidences. I promised her."

He stops talking and brings his hand to his lips. "Oh dear. And now I haven't. Never let on, please. Don't ever tell her I have told you any of this."

Constance nods.

"You see, I was no threat to her at all, just a boy. She might as well have been talking to herself. But she smiled at me and I stood up and took her hand and helped her up. And then she did something extraordinary. She bent down and kissed my cheek and said, 'Thank you.' I must admit I still feel that kiss today, I do. It's as though it landed on me and became part of me. Even the gas didn't burn it off." He touches his damaged fingers to the scars on the side of his face.

"I wanted to do something for her, so I built her the bench, right where we talked. I wanted her to think of me when she sat there. It seemed to be a place she liked to go. And then before you know it, we were in the war and her brothers were overseas and there were no more suitors anymore and she seemed to have her wish. It was just Alden and her father. The battles they fought! I'd hear them all the way outside. I wanted to go in the house and come to her rescue like a knight in dusty overalls. I thought of myself as a man already, I really did. I was as grown up as you."

It is hard for Constance to see Mr. Hunt as a young man, in love, and in love with Alden of all people. Constance has never seen a picture of him before the war, but she likes to think he was handsome.

"I thought if I went to war and distinguished myself, I could return and be worthy of her. It was a story for the flickers. I didn't wait until I turned sixteen. They were already running the well dry when it came to men and in their desperation, turned a blind eye. I told my Uncle Reggie I was signing up and off I went to 'hunt the Hun.' I thought that was pretty funny, with my name being Hunt and all. It was a big lark to me, an adventure. I said goodbye to Alden and I asked her if I could write to her. She said yes and took my hand and held it and told me to be careful. She was teary. She said I was too young to go. She said she could report me. She really cared."

He stops there as if to emphasize the point.

Constance can see the whole story playing out, but already knows the end.

"And then you got hurt."

"Yes, I did. But I'm getting ahead of myself. She asked me to keep my eyes open for her brothers and to send word if I heard anything. I imagined myself fighting the enemy and finding the Patterson brothers trapped somewhere, freeing them, bringing them home. They died of course, at Ypres. Their bodies were never found. Lost in the mud. Poor souls."

Hunt seems to be talking to himself now, looking right through Constance. "The bus dropped us off. A red double-decker. It was like we were on a sightseeing tour, all the boys jolly and full of bluster. I was only at the front for four days. Four days. A lifetime. My job was to dig trenches. We would dig up wrecked gun cartridges and ration carts, helmets, bully-beef tins, broken rifles, barbed wire, the swollen carcasses of livestock, pieces...." His voice trails off and he stares.

Constance has seen this stare on plenty of the boarders' faces before. She wants to crawl into Mr. Hunt's lap and hold him, but he is far away from her, somewhere in France, his face damp with sweat.

"We were spleen deep in it. The earth was full of us. I'd say a prayer every time my shovel went into the earth. I'd say, 'God bless the souls of these good men,' over and over. And the trenches would reveal unimaginable things and I would dig and dig. On the fourth day, I didn't hear the trench whistle. Maybe it never went. Maybe no one knew what was coming. The fellow beside me pushed me down. My face was in the mud, my mouth full of filth. I remember opening my eyes and trying to focus. Right in front of me was an uprooted plant. Asparagus. I knew it right away. I've told you about asparagus." He almost smiles.

This is the Mr. Hunt she knows, the Mr. Hunt that talks about plants. Asparagus is Mr. Hunt's favourite of all the plants in the garden, the first to come up in the spring with a green so vivid it wakes up the other plants. Asparagus takes years to establish. Planting it is an investment in the future, he says.

"For the first time, I thought about the farmers who were on the land before it became a battlefield. All that effort establishing the plants, just to see them blown to bits. I held on to that asparagus like a baby, cradled it in my arms. I wanted to plant it again. I looked around for a good spot. In the fall, when asparagus is done, it turns bright gold, so gold it's almost red, just like Alden's hair. I was out of my mind. Amid the chaos and the stench of cordite, I took Alden's hand again, just like when we were in the garden and I helped her up, and she kissed my cheek. But it wasn't Alden's hand I was holding. It was the fellow who'd pushed me down. Someone else yelled, 'Leave him; he's dead.'"

Constance shivers with the thought of holding the hand of a dead man.

"Then a sound we had never heard before—a hissing." Hunt stops talking for a minute and Constance waits, almost afraid to breathe.

She whispers, "What was it?"

"Someone said, 'Run!' so I ran, and I stumbled, ran straight into no man's land, with the asparagus plant still in my hands. I ran into the gas."

Constance gets up, kneels at Mr. Hunt's feet and takes his ruined hands in hers. "Don't say any more."

He shakes his head and pulls his hand away. "You see, I didn't do anything brave. I did something incredibly stupid. How could I come back to Alden having done something so stupid, after only four days at war? Nothing heroic in my service at all."

"You couldn't think. You had been shelled. You can't blame yourself."

Constance knows about shell shock. Everyone does.

Mr. Hunt finds his handkerchief and pats his eyes. "In the hospital, they were keeping me comfortable until I died. My eyes were bandaged. I couldn't talk. The inside of my throat was burned. My fingers." He holds his hands up and looks at them. "I still don't know what happened to me. I will never know. All I know is that I dreamed of Alden.

"A nurse argued with the doctor about me, certain I might live. Nurse Pascal. Oh, how she fought for me and encouraged me. If I weren't already in love with Alden, I may have fallen in love with her. She applied a salve she made herself from lily-of-the-valley. She said it was healing. The doctor said it was poisonous and told her she could not use it. But she continued. She swore by it and explained to me that her grandmother used it on burns. They were short of nurses and she confided that she was fairly sure she wouldn't be fired. Finally, the doctor let her experiment, so long as I didn't eat it. After all, he thought I was going to die anyway, and if it gave me some relief, even if it was imaginary, where was the harm?

"She whispered to me, 'You aren't going to die,' and I believed her. And the salve helped. To me though, it was more than an ointment; it was a sign, not just that my life was worth fighting for but another sign of Alden and Patterson House.

"Then they moved me to a different hospital, one where men were expected to live, and I left Nurse Pascal. She tucked a jar of the salve into my cot. Eventually I was sent to England. The worst winter in living memory. That's what people said. If that was the weather or the war, I can't say. Every day I wondered why I was still alive.

"The fellow beside me used to read the newspapers out loud to those of us who were blind or had our eyes bandaged. One day he read a piece about Rogers Patterson's daughter finding a baby. It said the family took it in." He pauses. "That's you. I could hardly believe my ears. I knew there was more to the story. The newspaper was already eleven months old. The fellow reading said there was a picture of Alden too, and I would have done anything to have seen it. He said, 'Don't worry, you're not missing anything. She's no pin-up.' All I can say is it was a good thing I still couldn't talk. I'd have given him a piece of my mind. I decided then that I would find a way to help her."

Constance did not expect this.

"I could never be a proper husband. When I arrived at Patterson House, I could barely walk. But I managed to get to the door on my own two feet. I didn't know if Alden would recognize me and I knew I was a fright. But she knew who I was. Her father had died, just a few weeks before. The Spanish flu. You were on her hip. The staff was gone. She was out of money and didn't know what to do. I really was needed here."

Constance tries to imagine Mr. Hunt at the door, all burned and raw. Was he wearing bandages or his balaclava? Did he have to say who he was? Did Alden recognize him right away? Did they embrace? No, he would have been too unsteady.

He rubs his thighs as if to signal he is coming to the end of his story. "You see, Alden will never marry Mr. Grant. They aren't flirting. Alden is simply being gracious. He might have designs on her, but they will lead nowhere. Alden and I, well, we have an understanding. She took me in. And I look after her. We look after each other. No, I couldn't marry her." He holds out his pitiable hands. "And besides, Alden never wanted to marry. She told me herself in the garden that day."

Mr. Hunt pulls himself up with his walking stick, wavers, and steadies himself against the chair. For a minute, Constance sees the young man he must have been, determined, proud, and in love. "We are a family, the three of us, odd though it might seem. Alden is as much a mother to you as she is a wife to me. She is the only mother you have, and she's done right by you." He leans down and kisses her cheek. "Mr. Grant will be gone soon enough. Make sure you get cleaned up before you come down for breakfast. Try to look respectable. And apologize."

Constance is too overwhelmed to speak at first. She touches her cheek where Mr. Hunt kissed her, his kiss replacing the sting of last night's slap. Then she says, "I'll apologize to Alden, but never to Carling Grant."

From the doorway, Mr. Hunt shrugs. "I can live with that. Tell Alden I won't be down for breakfast this morning. I'm going back to bed for a while." With this, he makes his way back down the stairs.

To think that Mr. Hunt has been in love with Alden all these years. But does Alden love Mr. Hunt? While Constance doesn't doubt Mr. Hunt's story, she finds it hard to imagine Alden in love.

Wait until she tells Gwen. Oh! Gwen! She almost forgot about Gwen. One thing is certain. Gwen is the one who needs help now. Constance has her savings, and if they both find jobs, even jobs that don't pay very well, they will be able to afford an apartment. There is no need to worry about Mr. Hunt. Alden will look out for him. And he for her. And she can look out for herself now. She can. She looks around the room, the ever-changing bloom of wet on the ceiling, the battered Windsor chair, her small washstand with a few trinkets on it. Constance will miss this place.

Carling Grant will leave eventually and will recede into the background just like every other boarder before him. Next to Gwen's terrible stepfather, Carling Grant is hardly more than a nuisance.

But that's not true either. In her heart, she knows he is more than a nuisance. She shudders at the thought of Carling Grant entering her room. Touching her. No. It can't be imagined. She thinks of Gwen, frozen at Gerald's touch, and she shivers.

Mr. Hunt made his own family. Constance can too. Hers will include Gwen. And it's not as though she'll never see Mr. Hunt or Alden again. They are family, too. They won't live under the same roof anymore, but it's right that she moves away eventually. It's simply a bit sooner than anyone expected. William Patterson did it. And Mr. Hunt. She can too.

Constance makes her way down the hall to the small third-floor washroom. It's not fancy but she has it all to herself. This is yet another way Alden has protected her. She is grateful for the ugly, dented, metal sink, the small tub that forces her to pull her knees up to bathe, and even the old toilet with the pull chain that breaks so often.

When she gets out of her nightdress, a dark stain on the back surprises her. A little "Oh!" escapes her mouth. She wipes between her legs. Brown like rust. Not red. It has begun. She cries, stifling her sobs so they will not be heard below.

PART FOUR

November 15, 1930

IT AMAZES ME how years can go by in a sort of hazy sameness in which nothing at all happens. Days and weeks pass empty of meaning. Events come and go, completely unremarked upon and unremarkable. It is easy to stay detached then, to come and go as I please, to attend when I want and drift off to thoughts of my own life when the story playing out before me is so mundane. I can skip through years in this way.

With all this time for reflection, I perseverate. I traded one scandal for another when I married Ruth, the second Mrs. Patterson. She was a dalliance. Just another girl. I did not realize her family was so influential. She never let on. I should have ridden out the storm. I failed to consider that marrying a papist would hinder my business. Of course, Bishop Strachan washed his hands of me entirely.

In truth, I found some solace in being close to the religion of my youth again even if I pretended I did not know anything of it. And Ruth was a kind-hearted girl. I did not appreciate her enough. She gave me a son. Another chance. I wasted it, ignoring them both and spending my days and nights trying to impress men who barely recognized my existence.

When I gave money to Macdonald's Conservatives, I imagined all kinds of new possibilities for myself, but instead I brought about my own end. I may have got the business without the donation. But what was wrong with supporting a government that supported me? I give you a donation for your campaign, and in return, you buy my lumber. Easy. "Quid pro quo," they said in their fancy Latin. But I would argue even today that this is how business works. A show of mutual support. A pledge to mutual benefit.

I wanted to be one of them. I wanted it more than I wanted anything else.

Hubris, Alden would say. Yes, it was hubris. I was only a small player. Why was I so worried? Sir Hugh Allen was awarded the contract to build the railroad in return for his donation. I was only providing the lumber. He was the one who would get rich. My part in the affair might have been entirely overlooked once the full extent of the scandal was out in the open. Or not.

I used to think that my accusers thought as much about me as I did about them. I used to imagine them in smoky, dimly lit rooms, strategizing against me in the wee hours of the night. Now I realize there were no secret meetings about me. Some probably could barely put my face to my name. I was a tool. I was there at the right time, to be exploited when they needed me.

I was certain I would be the scapegoat and the full extent of the scandal would fall upon me. I couldn't face it.

And then, I was wrong.

Oh well. It's over now.

Rogers, for all his other failings, was more of a realist than I ever was. He knew what the distillery business would do to the family reputation and he didn't care. I wanted influence and thought money was a path to it. He wanted money for its own sake and thought nothing more about it. But then again, he was lost, too. Lost after his wife died. Money was never a substitute for her.

Bah! And don't we hate how we depend on the women, how we need them? We call *them* the weak ones. We transfer our hate of ourselves and our own weaknesses onto them. The women are our scapegoats. It's a sickness.

Now, time slows down. My own life is of less interest to me. The minutes count again. Alden is in more danger than she understands. I want to be able to intervene, urge one thing on and stop another.

The girl thinks the bastard has a master plan. She gives him too much credit, as I gave too much credit to my accusers. He has no plan. He simply sees the next step and exploits it. And Alden! Instead of worrying about Constance, she should have her eye on the bastard. The woman seems to have no instincts. Or all the wrong ones. Take that Pellatt cousin. I'll be clear: I am no prude. As a man of appetites, all kinds of appetites, which I used to satisfy with glee (oh—the very idea of the flesh now, the haunting scent of a woman's darkness, the fullness of a breast in my hand, the stiffness of a pert nipple under my tongue—of, dear God— the weight of my stiff cock in my own hands—oh! Remembering is too much to bear!), I certainly understand. And Alden was hardly a child. Sixteen. The same age as the second Mrs. Patterson when we met. It is only natural that Alden's passions were rising. She is, after all, a Patterson.

Alden's mistake with the Pellatt cousin was that she did not pretend to succumb. Instead, she showed an enthusiasm that startled the boy. A woman cannot be overt about her desires. She was a far cry from the scared maids and schoolgirls he had fumbled with before. The boy was not ready. It was the boy who, feeling the eagerness in Alden and being unable to match her passion, decided that she must have experience beyond his. His inadequacy, his fear, his inability to respond in kind, became reason enough for him to spread rumours that she was used goods.

Scandal. I have known my share. Scandal has only two possible sources: flesh or money. The second Mrs. Patterson's family drove a hard bargain. Rogers should have done the same for Alden. It would have been easy enough. A trip to the Pellatt family with an oblique version of Alden's story, the implication of a promise broken and a straight-backed refusal to be shamed, some suggestion that Rogers would make known the cousin's shortcomings along with some ill-masked innuendo.

In life, I used to say that there was no wrong that could not be righted by money. What did I know? In death, I have learned that time is the only true currency. It is time that has been stolen from Alden. Her youth is gone. She cannot get it back. There is hardly any sign of the firebrand she used to be. Her fury is turned inward, a mighty oak tamped down to the size of an acorn deep in her soul. It is only a matter of time.

*

Alden is already in the kitchen when Constance appears.

"Mr. Hunt has gone back to bed. He told me to tell you not to expect him for breakfast."

"You're late," she scolds. "I need you to run to Schiffley's this morning. The snow is going to change to rain. Take an umbrella. And you were rude last night. Rude and disobedient." One thing Constance can count on with Alden is that she will get right to the point.

Constance heeds Mr. Hunt's advice and starts with an apology. "I'm sorry."

"Don't ever contradict me like that again." Alden picks up a bag of flour and sets it down on the counter again. A small fog of dust rises and then settles around it. "You will not be rude to Mr. Grant. He is our only boarder. Until things turn around, we're lucky to have him."

Constance does not reply. Alden hands Constance the bowl holding the dough she is working. "Finish these scones. Divide the dough into ten instead of eight. Maybe we'll be able to stretch it a bit. He'll be down soon. You'll have to apologize to him."

"I won't." Constance drops the dough with a thud. She meant what she said to Mr. Hunt. She will never apologize to Carling Grant.

"What did I just say?" Alden stops and folds her arms across her chest.

Constance turns her back on Alden, picks up the dough, shapes it, turns it over, and drops it with another thud on the floured work table; then she shapes it again into a round and flattens it far too vigorously until it is an inch thick.

"Watch it. You'll make the scones tough."

Constance fumes, her back still turned. She sees the small, chipped bowl in which Alden has reserved a little egg white and spills it over the top of the dough, spreading it roughly with her hands. She exaggerates the motion of the knife as she divides the round into ten triangles and separates them to give them room to rise on the baking sheet. Alden opens the oven and motions Constance to slide the scones in, which she does with another exaggerated gesture.

Alden closes the oven door with a bang. "I will not tolerate defiance."

Constance faces her again with her lips pursed and arms crossed over her chest.

"Try to understand." Alden's voice has a pleading tone that Constance has never heard before. "He paid me six months in advance. That money is almost gone and not four months have passed. His rent is what has kept us going. There is no giving it back. I have to make the rest of it stretch."

Alden rarely explains herself. That she is doing it now is akin to an apology. She picks up the flour again, stores it with the rest of the baking supplies, and noisily rearranges a few pans. They can hear the wind gusting in the chimney. When Alden turns back to Constance, she pulls her sweater close around herself and does not make eye contact. Admitting the truth has cost her. Alden's stooped shoulders knock the fury out of Constance and she will not make her pay anymore.

Constance bows her head and speaks with sincerity. "I'm sorry. I'll try harder. But I will not apologize to him." She grips the table edge. An unfamiliar abdominal cramp threatens to double her over.

Alden's eyes sharpen. "What's wrong?"

Constance stares out the window. "Nothing."

"Tell me. Dear God. I can't afford the doctor now."

"I don't need a doctor." She hesitates, looks to the floor again, and mumbles, "It started."

Alden's face registers recognition. "No wonder." She leans against the sink and her posture softens. Her tone turns to sympathy, or at least to what passes for sympathy with Alden. "I understand. But having your time is no excuse for your behaviour last night. You are a woman now." Her words are meant to reassure, but they almost bring Constance to tears. "You have to learn to get a hold of yourself." She straightens her apron and reties it at the back. "I'll finish breakfast. You are excused. Go rest. I can manage for the rest of the morning. I'll see you at lunch."

Constance trudges up the back stairs to her bedroom and lies down on her bed. The spot on her ceiling is more yellow than usual. Today, it looks like a carnation, the rough edge of the concentric circular edges building outward from the centre. She has never told Alden about the leak and now there is no point. There's no money to fix the roof. And anyway, Mr. Hunt would probably have to climb the ladder to fix it. It is one thing to have him on the porch roof over the side entrance but quite another for him to climb all the way up to the top of the house. She lies down and naps and wakes thinking of her savings. Almost twenty-three dollars. That's just a little more than three weeks' room and board at Patterson House. She should offer it to Alden. Maybe. Maybe not. It would be a drop in the bucket.

But it would make all the difference in the world to Gwen.

If only she hadn't been so selfish and had acted sooner maybe she could have spared Gwen her—situation. She imagines Gwen's excitement at the windfall. Not excitement. Relief. She glances at the time. Not even ten yet. Gerald will not be home. They will not need to talk about it. But Gwen will not be able to turn her back to her like she did last night.

Constance can't stop seeing her face, the blankness, and then, Gwen's recognition of Constance in the shadows. Gwen's tears. Embarrassment.

No. Shame. And what did she have to be ashamed of? Nothing. She tries to put herself in Gwen's shoes. It isn't easy. What would she want if it were her? She would want to escape, just like Gwen. She would want to forget. It will be important not to pity her. To be forthright. This is an attitude Alden has taught her. She will do as Alden would do—get down to business.

Feeling the unfamiliar bloat in her stomach, she gets up with effort and goes to her closet and reaches for the hatbox in the back. The small tobacco tin inside is weightless. There is no jingle of coins against the tin. She pries open the lid and her worst fear is confirmed. It is empty. Her savings are gone. Gone.

When did he steal it? How did he find it? She feels a cold chill run through her with the thought of him in her room again.

She should have asked for a lock. But how could she have explained it?

She throws the tin against the wall and it bounces on the floor, still empty. She stumbles to her knees and pounds the bed. "Goddammit," she says aloud. It is the worst thing she can think of saying, and then, "Goddammit all to hell." The swearing gives her courage, and she rises and says, "He's not getting away with this."

Her feet barely touch the back stairs.

The kitchen is empty, the dish towel folded and hung straight on its rack beneath the kitchen sink, the teapot and cups stacked on the blue tray and ready for lunch.

The rest of the main floor is just as empty. With the next meal still an hour away, Mr. Grant is not lurking near the dining room. Nor is he in the parlour pawing over the Patterson library. His coat and hat are not in the closet in the foyer. Alden's coat is gone too.

She tears up the main stairs. Mr. Hunt's door is closed. She walks down to the end of the hallway and taps on Mr. Grant's bedroom door. Her knock sounds too loud to her own ear. There is no answer.

She eases the door open and slips inside. It is hopeless. Money won't be easy to find—he could have changed her dimes and nickels and quarters to bills or even spent it all already. Constance stops in the centre of the room. Think like Sherlock Holmes. Decide which things are essential and which are immaterial. Most of what is around her is immaterial. Anything essential will be hidden. She imagines Holmes saying, "Or hidden in plain sight, Watson."

She must conduct a thorough search. Orderly. Carefully. In his top drawer are his undergarments. Lifting them makes her feel ill. There is an odour, slightly oniony and dank. Trying not to breathe too deeply, she puts everything back exactly where it was. Socks, garters, briefs. In the second drawer she finds the missing picture of William Patterson and his second wife in its silver frame. She was right. He took it. Sherlock Holmes would be proud of her.

In the closet, no pocket goes unexplored. In one suit jacket there is a program from Woodbine racetrack. In another there are torn tickets from three movie houses. So that is how the man spends his days. She replaces everything.

There is still liquor in his closet, but the bottles have changed. The whisky bottle is new and almost full, and the brandy has only an ounce or two left. His valise is still locked and there is no way to open it without damaging it.

Four quarters sit out in the open on his desk. She slides them into her pocket. Why not? Now he has stolen only twenty-one dollars and sixty-five cents from her. She is merely retrieving what is hers. Then she hears the front door open and Mr. Grant humming what is supposed to be "The Sheik of Araby" in the foyer. A quick glance assures her that she has left no clues of her presence and she closes the door behind her without a sound. She descends the stairs to confront him, her eyes narrowed.

"What is this? Not in school today? Does Alden know?"

As he says this, Alden bursts through the door, wet and annoyed.

"The girl is a truant," he says to Alden, his hand gesturing to exhibit A.

Both Constance and Alden say, "It's Saturday," at the same time."

There will be no confrontation between Constance and Carling Grant today.

"You're limping," says Constance.

"Slipped on the ice," she says. Mr. Grant frowns but offers no assistance.

"Let me get this." Constance lifts a bag of groceries from Alden's arms. In the kitchen, Alden sits and pulls a chair over to elevate her foot.

"Go upstairs and get my slippers, please. I'm afraid my whole foot is swelling." Alden reaches into her pocket and hands over the key to her room.

"You'll need an ice pack," says Constance, going to the icebox.

"Later. Just get my slippers and come back and put the groceries away."

Opening the door to Alden's room, she realizes how seldom she has been inside it lately. It smells exactly like Alden. Talc. Soap. It is so orderly. She scolds herself. She is not here to snoop. She finds Alden's slippers tucked under the other side of the bed. One of Constance's skirts is crumpled on the floor beside Alden's slipper chair. She picks it up to fold and a small pair of scissors drops from it. She examines it. Alden has been working on the hem. She brings it downstairs with the slippers.

Back in the kitchen, she holds out the skirt and says, "I can do this," and offers Alden her slippers.

Alden nods, slides them on to her feet, stands, winces, and takes the sewing from her. "I'll need something to do. I poked a hole in the fabric last night. That will have to be mended too."

When the groceries are away, Constance makes tea, sets it down on the table for Alden, and makes an ice pack, which she places gingerly over Alden's ankle.

"Thank you. You're a good girl."

"If you're all right for a bit, I'd like to get out for a walk before lunch. I'll be back in time to get everything ready."

"Exercise is always good for you. Even at your time of the month." Alden looks around to ensure they are alone. This is not a conversation for men to overhear. "I have thought twice about telling you to rest this morning. We don't often have that luxury. It's important to be able to work through these minor inconveniences. The world can't stop turning." With that, she picks up the sewing.

This is the Alden she knows. "I understand."

"It's icy out there. Be careful." Alden reaches down and assesses her ankle. "Foolish of me. I should have been watching where I was going."

At the doorstep, Constance looks out into the greyness, reconsiders what she is wearing, and steps back inside to find a pair of mittens and a hat. Outside, she tightens the belt on her coat and slips, landing on her behind, even before she arrives at the gate. She realizes to her own surprise that she might start to cry. What is wrong with her? No one is on the street and she feels terribly alone.

Desperate as she is to talk to Gwen, she is also scared. What can she say? Her plan to save Gwen is ruined.

She can't ask Gwen any advice about Mr. Grant. Gwen has bigger problems. And anyways, now that the money is gone, she doesn't want to admit she had money all this time and failed to offer it. She feels bad enough about that. She will wait and talk to Mr. Hunt. Maybe he will know what to do, but in the very pit of her stomach, she knows she will never get her savings back. She wonders if that is how Mrs. Hughes felt turning over her money to Mr. Hughes.

On the slope down to the lake, she slides and must hold the edges of fences and gates, even clutching on to some branches to steady herself. It is a relief to turn onto the flat of Gwen's walkway.

Mrs. Hughes answers the door, distracted, and turns toward the baby crying in the background. She looks older than Alden now. The change in her is shocking. Her hair pokes out from a kerchief, and she has come to the door in an apron.

"She's not home. Come in. I have to get the baby." Mrs. Hughes returns with the red-faced Judith, the apples of her cheeks inflamed. "Judith has a cold." Judith is such a mature sounding name for such a little baby. Mrs. Hughes uses the edge of her apron to wipe Judith's nose. "Gwen was gone when I got up this morning. Maybe she heard about a job. You'd think she would have told me. If you see her, tell her I need her at home, please. Judith won't go down."

Constance wants to take Mrs. Hughes's hand and lead her to the chesterfield in the parlour and tell her exactly what she saw the night before. And what did she see, exactly? How can she explain it? Constance wants to tell her about her stomach cramps and about Carling Grant. She wants to tell her that he stole all of her money, that he's up to something, but the baby wails again and Mrs. Hughes says, "I'm sorry, dear, I've got my hands full this morning. I'll tell her you came by."

And then with a flash of intuition, Constance knows that Gwen is gone. Gone like her money. Gone for good. "Did you look in her room?"

Mrs. Hughes shifts the baby onto her other hip and says, "Just to get the baby. Why?" As she says it, her eyes are wide with recognition and she moves down the hall and opens Gwen's door, opens the closet and gasps. Gwen's clothes are gone. Mrs. Hughes pulls open a dresser drawer. Empty. On the dresser is a piece of paper, folded in three that says, "Mum" on it. "I didn't see this when I came in for Judith. How could I have missed it?" She lays the crying baby on Gwen's bed and reads the paper, which then falls from her hand to the floor. Constance picks it up and reads it. *Dear Mum, I'm sorry to leave without telling you. I thought it would be best for everyone if I got a place on my own. Don't worry about me. I'll send word when I'm settled. Love, Gwen.*

The silence between them has a physical quality, a thickness and weight. It seems to slow the baby, who snuffles to silence.

Mrs. Hughes looks up at Constance and says, "Did you know?"

"No." Even if she knew, Constance would not have tried to stop her. She would have helped her pack.

Tears well up in Mrs. Hughes's eyes. "Why?"

Constance looks away, unsure of what to say. If Gwen had wanted her mother to know about Mr. Hughes, she would have told her. "I'm sorry, Mrs. Hughes, I'll go now. I'll let you know if I hear anything from her." As she says the words, she knows they are untrue. She will keep Gwen's secrets like her own.

This afternoon, Constance will go downtown and find Midmaples. She will see if Gwen rented a room or if anyone has seen her. If she cannot find her there, she will go to Eaton's and see if she has been in the employment office. She will find her. On her way back to Patterson House, freezing rain makes the streets even more slick and dangerous. A car comes down the slope and, ever so slowly, begins to slide sideways, stopping just before hitting Mrs. Parkinson's front gate.

Maybe she won't be able to go downtown today after all. But Gwen is out in this somewhere.

Back in the kitchen Alden is on one foot at the counter. "How was your walk?" asks Alden. "The weather is terrible." Small talk is unnatural from Alden.

"Fine. The weather is getting worse. I'm not surprised you fell. I saw a car slide sideways in front of Parkinson's."

"How are you feeling?"

For a moment, Constance cannot figure out what Alden is talking about and then she remembers. Her time. Isn't that what Alden called it? She has barely noticed the cramps since going to Gwen's house. "I'm fine."

"That's the spirit." Alden drops a jar of pickles on the floor and it smashes. "Oh, dear God," she says, looking at the mess with her hands in the air. This is unlike Alden. Neither of them is herself today.

Wordlessly, Constance picks up the mess of pickles and glass.

"Watch your hands," Alden says. She hobbles to the cupboard to get out a bucket, mop, and some soap.

"Sit down. I'll do this."

In a few minutes, the mess is cleared and the air between them seems more amiable.

"A whole jar of pickles," Alden laments.

"It was an accident," says Constance, putting everything back where it belongs. On a shelf in front of her are the cleaning supplies. It would be easy to poison Mr. Grant's lunch.

What a thought! She picks up a box of borax and looks at it. Borax might do the job. There is bleach in a jug on the floor of the closet. Mary Pickford's sister-in-law, Olive Thomas, was poisoned with mercury bichloride. It was a terrific scandal. The papers covered it for days. But no one could ever prove whether it was an accident, a suicide, or murder. Ever since then, the odourless and colourless concoction was more tightly controlled. Mr. Baxter, the druggist, would never sell her any. Maybe she could steal it. She shakes her head.

Mr. Carling Grant has made her think of poison. Of murder. And theft. He has caused a cascade of sin in her, sins she will never confess to Father Moore.

When Mr. Grant takes his place at the table for lunch, licking his lips in anticipation of another meal, Constance thinks of the bleach again. She needs help. She might have to tell Mr. Hunt everything after all.

They wait a minute for Mr. Hunt. "Is he home?" asks Constance. "I hope he's not out in this ice."

"I believe so. Haven't you seen him?"

"Not since before breakfast."

Mr. Grant sits, impatiently adjusting the position of his plate and napkin.

"Go check and see if he's in his room."

Constance runs up the stairs and taps on his door and when there is no answer, she opens it a crack. He is atop his bed, fully clothed, perspiring, and his breath sounds wet and heavy. With her light touch on his shoulder, he wakes and smiles weakly. Damp tufts of hair stick out above his forehead. He attempts to rise but starts coughing and falls back.

"Oh dear," says Constance, her hand on his shoulder. "I'm going to get Alden. I'll be right back."

Seeing Constance rush down the stairs, Alden stands, wincing again. "What is it?"

"You'd better come."

Alden struggles up the stairs, leaning heavily on the railing. When she reaches Mr. Hunt's side, his coughing subsides, and he says, "I'm sorry to be a bother. What's happened to you? You're limping." He can barely squeak the words out. It is just like him to think of her first.

"It's nothing. Don't worry about me." Alden lays the back of her hand on his forehead. "How long have you been feeling poorly, John?"

He answers her with a coughing spasm.

Constance steps forward again. "What should we do?"

"I'll call the doctor."

Just this morning, Alden said she could not afford a doctor, but they can't think about that now.

Alden stands and winces. "You'll be faster. The number is in the book. Tell Mr. Grant to serve himself. And bring a hot water bottle back with you. And a jar of camphor plaster." Then, to Mr. Hunt, she says, "Don't worry," as she gets him sitting up. "We'll get you sorted out." A look passes between them, Alden's hand patting Mr. Hunt's arm, Mr. Hunt's hand grasping hers, only for a second, before he lets it drop as another spasm of coughing wracks his body.

Mr. Grant doesn't have a chance here.

Constance doesn't have to tell Mr. Grant to begin lunch without them. The tray of sandwiches is rapidly disappearing. "Alden says to serve yourself, but I see you already have."

Mr. Grant is impassive, ignoring her tone. "Are there any pickles?"

*

Constance spends the afternoon at Mr. Hunt's side watching his condition worsen as the weather worsens outside. Wind pushes the rain against the windows and the icy mess outside keeps the streets empty. She finds a hand towel, rolls it up, and uses it to line the bottom of the windowsill to keep the draft out.

While Mr. Hunt sleeps, she allows her thoughts to go to Gwen. Gwen is still out somewhere in this terrible weather. If Gwen has gone to Midmaples, she will find her there tomorrow as easily as she will today. When Mr. Hunt is awake, she fusses, brings tea to his lips, straightens his quilt, tucks and re-tucks. A cool cloth she uses on his forehead makes him shiver so she finds the bed warmer, fills it with hot water, and wraps it in a soft towel before putting it at his feet. His stack of Zane Grey novels is handy, and she reads aloud to him from *Riders of the Purple Sage*.

By four o'clock, she is desperately concerned that the doctor has not arrived and goes downstairs to urge Alden to call again.

"It's the weather. He will come as soon as he is able," says Alden, but the furrow in her brow tells Constance that she is worried too. Her foot is up on a chair, which she has pulled close to her. There is a purple hue along her ankle.

"It looks bad," says Constance.

"It will be fine. Just a sprain."

At five o'clock, Mr. Hunt's temperature spikes a second time. His dozing is broken by his wet cough, and he spits a thick green mucus into a handkerchief that Constance replaces often. When she takes the used hankies from him, she imagines herself an impassive nurse, Amelia Earhart before she took to flying. Another coughing spasm. Constance helps Mr. Hunt lean forward and pats his back so that he can cough up the sputum.

When the coughing fit ends, he motions her to open his top drawer. "Get me a candy, dear, and one for yourself." It's the last thing she feels like. The front face of his top drawer is on hinges and can be let down to make a small writing desk. Inside, a sweet musty scent greets her. There are orderly slots full of letters, a black leather-covered diary, a chequebook, ticket stubs, and other oddments that make up the written record of a life. On the right side are two small paper bags of candy, one with humbugs and another with licorice allsorts. Constance plucks two humbugs, passes him one, and he tucks it into his cheek.

"I'm so sorry. It's my fault. If I hadn't run off last night, you wouldn't have come after me and you wouldn't be sick now." Constance's head sinks into her hands. But Mr. Hunt's next rattling exhale starts another bout of coughing, which expels the candy, and Constance pats his back again. With all the coughing, she does not hear Alden and the doctor until they are up the stairs.

"Not your fault, dear," he says, wiping his mouth with the handkerchief.

Alden holds one of Mr. Hunt's canes that he keeps in the closet in the foyer. She motions for Constance to leave the room, but Constance only goes as far as the threshold. The doctor listens to Mr. Hunt's chest, takes his temperature, looks inside a handkerchief, in his mouth and in his ears. Alden tries to shoo Constance away again.

"Isn't there anything I can do? Can I bring in warm water for steam?"

The doctor waves his hand. "No, that's not what's called for here. Oxygen would do him some good." He says this almost to himself. "The good news, Mr. Hunt, is that this is not pneumonia. Rest is what you need. I'll go downstairs and talk with Miss Patterson." Mr. Hunt smiles weakly and closes his eyes in relief.

Constance follows them down, refusing to be excluded from the discussion. They step into the little parlour and the doctor, pointing at Alden's ankle, says, "Sit down and let me look at that."

"I'm fine. It's Mr. Hunt I'm worried about."

"You're no good to anyone if you don't look after yourself," he says.

Alden limps over to a chair, puts her foot up on an ottoman, and the doctor inspects her ankle, moving it gently this way and that. "I don't think it's broken, but it is a serious sprain. You'll have to keep off it as much as possible. Do you have crutches?"

"I'm sure there are some somewhere in this house."

Constance stands in the doorway and listens for Mr. Hunt above while also attending to their conversation. Mr. Grant rustles his paper in the blue parlour. He is surely eavesdropping. Constance goes across the hall and closes the double doors. A minute later, he opens them, and makes no pretence that he is minding his own business, joining her at the door to the small parlour. Constance would like to elbow him in his giant stomach.

The doctor sets Alden's foot down. The gloom of the day makes the parlour look shabbier than usual. The chairs, all of them, are worn, their piping bare of fabric. The wallpaper, once a jolly floral, is now yellowed and faded. "Well, as I said, it isn't pneumonia. Not yet, anyway. His scars are not only on the outside. His lungs are badly damaged. These gas cases. Really," he says, gesturing back toward Mr. Hunt's room, "it's a miracle he has managed for so long. But a situation like this is serious for a man in his condition. All we can do is try to keep him comfortable, keep this cold from getting worse, and hope that it passes. You'll have to keep a constant eye on him. Keep his head elevated. Lots of fluids, especially warm fluids like tea and broth to keep the chest loose. If you hear it tightening up, if he has more trouble breathing, call me. I'll write out a list of what you'll need."

Alden pales. "I'm not equipped to care for an invalid."

The doctor is surprised. "But you're well known for housing war vets with all kinds of injuries."

"Working men," corrects Alden, "all able to look after themselves. Not men in need of nursing care."

"I'll take care of him," says Constance.

"And how will you do that? With all of your nursing skills?" One of her eyebrows is raised and her tone is dismissive. It's not like Alden to be sarcastic. She turns toward the doctor and away from Constance, indicating that Constance is not part of the conversation.

But Constance demands to be a part of it. "I'll learn. There's not much to do in the house now with only one boarder."

The doctor shakes his head. "Miss Patterson might be right. There is more to it than you understand. He's weak. He must be kept clean and toileted. You can't keep lifting him. And this ankle of yours."

"Mr. Hunt is entitled to go to the Christie Street Veterans' Hospital," Alden says. "I spoke to them the last time he was sick. If you'll recommend it, they'll admit him."

"What? You'd send him away? Because he's sick?" Constance feels unbalanced. The idea of Patterson House without Mr. Hunt is impossible.

Mr. Grant interjects. "It's where our bravest men go to be looked after." He nods at the doctor and introduces himself. "Miss Patterson discussed it with me while we were waiting for your arrival and I think it's the right idea."

Turning to face Mr. Grant, Constance says, "With you?" Her fists are clenched at her sides and she turns on Alden. "You discussed it with him but not with me?"

Alden warns, "Remember yourself."

Constance almost stamps her foot. "You're sending him there to die."

"Lower your voice," Alden scolds. "Do you want Mr. Hunt to hear you?"

The doctor, Alden, and Mr. Grant are silent for a minute. The doctor speaks first. "Yes, often that is the case." Constance pales. The doctor looks at Mr. Grant and Alden, who stare at him in amazement. "Well, it's no use lying to the girl." He turns his attention back to Constance. "But it's been a long time since the war. The men who live there now are there to live, not to die, and this will be the case for Mr. Hunt. He can receive oxygen there, which will benefit him greatly. He has defied the odds at every turn, and there is every reason to hope that with proper care, he will get past this. That's what we all want. I think the vet hospital is an excellent option. I'll make the arrangements, Miss Patterson. And in all likelihood, it will be temporary. If I could use your telephone, please." Alden directs him to the telephone in the parlour.

While the doctor makes his arrangements, Constance glares at Alden. "You're going to let him go. Just like that?"

"What choice do I have? You heard the doctor." She gestures to him and puts her fingers to her lips. She does not want a scene in front of him.

"You can't abandon Mr. Hunt."

Mr. Grant attempts to lay his hand on her shoulder and she jerks away from him. "Don't touch me."

"Mr. Grant," says Alden. "Please, leave this to me."

His eyebrows rise. He does not speak, but neither does he leave.

Annoyance flashes across Alden's face. To Constance, she says, "He's hardly being abandoned."

"He will be well cared for," says Mr. Grant. Alden's annoyance is completely visible for anyone who cares to see. "Mr. Grant, again, perhaps it would be best if you leave this to me." He looks down his nose at Constance and nods at Alden before retreating to the blue parlour.

Alden whispers with considerable vehemence. "I don't expect you to understand."

Constance is equally vehement. "This morning I was a grown woman and now I'm back to being a child. Which is it? I'm not a child. I can look after Mr. Hunt."

Alden motions sharply for Constance to follow her. She hops into the kitchen where she closes the pass-through door behind her and says,

"I can't afford to pay for his medical care. I have no money for the things he needs. If he goes to the Veterans' Hospital, it will all be taken care of. I won't have to pay for it."

"What do you mean? Of course, you can. Look at all this stuff." Her arms flail in front of her like propellers. "Sell something. You don't need half of this."

"No one has any money to buy it. Don't you think I've tried? It's worse than worthless."

"But it's Mr. Hunt." She is pleading. "I thought he was special to you."

"Of course, he is. He's a very fine man and he's been with the family such a long time."

"*With* the family? He is part of the family."

Alden bristles. "Certainly not."

"He thinks he is. I know that for sure. I think he is. He's part of *my* family."

Alden's eyebrows arch and she sits and rubs her ankle. "I don't know whatever gave you such an idea. He was the gardener, for goodness' sake, and not even the head gardener. He was a helping hand. And don't you dare suggest I haven't done well by him. Why, he's lived here for almost twelve years, Constance. I've looked after him, housed him, and fed him for a dozen years."

"And he has helped you, too. Don't deny it. He has looked after you, too."

"How?" Alden's voice rises. "By fiddling in the garden? By giving me his pittance of an allowance every month? It hardly pays for tea." This is news to Constance. She had no idea that Mr. Hunt got any sort of allowance or that he gave it to Alden. But it doesn't matter; he is still not like other boarders.

"That's not all he's done."

"Oh really? And you know so much about it, do you?"

Constance drops her head, turns away from Alden, and walks toward the door. Her voice comes out as a whisper. "He has looked after me."

The simple truth of the statement sweeps the tide of vitriol from Alden. Her mouth opens and then closes. Her lips purse. Constance leaves, somehow sorry to have won the point. Nevertheless, she already knows she has lost the match. Alden will send Mr. Hunt away. She returns to his room where he has fallen into a rattling sleep.

From her perch beside Mr. Hunt, Constance hears the doctor confer with Alden, hears the goodbye, the closing door, and more murmuring with Mr. Grant. She looks at Mr. Hunt's watch, sitting on his bedside table. It is half past six already. Constance is not hungry although she has also missed lunch. She has no idea if Alden has prepared a supper for Mr. Grant or how she will manage on one foot; nor does she care. Not one whit. Unless Alden demands it, she won't go down. She will stay at Mr. Hunt's side. From his chair, she watches a feverish dampness spread across his face and chest.

*

Constance is still in Mr. Hunt's room the next morning, rumpled and half-asleep in his chair, when Alden finds her there, nudges her shoulder to wake her, and tells her it is time. The ambulance has arrived. Somewhere, she has found a proper crutch and is using it. Yesterday's bad weather seems to have passed and there is some brightness in the morning sky.

She can barely straighten up; she pulls her fingers through her hair and wipes the sleep from her eyes. Her mouth tastes stale and her teeth feel fuzzy. The ambulance attendants arrive at Mr. Hunt's door and he opens his eyes and offers a weak smile while trying to raise his hand. They move him to a stretcher and carry him down the stairs and outside with practically no effort at all. He is so light.

It is still icy outside and the way to the ambulance is treacherous. Constance has not bothered to put a coat on, and Alden waits by the service door, unwilling to risk her ankle again.

Mr. Hunt's balaclava has been left behind and Constance wants to bolt back into the house and make everything stop so that she can cover him the way he likes. But it is too late. Because the ambulance doubles as a hearse and because of the early hour, curious neighbours peer through drapes and open doors to see if anyone has died. Hardly anyone ventures all the way out onto the icy sidewalks until they realize it is Mr. Hunt. Mr. Parkinson and Mrs. Shields from across the street come over to wish him well, not realizing he is in no condition to talk. The state of his face will become a new story in the community.

Constance is not permitted to go with him in the ambulance. "There are no children allowed at the Veterans' Hospital," the attendant tells Constance, showing a greater measure of sympathy for her than does Alden, who is calling to her from the doorway.

Constance grips Mr. Hunt's hand too tightly and says, "I'll see you soon," although at that moment, she is quite afraid she will never see him again. She looks down the street as though Gwen might appear and is doubly desolate. At least Mr. Grant has not come outside to pretend any decency.

As the ambulance drives off, the neighbours' talk turns to the bad weather. A few have lost tree branches to the ice. This is the kind of conversation Mr. Hunt would love. Constance leaves them, freezing as she is without a coat, and returns to the house.

Back in the kitchen, Alden announces they will not be going to Mass. "We are late, and I don't know how I would get there," she says, struggling with her crutch.

Constance cannot even revel in the idea of a Sunday morning to herself. She lets spoons and forks clatter against one another and bowls bang on the countertops.

"Banging cutlery around isn't going to change anything." Alden, balanced on her crutch, ties her apron with difficulty, lifts bread dough down from the shelf over the stove where it has proofed, and passes it to Constance. There is less than usual. Of course. They will need fewer loaves of bread without Mr. Hunt.

Alden notes her hesitation. "Only five loaves this week."

"The savings have started already," says Constance.

"I won't tolerate this attitude."

Constance sprinkles a little flour on the counter, lifts the dough out of the bowl, gives it a perfunctory punch, kneads it carelessly, and shapes the loaves.

"Make them uniform," says Alden.

What does it matter how the bread looks if it is for Mr. Grant? He'll eat it so fast he won't even notice. She lets the loaf pans land with a thud beside the oven to rest for a while.

Alden covers them with a tea towel and says, "If you have something to say, just say it."

"When can we go to the hospital to visit?"

"Children are not allowed."

"Why did you tell them I'm only fourteen? If you hadn't said anything, I could have gone."

"You think I should have lied?" says Alden, sitting back down in a chair. She lifts her foot onto the chair opposite her.

A lie seems like such a small thing in these circumstances. "Surely some of the men there have children. Are they never to see their children?"

"You are not Mr. Hunt's child." Alden polishes the flatware with her apron and sorts it on the table. Finishing her inspection of the knives and forks, she says, "Set the table, please. Think of the other men. There are things you don't want to see and men who don't want to be seen. Let them have their privacy."

What a horrible thought. Mr. Hunt is in some asylum of monsters. No matter how awful any of these men look, they must want to have a loved one to talk to. "When are you going to go?"

"Let's give Mr. Hunt some time to get better."

"You're not going today?"

Alden points at her ankle. "How would I do that? No. Not today. And likely not tomorrow."

"When, then? When will you go visit him?"

Alden does not answer.

"Will you let him come back when he gets better?"

"Let's pray that he does get better."

That is not an answer. It breaks something in Constance. Tears flow down her cheeks. Alden's stern expression softens. She is about to speak again when they both hear the stairs creak under Mr. Grant's weight, every step a challenge to the workmanship of William Patterson's carpenters.

Alden directs her from her chair. "Quick, get the table set." She hands her the cutlery. "And then the porridge and the rest."

In the dining room, Mr. Grant has seated himself at Mr. Hunt's usual place.

"That's not your spot," says Constance.

Alden joins them in the dining room and quickly assesses the scene. "It makes sense for Mr. Grant to sit at this end of the table while Mr. Hunt is gone. To leave a space is—disorganized."

Constance sets the porridge in front of Mr. Grant, wondering if there will be any left for her after he helps himself. He serves himself before she has finished setting everything else down, reaches for the cream, and adds a spoonful of raspberry jam and swirls that in too. Alden's eyelids become like hoods, but Constance has seen what she has seen. The man disgusts her.

Constance and Alden sit at their usual places and pass the porridge between them.

Mr. Grant surveys the table and says, "Is this everything?"

"A light meal today. Busy morning, what with—well, everything."

He makes a slightly disgruntled sound. "Understandable, I suppose. I trust it all went smoothly."

"Yes, as well as can be expected."

Constance pours herself tea and when she asks to have the sugar passed, Alden gives her a withering stare and does not move. Constance reaches over for the bowl herself, takes a spoonful, and sets it back down where Mr. Grant will have to ask for it. She knows that Alden would love to criticize her for taking sugar but cannot since she would also be criticizing Mr. Grant. When he asks for sugar a moment later, Alden passes it to him.

"Do you think I could pack up a few of Mr. Hunt's things and take them to the hospital? Maybe his dressing gown and slippers? To make him comfortable?" Constance has purposely asked this question in front of Mr. Grant believing that Alden would not want to say no and risk appearing callous in front of him.

Mr. Grant serves himself another spoonful of jam and plops it into his porridge. "I don't think he'll be in much need of those. They'll have everything he needs at the hospital."

"I'm sure he'll need them," says Constance. "He'll be up and around before the end of the week and will want to have his own clothes when he comes back."

Alden sets her spoon down. "I have already told you. They won't let you in."

"But we could send his things over. Or I could just deliver them and leave. Then he'll know we're thinking of him." Mr. Grant and Alden exchange glances as though this is a decision they are to make together. "Surely you want him to know we're thinking of him."

Alden's smile is thin and dry. "Yes, of course. You put everything together."

Mr. Grant talks with his mouth full. "Do you think she should be going through his things? Perhaps I should supervise."

Constance wants to pour what's left of the sugar over his head.

Alden bristles. "Constance is perfectly capable."

For a moment, Constance forgets how angry she is with Alden and lets a smile escape. She catches herself and stops.

*

While Constance undertakes her mission in Mr. Hunt's room, Mr. Grant walks the hall far too often. She leaves the door open just a crack, a move meant to infuriate him. He would have to move the door himself to keep an eye on her and that would make his intentions too overt. She collects a few personal items from beside the wash basin and wraps them in a small hand towel. While Mr. Grant is at the end of the hall pretending to use the washroom, she goes into the little hidden desk in his top drawer and collects his diary and chequebook. There is a five-dollar bill folded inside. She slips everything into her apron pocket. No sense letting Mr. Grant get his hands on that. It will be safer in the hospital with Mr. Hunt. She finds his billfold on his bedside table, but it is empty, so she leaves it. Perhaps he has already been here. She adds two Zane Grey novels to her package and the magnifying glass that Mr. Hunt uses to read. And his balaclava, of course.

From the top of the dresser, she picks up a framed photograph of the three of them, which was taken in front of Patterson House when Constance was no more than three or four. She doesn't know the occasion. She is wearing a pale dress with a white lace collar. The sash of the dress is trailing behind her. In her left hand, she holds a white porcelain doll she does not recognize. Alden looks grim, as always, in her severely cut dark clothes. She is not smiling for the camera. Mr. Hunt appears oblivious to Alden's mood and is crouched on one knee, holding Constance beside him, his arm circling her waist. He has a hat on that covers his patchy hair and he is not wearing his balaclava. His face is shaded and slightly blurred as though he turned his head at the moment the picture was taken. In this photo, he can be mistaken for a normal-looking man.

The photo is like a miracle, a picture of Mr. Hunt's dream, his little family. Wrapping it in another handkerchief, she adds it to the box.

Mr. Grant creaks past one more time while Constance checks the room one last time. His watch. He'd want it. She buckles it on her own wrist, only one buckle notch separating where it fits him and where it fits her. She looks again at his bedside table and adds two seed catalogues to the box. When she leaves the room, Mr. Grant is waiting outside his own door. "Do you want me to have a look, see if you've got everything a man might need? Toothbrush, shaving kit? Razor?"

Alden comes out of her own bedroom door and answers before Constance is able.

"Mr. Hunt doesn't require a razor," says Alden.

"Oh. Of course." He is momentarily chastised.

Constance is grateful for Alden's intervention again. Mr. Hunt is right. She can't let Mr. Grant get between them. Mr. Grant goes into his room leaving the door ajar.

"Do you have his toothbrush?" asks Alden.

"Yes, of course."

"I don't know why I didn't think to gather these things this morning. The ambulance could have taken it and saved us all the trouble. I don't know what I was thinking," she repeats, her voice trailing off. The display of uncertainty lasts only a second. "Send his quilt."

"I have his coverlet," Constance says.

"Let's send both." Alden enters his room and folds his quilt. "I might as well strip this bed and get his sheets done too."

"That way they'll be fresh when he comes home," says Constance, still waiting for some indication of Alden's intentions. Pointless. Alden offers nothing, closing Mr. Hunt's door behind her.

Alden bundles the sheets and puts them at the end of the bed. "Come back for these later. There's some twine in the kitchen we can use to tie the box."

In the kitchen, just before Alden ties the knot on the twine, Constance says, "I forgot. Candy. He keeps some candy in his dresser. Should I get that too?"

Alden smiles. "Why not? I'll go downstairs and get one of his jars of lily-of-the-valley salve and camphor plaster too. Perhaps they will let him use it there."

"I'll do it. You sit down."

Constance runs back upstairs. Mr. Hunt's door is wide open again. Mr. Grant is already inside. She creeps along the hall to see what she can catch him at. He has the billfold in his hand and is looking inside it. He puts it back on the dresser. That he needed to look in the billfold means he has not looked through this room before and now he is unsure. Constance stands in the doorway until he notices her. He spots the watch on her wrist. "You can leave the watch here. He won't need it."

"I don't think so," she says defiantly. "It's safer in the hospital."

His eyes narrow. This is how it will be now, their enmity out in the open. She brushes past him, opens Mr. Hunt's top drawer and takes out his two bags of candies. "Close the door when you're finished," she says.

Back in the kitchen, Constance tells Alden that Mr. Grant was in Mr. Hunt's room.

"Men," Alden mumbles under her breath.

The picture of the three of them is in Alden's hand. "Where was this?"

"On his dresser."

Alden sits at Mr. Hunt's desk chair, her shoulders rounded. "I don't remember this being taken," she says. "Are there others?"

"I didn't see any."

Alden looks out the window in silence, the picture still in her hand. "The starlings are back. Mr. Hunt would be annoyed."

It is impossible to know what she is thinking, but instead of her perpetual frown, she looks genuinely sad. There is a softness around her normally tight lips, a slight opening of her mouth. For an instant, she looks much older. She shines the glass and frame with the end of her apron and wraps the photograph back up in the handkerchief. "It was a good idea to take it to him." She smiles weakly at Constance and picks up the Zane Grey novels. "I didn't know he read these." She turns one over and reads the back cover and puts it back.

"He likes a good western," says Constance.

"You take the things to the hospital if you want. I know you want to do something to help. I appreciate it. And so will Mr. Hunt. Write a note to him too and add it to the box." She pretends a smile, stands unsteadily, hops to the baking cupboard, takes two nickels out of a baking powder tin, and pushes them into Constance's hand.

Constance is momentarily baffled. "For the streetcar," says Alden. This is an unusual kindness from Alden. She is doing what Mr. Hunt would have done. She feels as though she must say something consoling but can think of nothing. Alden speaks instead. "Oh well. No use dwelling. Let's finish up."

*

Constance walks all the way up to Queen Street, box in hand, when she has a thought. She could try the very same trick she suggested for Gwen. If she were to dress as a delivery boy, they might let her go right to Mr. Hunt's room.

The clothes are still in the carriage house. There's no reason not to try.

She backtracks until she reaches the carriage house and glances up at Mr. Grant's window. There is no sign of him.

The clothes are waiting exactly where she left them. There is a blanket lying across the bottom of the cot that she doesn't remember. Nothing else is amiss. She must have simply forgotten about it. Maybe a hobo has found this spot and is using it. She sure hopes not. Alden would have a fit.

Once she is dressed, she tries to get an impression of herself. Lucky for her, her shoes are unfashionable enough to be men's. She braids her hair. She can't do it nearly as well as Gwen, but after she secures it under the cap, she thinks she looks passable. She has the chequebook with the five dollars and slips it into the pocket inside her jacket and makes sure she has her two nickels. There are all kinds of pockets in the jacket. So much more convenient than women's clothes, which often have no pockets at all. She squats a few times, allowing her knees to widen each time. Although there is no mirror in the loft, she can see her reflection in the glass of the small window nestled beneath the ridge of the roof. The pants are a bit short. She is taller than Gwen, but so many boys are wearing ill-fitting clothes now that it hardly matters. She finds a piece of rope and uses it as a belt, hiding the makeshift solution with the jacket buttoned up. A wool scarf hanging on a hook by the door will hide any stray hairs and the looseness of her collar. But again, what does that matter when so many men are rumpled now?

There is a note on the workbench in Mr. Hunt's handwriting. She glances at it. Someone has offered to buy the Lozier and will call about it before Christmas, it says. No number and only a last name. She slips the paper in her pocket to ask Mr. Hunt about it. With her box in her hands, she makes her way back up the alley and toward the streetcar.

The box slows her down but is also a godsend because it hides much of her awkwardness. Pants continue to be a revelation. They are so much more secure and somehow freeing at the same time. And warm. If she could, she would wear pants every day. And why can't she? The answer is Alden. Alden would never agree. Once she moves out of Patterson House with Gwen, she will wear pants whenever she wants.

A hobo checks the trash bins, his eyes hungry and defeated, looks at her and laughs. "What are you playing at, girlie?" He comes closer.

"School play," she says, skittering past him. She's not fooling anyone. Her enthusiasm for the caper evaporates.

At the streetcar stop, she observes the men carefully. She knows more about the ways of men than women, having lived with them her whole life. She adjusts her posture, stands with her legs farther apart, and looks straight ahead instead of down. While Alden has always been annoyed by the men, Constance has felt something different. Envy. Constance likes the way they sit with their knees apart and their arms across the backs of the chairs in the movie theatre, sometimes taking up three seats instead of one. They say what they think at the dinner table and their opinions are considered, even opinions so idiotic and ill-informed that they leave Alden fuming later in the kitchen. Men never wonder if they are right. They are right. They don't wonder if they belong, even in someone else's house. Men always belong.

At the streetcar stop, Constance doesn't merit a second look from anyone. No one speaks to her, comments on the day, the box she carries, or her possible destination. She is neither invisible nor too visible. She is simply unremarkable. This must be what it is like for men. How wonderful it is to be unremarkable.

When the streetcar comes, she steps in awkwardly with the box, and fumbles with her fare, suddenly conscious of the smallness of her hands.

The driver does not seem to notice. If she were a girl, he would have asked her if she needed assistance or some man would have taken the box from her already and carried it to her seat. She picks up the box again and sits with it in her lap. Realizing her legs are together and her feet are crossed at the ankle, she rearranges herself. A young woman stands in front of her, clearing her throat lightly. Constance understands and offers her seat with a gesture, afraid to talk and reveal her voice. She moves with her box toward the back of the car where there is more space and where more men stand.

The men are all accustomed to standing on the streetcar and shift their weight easily in the turns, some while holding a newspaper. They appear to be in their own impenetrable spot, untouchable and untouched, oblivious to their surroundings. What must it be like to feel that way? Adjusting her posture, she tries to emulate their stance. The secret to riding easily through the bumps seems to be to keep the knees loose. After a transfer at Dupont, she gets off at the Christie Loop to walk the rest of the way to the Veterans' Hospital, making her way through the unfamiliar streets.

Only once does anyone give her a second look, a shifty-looking fellow smoking in a doorway. He seems more interested in the box than in her, though, probably imagining there is something of worth in it.

After only one wrong turn, she sees the hospital and her pace quickens. Inside, ammonia and camphor taint the dim entrance. The tile floor is worn and the whole atmosphere is shabby. This is what "our bravest men" get. Not much. She wonders what that darn Carling Grant would have to say about this place if he saw it. According to the lettering still visible on the brick outside, it used to be a National Cash Register factory. A sign in the lobby says, "All Visitors Please Check with the Front Desk." Was that for the cash register company or for the hospital? Erring on the side of caution, she coughs to get the attention of a white starched woman behind a desk at the back of the lobby.

From above her reading glasses she says, "Yes?"

"I have a delivery for a patient who came in this morning. Mr. John Hunt." Constance tries to sound bored and hesitates at the name, as though it is an effort to remember. If anyone asks for her name, she has already decided to say it is Con. Why not? It will be enough for Mr. Hunt to guess it is her. But no one asks. No one is interested in the name of the delivery boy. The nurse is more interested in the box she hugs to her chest. After several questions about the contents, which Constance pretends not to know, she takes it from her and looks inside. Perhaps Constance will not get to see Mr. Hunt after all. The nurse shakes her head at the candy, removes the jars of lily-of-the-valley salve and camphor plaster to study them, opens them, sniffs, wrinkles her nose, and sets them aside. "Yes, you can leave it here."

"I've been instructed to deliver it right to him." She applauds herself for her quick thinking.

The nurse waves her hand. "Saves me a trip. To the left. Ward 10. At the end."

The ring of the telephone bounces off the dull beige walls, and the nurse shifts her attention to it.

Once in the hallway, Constance realizes she should remove her cap, but she can't. Every plan has a flaw. She takes a deep breath and tells herself that no one expects fine manners from the delivery boy.

A few patients are in the hall, all amputees. Nothing she has not seen before.

This was probably an open factory floor once, part of some sort of assembly place. The walls are recent additions and likely thin enough that the men can hear each other snore. Through the open doors, she hears voices and a radio on low. Men are playing cards, cribbage, chess. It must be so boring. Further down, more and more men are outside of their rooms, socializing in their wheelchairs. Those who have both legs intact shuffle along the hall. Then one man turns around and faces her. His mouth opens to a gaping hole where his cheek once was. She does not allow her expression to change. In the city, a man like this would wear a mask carefully painted to match the rest of his face. But a living face cannot be faked. These men can pass, but only from a distance. Close up, they are always startling.

And how is what she is trying to do any different? From a distance, she can pass as a boy, but like the men in masks, once anyone comes close to her, she will be discovered. And what would these men do if they found her out? What is the worst that could happen? They might laugh at her. She can live with that. But something in her knows much worse can happen even though she doesn't know why she knows it, or exactly what that "worse" might be. Alden's ongoing concern about "the men" is part of her now. Who knows what a man might do?

One of the patients calls out from behind her, "Are you lost?" She realizes she has stopped walking and is standing stock-still in the hall, lost in thought.

A man missing both arms and both legs is perched in a wheelchair in the hall. "Yes, you. Are you lost?" He says to the others, "Looks like someone's getting something new. The lucky bastard." She almost smiles and then recovers herself and nods, a slight acknowledgement from a busy errand boy.

"Ward 10?" she says, her voice as deep as she can make it.

"Ah, the gassed fellows. Two more doors."

Given a few more visits, she is certain she could get used to all these men. Are they really to be feared?

The man without arms and legs tries to engage her in conversation. Alden was wrong. The men, at least some of the men, do want visitors. "What's the news?"

"They're talking about more snow."

The man laughs and says, "I'd better get my shovel out." A few of the others chuckle. Constance cannot help but smile.

Ward 10 has oxygen tanks with tubes and breathing masks attached. Three of the eight beds are occupied, and the others are made up. Mr. Hunt is in the corner by the window, an oxygen mask over his face. He is so slight that his body barely creates a bump under the thin covers. Through the window are a large pine and maple trees. There is a good view of the street, which he could see if he were able to stand up. On a better day, he'll get the sunshine in the morning.

As she approaches the bed, she can feel the chill through the window. It's a good thing she brought both quilt and coverlet. His breathing seems less laboured already. She leans in and whispers, "Mr. Hunt, it's me. Constance."

When he opens his eyes, he is confused for a moment but then starts to laugh. He lowers the mask under his chin and his laughter brings on a terrible coughing fit. He waves his hands in front of him and Constance helps him sit up. He catches his breath and says, "What's this about?"

"I figured if I dressed like a delivery boy, they'd let me in. They said I couldn't see you because children aren't allowed."

"Pretty clever," he says.

"I brought you some things." She starts to open the box.

"Don't worry about that now. Tell me how you are."

"I came all the way here on the streetcar and not a single person noticed I'm a girl."

Mr. Hunt sits up a bit and asks for some water. There is a cup on his bedside table that she brings to his lips.

"You're looking better."

"It's the oxygen. A wonder. Don't be angry with Alden." Constance is shocked that he knows of their spat. "She did the right thing. I feel better already."

She investigates her jacket and hands him his chequebook and five dollars. "I thought you might need this."

He pushes the bill back into her hand. "You keep this. Put the chequebook in the drawer here."

The note about the car is stuck to the back of the cheques. "Oh, and I found this in the garage. You sold the car?"

"Yes. A handshake deal." He checks the note. "I haven't told Alden. You can't count on these things until the money is in hand. But you should give this to her and let her know she might get a call, and if she does, it's on the up and up. She'll be thrilled. I got a pretty penny for it."

"Really?"

"It should keep her going till the spring."

"You said no one has money for something like this."

Mr. Hunt laughs. "Well, we'll see, won't we? I guess the hard times never hurt the truly rich. Just the likes of us have to tighten our belts."

Constance remembers the rope holding her pants, shows it to him, and he laughs again. She tucks the note back in her pocket. "How is everything? Is Mr. Grant behaving himself?" Constance stiffens, turns her back, and fiddles with untying the string on the box. Mr. Hunt says, "Tell me. What is it?"

"This isn't the time."

"Tell me. I'll just worry."

"I have—well, I had—some money saved. I kept it in the back of my closet. Hidden. I've saved my whole life. It's gone. He took it. I know he did."

"How do you know it was him?" He shakes his head. "What am I saying? Never mind."

"What should I do?"

"Let me think on it. For now, don't do anything. You promise?"

Constance nods.

"How much?"

"Almost twenty-three dollars."

Mr. Hunt whistles, and it makes him start to cough. When he recovers, he asks, "What was it for?"

"I was going to give it to Gwen. She needs to get a place. Right now. Trouble at home."

Mr. Hunt nods. "The new baby?"

"No. Worse than that."

He nods again. "Give me my chequebook." Good old Mr. Hunt. He never asks too many questions. "I don't have twenty-three dollars. But you're welcome to what I have. I won't need it here." He writes a cheque for sixteen dollars and hands it to her. "Take care of it. Fold that up and stick it in your pocket, young man."

"We'll pay you back. I promise."

"I know."

Constance leans in conspiratorially. "I'm going to get a job too. Gwen and I talked about applying for men's jobs. What do you think? Could I get away with it?"

He frowns. "Pretty risky, my dear. Playing a bit fast and loose. It's always easier to tell the truth. Although, your disguise is pretty convincing."

Constance can't help feeling a bit deflated and tries to hide her disappointment. "Your coverlet, quilt, and robe, and a few other things are in the box." Unable to untie the knot, she breaks the twine with her teeth and brings out a quilt to lay over him.

A nurse enters and is surprised to find a delivery boy fixing a patient's bedding. "You there, boy! What are you doing?"

Mr. Hunt winks. "Don't mind the boy, nurse. I asked him to. Now that you're here I'll send him on his way." He starts to cough again, expelling phlegm. The nurse forgets about Constance and she uses the opportunity to slip away.

Walking back to the Christie Loop without the box, she has nothing to hide behind. Falling into step behind another man, she imitates his gait. Long confident strides, hands in pockets, shoulders hunched against the cold.

At the bus stop, she flicks her Zippo lighter open, lights it, and shuts it again. No one, not a man or a woman, gives her a second glance. Then a mother with a red-cheeked toddler in tow arrives and the little boy looks up at Constance with grave intensity. A woman would respond and engage with the little boy, maybe ask him his name, but she doesn't know what a man would do. The other men ignore him, and she takes her cue from them. The boy tugs at his mother's sleeve and says, "Why is the lady wearing pants?" The mother shushes him and looks embarrassed. Constance pretends not to notice. When the streetcar comes, one of the men touches the young mother's elbow and helps her up the step with her son. It annoys Constance when men do this, even if it is done in the most polite way. And if the woman in question doesn't smile pleasantly and say thank you, she is considered the rude one.

On the streetcar, she stands near the back again and watches the passengers from her new male perspective and notices that men don't necessarily sit down when they are only aboard for a few stops. Fearful of being recognized as she gets closer to home, she gets off the streetcar early and she lets three women exit before her. One is the cashier at the Prince Edward Theatre. She doesn't recognize Constance, although she has probably sold Constance twenty movie tickets on her travels with Mr. Hunt. *Double Danger*, *The Ramblin' Kid*, *Thundering Thompson*, and most recently, *The Virginian* with Gary Cooper. That was her favourite. For weeks afterwards, she and Mr. Hunt re-enacted the scene in the bar between Gary Cooper and Walter Huston. He would say, "I'm talking to you, Trampas." Then Constance would get to say, "When I want to know anything from you, I'll tell you, you long-legged son-of-a...." Not playing Gary Cooper was worth it just to get to say that line. It would be a lot more convincing coming from a person in pants.

Everything is more convincing in pants.

She zigzags her way past the racetrack and to Kippendavie Avenue with her head down. On the side street, mothers are calling children in to supper. Few people are out walking. The hobo who was in the alley earlier is gone.

As she approaches the carriage house in the alley, a flock of starlings descends on the roof. She picks up some gravel and throws it at them and a few flutter upwards. Her effort is unconvincing, and they land back on the same perches.

Inside the carriage house, Mr. Grant leans against the workbench, waiting. "Caught you."

*

Alden has minced the onion for the shepherd's pie to a pulp before she realizes what she has done. Oh well. She'll use it anyway. She wipes the knife edge with her dishcloth and leaves both by the edge of the sink. Standing on one foot preparing dinner is, strangely, exhausting.

The child doesn't understand. The situation is impossible. She cannot keep an invalid.

She slides the onion from the cutting board and into a bowl with tears in her eyes and wipes her cheeks with the back of her hand. Honestly, if she never cooked another meal in her life, she would be glad. She's not even sure she gets hungry anymore. Her mathematical mind makes it impossible for her to keep from making a calculation of the number of meals she has made. December 1918 to now. Roughly four thousand three hundred dinners. And lunches. And breakfasts. The monotony of it. How has she borne it?

That photograph from John's bedside table rattled her. She looked like the dour old aunt. And that was eleven years ago. The moment animated both Constance and John. They were movement and life. She was a grim gargoyle, looming.

Grim indeed. At the possibility of John's departure from Patterson House, she did not feel sadness, but relief. Yes. Relief. It weighs on her. She cannot imagine sitting before her confessor and admitting, "I felt relief that the poor man was too sick to stay." She whispers the words aloud, needing to admit them to someone, to anyone. Her heart is dark. Such callousness must be a terrible stain on her soul.

Why is it that no matter how much she has done for others, she is afraid it will not, in the end, be understood as enough? It is not as though she has thrown him into the street or left him without care. He is where he should be, a man in his condition. Even the doctor said so.

She drops the cutting board into the sink with a clatter. At the very least, she can be honest with herself. With John away, she will not be required to explain her decision to marry Carling Grant. She will not have to see his face. And if he dies—she stops herself from completing the thought.

She is a wicked, wicked woman. She remembers the taunt aimed at her by a boarder. Not a drop of human kindness. What was his name? What difference does it make? They probably all thought the same of her. And they were right.

Constance's dislike of Mr. Grant is far too obvious. As is his of her. They will simply have to put up with each other. Hard enough as it is to imagine Patterson House without John, it is harder for Alden to imagine it without Constance. Harder still to imagine it with Carling Grant as a permanent fixture. Yet all of this is easier to imagine than having to leave.

The tap drips, a long slow drip. At the same moment she makes a mental note to tell John about it, she is crushed again by the realization that he is gone.

The door from the kitchen to the garden lurches open, its hinges squeaking. Alden turns with a start to find Mr. Grant hustling a young boy into the kitchen. She knocks a measuring cup full of flour off the counter and it clatters to the floor, a cloud of dust rising. "Why, Mr. Grant? What is the meaning of this? Who—" And then recognition dawns. "Constance. What have you done?"

*

Mr. Grant is as satisfied as Sunday dinner. No matter how Constance tries to explain herself, she realizes that there is no explaining. Not really.

The facts are indisputable. She is dressed in men's clothes.

Alden's hands are on her cheeks. "What if someone saw you? What on earth would I say?"

"I was only trying to see Mr. Hunt."

"Look at how convincing she is." He leers at her and the look makes Constance want to become invisible. "Well-practised, obviously. So well-practised you didn't recognize her at first. You are not a woman of the world. You have not seen what I have seen. There are *women* like this," he sneers. "Women who pretend, women who *consort* with other women. Women who go to jazz clubs."

At this, Alden pulls a kitchen chair to her and sits. "Jazz clubs?"

Constance feels as though she is watching the scene from somewhere outside her body and is simultaneously amused and aghast. "When on earth would I have gone to a jazz club?" Her hands are spread in front of her, palms up. He is pulling out all the stops, preying on Alden's greatest fears.

"Don't allow your good name to be tainted by this...this...foundling," says Mr. Grant, pointing an accusing finger at Constance.

He makes the word "foundling" sound as bad as "bastard."

"Look at her. It's ungodly," he sniffs, gesturing to the heavens as if inviting the Lord Himself to agree.

Constance feels utterly ridiculous in her outfit. If only the earth could swallow her up right now.

Alden is red-faced, her hands at her neck, but she says nothing.

Mr. Grant makes his next gambit. "You have not been paying attention," he says. "She is a pilferer. A dollar is missing from my dresser. Four quarters. Who else would have taken it?"

Alden looks grave. "Is this true, Constance? Have you stolen money from Mr. Grant?"

Constance has always been a terrible liar, a fact that should play in her favour but does not. "You don't understand. *He* stole money from *me*. My savings. From my closet. I was only trying to get some of it back."

Alden's head moves back. Her expression is one of disbelief.

"He doesn't even work for the BAS. He never worked for the BAS. He's been faking it all this time. When he leaves, he goes to the racetrack or the movies. His pockets are full of ticket stubs."

Alden's eyes are getting wider. Mr. Grant looks from one to the other, barely moving.

"And he drinks. He has liquor in his room. Brandy, whisky, gin." Her hands are flailing. "He's a grifter, a four-flusher, a chiseller, cheater, a liar," she sputters, trying hard to think of every name she has ever heard in every western she has ever been to with Mr. Hunt. But the look on Alden's face stills her.

Mr. Grant crosses his arms over his chest, and there is a smirk on his face. He has stood back and let her rant. Constance realizes Alden will not believe her. She tries once more. "If you don't believe me, go look in his room."

Alden stands. She looks to Mr. Grant, "I don't know what to say, Mr. Grant. I am so sorry. Constance, you must apologize at once."

"Apologize?" She points an accusing finger. "No. He has to apologize. And I want my money back." She stomps her foot.

Mr. Grant says, "A girl with over twenty dollars must have been stealing all along."

Constance says, "How did you know it was over twenty dollars? I never said so." She turns, pleading to Alden. "Alden, I never said so. He couldn't know unless he was the one who took it."

In response, Mr. Grant affects disdain, looks at his pocket watch, holds it to his ear, winds it, listens, and tucks it away again. He is biding his time, waiting for the right moment, assessing.

"I'm not a thief. Alden, you know me better than this. You know I'm honest. I earned that money running errands for boarders, for mending, for all kinds of things. I've been saving it my whole life."

Mr. Grant waves his hand. "Don't be so foolish, Alden. The proof is right in front of you." He slaps his hand on the work table for emphasis. "You know nothing about this girl. For crying out loud, you found her in the trash." With that, he storms out of the kitchen.

It takes Constance a minute to hear the words, and then another to understand them. There is a moment of stillness in which anything, absolutely anything, might happen. Constance and Alden stare across the kitchen at each other, the linoleum between them an abyss.

"In the trash. You found me in the trash?"

The scaffolding Constance has built to support her story crashes to the ground, and with it, her understanding of who she is. She pulls her cap off and unwinds her hair.

Alden attempts to deflect. "This is not the matter under discussion. What we are discussing is you and your behaviour today, in the here and now."

Constance places her cap deliberately on the kitchen table and unbuttons her jacket as she sits in a kitchen chair. She no longer feels guilty. Alden's lie has absolved her of any sin of her own. She makes eye contact with Alden, but Alden falters and looks down at the table.

Constance rests her elbows on her thighs and bends down, almost putting her head between her knees, and then interlaces her fingers behind her neck. She might pass out. Her head fills with images from *The Kid*, the moment when Chaplin, ambling along the alleys and minding his own business, gets hit by a bunch of trash thrown from a window and then hears a baby, looks down, and sees it lying beneath the fallen trash. The life seems to drain out of her.

"I thought you found me on the church steps." She says this without raising her head.

"I never said that."

Didn't she? Constance is not certain. "You let me think it. Why?"

Alden does not answer, but smooths her apron over her hips.

"Tell me the truth."

"It's true. I found you in The Ward. You were abandoned."

"In the trash."

"No. You were in a box."

"In a box in the trash."

"The whole street was trash. You were left in the street, not in the trash." Alden cannot look her in the eye. Her gaze falters.

"Oh," says Constance. And then again, with greater understanding, "Oh." So, it was just like in *The Kid*.

Constance rises, picks up her cap from the table, looks to Alden, and can think of nothing to say. She turns back toward the service stairs, her chin lowered, her hands limp at her sides.

"Oh dear," says Alden, as though milk has been spilled. She is flustered. "Why would I tell you that? What good would it do? It makes no difference where I found you. It only matters *that* I found you."

The stories she has made up of her mother watching over her, making sure she was safe until she was found, blow away like dead leaves in autumn. Her mother left her in the trash.

She turns and climbs the back stairs and Alden's voice follows her, calling her name.

*

Constance has been in her room at least a half an hour when she checks Mr. Hunt's watch. She forgot to give it to him. Does Mr. Hunt know? Does everyone know except her?

She opens her door, descends the back stairs and opens the deadbolt to the second floor. She hears nothing and redirects her ear to the kitchen. There is a slight murmur. Mr. Grant and Alden are talking together and are barely audible. Constance creeps further down and listens through the service door to the blue parlour. Mr. Grant is giving Alden an ultimatum. "You brought her into your home, a fine home, a wealthy home, have offered her every advantage and this is how she repays you." Alden hisses something in response. "You don't know the stock," he says. "It's nothing you have done, but by God, if you keep her on now, I won't know what to make of it."

Constance creeps back through the hall and up the stairs to her room to further dismantle the fables she has told herself. The sleeve of the men's shirt she still wears is rough against her wet cheeks. Nothing can be worse than your own mother leaving you in the garbage.

Better to have never been born. Then, at least, you would never know.

She hears the front door close and knows that Alden is gone. She stands on the chair and looks out her window. Alden has her best coat and hat on and is making her way slowly down the street with her crutch. She is going to see Father Moore, no doubt. Listening, she cannot discern the whereabouts of Mr. Grant. And suddenly she does not care. Not about Mr. Grant or Alden or even Mr. Hunt. All she wants to do is leave.

Where will she go?

It is already dark.

"Think," she says to herself. She can't go to the Veterans' Hospital, and besides, she is loath to tell Mr. Hunt and find out he knew all along. That would be too much right now. She can go to find Gwen at Midmaples, but it is already dark and she's not sure where it is.

"The carriage house," she says aloud. No one will know. No one will look there, not tonight. Mr. Grant has found all he needs to find there. Tomorrow, she can figure out the rest. She goes into the room next door, digs out an ancient valise from the closet, and packs haphazardly. She finds an overcoat in another of the spare rooms, checks it for size, and throws it over her arm.

Miraculously, Mr. Grant does not appear while she comes down the stairs and is not waiting for her at the door to the kitchen. As quietly as she can, she opens the door and sets her valise down, hesitates, and goes back into the kitchen. She's not hungry now, but she will be later. Or tomorrow. She stuffs half a loaf of bread, some cheese, and two apples in a bag. She will leave no note. It is pointless. Then she hears Mr. Grant grunt as he rises from a chair in the parlour. She slips through the kitchen entrance to the outside, closing the door so the latch barely clicks, staying in the shadows on her way to the carriage house.

Inside, the Lozier gleams. She whispers, "Hello?" and wonders what she expects to hear back.

What she does not expect is to hear Gwen's voice. "Con?"

"Gwen?"

"I'm up here!" Her head pops out from the loft and they both practically jump with joy.

"Look at you!" cries Gwen. "You did it! Did you get a job?"

"Shhh! Quiet," warns Constance, pointing back at Patterson House.

Constance drops her suitcase and climbs the ladder. She embraces Gwen, who is wrapped in the moth-eaten blanket that was at the bottom of the cot that morning. She has not seen Gwen since that terrible night. Was it only two days ago? Is it possible?

"I was so worried about you."

Gwen's smile disappears. "Don't say anything. I don't want to talk about it. I don't ever want to talk about it."

"But—"

"No. Never. If you're my friend, you'll never talk about it. Ever."

Constance hugs her again. "I won't ever. I promise. I went to see you. Your mother—"

"She's upset."

Constance nods.

"She'll get used to it." She tries her best to look resolute. "I couldn't stay. You know I couldn't stay."

"I understand."

"You didn't tell her, did you?" Gwen's eyes are wide.

"No. I wouldn't. Ever. I promise."

Gwen hugs her again.

"I was going to go find you."

"Dressed like that?" Gwen laughs, and they sit together on the old cot.

"It's a long, very long, story." Constance tells her about Mr. Hunt, how he fell ill and how Alden sent him away to the Veterans' Hospital. She talks about Alden and Carling Grant as though they are in cahoots. Then she tells her about her plan to go and visit Mr. Hunt. "That's why I couldn't find you right away," she says. "I'm so sorry. I wanted to go straight to Midmaples, but how could I with Mr. Hunt so sick?"

"I understand," Gwen says "I wasn't there anyway. And you can't go see him? That's not fair."

"I know. But you—how long have you been here?"

"I've been here every night."

"What? You must have frozen."

"I didn't know where else to go. I figured no one would find me here. It's been pretty cold," she admitted. "I waited until it was dark to come in. No one saw."

"You're lucky Carling Grant didn't find you."

"If only I'd been back a bit sooner, I could have waited in the alley and warned you not to come in."

"Bad luck," says Constance. "Why didn't you go to Midmaples? Why did you stay here?"

"I did. But there was no room available until Tuesday."

She passes the cheque for sixteen dollars to Gwen. "From Mr. Hunt."

"Oh, the dear." Gwen clutches the cheque to her chest. "We'll cash it tomorrow when the banks are open." She puts it in her own pocket. "Too bad I didn't know about that."

"Why?" asks Constance.

Gwen averts her eyes and says evenly, "I stole money from Gerald. And I don't care. I'd do it again." Her defiance emboldens Constance.

"And I stole money from Carling Grant." Gwen listens as Constance explains about her savings. She never says how much it was. She'll take that to her grave.

"What did Alden say?"

218

"As it turns out I can't stay either." Constance shrugs and unsuccessfully tries to fend off the tears that are rising. "It's a mess." She does not tell her about being found in the trash.

"It's okay." She pats the pocket where the cheque is. "We'll go to Midmaples and pay our deposit tomorrow. It's just like we planned."

"Not exactly." They silently acknowledge the truth of the statement.

Constance remembers the bread and cheese and apples she took from the kitchen. "Are you hungry?"

"Famished." They spread out a feast for themselves on the cot.

"We'd better leave early. Let's go before dawn so no one sees us."

"Where will we go?"

"How much money have you got left?"

Gwen says, "Keeping back the first two weeks at Midmaples, I've got two dollars and eighty cents."

"I've got Mr. Hunt's five, and Carling Grant's four quarters. We'll be fine."

"And the cheque. Let's not forget the cheque. And if you stay dressed as a boy, you're sure to get work."

Constance nods. "Better chance, I guess. Hold on a minute." She runs down the ladder and finds a pair of sharp scissors in a drawer in the workbench and brings them back to the loft with a hairbrush from her valise.

"Do it. Cut my hair."

"Are you sure?" asks Gwen.

"Yep. I can't take off my hat with this hair. I'll be found out for sure."

"You want me to cut it in the dark?"

"Can you see well enough?" The moonlight shines through the small window in the peak of the roof.

"I guess so." She hesitates. "But how can you live in an apartment for girls *and* pretend to be a boy?"

"I won't be the only girl in the world with short hair."

"I don't know."

"So, don't cut it too short and I'll slick it back when I'm looking for work."

"You're sure?"

"Yes."

First, Gwen ties it with a piece of string and then she cuts the whole ponytail off. Constance loves the feeling of Gwen brushing her hair and running locks of it between her fingers as she snips. Constance's head feels light, like it might lift off her neck and float away. There is another half hour of trimming and shaping. Constance surprises herself by not feeling any remorse whatsoever watching the semicircle of her hair fall around her.

"How is it?"

"I'm afraid I'm not as good at this as my mother is, but I think it will be fine. A little pomade would help. You really do make a good-looking boy." Gwen considers her for a moment. "I swear, no one would know."

"Oh, some people know right away." She tells her about the hobo in the alley and the little boy. "I don't know if I'll get away with this."

"Confidence! It's all about confidence." Gwen's words remind her of Mr. Hunt's observation about Mr. Grant. She's right. "And remember, men don't look down. Men look you right in the eye—or in the chest," says Gwen. "And now, without your hair to trip you up, you'll have more confidence than ever." Gwen takes Constance's hand in her own and turns it palm up. "I see a bright future for you." It has been ages since they read palms, and they both laugh.

If only Constance could be as certain as Gwen. "I think we better get some sleep," she says, as they sweep the last of the hair into a dustpan only to realize there is nowhere to throw it except outside in the garden. Constance carries it down the ladder and opens the door a sliver, careful to make sure there is no one around.

Mr. Grant's light is on and so is the light in the kitchen. Alden will be back by now. What must she have thought when Constance was not home? Maybe Alden has not realized Constance is gone yet. A sudden urge to creep to the house and look in the window seizes her, but she remembers what happened the last time she looked in a window.

The wind picks up taking most of her hair off the dustpan and she shakes out what is left. If Mr. Hunt were here, he would say it would make fine nesting material for the birds.

Back in the loft, neither of them wants to take the cot from the other. Instead, they curl up together on the blanket on the floor and Constance lays her overcoat on top of them. When Constance wakes before dawn, Gwen's arm is over her and she dares not move. The forked blue veins running along the pale skin inside her wrist disappear at her hand. Her life line is the same length it has always been, her head line strong and straight. Gwen will know what to do. When Gwen stirs, they gather their things, tidy everything so the loft looks the same as it did before Gwen arrived, and leave through the alley.

*

In the distance, walking hand in hand, Constance and Gwen look like a young couple in love, arm in arm. Oh, how I wish I could follow them.

This is an adventure of the first order, circumstances be damned! They are out to start their lives together. What could be more exciting!

But I'm stuck here to watch Alden's life fall to ruins. Alden can't bear the idea of a scandal. I understand that, but it's hardly a scandal on the scale I faced. Barely a ripple beyond her own neighbourhood. She will not be pilloried in the papers or sued by pernicious lawyers. Certainly, at Schiffley's, the neighbours will twitter about Constance the same way they twitter about Gwen. Word will spread like pollen on the wind, but that wind won't go very far. That is unfair, perhaps. Small though it may be, this is her world. Her scandal will be felt as deeply by her as I felt my own.

So, Alden will speak to no one about Constance's departure—no one except the bastard and, of course, the priest—and she will wither in her heartbreak, alone. She will call the school and tell them she is taking Constance out for the foreseeable future because she is needed at home.

Her ankle provides a good enough excuse for her to stay in rather than search the streets for the girl. The bastard will offer to call the police on her behalf and she will accept his assistance with gratitude. He will inform the police that the missing girl is a thief and is known to go about in men's clothes. He will paint quite a picture, emphasizing her origin as a foundling and the darkness of her skin. He will instruct the police not to bring the girl home if they find her but to keep her. He will tell them to call him, not Miss Patterson. He will tell them that Miss Patterson, who has been the girl's careful guardian, is distraught because of recent events. He will speak on her behalf.

"And who are you again?" the policeman will ask.

"I am Mr. Carling Grant," he will say. "Miss Patterson and I will be married in a few weeks. I can assure you, I speak for her."

There is nothing I can do to stop him. Nothing.

*

Constance and Gwen lurk around the edges of their school, St. Joseph's, as darkness nears. They hope to find an open door somewhere so they can stay warm for one more night before getting Gwen's apartment at Midmaples. It has been a long, aimless day spent mostly in the ravine. They walk around the playing field, go a few blocks in every direction, and try to look purposeful. Thank goodness the school isn't attached to the convent anymore. At least there is a chance of them escaping the notice of the nuns. But what if some of the nuns are inside? They used to joke that Sister Mary Agnes lived in her office. What if she really does? They will be discovered for sure.

Once they feel it is dark enough and they are sure they will not be seen, they start trying doors. One after the other is locked. Finally, they find a small set of stairs to a basement with an unlocked door that leads to the furnace. Inside it is barely warmer than outside, and they realize the door is unlocked because the inside door that would get them into the school is locked tight. Further, when Constance lights her Zippo, they realize the place is covered in coal dust, and the longer they stay in it, the blacker they will get. They leave and go back to the schoolyard.

"Well, that was a bust," says Gwen, trying to clean her hands in a pile of snow. "You look like a miner. There's a big smudge of coal on your cheek."

"How did that get there?" Constance picks up some snow and tries to rub her face clean.

"You're only spreading it around."

"Where are we going to sleep?"

They look at each other and into the dark night.

"A hotel?"

"Do you know how to do that?"

"Nope."

"It might cost a lot."

They have not spent any money yet and are so afraid of using it up that they have not even bought anything to eat. A hotel is out of the question.

"It's getting cold." Constance runs her hands along her arms, hugging herself. "We've got to find some place to get warm."

"How about a church?"

"As long as it's not St. Michael's or Corpus Christi, that might work."

"St. Basil's. It's big. No one knows you there." They walk to the huge church and try the main door. They are in luck. It's open.

Kneeling in pews in the darkest corner of the church, they pretend to pray. It is not long before Gwen is asleep, still kneeling and slumped over the pew ahead. Constance—determined to keep vigil—yawns and kneels beside her in the pew while her stomach growls.

The next thing she knows, she is waking to the sound of voices. "Probably runaways," she hears a man's voice say. When she opens her eyes, a Jesuit is standing over her and behind him is a bored-looking policeman. It is still dark, and she has no idea what time of night it is. They have been discovered and it's all her fault for falling asleep. If she had been awake pretending to pray, no one would have bothered them.

She nudges Gwen, who has, at some point, slumped down to the floor. Her head is resting on the kneeler. She yawns and opens her eyes to the same scene and scrambles to stand.

"Come with me," says the policeman, sighing.

"It's unholy, the two of them spending the night here in the church," says the Jesuit, practically spitting with outrage.

"Young man, you have a lot of explaining to do," says the policeman.

Constance realizes they think there has been some sort of shenanigans going on and she says, "I'm a girl."

The police officer and the Jesuit stare at Constance, and she realizes that with this admission she has, somehow, made matters even worse.

The policeman whips the cap off her hair, shakes his head and rubs his chin. "I don't like this one bit."

In the police car, the policeman says, "All right. I can't see that you've done anything other than be out too late. I'm taking you home. Where do you live?"

They look at each other and silently agree not to say.

"Don't get cute with me. Your only other choice is to come to the police station. I'll have you arrested for vagrancy. Or worse. It will be on your permanent records. Your *permanent* records," he says again.

Gwen reaches for Constance's hand and squeezes. "If that's how it has to be."

The policeman sighs, a world of weariness in his exhale. "Fine. I wanted to go easy on you, but here we go." He looks behind his shoulder at them and Constance tries to see herself and Gwen through his eyes. They are sooty. They must look like waifs. Or worse. Maybe he thinks they have been living rough. Maybe he thinks nothing at all about them. Maybe he is simply doing his job. He drives to the police station, opens the car door, and directs them inside.

At the front desk, another policeman asks their names. Constance refuses to answer. If they don't know who she is, they can't call Alden. Gwen's face brightens and she also refuses to give her name. The policeman says, "Jesus, Mary, and Joseph" under his breath.

"Sit here." He points at two chairs in the foyer and says, "Don't move." They glance sideways at each other, not certain if they are allowed to talk.

"At least it's warm," whispers Gwen.

"We should run for it. While no one is paying attention."

"We'd never get away with it," Gwen whispers back.

When light begins to brighten the windows, the same policeman who brought them in returns to them and says, "Constance Patterson and Gwen Hughes."

They look up, shocked that they have been found out. "You've both been reported missing."

Constance never thought of that.

"Uh-oh," says Gwen.

The policeman locks them up in a spartan cell with one narrow cot and a bucket to relieve themselves.

They soon learn that neither of them needs to worry about being sent home. A different policeman finally comes back and says, "I don't know what you girls did, but no one wants you back. You'll be going on to the Reformatory." He looks at them as though they are stray dogs and shakes his head again.

Constance has no idea what the Reformatory is, but she is certain it is not a place she wants to go. "Excuse me. Did you talk to Alden? Alden Patterson?"

"Did you talk to my mother?" asks Gwen.

The policeman does not answer. "The Reformatory will set the two of you to rights."

Surely, Alden is just trying to scare her.

Constance and Gwen sit and shiver together, too scared to ask questions, and they let their imaginations run away with them. Another girl is brought in. Her lips are scabby. Her clothes are dirty and so are her hands and face. Her neck beneath her yellowed collar is grey. She smells terrible.

She looks them up and down and smirks. Somehow, in this upside-down world, she is superior to them. Gwen clasps Constance's hand and holds it so tight that it hurts.

"What are you dressed up as?"

Constance refuses to answer.

"Oh, I get it. You're one of them girls. You'll meet plenty like you at Mercer's."

"What's Mercer's?" asks Gwen, still trembling.

The girl guffaws. "The Reformatory. Mercer's Reformatory for Females." She says "Females" with particular vehemence. "Otherwise known as finishing school." She turns her back on them and looks between the bars down the hall. "Hey! I'm hungry!" she yells.

Constance and Gwen look with amazement at each other. Constance almost forgot how hungry she is, and with this reminder, it is the only thought in her head.

"Do they feed us here?" Constance asks.

"Most times, yeah."

"You've been here before?"

The girl just laughs. She holds out her dirty hand with her chewed nails and says, "Eleonore."

"Constance." They shake hands. Constance gives Gwen a nudge.

"Gwen." They shake hands, too.

"Charmed, I'm sure." She does a little curtsy. She is making fun of them.

"Well, I can see what one of you did to get yourself in here. What about that one?" she motions toward Gwen but speaks only to Constance.

"We both ran away."

"Yup. That sounds right. What's with the getup?"

Constance sighs. There's nothing for it but to tell the truth. "I thought I'd have an easier time getting a job if I dressed like a boy."

Eleonore whistles and then smiles. "Not a bad idea, really. Wish I'd thought of it." She assesses Constance. "It could work. You look pretty good. Who cut your hair?"

Constance motions toward Gwen, who nods.

"Not bad. You'll have lots to do in Mercer. The trick will be getting scissors. I'll work that out. You'll charge them girls for it. Not money. Whatever they've got. Food, usually. I'll set up the appointments. And we'll split it."

Gwen is wide-eyed and says nothing.

"Okay, sixty-forty."

Constance holds Gwen's hand a bit tighter. "Thanks for the offer. We'll talk it over and get back to you."

"Whatever you say, boss." Eleonore looks down the hall and hollers again for food.

By the time food comes, Constance is beyond hunger.

Gwen pushes it away. "I don't feel so good," she says.

Maybe she's too scared to eat. "You should eat something."

Gwen shakes her head.

"Are you sure?" Constance eats Gwen's meal. She's eating as fast as Carling Grant.

"You're right to eat," says Eleonore. "This here is better than anything you'll get there."

"But it's just bread and broth," says Gwen.

"Yeah, but the bread isn't mouldy or anything. No maggots."

Gwen dashes over to the bucket and vomits.

Constance pats her back and looks over at Eleonore and says, "Cut it out, will ya?"

Eleonore shrugs.

"Sorry," says Gwen, wiping her mouth. The smell of her vomit wafts through the cell.

"What's wrong with you?" asks Constance.

"I don't know." Gwen pulls the scratchy wool blanket off the cot and wraps it around herself and sits with her knees to her chest in the corner, as far away from the smell of the vomit as she can get. The other girls join her.

Constance shivers.

Why would Alden let this happen to her? She tries to think clearly. What does she know? The policeman said Alden won't have her back. They are going to the Mercer Reformatory for Females. Maybe Alden is trying to teach her a lesson. She turns to Gwen, who is biting her nails.

"I understand why Alden might not come for me. But I can't understand why your mum hasn't come for you."

"It's Gerald," says Gwen. "I bet he said no."

"Did the policeman say who he talked to?" She can't remember.

"I'm not sure," says Gwen. "I don't think so. I don't know."

Eleonore jumps into the conversation. "They're just trying to scare you."

"It's working," croaks Constance.

"Don't worry. You'll be out in no time."

"What about you?" asks Constance. "Do you have someone who could get you out?"

Eleonore closes her eyes. "I don't have any people."

"I'm sorry. I…." Constance has no idea how to finish the sentence. No people.

Eleonore shrugs. "Sometimes no people is better than people if your people always let you down." She pulls her arms across her chest, closes her eyes, and lets her head rest on the side of the cell.

Constance pulls off her jacket and tries to cover herself and Gwen. Gwen has tears trembling along her lower lids. They fall from her eyes and down her cheeks. "I'm afraid," she says.

For as long as they have known each other, Gwen has been the fearless one. Not anymore. Constance's world really has turned upside down.

*

Late in the afternoon, a balding man wearing a uniform with dirty cuffs escorts the three of them to a bus where two other guards load them in the back and sit between them and the door. Gwen bonks her head getting in, and one of the guards snickers.

"Where is it?" Constance asks Eleonore, a question she certainly should have asked already.

"King and Dufferin."

"Dufferin?" Gwen asks.

Constance shrugs. "I don't know." She's only been as far west as Christie, to the Veterans' Hospital, and that was far.

"Not so easy to walk back from. Let me tell you. I've tried it."

One of the guards says, "Quiet."

The drive seems interminable with Gwen teary and touching her forehead where she hit it. Eleonore looks past the guard out the window at the back. By the time they reach the Reformatory, Gwen is openly weeping. The building is huge and frightening, like something from a movie. Gothic with iron gates. It is almost a block long.

"Get out." The guard's grip on Constance's arm is like a vice. Another guard grips Eleonore by the shoulders. No one worries too much about the snivelling, limping Gwen. They are hustled into a cavernous, dark entryway. It takes a minute for Constance's eyes to adjust. The guards pass papers to a uniformed matron who barely looks at them. Her eyes rest on something and she looks up at Eleonore. "Back again." A statement, not a question.

"Yes Matron," says Eleonore.

"And in the family way again, I see."

Eleonore sticks her chin out defiantly. She looks over to Constance and Gwen and smiles lopsidedly. "See you," she says, as another attendant leads her out of the entryway and through a dark doorway. Constance and Gwen exchange glances, too afraid to speak.

December 13, 1930

ALDEN IS SEATED in the front pew of Corpus Christi beside Mr. Carling Grant. Her legs twitch with the urge to bolt. Marrying this man in front of Father Moore at St. Michael's would be too much to bear. Father Moore would see the blackness in her heart.

Constance always preferred this church. She shakes her head. She is thinking about her as if she were dead. She's not dead. She can't be dead.

Fidgeting with the pages of the Missal, she sits, stands, and kneels without listening to Father Henry's words. The church will soon be decorated for Christmas. That is something. Christmas. She can hardly believe that this terrible year, 1930, is almost over. Auld Lang Syne.

Since the day when Constance ran away, she has spent hours in front of the window, feeling empty and listless. To lose them both, John and Constance, on the same day—it's too much.

Constance left her without a word. But of course, she did. And what must she think, having learned the truth of her origins in such an awful way? And what of Carling Grant? He could not possibly have understood the damage he was doing. But his intentions were unkind. Spiteful. A part of her hopes Constance never comes back because she will never forgive Alden for what she is about to do.

But the bigger part of her finds the stillness in Patterson House unnerving. She misses the sound of Constance's voice chattering away to Mr. Hunt in the garden, her humming on the stairs, her shoes clattering in the foyer. She misses tidying her hair, a task that she pretended to find tiresome. Now the only sound is Carling Grant, up and down the stairs, chewing, turning pages, flicking his pocket watch open and closed, talking about things that do not interest her in the slightest.

Constance's face in the kitchen, her hair up under that hat, dressed like a boy. To think she had not recognized her. What kind of woman doesn't know her own…her own…what? The word "daughter" springs to her mind and she dismisses it. "She is not my daughter," she says to herself. "Not my daughter." She chants it like she used to chant "temperance" to herself.

Father Moore, shocked by the news of Constance's disappearance, asked what measures Alden was taking to find her. "You must report it to the police. A young girl alone. Anything can happen!"

Alden had wanted his sympathy. But instead, she was being scolded. "Father, it was she who left me."

Father Moore narrowed his eyes. "She is a child. You are responsible. You have to do something." She hasn't spoken to him since. Why does no one other than Mr. Grant understand how difficult this is for her and how she has been hurt?

Thank goodness for Carling Grant. He has been steadfast. He contacted the police to report the girl missing. He visited Mr. Hunt, checked with Mr. and Mrs. Hughes to see if they had heard from Gwen or Constance. He did everything she should have done but was too shattered to do.

He has been so understanding. "Not your fault, my dear. It's in the blood, and it's not your blood. You did everything you could." He is a coarse man, yet he did everything right in her time of crisis. That helps, some. He even helped carry dishes to and from the dining room while her ankle mended, told her to sit down when he saw her working, and didn't bat an eye at their simple meals.

When she takes Communion, Alden's stomach tightens. Then it is time for the vows. She cannot meet Mr. Grant's eyes. Or Father Henry's. The word "obey" leaves her lips dry as a whisper.

Without family, friends, or acquaintances to join them, they ask the rectory's housekeeper to act as the witness along with a visiting Jesuit. Alden cannot even remember their names.

He does not kiss her at the end of the ceremony, and she is relieved. They have not kissed yet, not even a peck on the cheek. Besides, a kiss would embarrass her in front of Father Henry.

Father Henry ushers them into a small room to sign the papers. As they prepare to leave the church, Carling Grant thanks Father Henry and gives him a hearty handshake, a broad smile on his face. Alden waits to see him pass along an offering for the church, but he does not. He must have forgotten. Father Henry squeezes her shoulder and says, "Good luck to you, dear."

The walk back to Patterson House is punctuated with small talk.

"A fine, bright day."

"Yes, indeed."

"Snow is expected later."

"Yes, it is."

Under her glove, Alden's ring is uncomfortably tight. He has not bought her a new ring, suggesting instead that she might have a family ring she would prefer to wear. It was a sensible suggestion, and she did have her mother's wedding ring. She didn't think to have it sized. Her mother's fingers must have been quite slim while Alden's are swollen with manual work. As soon as they get home and they have removed their coats and hats, Alden goes into the kitchen, smears butter around the ring, and struggles to pull it off. When she is finally free of it, she sets it on the windowsill and rubs her bruised knuckle.

He did not want a honeymoon. "That's not really our style, is it?" A trip abroad would remind him too much of the war, he said. Alden didn't mention it again. An overnight trip to Niagara Falls would have been a treat. She has never been outside Toronto. But not wanting to appear flighty, she kept silent.

Instead, Alden does what she can to make the day special. She wears her best dress. He complimented her appearance when she came down the stairs, ready to go to the church with him. He gave her a corsage with three white roses. A nice gesture. She pinned it to her dress herself and takes it off now so that it will not be crushed by her apron. It cannot stand up in a vase, so she lays it down carefully in a crystal pudding dish in a bit of water. It makes a nice centrepiece on the kitchen table. Maybe now that it is just the two of them, they will take their breakfast in the kitchen.

Dinner is already prepared. A roast. His favourite. All she must do is finish it in the oven. It cost a small fortune. When she picked up the meat from Mrs. Schiffley yesterday, the butcher's wife shook her head, looked around the shop to make sure no one was listening, and said, "Are you sure?"

At first, Alden thought she was talking about the meat. Then she realized she was talking about the marriage. Despite Alden's best efforts to keep it quiet, word got out. Word always gets out. After all, the banns were read at Mass for three weeks in a row. Everybody knew, even the Protestants.

Alden was curt with her, pursed her lips, and refused to answer.

In response, Mrs. Schiffley sighed and said, "I hate to tell you, today of all days, but you've gone through your credit with me. I'll start a new bill under Mr. Grant's name for you."

Was she sure? Of course she was. How else was she supposed to eat?

She goes to the dining room and fusses with the table, adjusts the position of the silver, and turns the dishes so that the patterns face the same way. Flowers this time of year are far too expensive, so earlier in the day, she found some greenery in the garden with berries attached and made a little display on the sideboard. The cedar smells fresh in the room. When she comes out from the kitchen to serve dinner, Carling Grant is in her usual place at the head of the table. Yes, this is how it is supposed to be now, she tells herself. She sits in her new place to his right.

There is a bottle of spirits sitting on the table beside him. "A little something to celebrate," he says. He pours her a glass as her eyes widen.

"I thought you knew. I don't use alcohol."

"Under the circumstances—" But Alden's scowl stops him. "I see. You won't mind if I do, though," he says as he pours a drink, two fingers deep. "To our marriage," he says, tipping his glass toward her. Then she realizes the bottle is already half empty. When did he bring that into the house?

Constance's accusations ring in her ears.

He compliments her on the roast, the smoothness of the mashed potatoes, and says the mint in the carrots reminds him of a meal he once ate at the King Edward Hotel, but their conversation is stilted. He pours a second drink and has a second helping of everything, including the trifle, for which she has used up the last of the jam.

The uncertainty of the evening ahead weighs heavily upon her, and perhaps upon him too. She knows what to expect. The Pellatt cousin. After dinner, she tidies the kitchen, hangs up her apron by the back door, and is about to sit in her chair in the little parlour and put her feet up when she realizes she should go meet him in the blue parlour. It has been years since she has sat in this room after dinner. A record is playing on the phonograph, something popular, something she doesn't know and finds irritating. He appears surprised to see her and says, "Oh, of course.

Yes, of course." He is not her boarder anymore; she is not his landlady. They will share this room, and all the rooms.

She picks up a book and reads the same paragraph over and over. She asks, "Would you like a fire?"

"It would take the chill off."

Alden waits for him to rise and get it ready, but he does not. She builds the fire herself and keeps it stoked throughout the evening. Tomorrow, she will speak with him about hiring staff, at least one person. Part time will do. Alden does not want to clean the fireplaces anymore. The house is too much work for her alone. Constance lifted so much of the burden from her, but this is the least of the reasons she misses the girl so much. Alden's breath catches in her throat. Her hands flutter to her eyes as if to catch tears, but she stops herself. She cannot cry on her wedding night.

Behind his newspaper, Carling Grant has not noticed. In their silence, they could be a couple who have been married for twenty years already. He lowers the paper and says, "The Canadian Bank of Commerce skyscraper is almost finished," as though this is of great interest to her. She nods. Perhaps this marriage will not be so bad. She looks up to her grandfather's portrait and feels his pitiless stare.

When Mr. Grant says it is time for bed, she breaks up the fire and sets the grate in place, noting all the burn marks on the carpet runner. They climb the stairs together. He says, "I will stop at my room to get changed. We can reorganize our things tomorrow." Alden feels herself flush and goes into her own room, hesitating before leaving the door open for the first time ever, and goes into the bathroom to change into her new peignoir set. She bought it from the same woman at Eaton's who fitted Constance for a brassiere. When she asked about "her daughter," Alden gave a forced smile and said she was fine, thank you. The woman showed her all manner of flowery, silky bedclothes. Alden settled on a full-length, light pink satin arrangement with a lace trim over the bodice and hem and a matching robe. She fusses with the sash.

When she emerges, Carling Grant, her husband, is already waiting, standing at the foot of her bed. Their bed. His nightshirt does not appear fresh. She has never seen him undressed before. Without his high collar, his jowls sag. His legs are oddly spindly compared to the rest of him. He is not wearing slippers. His toenails are misshapen and thick.

Another whisky bottle, this one almost full, sits on her dressing table beside her hair brush and comb. He looks at her looking at it and neither of them comment. The smell of alcohol is strange in her room. Perhaps he needs it to settle his own nerves. She is inclined to forgive him this sin. Just this time. Besides, she has something much more urgent to worry about now.

Alden has dreaded this moment. But this is the cost of marriage—consummation—as Father Henry so delicately put it while trying to offer her guidance during their brief time in the confessional. She could not have been more mortified and more grateful to have the screen between them.

She fears his weight upon her. She will be crushed. Alden is too embarrassed to get into bed first.

His face is pinched. "Well, we'd best get on with it."

He walks to her, takes her hand and, to her surprise, brings her to the foot of the bed. There, he turns her around so that her back is to him. Looking down, she can see his hairy legs and gnarled toes. He runs his cold hands along her shoulders, down her arms, and to her hips, assessing, and lifts her robe and nightdress. Alden stands rigid, her backside exposed, desperately wishing the lights were off. He nudges her forward slightly. When he tells her to bend over the bed, she does. When he tells her to crouch a little, she does. When he fumbles for her opening, she spreads her legs and reaches down to direct his hand to the right place. He is going to take her from behind, like a dog. At least she will not have to bear his weight. There is that. His hard stomach presses against her back. When she feels him enter her, she closes her eyes tight and bites her lip. When he is finished, his grunts still hanging in the air, he says, "Well, then," as though he has just finished another meal or closed a book. He pats her on the shoulder, goes into the bathroom, and shuts the door.

While he washes in the sink, she feels his mess sticky between her legs. She smells him on her. When he opens the bathroom door, still drying his hands on her towel, the fresh one she laid out for tonight, she is still in the same place, but upright.

He says, "You don't have to stay."

Alden, uncomprehending, stammers. Her grip tightens on the bedpost.

"I don't expect us to sleep in the same bed," he says, a cool practicality in his voice. "We are married now, I have done my duty as a husband. We have fulfilled all the obligations. It cannot be undone. You need not concern yourself that this will happen again. I have as little interest in the carnal aspect of marriage as you."

Alden feels a drip run down between her legs.

"We are both set in our ways. I'm sure you would rather keep a bed to yourself, and I know I would. There are seven other rooms for you to choose from." He gestures for her to leave as though he is shooing away a pigeon. "Go ahead."

"But this is my room." She looks around at her sanctuary, the place that has been hers and hers alone since her father died.

"This is the master bedroom, yes?"

Alden nods.

He pulls back the covers on her bed, the bed she made so carefully that morning with fresh sheets and the coverlet that she has used since she was a girl, and he sits on the edge. The frame strains with his weight. "In the morning, when you clean, you may get your personal things and move them into the room you have chosen." When Alden remains unmoving at the end of the bed, he says, "There is a nice view of the garden from my old room. You might like it. Please go now. I'm quite tired."

And to her own astonishment, Alden leaves. It is as though she is watching herself from above, a scolded child sent to the Mother Superior's office. Once she is in the hall, he says, "Close the door, please," and again, she does what she is told. She hears him rise and turn the lock on the door, and it is this click that wakes her up. They will not be man and wife; they will be man and maid. She runs to the boarder's bathroom and retches into the toilet. When her stomach can expel no more, she locks the door behind her and runs the bath.

The water begins to warm and Alden pulls her clothes off, squats, and washes between her legs and her buttocks, retches again inside the bath, and watches the sick go down the drain. She cannot bear the sight of the peignoir set. To think, she was concerned about how she might look to him. Naked and shivering, she sits on the edge of the tub in a stupor.

What was she expecting? Father Moore registered surprise when they came to the church to announce their intentions. He was concerned for her, not happy. The next time he was alone with her, he asked if this was what she really wanted. She shook her head and said, "Father, I'm thirty-six years old. I'm not going to get another offer."

"But you don't have to marry, Alden. You've done well on your own. You've managed. Times are changing. I know the last few weeks have been hard on you. Mr. Hunt in hospital. Constance gone. You don't have to do this. You have other options."

But he proffered no suggestions, and she could think of none.

The porcelain of the tub is cold against her backside. She cannot stay here, cowering in the bathroom. In the morning, she can go to Father Henry and ask for an annulment.

No. She can't.

It is too humiliating. And on what grounds? The marriage has been consummated. She stands and feels more of the stickiness ooze out from within her and retches again.

My God. What if she has a child? She is only thirty-six. She thought about the possibility before they were married, but only abstractly. A child would be truly disastrous. She rinses the tub, draws a proper hot bath, and does her best to wash again, completely, inside and out. At least he has promised there will be no more of this. Assuming her time comes next week as expected, she will never have to worry about it again. If he keeps his word.

Steeling herself, she slips the peignoir set over her head and uses it to dry herself. It is that or walk through the house naked and wet. When she opens the bathroom door, she checks the hallway. There is a light under her door. He is up and moving about. She walks past it as silently as she used to when her father was alive and goes down the stairs, through the foyer, into the kitchen, to the back stairs, and down to the basement. There, she strips and finds herself some clothes from the laundry. They are still unwashed but clean enough, given the circumstances.

The peignoir set goes into the furnace. She stands for a moment and watches the flames catch the lace, eat into the pink satin, and swallow the bodice before she closes the furnace door.

It is eleven o'clock, still the same day of her marriage. This morning, she awoke in her own room, still herself. Now she is someone she does not know. She is Mrs. Carling Grant. Taken from behind. Evicted from her own bedroom.

In the storeroom, she pulls the turnip bin over to find what little money is left, counts it, brushes it off, wraps it in a handkerchief, and slides it into her corset.

Climbing the back stairs, her intention is to go to the third floor and stay in Constance's room. It is the furthest she can get from that man, and with the door from the second floor to the back stairway locked, he would have to go down to the first floor by the main stairs and all the way up three flights to find her there. She would surely hear him coming. She never imagined she would use the lock she installed on the second-floor door for herself.

At the threshold of Constance's room, she cannot pass. It is unbearable that the girl has left her.

The room has a narrow single bed across from a small, high window, a crucifix above it, a nondescript lamp on a too-small bedside table, and an old, scarred dresser. There are few keepsakes. There are no dolls. No toys. She has made the girl live in a nun's cell. The servants' quarters. No wonder Constance left her. For the second time in one evening, she wants to sink to the floor and weep. But there is no time for that now. She knows: she was a terrible mother, or whatever it was she was supposed to be. She cannot sleep here amongst the evidence of her neglect.

If the girl ever returns, she will treat her like the prodigal son. Prodigal daughter. She remembers the men's clothes and chastises herself. The girl committed her misdemeanours innocently enough; at least that's what Father Moore thought. Yes, she was trying to get away with something and she deliberately deceived people, but she did it to see Mr. Hunt. Father Moore doubted there was any immorality at the root of her antics. Just the faulty judgment of the young.

It is time to take matters into her own hands. Who knows if that man pursued every lead to find her? He may not have pursued any. The truth of the thought doubles her over. In the morning, she will go to the police herself.

From the landing to the second floor in the back stairway, she opens the deadbolt to the second-floor hallway. At the other end, light leaks from under her door. He coughs and mumbles to himself. She looks inside three bedrooms before opening the door to John's room. When she was a child, this room belonged to her. She never told John that.

The smell of camphor, herbs, and earth persists and comforts her. She has not watered his herbs. Now they are dead. How could she have been so careless?

John's log cabin quilt is with him at the hospital. She has not bothered to replace it. She looks at the dresser where his photograph of the three of them used to sit. It is John she should go to first tomorrow, not the police or the priest or anyone else. It is John who must hear her confession, not Father Moore.

*

The bastard took Alden the same way I used to take Maudie. I used to bend the girl over the old battered Windsor chair, lift her skirts, and have my way. I do not know if she, like Alden, was pained. I never bothered to look at her face. I never thought about what she felt at all.

Every day, this purgatory finds new ways to enumerate my sins. I experience their echo all around me. If only they didn't all have to be played out upon my poor granddaughter. But what can I do?

Oh! Of all the things I miss, fornicating is surely the thing I miss most. And I was so mechanical and passionless about it. Such a fool. Often, I would not even bother to get undressed; I would only unbutton my pants and open the front. Now, I would like nothing more than to revel in the warmth of another body, to feel skin against skin, to linger in an embrace. The longing is impossible to bear.

The bastard empties every drawer of Alden's dresser and looks at every paper in her desk. He pours himself a large whisky and reads a stack of letters John Hunt sent during the war. He guffaws. "The fool was in love. With that cold fish." As he finds jewellery, he evaluates it briefly and sets it aside in a pile on the dresser top. He tosses my first wife's wedding ring on the heap like it is worthless.

Dear, dear Agnes. There was a tender woman. And fool that I was, I criticized her constantly, often for nothing at all. I was angry that she came to me sick and spent, and instead of trying to bring her back to health, I wore her down even more. If I had been kinder and more attentive, would she have lived?

The bastard throws a necklace on the pile and it bumps against Agnes's ring, shoving it off the edge of the table and onto the floor. It rolls on the rug and drops off the edge to the hardwood floor behind a chair. He does not notice. The bastard will not have this, at least.

It feels like divine intervention. It can't be. Can it?

I can't help but ask, "Agnes, is that you?"

There is, of course, no answer. Such a foolish thought.

A raccoon runs across the roof and chews at the shingles, widening the entry he has created to his winter home. First the raccoons and then the squirrels and then the bats. My house is a wreck.

Finally, the bastard finds what he is looking for—the locked cupboard built into the closet. He breaks the lock easily enough and scans file after file. As he reads, he drinks, not bothering with a glass anymore. The whisky draws me over and I go through the motions of inhaling the aroma, imagining caramel and peat, and pretending to raise a glass.

*

Alden listens from John's bed, her back against the headboard and her knees pulled to her chest like a girl. She hears something run across the roof. A raccoon probably. The roof needs attention, desperately. Like the rest of Patterson House.

When this was her bedroom, her bed was against the other wall, the head facing the window. It is comfortable both ways. John's lingering presence in the room is comforting: a friendly ghost. It is as though he is with her saying, "It's not so bad. We'll figure this out, Alden dear."

I deserve this, she says to herself. I married the man for money. I married him to keep Patterson House. This damned house. I do not deserve my own sympathy.

As Alden rises from the bed, the clock in the foyer below strikes four. That man, that horrible man, is still moving about in her room. She imagines him examining every facet of her life, his hands on all her possessions. How could that feel worse than where his hands have already been? The bile rises in her throat again, but she steadies herself. All night she has run through a mental inventory of everything he will find. There are letters, all quite dull. He will have no interest in those. She has not kept a diary, thank God. Financial papers, a whole Patterson history of bad choices and bad luck, are locked in the cupboard in her closet, not a safe, but a cupboard that is not easy to see at a glance. He may miss it. And if he finds it, he will soon know the truth.

There is a loud thud, the sound of a chair overturned, cursing, and her door opening at the end of the hall and hitting the wall. Carling Grant lumbers down the hallway, opening every door and bellowing her name.

He knows.

For a moment, Alden cowers. She stops herself. He will not touch her again. She won't allow it. John's letter opener is on his desk and she slides it into her pocket, just in case. She is ready. A shard of pleasure pierces her. Whatever punishment she deserves, he surely deserves learning that there is no fortune at Patterson House.

Alden opens the door to the hallway and waits for him to see her.

"I should have known you would be in *his* room."

He is dishevelled, drunk, stinking, grasping papers that he wrinkles in his sweaty hands. With slurred words he says, "Where is it? Where is the money?" He gives the papers an insolent toss and they scatter around him like feathers.

How could she have let herself be laid low by this disaster of a man?

"You're drunk."

"Where is it? Tell me now."

"Where is what?"

"The money, damn you."

"There isn't any money. But you know that now," she says, gesturing to the papers all around him. "You've gone through my things." She strides past him into the hallway, her hand on the letter opener in her pocket, and walks down the stairs as though this is an early beginning to an otherwise normal day. "It's gone. It's been gone for years."

"How can it be gone?" He is still at the top of the stairs and he spreads his arms out to indicate their surroundings.

"It was gone when my father died. For all I know, it might have been gone when *his* father died."

"You lied to me."

"Lied?"

"You led me to believe you were well off."

"I was not obliged to tell you anything. You made assumptions."

"You led me to believe—"

"I did no such thing."

He looks around him. "There is a second mortgage on the house."

"But not a third." She can't help smiling. He is just like the boys her father wanted her to marry all those years ago. "Had you never asked yourself why I would have boarders if I were well off?"

"There is nothing in the bank. Nothing." He stamps his foot like a child. "How do you pay the bills?"

"Since you arrived, I've been paying them with your rent money. I rob Peter to pay Paul. I trade china for meat at the butcher."

He pales.

"The taxes are due again. I've put them off for as long as I can. You can pay that." She could spit on him.

"And how will I do that?"

"You're well off."

He grabs at the papers on the floor and tries to throw them at her. They scatter, again, some over the banister and onto the foyer floor, some along the stairs. He lurches toward her and his foot slips on an overdue notice. He lands on his backside and groans.

She could push him down the stairs. He is so drunk anyone would believe he fell. The thought is treacherous, malicious, venomous. She dismisses it. This is not who she is.

The alcohol has made him volatile, like her own father used to be. She feels the letter opener against her thigh in her skirt pocket. "We will talk about it in the morning." She hears the catch in her voice. "When you've sobered up."

She will find every bottle he has stashed in the house and pour it down the sink. For now, her instinct for self-preservation asserts itself. She edges closer to the front door, while continuing to face him. Turning her back would be foolish.

He surprises her by staying seated and starting to sob. "And my rent money?"

"I spent it feeding you. Your appetite—" She shakes her head. "I owe every grocer in a five-mile radius because of your appetite. I have had sixty-three men in this house before you and none has ever cost me as much as you."

That man, that wreck of a man, sits on the stairs and puts his head in his hands. "It's all gone? Everything? Gone?"

Alden begins to understand. "What are you saying? Is it all you had?" Alden can hardly believe it. "But you, you…" She lets the point drop. He led her to believe he had money. It is the very same accusation he levelled against her.

It was all for nothing.

They are the same.

She tries to remember when, exactly, he proposed to her. Did he ever properly propose? He said, "You need someone to look after things here," and took her hand. Is that a proposal? In the weeks after Constance left, Alden was so awash in grief she was not thinking straight. Maybe this is reason enough for annulment. Yes, she will go to see Father Henry. She will wait in the church until he appears for six o'clock Mass. She puts her coat and boots on and gathers her purse, hat, and gloves. Carling Grant is still on the stairs, head still in his hands, groaning.

"After all I've been through," he moans. "Can't you understand what it was like? A three-room shack and the stench of the tannery after this?" He hiccups and swallows, as though he is trying not to vomit.

Alden wants nothing more than to escape.

"Aunty Pat promised." He looks down as forlorn as any hobo. He is nothing more than a pleading little boy. Suddenly angry again, he says, "She promised we would always have a home here, and then that son of hers turned us out. It was humiliating."

"What son?"

"Rogers, dammit. Who else?" He uses the banister to pull himself up and descends the remaining stairs. "Your father, Rogers Patterson."

Alden's hand is on the doorknob before he reaches the landing.

"Oh, I don't blame her. She was dead. Mother said she was a saint, a genuine saint. She probably didn't think to write anything into the will. Women don't, you know. No, it wasn't Auntie Pat's fault."

"I don't know what you are talking about."

"You weren't even born yet," he sneers. "I was special to her, she always told me so."

"Who on earth is Auntie Pat?" She slips her hands into gloves.

"Mrs. Patterson, of course. Don't you understand?" He points at Alden, accusing. "You've had every benefit, every opportunity." He comes close enough that the stench of alcohol assaults her. "He was protecting himself. Protecting his children. Except for me. I was cast out into the wilderness. But he was my father too."

Alden stamps her foot. "Who?"

"William Patterson."

Alden could crumple to the ground. She sets her hand on the head of one of the trophy wolves to steady herself.

The resemblance is there. It's in the eyes. Predatory, hawk-like, even when he is lit like a blue flame. And dangerous.

A loud creak travels through the house, a sudden settling that sometimes happens in the cold or rain. Alden summons everything within her to remain calm, an antidote to Carling Grant's derangement. "Where is the proof?"

The proof is right before her, in his eyes, in his hairline, his temperament.

He spins around, arms outstretched. "Proof? My mother. She told me on her deathbed."

"Who is your mother?"

"Maudie Grant."

"Never heard of her," Alden says. "And even if it were true, you are a bastard." The use of such a terrible word emboldens her. "For all I know, there could be hundreds of you. There's a reason the law doesn't recognize you. You have no rights here."

Alden spies the umbrella stand to her right and takes hold of a sturdy looking instrument with a wooden handle. She will bring it down over his head if she must.

"No rights? You forget. I am your husband." He is suddenly cogent again.

She holds the door handle for support. Yes, he is. It is she who has no rights. She feels dizzy with the realization of what he has done. The puzzle of the last few months rearranges itself in her mind. He knew. He always knew, and she did not. He was never just another boarder. He was calculating. He could never prove his claim. The only way for him to get control of Patterson House was to marry her. Which he has done. Which he could not have done without her agreement. She has been duped.

This man is not her saviour. He is not, as she suspected throughout the night, a man merely in search of a maid. He is her usurper.

No. It is worse than that. William Patterson is his father. He is her uncle. And she has fornicated with him. She clutches at her stomach.

Bile rises in her throat. Half-uncle. Is that any less of a sin? She tries to speak and falters, then tries again. "I'll have it annulled."

"On what grounds?"

If she could stab him through the heart she would. "You know the grounds."

"Do you mean incest?" He laughs and repeats the word, lets it roll around his mouth like a spoonful of pudding. "Incest." He practically smacks his lips with it. "Let's go, then. Let's go now to your blessed Father Henry and tell him all about it, how you've married your uncle, shall we? Half-uncle, actually, which, by the way, there's no law against. Civil or canon. I checked. And when he asks if we've consummated the marriage," he stops to lick his lips, "I'll be sure to let him know the answer is yes. Let's call the papers with it."

Alden falters. Her face crumbles.

"Oh, you don't want anyone to know?" He smirks.

"We'll see about this," she says as she turns and goes through the front door, slamming it behind her.

What is there to see about? She has lost everything. She presumed he was weak, a fool. She presumed she could manage and manipulate him. It is she who has been a fool.

Her shoulders droop and she sways slightly on the stone path to the street. She holds the post of the gate while a terrible thought comes to her.

What if he never lets her back in?

PART FIVE

December 14, 1930

HARRIET BECHNER stands before the ruddy-faced matron of the Mercer Reformatory and accepts her scolding while trying to maintain an impassive face.

The matron's office is awash in paperwork. A mess. The matron does not practise what she preaches, but that is no surprise. No one does. A clock ticks far too loudly on the wall and another on the credenza behind her is seven minutes faster. For a woman who demands order, Harriet cannot understand how the lack of synchronicity goes unnoticed.

Harriet might be fired. Again. First from the insane asylum, now from the Reformatory.

Her failings are enumerated. She has been too friendly with the girls. Talked to them as though they are normal, which they are. At least, most of them are, she thinks. She tries not to fear them. Mostly, she doesn't see a thing wrong with them. Not one thing. Except maybe they don't do what they're told. She and the inmates have that in common, at least. The Female Refuges Act lets them incarcerate any woman or girl they want. For any reason. There's no trial. Nothing. It's not right. A lot of them are simply worn out from too many babies, like her own dear Ma. But her Ma has her to rely on. The women in the asylum and at Mercer have no one.

The odd one has fallen right off her front porch, as it were. Harriet likes thinking up euphemisms for crazy. Not two thoughts to rub together, is another favourite. Or drinking from the wrong side of the cup. She almost giggles in front of the matron and catches herself.

They're not dangerous, though. They're not going to hurt anyone. They're just girls, after all. Harriet wishes the others who worked here felt the same.

The matron's face is getting red. The Mercer is nothing but another warehouse for unwanted women.

Harriet wants to talk back to the matron but is aware that her finances will not support such an indulgence. If only she could say, "I know what it's like. You don't understand these girls." They have been hurt. Sometimes by their fathers. Sometimes by other men. They have been neglected. And they are not helped by coming here. They hardly let them rest. They are not allowed outside to enjoy the healing sunshine or sit under a tree and think. There's no schooling. Instead, they are put to work, scrubbing the pots, the toilets, and the floors, or doing the laundry. With the overcrowding, there is talk that the new girls are going to be sent to the asylum. It's not right.

She is being chastised for giving an extra slice of bread to that one doing so poorly and smuggling in an apple for another.

"Are you listening to me?"

"Yes, Matron."

If the matron knew she took a letter out for that new one, the one who came in wearing men's clothes, she would be out for sure. There might really be something wrong with that one. But who is to say? The girl swore it was all a big misunderstanding. She pleaded with her for a paper and pencil. She has fancy manners and is obviously from a good home. But she would not say where she came from. She only said that this fellow at the Veterans' Hospital would vouch for her. Harriet even paid the postage for the letter herself.

The matron continues to scold. "There are rules for a reason. You do not make the rules. You obey the rules."

"Yes, Matron."

She does some calculations in her head. She will stay another two weeks and save whatever wages she can. Surely there is other work, even in these times.

"These girls are dangerous. They are not harmless stray dogs. They bite. They have rabies." The matron sounds just like her ma sometimes. Ma always complains when Harriet brings strays home. When she was a girl, she would capture grasshoppers in jars. Ma said grasshoppers weren't meant to be in jars and that she was killing them with kindness. The crickets died too. But it didn't stop her from trying again and again. A baby squirrel died before it got fur. And kittens. She was more successful with the kittens. There seemed to be kittens under every porch in The Ward. Ma always warned her: "Don't name them. They're not yours to name."

"Well?" asks the matron. "Do I make myself understood?"

It's now or never: resign her post or stick with it. She crosses her fingers behind her back and lies. "I understand, Matron."

The matron looks unconvinced.

"I will not deviate from the rules again. My mother always says you can kill something with kindness."

"Exactly," the matron says, satisfied she has finally made Harriet see her mistake.

As Harriet turns and walks out the door of the matron's office, she thinks ahead. Maybe that letter will do some good. She will do whatever good she can until her next pay. Maybe she could go to work for a veterinarian. She would probably be better with stray dogs than stray people.

*

On his early morning check of the church, Father Henry sees Alden kneeling in a pew in the back. As he makes his way down the centre aisle to the nave, he realizes she is weeping. It has not even been twenty-four hours since he married them.

He whisks her through the vestibule and into the rectory to his study. As he opens the drapes, the early eastern sun animates the dust motes. The normally comforting scent of books and tobacco feels off so early in the day. There are at least six volumes open on his desk, evidence of his difficulty preparing this week's sermon. This time of year, the children are so excited. They squirm and fidget. It is almost impossible to hold their attention. But is that his goal? He pulls an oak armchair to the desk for Alden and motions her to sit down while he clears the space between them.

The rectory housekeeper pops her head in the other door. "Good morning, Father. You're in early today. Do you want your tea in here—" She stops short when she sees Alden. "Oh dear. Pardon me." Father Henry motions her away and she nods, shutting the door behind her. Alden's presence here this morning will be all over the parish by noon. He really needs to find a housekeeper with a bit more discretion.

Alden has looked away, probably hoping not to have been caught crying, and her gaze is fixed out the window where common redpolls and chickadees skitter from branch to ground looking for their morning meal.

Obviously, the wedding night did not go well. Alden will not speak, and he is anxious to get back to his sermon.

"Oh, Father—" She wipes her nose with her handkerchief. "I've made a terrible mistake." With this admission, she makes eye contact—briefly— and drops her gaze again.

"Child, I know it must have been a shock to you, but the relations between man and wife happen as God intended, difficult as that might be to fathom." The poor woman probably had only the most abstract idea. Alden Patterson is not a woman of fleshly desires. If anyone knows this, it is he. He has been her confessor. Not her preferred one. He knows that. Given her druthers, she would rather see Father Moore. He won't pretend he and Father Moore haven't discussed her together, the sanctity of the confessional notwithstanding. It is good to have a colleague to consider the tough cases with. Father Henry thinks Alden might have made a good nun. Father Moore disagrees. She has a natural inclination against authority.

Father Moore said this wedding would be a disaster. Father Henry was more optimistic. He could never have imagined Alden would end up in his office quite so soon. He is no fan of Mr. Carling Grant. He has never heard the man's confession and suspects he does not partake of the sacrament. He has a strange manner during Mass. He is a step behind everyone else, just by a second or two. He rarely speaks any prayers out loud. It is almost as though he isn't really a Catholic, as though he is following along and pretending. But then when he took Communion, Father Henry knew he must be wrong. No one would receive the sacrament if they were not among the faithful. Still, something about the man bothers him.

And now he will have to find some words of consolation for this unhappy, unlikely, bride.

"Alden, dear child, what has happened?"

"Father, he only wants the house." She looks to him, her desolate heart visible in her red-rimmed eyes. They sit in awkward silence for a full minute while she regains enough composure to continue. She clears her throat and sits slightly taller.

Father Henry offers her his handkerchief, an unnecessary and empty gesture since she clutches her own in her hand.

"Can I undo it? Can I get it annulled?" She meets his eyes.

Father Henry looks away, makes a steeple with his fingertips and touches them to the underside of his chin. Annulments are such a lot of work.

"What has been done cannot be undone so easily. Matthew 19 tells us, 'What therefore God hath joined together, let not man put asunder.'" He struggles to come up with additional advice. "It takes time for two people to learn to live together under one roof."

"Father, he has been under my roof since August."

"That is not the same. He has been a boarder. And here I see a problem. You say, 'my roof.' You have been alone a long time, child. It will be a challenge for you to learn to open your life to another. But this you must do." He is pleased to have found the right answer. His tone assumes the more assured cadence of a sermon. "For you are married now. You are his wife. You have made vows. Those vows are sacred."

Alden shakes her head. The uncertainty in her eyes changes. Her hands tremble. She fidgets with her handkerchief. Finally, she speaks. "Father, the vows are not sacred to him."

"Only God can know what is in his heart. I urge you to go home and to try. Try to be a good wife."

Alden gathers up her purse, coat, and scarf and goes to the door. She is too proud.

She turns back to him, opens her mouth to speak, and then does not.

"I will see you at Mass later." It is a statement, not a question.

Alden turns back to him and says, "No, you will not," and he recognizes that she is not sad, not dejected, not rejected; she is furious. He knows in that instant that he will never see her again.

Oh dear. He must call Father Moore. Maybe he will know what to do.

*

Alden leaves the rectory walking far too fast. The very idea of Father Henry sending her back to Patterson House with instructions to be a better wife leaves her breathless. He implied that she is to blame, that she is selfish. All because she said, "My house." It *is* her house. What is done *can* be undone, and if God won't do it, she will do it herself.

The enormity of what has happened washes over her in yet another wave.

And the church will not save her.

Walking clears her mind. With walking, there is always a path forward. At Kingston Road, she says out loud, "Ruination Road indeed." She has been on the road to ruin for some time.

The temperature hovers around freezing, and a thin layer of ice under the snow keeps her steps short and her posture tense. Her ankle has just healed; she cannot go through that again.

Everything about this morning reminds her of the day of the temperance march so long ago, the day she found Constance. The greyness, the cold, the snow. Even the time of day, so early in the morning. Her distraction is the same too; she goes further north than she needs to and decides to cross the river at Bloor. She tells herself there is no point arriving at the Veterans' Hospital before visitors are allowed, but she knows she is procrastinating.

What if Mr. Hunt blames her, just as Father Henry did?

Few cars cross the Bloor Viaduct at this early hour. Northward, the ruined Don Valley is dark, deep, and inviting, the river's typical stench almost indiscernible now that it is frozen. It looks almost beautiful, a trickle in the ice far below. From her place on the bridge, she feels as though she is suspended in space with snowflakes above and below. She is weightless. Falling would be easy. So easy. And she would be free of it all. Free of everything she has done.

A car pulls up and the driver toots its horn at her. A grey-haired man with wire-rimmed glasses and a kind face leans across and opens the passenger door. Two girls in the back dressed for church look at her with open curiosity. "Do you need a lift, Ma'am?"

She adjusts her hat. "No, thank you."

He frowns and hesitates.

Alden forces herself to smile broadly. What must she look like out here alone, so early in the morning, leaning into the valley? "I'm fine. Thank you, Sir. It's a grand day, if you like the snow."

His head tilts again and he smiles. "All right then. We're off. Be careful."

A quick burst of huge white flakes obliterates the river and valley as he drives away. If she were to stay still, she would be covered in white. She might become invisible to passersby. Is it invisibility she wants? She brushes herself off.

"Buck up," she says aloud and stomps her boots. It will be at least another hour before she arrives at the hospital. Maybe longer. The regularity of her footfalls calms her. Like her heartbeat. Like the waves on the lake.

The streets are quiet, and not simply Sunday quiet. New snow absorbs the clink and clank of doors, the trot of horses' hooves, the whirr of motors. It is quiet enough to think. She gets off Bloor Street, skirts houses and buildings, and makes her way to the edge of the ravine where the trees are her only company. Remembering the hobo camps far below, she decides to keep to boot-beaten paths on the higher reaches. Finding herself on a widening trail, she realizes the Necropolis is ahead. She almost turns away, but a graveyard is as good a place as any to contemplate the disaster her life has become.

The Necropolis used to be on the outskirts of the city, but, like Patterson House, it's been swallowed up. Long before Alden was born, the dead of Potter's Field at Bloor and Yonge had been re-interred here. No one could have imagined Toronto would grow so large. Somewhere, there is a monument that commemorates William Patterson for funding the terrible work. Gravestones tilt toward the depths of the ravine along the edge of the cemetery. Perhaps the bones of the dead are sliding into the valley as the slope erodes. What a grisly thought. Some of these souls may have to be moved yet again. Even in death, one's circumstances can change.

Squirrels run about in the snow between the headstones, oblivious to their sombre surroundings. The inscriptions are terse. So many women die in their twenties and thirties. Childbirth, probably. Like the first Mrs. Patterson, and the child right afterwards. A squirrel chatters atop a slim headstone of a private who died in 1917. He was the same age as her youngest brother, Arthur. How would her life have been different if her dear brothers were alive?

At the cemetery's entrance on Winchester Street, she takes refuge under the alcove of the chapel and watches the snow accumulate. Mourning doves land on the wire across the street and their long, low laments speak to her.

Just inside the gate, a thick-trunked tree with smooth, elephant-coloured bark reaches its perfectly symmetrical branches upwards. If

John were here, he would tell her the species of the tree and all manner of facts about it, what birds like to live in it, what fruits or nuts it bears. His eyes would see it in its full flower.

Dear John. What will she say to him? How will she explain? She begins to walk again.

That man came to Patterson House with a plan. It was in his interest to create a division between her and Constance. And between her and John. Even if sending John to the hospital was the right thing to do, her motives were far from pure. She knows that. But that does not alter the fact that he manipulated her. He played her for a fool. And she obliged.

How could she have allowed herself to have been brought so very low?

And there is more to admit. His disapproval of everyone she knew, neighbours, parishioners, shopkeepers—people she has known her whole life—his disdain for this person's clothing or that person's manners, created new reasons for her to avoid the company of others. He took her natural inclination toward solitude and snobbishness and compounded it. She stopped participating in the charity drives. It has been months since Father Moore or Father Henry came for dinner. Not that it matters anymore. Why, she didn't even go over to see Mrs. Hughes after Gwen left. How could she have been so mean-spirited? She has been utterly self-absorbed.

Admitting this to herself is hard. Confessing to Mr. Hunt will be crushing. But she must.

A church clock strikes ten. She has been away from Patterson House for more than five hours and she feels she left only minutes ago. Her ankle should be aching with the long walk, but she feels nothing at all. She passes the newly built Spruce Court Apartments on the edge of Cabbagetown. In the WCTU, she met two mothers who lived there raising children on their own. She did not inquire about their circumstances but assumed them to be war widows. They were entirely respectable and their children clean and orderly. Constance once suggested she have women at Patterson House. Why did she reject the notion? It makes so much sense. Women need places to live, too.

Alden has lived too long among men. She has absorbed men's ideas, including their ideas about women, and she has dismissed her own sex. She has dismissed herself.

A hare, its winter coat thick and white, darts across the path, stops, looks at her, and she asks aloud, "What should I do?" The hare stares back, as if to answer, "What do you want to do?" She does not know. But she knows that she will procrastinate no longer.

She can make things right. She will find Constance. Constance and Gwen are together. They must be. She will bring them both back. If they will come.

*

John wakes to Nurse Doris opening the drapes beside his bed. It's a grey day. Snowy. He is not sure if Doris is her first or last name, and hopes it is her first. She has lovely auburn hair like Alden, although Alden's is a bit flecked with grey these days. He pushes himself up and swings his legs over the side of the bed. "Good morning, Nurse Doris."

Because he is by the window and because the first thing Nurse Doris does in the morning is open the drapes, he gets her attention first. "Look at the snow, Mr. Hunt. I can hardly believe it's almost Christmas."

The three other men who share this ward begin to rise with the groans and gripes to which he has become accustomed over the last month. All three of them are going to their respective homes for Christmas Day, including Mr. Wilson, the one with shell shock so bad he dives under his own bed if someone accidentally closes a book too fast. John has made no plans. Nurse Doris keeps bringing it up. It occurs to him that if he is here, she must be here too. She probably wants the day with her own family.

Sure enough, she asks him about it again. "Have you made plans to go home for a few days? You're doing so well. They might discharge you altogether. What a Christmas gift that would be."

"No plans yet, Nurse Doris. I'll work it out soon." It would be good to be out. He could take Constance to see the window displays at Eaton's like he always has.

Perhaps she has gone already, without him. A dark thought. He's had too many of these lately. He does not understand why no one has been to see him and he's been feeling a bit sorry for himself.

Nurse Doris becomes excessively cheerful, something she does whenever she senses any sadness among the men. Her voice gets a bit higher and her smile a bit forced.

"I don't see any reason why you couldn't. The doctor has said you are ready. He's bound to discharge you any day now, and you are well enough to decide to go on your own." She pulls an envelope from her apron. "Oh, I almost forgot. A letter for you was in with Mr. Huntley's mail—here it is. Sorry about the mix-up. It's all the extra mail with the Christmas cards and such."

Not a single card decorates his bedside table or is tacked to his wall. It hurts him to think of Patterson House and know that no one has thought to visit or send a note or forward his mail. His spring seed catalogues will be arriving soon, and he would like nothing more than to pass his time planning the garden.

"Perhaps this is a Christmas letter for you." She changes the subject swiftly. "Do you need help getting into the biffy this morning?"

"I'll be fine, thank you."

"See? You're ready to go home."

One of the other patients calls to her.

"Back in a minute."

The envelope has unfamiliar handwriting on it and no return address. In it is a single-page letter, folded in three, and written in Constance's tidy script dated almost two weeks before.

Dear Mr. Hunt,

I need your help. I'm in the Mercer Reformatory for Females. I ran away with Gwen and was caught and now I'm here. It is a terrible place. Alden and I had an awful fight. So many things have happened. I got picked up by the police while I was wearing the delivery boy disguise. Instead of sending me back to Alden, they sent me here. They say there is something wrong with me. Alden won't take me back. I know you are not well and I don't want to burden you, but I don't know what to do. This is a terrible place. Can you get me out of here? Please? If you can't

*come, can you send Father Moore? Anyone who knows
me. But please, don't talk to Mrs. Hughes. Gwen really
can't go home.*

Love, Constance

On the other side of the page, there is another note in the same handwriting as the envelope. "Please hurry. They're going to move her to 999 Queen." Mr. Hunt's mouth falls open and his fingers touch where his lips should be. 999 Queen. The Provincial Lunatic Asylum. There isn't a soul in Toronto—maybe not in the province—who doesn't know that notorious address. Stories about riots, overcrowding, terrible conditions, and, worst of all, escapees come up regularly in the papers. Children are as afraid of the place as they are of monsters under their beds.

Good Lord. How on earth did that happen? Turning the page over several times reveals no more answers, nor does looking in the envelope again.

"Nurse Doris," he calls out. "You are right. It is time for me to go. I'm needed."

"That's the spirit. Must have been quite a letter. The doctor will want to say something about it, but we'll work that out." Nurse Doris isn't going to put any bureaucratic roadblocks in the way of his departure if it gets her one step closer to being home at Christmas.

The box that Constance brought is in the closet and he finds his clothes. A terrible mistake has been made. Alden would never send the girl to the Reformatory. And the asylum? Impossible. Are both girls at Mercer or only Constance? He rereads the letter yet again and cannot tell for certain. Hard as it for him to guess what has happened, he knows Carling Grant has something to do with it. And if he had stopped feeling sorry for himself long enough to think about why Constance didn't come back or send a note, or why Alden didn't visit, or why his mail wasn't forwarded, he would have realized sooner that there was trouble.

After he is dressed and readying himself to call for a taxi, Alden walks through the door of the ward with Nurse Doris. "Someone is here for you," she says jovially, oblivious to the fact that Alden is ashen and unsteady. John has not seen her like this since the day he arrived at

Patterson House after the war. Her movements are tentative, guarded.

Stepping forward, he stops short of embracing her and says, "It is so good to see you. I've just heard."

"You know?"

"Yes, I got a letter from her."

Alden's face is uncomprehending. "From whom?"

"Constance, of course."

"Constance? Where is she?"

"The Mercer Reformatory."

The news stills her hands.

"The Reformatory? Good heavens. How?"

"She said the police picked her up and that you wouldn't take her back."

Alden sputters. "Wouldn't take her back? I didn't know where she was!"

John passes her the letter. "I don't doubt you. I do think, though, that Mr. Grant has been at work behind the scenes somehow."

Alden scans the letter, turns it over, sees the other message, and says, "Dear God. Why did I ever let that snake into our lives?"

"Tell me what happened." He walks to his bed and sits on the edge facing the window and motions her over. She pulls a chair up and sits with him.

"I don't know where to start."

"Start anywhere."

"We had a row."

As the story spills out of her, John realizes the argument was the very same day that he was sent to the hospital and about the very same suit of clothes that Constance wore to sneak in to see him. "She did it to see me," he says. "She told me herself."

"I know that now."

"Didn't she tell you?"

"She did, but I didn't believe her."

The various morning noises of the men in the ward are behind him. He hears his fellow patients gather themselves and leave the room. He and Alden are alone.

"What else?" asks Mr. Hunt, knowing there is more she is not saying.

"Oh dear. He blurted out that I found her in The Ward. In the trash."

"What?"

"I've always suggested to her—for her own sake—that I found her at the church. You know it's not true. You know I found her on my way to the temperance march. What I never said was that she had been left in the trash."

The words leave him keening with a heartache so exquisite, he fears for a moment he might faint. Who would leave a baby in the trash? What kind of callous, indurate heart could do that? His own knowledge of abandonment engulfs him, and he remembers the ride to his uncle's house, the curt goodbye from his mother and father, their brief, "Be good, boy," and his devastation at being left behind. And this is how Constance must feel, but worse. She was not left in the care of a relative or even a stranger. She was simply left. It is too much to bear. All he can manage to say is, "Oh dear."

Alden is wringing her hands. "I'm sorry I never told you. Do you understand why? It is so awful."

"You never told me this, but you told Mr. Grant?"

"I never should have told him."

"Why did you?"

"I don't know. I was trying to explain how she came to Patterson House." She clutches the fabric of her skirt.

Alden is still not saying everything there is to say. "And why would you need to explain anything to Mr. Grant?"

"He kept questioning me, wanting to know why I took on a foundling." Alden smooths her skirt, turns away, wipes her hand across the windowsill, and looks at the dust on her palm and fingertips.

"I still don't understand why you felt a need to justify yourself to him."

"Constance thought I'd been lying to her. I have been, I guess, but not out of malice. How must it have felt to learn…to know…." Her voice trails off.

"And that's when she left?"

"I sent her to her room."

He shakes his head. "She's too old for that now."

Alden nods, her eyes to the floor again. "I went to see Father Moore, and by the time I got back she was gone." Her fists are tight in her lap.

"I wish you had come to see me." He rubs his chin. "That's almost a month now. Didn't you look for her? Speak to Mrs. Hughes? Ask around the neighbourhood? See what Mrs. Schiffley knew?"

Alden shakes her head, miserable.

"Why not?"

"I felt terrible. You were gone. Constance was gone. I couldn't think." She pauses. "I could hardly walk on my ankle. And I was angry. I thought, 'Let her see what it's like out there. She'll be back.' I was so wrong."

"Stubborn. It's your downfall." This is as close to a scold as he can muster with Alden.

"There's something else." She hesitates. "Mr. Grant offered to call the police for me and I let him. I left him in charge of finding her."

"Why on earth?"

Alden bites her lower lip and looks him in the eye. "I've done a terrible thing, John."

"Yes, you have."

"No. There's more. There's something else."

"I don't think I want to know."

"I married him."

He cannot look at her. Instead, he moves to the window and keeps his back to her for several minutes.

Constance was right again.

Once he trusts his voice to speak, he says, "When?" As he asks the question, he wonders why that matters.

"Yesterday." She drops from her chair to her knees beside him, rests her face in her hands and says, "Forgive me."

This is not the woman he knows. He puts his hand on her shoulder and this small act of kindness starts a flood of tears. As the story spills from her, he is hardly listening. Carling Grant wanted the house. Of course. That should have been obvious to anyone. Even Alden. It should have been obvious to him. He had been oblivious. Alden's hair has gone more than a little grey. It is quite grey. She is far too thin, her shoulders as sharp as the wings of a bird. What was powerful in her frame before is gone, vanished like snow in the first driving spring rain.

When Alden's tears are spent, he rises and holds out his hand and helps her stand. He has done this before. She dabs at her eyes and nose.

"Don't worry, dear Alden. We'll sort it all out. First things first. Let's go get Constance."

*

The taxi lets them off at the main gate of the Mercer Reformatory, a mammoth and foreboding gothic structure. The driver whistles and says, "Never been here before. 'Abandon all hope, ye who enter here.'"

"I beg your pardon?" asks Alden.

"Dante," he says, matter-of-factly.

Neither Alden nor John have been here before either. Alden had been unaware of the existence of this fearsome place. The small, barred windows send a chill through her. Constance could be looking out of one of these right now. She could have seen them arrive. She chides herself. The place is massive. The odds are against it.

If Constance committed murder, she would not send her here. It is, to her eye, more frightful than the lunatic asylum.

"She's in there somewhere," says John, scanning the length of the building.

The entryway is vast and hollow. There is not a stick of furniture aside from the desk and chair the attendant uses. This is not a place that sees visitors. The floors are polished to gleaming, but the air smells of rot and mould. There is filth beyond this facade.

The sound of their footsteps bounces around the room. There is a hallway to the left and a wide, padlocked doorway to the right. Two spiral staircases rise and meet on a landing above. They seem to lead to a tower. Probably a locked tower. This is the architecture of nightmares.

Getting Constance released from the Reformatory is a much more difficult endeavour than getting John from the Veterans' Hospital. He could leave of his own volition, but Constance cannot. As her guardian, Alden thinks she has every right to demand her back. She doesn't realize at first that the girl has been arrested and placed here, that there is a rigid bureaucracy behind her incarceration, a bureaucracy that moves slowly at the best of times, and not at all on a Sunday.

Alden musters every inch of her height and disdain to weaken the will of anyone trying to thwart her. Finally, the matron stands before her. But Alden's outrage is not enough to get the girl released. Mr. Hunt whispers that she might want to call in one of her father's lawyers to get the job done.

She balks. "It's Sunday."

"It won't hurt to try."

"I was quite sharp with them after my father died."

"Stubborn."

"Yes, you're quite right, John, as usual. What choice do we have?"

Had the matron realized how much more contentious Alden would become, she might never have let her use the phone. While they wait for the lawyer, they get a sense of the place. They hear footsteps behind closed doors. Alden wonders if Constance is among those shuffling by, just out of her sight, and begins to call out to her. The matron threatens to have her removed. Alden says, "Try it." Staff rarely enter the foyer, but when they do, Alden demands to know if they know the whereabouts of Constance Patterson. The matron inevitably shoos the staff member out and Alden yells after them. "Tell her we are here. We are here for her!" John takes her arm and pats it more than once. Alden suspects he is embarrassed by her outbursts, but she cannot worry about that. She is past worrying about things like that.

When the lawyer arrives, he is armed with paperwork and all manner of legalese. Constance has been charged with no crime, but has been listed as "incorrigible," a catch-all that has no merit in the Criminal Code, a point that the lawyer emphasizes with a sharp rap of his cane on the polished floor.

After a telephone call to a judge, the matron shakes her head and says, "You can have her. What do I care? And good luck to you."

It is amazing what they have been forced to learn in one day. How many other women are incarcerated here under similar circumstances and without the means or connections to get out?

While an attendant finds Constance, the lawyer leans against his cane and waits.

"I thank you," says Alden, her posture straight and her chin raised. It is difficult, after making such a scene, to regain a sense of dignity. She has been on her feet almost all day. She has not given a thought to her appearance and it is too late now. She imagines her hair loosening from its bun, her clothes wrinkled, pulled from the laundry in the middle of last night. Was it only last night?

"You are your father's daughter. There is no doubt about that." He looks at his watch. "I don't imagine there will be any more trouble. I'll be off." He tips his hat. "I'll send the bill."

"Thank you," says Alden. "I'll need your services again." He already knows what has become of her charge. The embarrassment of disclosing her desire for a divorce can be no worse. If divorce is out of the question, she can, at minimum, discern her rights, if she has any at all.

"Call tomorrow in business hours," he says, walking out the door.

John says quietly, "A divorce?"

Alden motions with her eyes toward the matron, who continues to watch them, and he stops his questioning.

When an attendant finally opens the door and Constance emerges, she is utterly dishevelled. Her hair is shorn short, her clothing is grey, baggy, and unfamiliar; she is dirty, and her shoes are far too big, causing her heels to drag with every shuffling step. When Constance sees Alden, she does not smile or rush forward. Life seems to have drained from her.

Alden is aghast. "What have they done to you?"

John says, "Thank God," and rushes forward. He tries to put his arm around her shoulder but she flinches and he stops himself.

Constance glances at the attendant, coughs, and wipes her nose with the back of her hand. She is utterly cowed.

"Look at her! She could have consumption," Alden scolds the matron. To Constance, she says, "I'll call the doctor the minute we get to Patterson House."

Constance flinches. "No more doctors."

John furrows his brow and glances at Alden, but she cannot investigate the comment now.

The attendant says, "You get to go home now. Is this the man from the Veterans' Hospital?"

Constance nods and the attendant moves forward to shake his hand. "Glad you could make it," she says with an easy smile.

The matron, eagle-eyed, says, "You! It was you? Get your things and get out."

The attendant shrugs, leans over, and gives Constance a pat on the shoulder and says, "You'll be fine now."

Turning to the matron, she says, "I was going to leave anyway." She extends her hand to Alden. "Harriet Bechner."

"Alden Patterson. I believe we are in your debt." Alden searches her purse for a calling card. "Please, do call us. We would like to thank you properly."

The matron rolls her eyes and says, "Let's get on with it, shall we?"

"We're taking you back to Patterson House," says John. "Let's go."

Constance takes a step back. "I'm not leaving without Gwen."

"So, Gwen *is* here too." says Alden.

"We were brought in together, but I haven't seen her in three weeks. We got split up."

Alden addresses the matron. "Find Gwen Hughes. We'll take her too."

The matron smirks. "Gwen Hughes is not yours to take, Ma'am."

Alden has dismissed the lawyer too soon.

"We can't solve every problem today," says John. "Constance, we'll talk to Mrs. Hughes and come back for Gwen tomorrow, I promise." He glances at the matron and attendant. "Let's talk about this outside."

"If Gwen hears I've left without her, she'll be worried sick."

"And don't you think I have been worried sick?" asks Alden.

"Have you?" Constance stares straight into Alden's eyes and Alden falters. "Of course, I have. Oh, dear God. I didn't know you were here."

Harriet Bechner whispers to Constance, "Don't you worry. I'll get word to her before I go." To the matron, she says, "I'll get my things and be gone," and she disappears behind the doors through which she'd brought Constance, uttering one last bit of encouragement to her. "Good luck!"

"Can we see Gwen Hughes? Is that allowed?" asks Alden.

The matron scowls. She will not give anything else today. "Visitors are allowed. But you've passed the time." It is true. Darkness has fallen without Alden noticing. They will get nothing more from this martinet today.

John whispers, "Could we just get out of here now?"

"Please, Constance. Let's leave here and sort this out elsewhere." The sound of Alden pleading is magnified in this huge empty room. Alden whispers to Constance, "I was wrong. About everything. I should have listened to you." Constance nods.

John herds them toward the door and Alden takes off her coat and puts it over Constance's shoulders. A blast of winter air welcomes them back into the world. Constance looks up at the sky and begins to weep.

Alden realizes they have no way to get home. After all this, she must go back inside and ask the matron to call her a taxi. Why should this day not contain yet another humiliation?

*

Settled in the back of a taxi between Alden and Mr. Hunt, Constance feels as though she can breathe for the first time in weeks. She closes her eyes and tries to get a hold of herself. Her relief at leaving the Reformatory is as huge as her guilt for leaving Gwen behind. While she doesn't hold a thing against Mr. Hunt, she is still wary of Alden. And so tired. She did not know it was possible to be this tired.

"Look at you. God only knows what happened in that place." Alden's hands haven't stopped moving. She is tucking her coat around Constance. "You can be sure they haven't heard the last of me."

"First things first, let's get her home and well," says Mr. Hunt.

The dry, hacking cough Constance got after her first week in the Reformatory seizes her. She leans forward, and Alden pats her back. There is no room for her to move away. When the coughing subsides, she says, "How could you do it? How could you leave me there?"

"It wasn't me. I didn't know. I thought you ran away with Gwen."

"I did."

Mr. Hunt interjects. "Constance, Alden did not know. It was Mr. Grant's doing."

"How?"

Alden straightens the front of her skirt over her legs, glances at the driver, and hugs her arms around herself. It is cold in the cab and she is shivering. Her tone is hushed. "I should have listened to you the day he arrived and turned him away. I rue the day I ever let him into Patterson House. You tried to tell me. He is the one who sent you to the Reformatory. I hope you know I would never do such a thing. I learned today that when the police called Patterson House to say they found you, he said he spoke for me. Nothing could be further from the truth. I'm so sorry," she says. "I can't imagine what it has been like to be, to feel," her voice catches, "abandoned."

The word seems to echo around the cab. The three of them are silent, awkwardly aware that the driver can hear everything. What secrets can they have from someone who has picked them up at the Mercer Reformatory? He has likely already made up a story of the wayward girl, the spinster, and the man in the balaclava. He will tell it over his Sunday supper. Any of the actual details don't really matter. If there is one thing Constance has learned in the past few weeks, it is that the truth does not matter.

The driver cannot know that this is certainly not the first time Constance has been abandoned. His story will not go back that far in her life. But Constance has imagined herself left in The Ward so vividly for the past few weeks, she feels as if she has a true memory of it.

Both Mr. Hunt and Alden are looking out their respective windows, deep in thought, and she realizes that they, too, know abandonment. Mr. Hunt was left with his old Uncle Reginald at the age of ten. He was left again, and finally found, on a battlefield in France. He probably felt abandoned in the Veterans' Hospital. Just as abandoned as she felt at the Reformatory.

And what of Alden? Her mother died when she was an infant. An accident, but a kind of abandonment, nonetheless. There was the story of her being jilted, or nearly jilted. Certainly, there is more, but Constance does not—cannot—know all the ways in which Alden has been hurt.

The abandoned cannot know if someone intends to come for them until someone does. All they can know is that they have been left alone to fend for themselves. She is not alone—not anymore—squashed between Mr. Hunt and Alden. She should feel better than she does. But she is wary. Another thing she has learned in the last few weeks is that intentions count for little.

Alden interrupts her thoughts and says, "I'm sorry I didn't tell you the truth. About how I found you. I hope you can forgive me."

"I've had time to think about it. I understand why you didn't tell me. To be honest, I wish I still didn't know."

She turns to Mr. Hunt. "Did you know?" He shakes his head.

"Why would you tell Mr. Grant such a thing? A thing about me that I didn't know myself? You *gave* him something about *me*. Something of mine. Even when you must have known how I hate him."

Alden nods and tears roll down her cheeks. She does nothing to hide them.

"I see now. It was a betrayal. I am so very sorry," she whispers.

She has never heard Alden apologize so much. "Can I ask you something?"

"Anything."

"Did you try to find my mother?"

Alden nods. "There was a little girl there when you were found. It was she who first heard you. She hadn't seen anyone. We went to see the girl's mother and she knew nothing. She had another baby. It was clear you were not hers. I took you to the police. I went back and forth from the hospital to the police station." Alden gestures and furrows her eyebrows. "The temperance march was on and there was a riot. It was such a strange and chaotic day. I went round and round with you and then the police asked me to keep you until they found your mother. I know they looked. The case was in the papers. But I guess she didn't want to be found. And it was wartime. Maybe they didn't try very hard. In the end, we kept you."

It occurs to Constance that the phrase "it was wartime" is used to excuse all manner of sins.

She runs her hands through her short hair. "Did you want me?"

Alden looks across to Mr. Hunt, searching for help with her answer. "It wasn't a question of want. There you were."

Duty. Alden would have done her duty.

Mr. Hunt adds, "You were a precious little baby. Of course, we wanted you. It was hard at first. Alden's father died, and she was alone with you, and then I came."

"And we made it work, didn't we?" Alden's voice is pleading again. "I know I wasn't a good mother. That's because I wasn't a mother and I never felt like a mother. I was not prepared. I never knew what I was supposed to be. But I made sure you were safe. Or tried to. Until now. I know that I have failed in my duty egregiously. I hope you can forgive me."

She can, but she does not want to say so quite yet. They pass the Annex. "You have to help me get Gwen out." She will not give up her advantage before she gets what she wants.

"We'll do everything we can. I'll call the lawyer back tomorrow. We'll go to see Mrs. Hughes tonight if you want."

Constance rubs her eyes, hoping the action will hide any tears. Her voice cracks. "It won't help. Mrs. Hughes already knows she's there. They called her. They don't want her back. Gwen is in the family way."

"What?" Both Alden and Mr. Hunt are incredulous.

She sees Gwen's face begging her not to talk about it. She cannot keep quiet any longer. She whispers. "It's Mr. Hughes," she says.

Alden, understanding dawning, gasps and her hands go to her heart. "Dear God."

God has little to do with what has happened to Gwen, Constance thinks.

Mr. Hunt is slower to understand. "What? What is it?"

Neither of them explains.

"Don't worry, we'll take care of Gwen," assures Alden, her voice hardening. "She won't have to go back there. We'll figure something out. She can come and live with us."

"Do you mean it?"

Alden takes Constance's hand and turns so that she can look into her eyes. "Yes, I do mean it."

"And what will we do about Mr. Grant?" Constance asks.

Too many questions. Alden looks away but does not let go of her hand.

Mr. Hunt squeezes his eyes shut and crinkles his scarred face. "Oh, poor Gwen." He has figured it out.

They are all silent as the taxi driver continues east. Constance gets the sense that there is something she doesn't know. "What else?"

"Dear God, I have failed in so many ways. If it is any consolation, I have harmed myself more than anyone." She swallows hard. "I must confess that I have married Carling Grant."

She was right. She knew it. She looks to Mr. Hunt and assesses his face. He will not look at her.

They are across the river and getting closer to Patterson House.

Alden says, "I'll fix it."

Constance knows it's not fixable. Everything is his now. Everything.

"I can't have him in charge of me. I won't."

"He won't be. I'll fix it, I promise."

Mr. Hunt directs the driver to turn and then speaks to Alden and Constance. "We're almost there. I suggest we all go in as though nothing has changed. He is unlikely to challenge us when we are all together. We will need each other's help through this, and we will get through it, somehow. Think before you speak. Try not to get into an argument." Constance can't help but feel that caution is directed at her. "We'll behave as if it were a month ago. We'll stick together—three against one. If nothing else, it will throw him off, and we will give ourselves enough time to find out his intentions."

Constance has never heard of a more unlikely scenario. Mr. Hunt is too optimistic. Mr. Grant will not allow them to do anything that sets his gains back.

Alden says, "He took my bedroom."

"I beg your pardon? I don't understand," says Mr. Hunt.

"He took it. He sent me out of it and told me to find another room. What am I supposed to do?"

Mr. Hunt says, "Take it back, of course."

That will never happen, thinks Constance. Mr. Hunt still does not understand what they are up against.

When they stop in front of Patterson House, Alden pays the driver and she and Mr. Hunt give Constance no opportunity to hesitate. They rush her into Patterson House so quickly that she feels as though her feet hardly touch the ground.

Inside, Constance begins to understand the gravity of what has happened. Papers are scattered down the stairs and into the foyer, as though they have been thrown there. Constance watches Mr. Hunt and Alden exchange glances. Exhaustion is getting the better of her, though, and she cannot bear to ask questions. Alden calls out several times for Mr. Grant and there is no answer.

Mr. Hunt says, "I'll look for him. Find Constance something to eat."

"I'm too tired to eat," she says.

"All right then," says Alden. "Upstairs to a bath and then bed." Alden is speaking to her as though she is a child, and she doesn't mind. Not much. She needs a bath. She is itchy and full of red bites. To her surprise, they go to Alden's room, despite Alden having said that Mr. Grant took it from her. She really is pretending everything is as it was a month ago. Alden says, "You'll use my tub. It's bigger. You'll be more comfortable."

Alden's door is ajar, a great rarity, and when they enter her room, they both come to a stop and look wide-eyed at the chaos. The room has been ransacked, the bed is unmade, and the smell of whisky lingers.

Alden holds the door frame.

"Alden, what happened?"

She cannot answer.

Constance approaches her carefully. "Did he hurt you?"

Alden nods. Constance is shocked to see tears forming in Alden's eyes. Her own problems are instantly forgotten, as is any anger she harboured toward Alden. She has never seen her so vulnerable and has never wanted to help anyone more, not even Gwen.

Alden straightens up, wipes her eyes, and pulls away from Constance's concern. "Let's worry about you now." She closes the bedroom door behind them and locks it. "I'm certain I have the only key. He'll have to break it down if he wants to get in here."

Judging by the state of the room, he would be quite capable of doing so.

Constance takes a chair and shoves it under the handle as she has done before. Alden nods. "Good idea," and ushers her into the bathroom where Constance leans against the sink and looks in the mirror, something she has not done for weeks. Her nose is red, her skin is dull and dirty, and she has dark circles under her eyes. Her hair—well, she never got a chance, really, to see her hair after Gwen cut it and it has been a few weeks now. It's not very good for a boy or a girl. She scratches at her head. She is so tired that her bones ache. She has heard old people say that. Do Alden's bones ache too? She's very thin. Her shoulders are sharp beneath her shirtwaist.

Constance looks back into the bedroom. She will never learn what happened in this room—Alden will never say. Of that she is certain.

Why is it that women will not speak of the wrongs against them? Even in the Reformatory. Such silence does not serve any of them. They should shout what happens to them to the moon. No, not to the moon. The moon can't hear them. To the doctor? But look at what the doctor at Mercer did. Who is there to shout to? To the police? Would the police help? The police didn't help her or Gwen. She has realized that even the laws are against them.

They could, at the very least, tell each other.

But instead of telling anyone else or even talking to each other, a wordless form of communication takes over. The girls at Mercer demonstrated their understanding by performing small acts of kindness, the only size available in that hellish place. Perhaps one girl might offer another a bit of her bread or brush another girl's hair. But the girls who needed such kindness the most, girls like Gwen, girls who flinched at the slightest touch or raised voice or loud noise, girls who shrank from the attendants like horses from the whip, were siphoned off to somewhere else. She cannot know what Gwen has been through but imagines it is worse than what she has experienced. It eats away at her.

Alden is doing much the same thing, trying to communicate with acts of kindness. She never stops moving. "Let me scrub the tub first," she says, getting on her hands and knees and reaching under the sink for some scouring powder and a cloth.

"I'll do that."

"No. You sit." Constance tips the lid of the toilet down and obeys. Alden makes quick work of it, and says, "God knows if that man used it or not, but just in case."

When she is done scrubbing and the tub is rinsed, she fills it with hot water and moves on to the sink. There won't be a speck of Mr. Carling Grant left by the time Alden is through. She collects his shaving cream and brush and razor with two fingers and drops them in the waste basket and sets it out the door. Then she pours some Epsom salts into the bathwater and swishes it around with her hand. "It will help." Finally, she takes a fresh towel out of the cupboard and lays it over the rack.

"Alden," Constance says, and waits for Alden to look at her. "Thank you for coming to find me."

Alden says, "I'm so sorry it took so long."

"Don't be sorry. You have been good to me. As good as any mother could be." The words have come out of her before she even knew she was going to say them.

Alden's eyes brim with tears. She tries to speak but cannot.

They hear Mr. Hunt knock gently on the bedroom door.

"I'll get that. You get into the bath while it's hot," says Alden and closes the bathroom door behind her.

Constance strips away her clothes and lowers herself into the steaming water. It is the first time she has been truly alone in weeks, but she doesn't trust it. She gets out of the bath and listens at the door and checks to see if there is a lock. There is not. Alden calls out to her from the other room. "He's not here. Don't worry. No one will bother you." It is as though Alden is reading her mind. She hears Alden's bedroom door close again and settles into the water.

*

Alden steps into the hallway and closes her bedroom door behind her.

"You're sure he's not here?"

John nods. "Gone. So is his coat and hat and his valise. But there are still a few clothes in his closet. It is hard to tell if he'll be back." He nods toward her bedroom, which he saw when she opened the door. "Downstairs looks much the same. Let me help you clean up. I suspect he's taken a few things with him—things that are easy to sell."

Alden wants very much to cry, but she will not. "Yes, my jewellery is probably gone." Not that she ever wore it anyway. All of it had been her mother's or the first Mrs. Patterson's. No one has ever given her a piece of jewellery meant for her.

"It won't take long if we all work together."

"No, we can do this later. Let's give Constance some privacy. I'll go up to her room and get some clothes for her and meet you in the kitchen."

Her legs ache on the stairs. In Constance's room, she finds pajamas and a robe and slippers. When she goes back to her own bedroom to drop them off, she calls out to her softly from the other side of the bathroom door. "He's not here. Don't worry. I've left some clothes for you outside the door here. Mr. Hunt and I are in the kitchen. Take your time."

Constance responds from behind the door with a quiet, "Thank you."

In the kitchen, everything appears normal except bread has been left out to get stale and there are crumbs across the counter and a few dirty dishes in the sink. Alden sits, and John moves about the kitchen. He wipes up crumbs, puts the kettle on, and slices the rest of the bread. He looks around in the cupboards for something as the water boils and the bread toasts.

"If it's jam you're after, we're all out."

"What's this doing here?" he asks, picking up an opened jar of his lily-of-the-valley salve.

"I have no idea," says Alden.

"Surely, no one has been eating it." They both realize that it must have been Mr. Grant. That man truly will eat anything.

"He must have found it in the cellar."

"Good heavens. It's poisonous," says John.

Alden almost laughs, but John is genuinely alarmed.

"Surely not just that wee bit," she says, looking at what is missing from the jar.

"No, probably not," he says with no certainty whatsoever.

Alden knows she would never be so lucky.

John asks, "Alden, is there something you are not telling me?"

Plenty. She will take most of it to the grave. Instead, she says, "You know, there was a moment last night when he was drunk and unsteady on the stairs. I could have pushed him. All day long I have wondered why I didn't."

John looks at the jar of salve again and tightens the lid. "Because that is not you, Alden."

"Isn't it?" She folds her hands on the kitchen table and rests her head on them, an action she would surely scold Constance for if she were to do it.

She is truly out of options. She and John could talk through to the next morning and it wouldn't change a thing. That man has every right to enter his own house. They cannot involve the police; what he has done is not criminal. Nothing he has taken is stolen.

She feels John place the teapot and cups gently on the table, hears the tinkle of the spoons, smells the toast, hears him scrape butter across the surface. When he sets the plate down before her, she raises her head and says, "Thank you."

"I'll take a plate up," he says.

"No. Leave her be. She will come down."

She could sleep here, her head on the table. The table top is cool, and she is so tired. She has been up more than twenty-four hours and has hardly eaten a thing. In that time, her life has been ruined. A life she already considered ruined has been ruined. How she wishes she could go back in time.

*

At some point, don't we all wish we could go back in time? If I could do it all over again, I would do things differently. I would be a better man.

Or would I?

In truth, I would probably make the same mistakes. Who wouldn't? Only if I knew then what I know now would I be able to change. But I did not. I could not.

Even so, it's a matter of character, is it not? I was grasping and greedy. I wanted to be among the powerful, to shape the events around me, to be known and recognized.

I'm still the same. I'm still trying to be heard and felt in Patterson House. I crave the greenish glow. I'm still trying to manipulate people and events. I have not changed at all. Perhaps that is why I am still here.

I never thought for a moment about the men I swindled, never thought that maybe they had wives and children. I never thought about it until this very second.

But I never stooped so low as to swindle a woman, though.

Or did I? I stole the virtue of more than one young girl. Does that count? Yes, it does. I think it does.

As for the bastard, I can guess where he is. He's out on a tear. He's got cash in his pocket and will have more tomorrow once he pawns the jewellery. He has already sold the clock from the mantel, the one I gave Agnes, the one with the exposed gears with delicate flowers painted on the clock face that sat under a glass dome. Agnes said it reminded her of a ballerina. She loved that clock.

The barometer is gone too, as are two pairs of binoculars. A man from the track came over and he has them now.

Perhaps he will leave a string of unpaid bills behind him at the King Edward Hotel, at several drinking establishments, and at a men's haberdashery. Perhaps, outside of Patterson House, he will go by several names. Who can know? One thing is certain though: greedy to the core, he won't be gone entirely until the house and everything in it has been turned into cash and spent.

*

In the morning, Alden wakes and remembers Constance is curled up on a mattress they made up on the floor beside her bed. Alden didn't want her in the cold upstairs. That man could return at any time. Best to stick together. Perhaps they were both afraid to be alone. And Constance refused to take Alden's bed. They are falling over each other to be kind.

Alden dresses swiftly and silently, creeps to the door, and opens it to find John asleep in a chair on the other side. It appears they were all concerned about what might happen in the night. Safety in numbers. Three against one.

She taps his shoulder. He wakes and nods, unfolds himself from his chair, and they make their way to the kitchen.

They spend their time in the kitchen wordlessly, making and eating breakfast and drinking tea. They do not discuss Mr. Carling Grant. They make no plans. They understand each other. They do not need to speak. Not yet.

When they hear Constance stirring, they look at each other and smile as if to say, "Now the talking will begin."

Constance arrives in the kitchen, still in her nightclothes.

"Sorry, I didn't go upstairs for my clothes yet."

"Not to worry." John reaches to touch Alden's arm, a gesture that Alden recognizes as a request for restraint, but no scolding will come from her. She brushes him off and motions Constance to the table. "Sit down. Mr. Hunt and I have started without you. I'll warm the porridge."

"Good morning, dear," says John. "I hope you slept well."

After serving Constance some breakfast, Alden fills the teapot again and takes a couple of deep breaths, preparing herself for her next words. "Now that we're all here, I have a few things to say. Firstly, I have missed you both and am so grateful you are back.

"Secondly, I have made terrible mistakes. You know most of them. One you may not know is that I should have sold Patterson House long ago, and certainly before that man came." His name is too hard to use. "I was ready. I should have kept with my plan and turned him away instead of thinking that he would offer some sort of reprieve. There is no reprieve in this house. It is stuck in the past and has left me mired there too." A stiff wind knocks the branches of the closest beech tree against the east windows.

"Times are not getting better." Her spoon clinks against her saucer. "We are tighter for money than ever before. Mr. Grant has none, by the way. He cannot save us, nor would he if he had the chance. He is our adversary in every possible way."

"Are you going to sell now?" asks John.

"I won't be able to, will I? I've missed my chance."

"What do you mean?"

Constance answers. "Patterson House isn't hers anymore."

He appears mystified. He is so naïve.

"It became his when they married," Constance explains.

Alden is surprised that Constance understands, then Constance adds, "The same thing happened to Mrs. Hughes."

Constance is more world-wise than she had understood. They are three adults at the table now. Three weary adults.

"I've made my bed. Now I must lie in it." With these words, Alden can no longer bear to look at them and turns her face to the sideboard. "I've been to Father Henry. There's no undoing it."

"But surely there is something that can be done." Mr. Hunt's optimism could become irritating.

Alden cuts him off. "There is nothing." And with this admission, a few tears escape.

John pats her arm again, his new expression of solidarity. It is almost intolerable, his willingness to forgive and forget. She uses her apron to dry her eyes.

Constance remains silent, but not unmoved.

"I've made a mess of everything."

"We'll sort it out."

"I know you mean well, John, but this is the time to face the truth in the cold light of day. Any possibilities that were open to me before are closed now. I can no longer make my own decisions. However, you two can. You are not constrained by what I have done. I want you both to know, I will understand if you leave. I am a prisoner here. You are not."

Constance shakes her head with annoyance. "Don't be ridiculous, Alden. No one is a prisoner here. No one. If anyone knows what it is like to be a prisoner, it's me."

Of course, she is correct. Alden understands that the events of the past few weeks have changed Constance. She has become an adult, careful and wary. Never again will she see the wild girl running down the streets with her socks around her ankles, off to play with Gwen. As the grief of this loss enters her, Constance says, "I might as well tell you now. I will not stay."

The words seem to make the air solid. Alden finds it hard to breathe. It is what she offered, what she expected, but it still comes as a blow. The tears rise again.

John breaks the silence. "Must you?"

"Don't make her feel bad."

"I've made promises to Gwen." She uncrosses her arms and lays her hands on the table as though showing her hand at cribbage. "I am grateful for everything you have done, Alden, truly. I don't leave in anger. Not at all. Not like before. I know you have said Gwen can live here, but I've thought it over and how can she live here with Gerald Hughes just a few doors down? How can I stay here with Mr. Grant?"

"I know," says Alden, nodding her head.

"I'll help you however I can until he comes back. But once he's back, I have to go."

"There's no changing your mind?" Mr. Hunt's fingers are interlaced on the edge of the table, his brow creased.

"John," she cautions, "she needs to go out in the world and discover herself. It is what I never did. If I could do it all over again," she sighs. The sentence is never finished. Directing her attention to Constance, she says, "I will help you. I've been thinking. You told me to sell things before and you were right. That man stole your savings. I'll make sure you leave with a little nest egg."

Constance interjects. "How will you get away with it? He knows what's here. I bet he's practically taken an inventory."

"I know, but I have a plan." Alden explains that she has decided to sell all the Jacques & Hay furniture. "It's still worth something. I know he will be furious, but the scale of the disruption will hide some of the smaller changes from his eye." There is a certain genius to her scheme, and she is pleased with herself. He will not be able to account for any smaller missing items, at least not right away. She will turn some of the money over to him (certainly not all of it) and claim that she needed the rest for housekeeping and to pay bills. "If he is angry, I will tell him that if he wants to manage the household, I would happily turn those tasks over to him. Meanwhile, everyone must eat, and bills need to be paid. Simple."

Constance and Mr. Hunt look skeptical.

"Can you think of anything better?"

Neither make any suggestions.

"If we're lucky, we will raise enough for you to rent a decent apartment. One with hot water. Something that you and Gwen can share. When you get work, you will be able to manage. And I'll speak to the lawyers and see if they have any ideas. Maybe they have work for you. Something in the office. You could train. I'll call an estate agent today and set up an appointment. Keep your fingers crossed that we get it done before that man comes back."

"He might never come back," says John, ever the optimist.

"We can't count on that."

Constance is shaking her head. "If you can do that for me, Alden, why not do it for yourself too?"

What is the girl saying? "Leave everything behind?"

"Yes," says Constance without even blinking. "You're not a prisoner. And as you said, it's not yours anymore anyway. Leave with me."

Leave it all. Is it even possible? A lightness enters her. She rises from the table and paces the kitchen. "You are right. What am I supposed to do? Wait for him to come back and serve him dinner? Live like a scullery maid?"

"Don't do anything rash," says John.

"John, I know this decision affects you too. There is a lot to consider. I don't know how we got so lucky last night to have the house to ourselves. But we can't count on him simply disappearing, can we?"

Constance brightens. "We should call a locksmith. Change the locks. At least then, when he comes back, he won't be able to walk right in. We'll know."

"Good idea. We'll keep the doors locked and try to make sure one of us is always here. But not Constance. Not alone."

Constance tries to object, and Alden waves her hands. "He could have you arrested again, and I won't have that."

"If I shouldn't be alone, Alden shouldn't be alone either," says Constance.

Alden reddens. She does not want to admit that Constance is right.

"I agree," says John. "But what if he comes back and I am alone, and he throws me out?"

"I don't know. Dodder away at packing until I get back. But you have raised an excellent point. What will we do if he demands that you leave?"

The three of them look to each other, waiting for one of them to come up with an idea. Finally, John says, "We can't solve every problem right now."

"Right you are. John, you arrange for the locksmith. We won't worry about things that haven't happened. Constance, as soon as you finish your breakfast, we'll go to see Mrs. Hughes."

"Maybe you should call first," suggests John.

His natural caution is a threat to her newfound determination. She must find the strength to urge the others forward. As she has always done. "No. The sooner the better. We'll finish our tea and be off. Besides, they have no telephone. And it's after nine o'clock already. Half the day is gone." She offers Constance some sugar. "Go ahead. I'm not saving it for that man anymore. One more thing. This afternoon, I'd like to ask the doctor to check on you."

"No, please—" Constance looks like she is about to bolt.

"I don't know what happened to you at that awful place, but I want you checked out."

John interjects. "I concur, completely. I heard you coughing all night, and," he hesitates, "I'm not sure how to say this politely, but I think you have lice."

Constance scratches her head and looks at her nails.

"Dear God," says Alden again. "I wish you told me yesterday." Her own hands float to her head and she fidgets with her hair. "Go put a cap on until we can get to the pharmacy. We'll do all the laundry and change the bedding and towels. We'll dry everything outside and freeze them to death in the cold."

Constance grimaces.

"Look at the bright side. With your hair this short, it won't take long to go through."

"I just—"

"Go get a cap."

"I've got one I can sacrifice," says John. "Excuse me." He leaves them at the kitchen table while he goes in search. Everyone is better with small tasks, things they can accomplish. She must remember this.

Once John is upstairs, Constance says, "About the doctor." She scratches again. "A doctor examined—I guess that's what it was—all of us."

"What kind of examination?"

Constance flushes a deep pink, looks down, and scratches some more. Alden does not make her finish. She can't bear to hear it. "I understand. Fine. We will wait and see how the cough goes and revisit in a few days. As Mr. Hunt says, we can't solve every problem today. Let's just pray Mr. Grant stays away a little while longer."

When John returns with a flat cap, Constance pops it on her head.

"There's another matter," he says. "The Lozier. Did Constance tell you?"

"Don't tell me he's stolen that too," says Alden.

Constance's eyes widen. "Oh no. The paper. It's in my jacket pocket. The one I had on when I was arrested. I never got it back."

"What are we talking about?" asks Alden.

"I had a buyer for the Lozier." John says. "At least, we shook hands. He said he'd be around before Christmas. I didn't tell you in case it fell through. I didn't want to disappoint. But when Constance came to the hospital, I asked her to let you know to be on the lookout for his call. I think I can track him down, even without the paper. I remember his name."

Alden can hardly believe it. "You sold it? How much?"

"Four hundred."

"Four hundred? Four hundred dollars?" She shakes her head and holds the edge of the table. Four hundred dollars could have made all the difference. It is as though her chest has been crushed.

"Have I done something wrong?" he asks.

Alden rises unsteadily and leaves the room.

In the blue parlour, she stares at the portrait of William Patterson, her face and ears hot.

Constance comes in a minute later. "What's the matter? Isn't this good news? I thought you wanted to sell it?"

Alden's hands grip the edge of the mantel. "I made decisions without knowing. I made decisions because I was out of money."

Constance considers what Alden has said, leans against the back of a chair, and thinks. "He had no way of knowing what you were going to do, did he?"

Alden shakes her head.

"You know, I told him once I thought you would marry Mr. Grant and he brushed the idea off. Not only did he brush it off, he said that the two of you had a kind of 'understanding.'"

Alden realizes she is being scolded and looks at her. "He did?"

"He's beside himself in there thinking he let you down somehow. You can't blame him. He was doing his best. If anyone owes anyone an apology, you owe one to him."

"I have given it."

"Give it again. We've only got each other, and there's been enough trouble to go around already without adding any more. Mr. Hunt doesn't deserve any of this. And besides," she continues, "the car isn't sold yet, is it? He was right not to get your hopes up. If you had been waiting for that money, you'd still be waiting. The buyer may never come back."

"You're right." Alden assesses Constance again. She is, indeed, an adult now.

*

As Constance and Alden walk toward Gwen's house, Constance coughs and coughs. The cold air seems to bring it on. Alden looks at her with concern and she holds up her hand and says, "No doctor," between gasps.

"Mustard plaster tonight then. We'll dig into Mr. Hunt's remedies. And we'll get some gasoline for the lice."

One thing Constance can say about Alden is that she is not squeamish. Constance has never been more grateful that Alden doesn't need to discuss a thing to death. She hasn't forced her into some excruciating explanation of the humiliation she endured at the hands of the doctor or forced her to tell her anything at all about Mercer. There's always a task to do. Dishes to wash. An errand to run. And there is something soothing about digging into household tasks; it shores her up, somehow.

When she is idle, she replays the day they were sent to the doctor; it tumbles over and over in her mind. It's even in her dreams. She can't seem to shake it. All the girls were frightened. Scared to death. But they all waited quietly together in line and did what they were told. She wanted to take hold of Gwen's hand and run but did not. Instead, they stood there in their old-fashioned, raggedy dresses, and for some reason she still cannot explain, they were obedient. Docile. It is this obedience that mystifies her. How could she not get past her own fear and act to protect herself? How could all of them not get past their fears, band together, swarm the attendants, and free themselves? She had wanted to run from the police station when they had the chance, but Gwen had put her off. She should have trusted her own instincts.

The attendant showed them what to do before the first girl went behind the curtain. Remove your clothes and undergarments, get on the table, slide your bottom to the end, put your feet in the stirrups, and spread your knees. A few of the older girls had been through this before. You could tell by the looks on their faces. False bravado and, sometimes, dread.

Constance could not imagine what was about to happen, and once it happened, she had no way to explain it. Not really. Why on earth was *that* necessary?

There was talk of a procedure, dark talk whispered late at night between the cells. It would happen after Christmas.

When Constance joined the other girls again, Gwen was missing.

"Where's Gwen?" she whispered to one of the older girls.

"They take the ones out who have syphilis," as though syphilis were a word one said every day.

"Take them where?"

Another girl said, "Your friend—she's in the family way. They take them too."

The family way? The expression revolted Constance.

As they approach the Hugheses' front door, Alden says, "It is possible that Mrs. Hughes does not know where Gwen is. I did not know where you were. It is possible she knows nothing at all. It could be Mr. Hughes behind all of this."

Constance considers this and nods. It is possible.

Constance and Alden knock on Gwen's door. There is movement inside, but no one answers. The baby cries. They knock again. Mrs. Hughes speaks to them from behind the door.

"It's not a good time, I'm sorry. The baby is fussy, and I'm not quite dressed yet."

Constance persists. "Mrs. Hughes, we know where Gwen is. You told me to tell you if I knew anything."

The door opens, and Mrs. Hughes is holding the baby, fully dressed after all. "I know where she is too," she hisses, surprising them both. "And I'll thank you to keep your voices down."

"If you know where she is, you also know we have to get her out of there," says Constance.

"Absolutely not. She's not coming back here. I won't have it."

This is not the Mrs. Hughes Constance knows. Something has happened to her. Gerald is what happened to her.

Alden says, "She doesn't have to come back here. I can take her. But I can't get her out without your help."

Mrs. Hughes hisses again. "So the whole world can know she's ruined?"

Constance bursts. "She's not ruined. She's the same as she always was."

Mrs. Hughes raises her nose in the air and shifts the baby in her arms. "I expected better of you girls." Her lips quiver and she looks a little more like her old self. "Constance, how you could have let her get into this kind of trouble, I'll never know."

"Me?" Constance blurts. "It should be Mr. Hughes who is locked up, not Gwen."

"Why should Gerald be locked up?" Even as she says the words, her face disassembles for an instant. She understands.

Alden holds up her hand. "Constance, go back to Patterson House." When Constance opens her mouth to speak again, Alden interjects. "Please. I'll discuss this with Mrs. Hughes. Alone."

She should not have blurted that out. It was a mistake. Yet, despite Alden's warning stare, Constance puts her hands together, pleading. "Gwen needs you. She needs all of us. You can't leave her there. You wouldn't if you knew what it was like."

Mrs. Hughes does not respond. It is as though she has not heard. Alden gestures at Constance to send her back to Patterson House. Constance must trust Alden. "Please," she says to Mrs. Hughes. "Listen to Alden."

*

Later that afternoon in Alden's bedroom, after the conversation about Gwen and Mrs. Hughes is exhausted, after Alden has scrubbed Constance's head with gasoline and gone through her hair with a fine-toothed comb, after they have gathered all of the bedding and washed it and hung it outside in the freezing cold, after they have burned the clothes she came back to Patterson House in (an act they both found particularly satisfying), and as they sort through the disaster left behind by "that man," as Alden calls him now, Constance can't help but raise the topic of Mrs. Hughes again. How can Alden be so calm?

"Mrs. Hughes needs time."

"You know who needs our help more? Gwen."

"I know. It's urgent. I am frustrated too. But my hands are tied. The matron was correct. I have no right to take her. I try to think about it from Mrs. Hughes's perspective. Look what she has just learned. Look at what she has learned about the man she married." Alden stops. "I know a little about that."

"That's different."

"Is it?"

Constance stops arguing. Maybe it is, maybe it isn't. She can't know. And arguing with Alden isn't going to get Gwen out.

They sort some more. Constance hands Alden any papers to do with the bank, and Alden hands Constance anything to do with Patterson House or the boarders. There are so many receipts. Alden is an excellent record-keeper. Constance says, "Here's a repair estimate for the chimney."

"Kitchen or blue parlour?"

"Kitchen."

"Throw it out. I sealed it off instead. Cheaper."

"Right," says Constance, nodding.

Alden sets aside the short stack of papers she's been sorting. "Mrs. Hughes may never believe it, you know. We see what we want to see."

Constance understands. Despite all the signs, Alden did not believe Mr. Grant would bamboozle her.

Alden stands and her knees crack loudly. A stack of books teeters. She steadies it against the slipper chair.

"Do you want to go to Schiffley's with me?" No matter what else is happening, the household chores never stop. It's so normal.

"Sure."

Alden goes down the hall to wake Mr. Hunt from his afternoon nap so he can keep watch for both the locksmith and Carling Grant.

"We won't be gone long," Alden reassures him as they leave.

They walk in silence until they get to Queen Street. Amid the bustle, it is somehow easier to talk. "I don't really need anything. I'm going to tell Mrs. Schiffley that Mr. Grant has left me."

"You are?"

"Yes. I want people to know. And I want to be the one to tell the story. I don't want him doing it, telling people I'm somehow deficient. Who knows what he would say?"

"And what about me? What do people know?"

"As far as I know, nothing. The school thinks you were home to help me. I didn't speak to anyone."

Except Carling Grant, she thinks, but keeps it to herself.

Alden continues. "If people pity me, so what. Pity isn't the worst thing that can happen." Her bravado, although mostly false, reveals a more familiar side of Alden and is as calming as thinking about making dinner.

As they walk, several people greet them with a quick nod or hello. Mrs. Fredrick, whose yard abuts the alley behind Patterson House says, "Oh, Constance dear, I haven't seen you in a while." Then, to Alden she says, "I hear congratulations are in order. How lovely."

Constance is mystified by the comment at first and then remembers. The wedding. Mrs. Fredrick has heard about the wedding. And so has everyone else. No wonder so many people are nodding and smiling at them today.

Alden looks to Constance and then responds, "Thank you, Mrs. Fredrick."

"Mr. Fredrick and I wish you every happiness," she says as she walks on. "We'll be celebrating twenty years this summer. You'll have to come by for tea and tell me all about it." She walks away without demanding any firm plans.

Constance looks up at her and Alden shrugs. "I can't go through this every day. If I tell Mrs. Schiffley, I only have to tell it once."

They enter Schiffley's butcher shop to the familiar smell of sawdust and raw meat. Mrs. Schiffley brings a hatchet down on a side of ribs behind the counter and welcomes them into the shop. "Good to see you, Constance," she says. "You haven't been around much. Heard anything about Gwen?"

Constance averts her eyes and studies the mustards on the shelf behind her, turning her back for a second. "Nothing new." It is not a lie.

"You must miss her," says Mrs. Schiffley. "You've cut your hair. I bet it feels good. You know, we all did during the war. I've never gone back." Short grey curls peek from under her scarf. "Who has time for it?" She snorts. "I think about all the time we ladies waste 'fixing our hair.' It's no wonder we never get anywhere." She whacks another side of ribs with a blow so fierce that the front window of the shop shakes. "You're not in school." It is a question that is phrased like a statement.

"I'm applying for work," says Constance. "Could you let me know if you hear of anything?"

"You and everyone else," she says. But she stops her bustling and looks at Constance and then to Alden. "I tell you what. I've lost my delivery boy for the rest of the season. Broke his leg playing hockey. You want the job? Just until Christmas, mind you. Or till he gets mended. I've promised him he can come back."

Constance looks to Alden for her response. Alden asks, "You wouldn't prefer a boy?"

Mrs. Schiffley looks Constance up and down and says, "She looks pretty capable."

Constance beams and says, "When can I start?"

"Now. I've got a dozen orders to get out this afternoon alone. Christmas. 'Tis the season."

Alden interjects, "Mrs. Schiffley, I need her for the rest of the day. Can she start tomorrow?" Constance gets a whiff of the gasoline smell coming from her hair and thinks it's just as well. Someone is bound to notice.

"Why not? Sure. It'll keep Mr. Schiffley out from underfoot this afternoon. Come at noon tomorrow. Last delivery is out by four and you can go home straight from it. You can sweep up and help around here if there's nothing to do. It's not much. But tips, if you get any, are yours. People tend to be a bit more generous at Christmas. Be friendly. You might be lucky."

She sets the ribs in the glass case at the front and asks Alden, "What'll you have today?"

Alden points at the glass. "The chicken, there, two pounds of stewing beef, and a rasher of bacon, please."

"I'll put it on Mr. Grant's account. I trust everything went well?"

Alden deflects. "Mr. Hunt is back."

"Lovely," says Mrs. Schiffley. "Fit as a fiddle, I hope?"

Alden says, "Yes. It's the oxygen. A miracle."

Constance gives her an encouraging look while Mrs. Schiffley's back is turned.

When three packages wrapped in brown butcher paper tied with string are on the top of the display case, Alden hesitates and Mrs. Schiffley asks, "Anything else?"

"Mrs. Schiffley, you can't put it on Mr. Grant's account. Mr. Grant is gone."

Mrs. Schiffley curses. "Flown the coop? Oh, I knew he was no good." She lifts the counter where it hinges to allow passage to the front of the shop, marches to the door, locks it, and turns the closed sign over. "You come into the kitchen and have a cup of tea with me." When Alden starts to refuse, she says, "I won't take no for an answer." She leads them both behind the counter and through to the kitchen behind the shop.

They sit on mismatched chairs at a scarred wooden table the right size for playing cards. There is no way the whole Schiffley family could fit around it. They must eat upstairs. Mrs. Schiffley lights the stove under the kettle. Alden's old china is stacked neatly in the corner cupboard. Mrs. Schiffley brings down the creamer and sugar, a few cups, and a teapot. Her rough, red hands and big knuckles seem incongruous against the fine bone china. But why shouldn't a hard-working woman like Mrs. Schiffley have nice things?

Mrs. Schiffley appears to take no pleasure in being right about Mr. Grant. Her concern feels utterly genuine. Two tow-headed children burst into the kitchen from upstairs as though they have sensed the arrival of cookies on the table. Mrs. Schiffley hands each of them a shortbread from a tin and says, "Be gone with you both." She yells up the stairs, "Christine, keep your brothers out of my hair. I've got company down here."

How many children does Mrs. Schiffley have? Christine, the oldest, is four years ahead of Constance, maybe five. How many are in between Christine and these younger ones? Five? Six? None were in Constance's class. And all the while, Mrs. Schiffley tends the shop. Alden has always talked about Mrs. Schiffley as though she is only a gossip. There is more to this woman.

"He's a rotter," says Mrs. Schiffley.

Alden's shame crawls up her cheeks. "Everyone told me, Mrs. Schiffley, including Constance here." Constance looks away.

"Hold your head high, my dear. You've done nothing wrong."

Mrs. Schiffley motions to Constance. "Would you like to join Christine upstairs while your mother and I talk?"

"No, Ma'am." Your mother.

"Oh dear, my apologies. Just a slip of the tongue."

Alden says, "No harm done."

A thud comes from above. Mrs. Schiffley laughs and says to Constance, "I can't blame you for not wanting to join them. It's mayhem."

Finally, she takes her blood-stained apron off, throws it over the back of her chair, and sits at the table with a heaving sigh to pour the tea. "I understand. Anyone would. A woman at your stage to have a man interested."

Alden motions to Constance and says, "Mrs. Schiffley, it's bad enough."

"Oh, I'm sorry, dear. So sorry. I meant no harm." The woman is so earnest. She continues. "I remember your poor dear mother, you know. So kind-hearted. She loved children. Mrs. Patterson knew the name of every child in the neighbourhood, I swear it. I'll never forget the day she died. You know, I was in the search party that found you."

"You were?"

"So many of us were, my dear. So many of the neighbours. I was just a girl. Maybe eleven or twelve. When the call came up that you were found, everyone cheered."

Alden's mouth is slightly open and her eyes are as wide as communion hosts. "I didn't know."

Alden has always approached the neighbours as though they are adversaries. They have been her allies all along. That means they are Constance's allies too. The idea cheers her immeasurably. And they will be allies to Gwen too. Even better.

Mrs. Schiffley continues. "I remember before that, just after you were born, we had a little dog that your mother loved. We gave her one of the pups."

"You did?"

"Yes, we did."

"I don't remember a dog."

Constance thinks about the dog in the photograph Alden gave her for her room. Maybe that is the forgotten dog.

"We all worried what would happen to you with only brothers and a father who only knew business."

"My father never spoke of my mother."

"That's a pity. She was lovely. I'll try to remember everything I can," she says. "You come around again, and I'll tell you stories. But for now, I know you've got more urgent business. Your head must be spinning. Is he selling the house out from under you?"

Alden pales. "Oh dear. I guess he could. I hadn't thought of that."

"Oh dear. I should keep my mouth shut. I'm sorry, dear. Nothing's to say he will."

Constance speaks up. "Well, I guess we'll find out soon enough. No use worrying about things before they happen." It's like the new Patterson motto.

"Wise beyond your years, you are," says Mrs. Schiffley.

"This is no time for pride." Alden looks Mrs. Schiffley in the eye and says, "I've no money. None at all. If you would like that second tea set, I'll have Constance bring it over tomorrow. We can trade again."

Mrs. Schiffley says, "That would be fine, dear. I do admire it. I was thinking I'll have it here for Christine. She's sure to be married someday."

"And I've decided to take in women now instead of men. Maybe you can put the word out." Mrs. Schiffley is better than any advertisement.

"Good idea. Men. They're more trouble than they're worth." Mrs. Schiffley winks at Constance, who smiles back at her. "But you wouldn't know about that yet, would you, dear Constance?"

"I'm beginning to figure it out."

There is an urgent knock on the shop door and Mrs. Schiffley says, "I'd better go see what that is."

As the bell over the shop door rings and they hear customers enter, Alden says, "That wasn't so bad, was it? Let's get back to Mr. Hunt." They leave the kitchen and enter the back of the shop and Alden says, "Thank you, Mrs. Schiffley. We'd best be going and we shouldn't keep you from your customers. Constance will be here at noon tomorrow."

She stops them. "Just a minute," she says, and motions them toward the walk-in icebox. The smell of raw meat is overwhelming when the massive door opens. It is no wonder Mrs. Schiffley didn't notice the gasoline smell emanating from Constance when her nose is full of this all day. With Constance holding the door, Mrs. Schiffley swings a side of beef out of her way and reaches up to a Dominion tobacco can on a top shelf and urges Alden to enter. She pulls out a few bills and stuffs them in her hand. "Take it," she says. "Till you get back on your feet. Pay me back later."

Only a few weeks earlier, Alden might have been offended and too proud to accept. Today, she takes her hand and says, "Thank you."

As they leave the icebox and Mrs. Schiffley closes the heavy door, Constance says, "I'll see you tomorrow, Mrs. Schiffley. I won't let you down."

"I know you won't." And then to Alden she says, "Chin up, dear."

Chin up indeed, thinks Constance, as they walk home together. Word will spread now. Alden might be an object of pity, yes, but Mr. Grant will be an object of scorn. Judging by Mrs. Schiffley's reaction, no one will be surprised. Mr. Grant will not have anyone in his corner when he returns.

At dinnertime, they settle around the kitchen table. Alden and Constance have made bacon, eggs, and toast. It's all they can muster, and Mr. Hunt looks delighted. They are together and that is all that matters. No one makes any mention of not eating in the dining room.

A sound at the front door sparks tension. They all listen, but it is nothing.

Constance broaches the topic of school. "I can't go back."

No one challenges her.

She will work for Mrs. Schiffley each afternoon until Christmas and will go to see Gwen every other morning. Alden insists that she be accompanied by either herself or Mr. Hunt. She is afraid they will keep her again without a guardian to protect her. "I can't risk it," she says. The locksmith came while they were at Schiffley's. Alden has an appointment to talk to the lawyer the next day. "Not that he will have any solutions," she says glumly. The morning after that, the estate agent is coming. Everything depends on Mr. Grant staying away just a little longer.

But despite all the new things they must do, Patterson House establishes something almost like a routine again. They discuss each day's events over dinner. Constance moves back to her usual room. Mr. Hunt continues his search for the buyer of the Lozier. Alden's visit to the lawyer is, as she knew it would be, decidedly unhelpful. She can proceed with a divorce, but she will lose everything. And there is no way for them to assume responsibility for Gwen. As an unwed mother, her incarceration at Mercer is entirely justified. The topics they consider over dinner together have certainly changed.

They all try their best to be in a festive spirit with Christmas coming, but it rings hollow. Every day, something happens to remind them that nothing is the same. It takes until Friday evening, but Alden and Constance finally finish tidying up the parlour, replacing the last of the books back on the shelves and standing back to admire their work.

Constance says, "It probably hasn't been this clean in years." It is true. Every surface is polished to gleaming, every shelf is clean. But Alden is not pleased. She is irritated.

Constance says, "What's wrong?"

Alden looks up at William Patterson, picks up a candlestick, and hurls it at the portrait. The candlestick tears the canvas and clatters to the floor. Constance folds her arms over her chest and nods slightly. She asks for no explanation.

Mr. Hunt comes in to investigate the commotion and takes in the scene. Without a word to Alden, he takes the torn canvas down and carries it out of the room. And that is the last of William Patterson.

Alden stands back and looks at her handiwork for a few moments. "It's much better this way, don't you agree?"

The room feels so much bigger without him.

*

Is it much better? I certainly don't think so. And where is that gardener taking me? Not out to the carriage house? Oh, how the mighty have fallen.

But I am not gone, am I? I'm still here. The joke is on Alden.

No. The joke is on me.

The blank space above the mantel goads. I'll never get used to it.

Hubris, as Alden would say. I still have plenty of that.

*

On Sunday, Alden wakes to discover her time has arrived. She sits on the toilet and weeps. Instead of fasting before Communion, she goes to the kitchen and cooks the last of the bacon and makes toast. This has become her favourite meal. She could eat it morning, noon, and night.

Constance and John come in, drawn by the cooking. Constance says, "We're not going to Mass?"

"No." She offers no further explanation. They can think what they want.

Constance, her chin up in defiance, says, "Pfft. If you're not going, I'm not going."

"Do what you want." It comes out sounding like a scold. "What I mean is, you should do what you want. Decide for yourself. Make your own decisions." Alden is unable to bring herself to the point of advising the girl not to go to Mass. Part of her waits for lightning to strike. It does not.

John and Constance look at each other and say nothing.

Constance, a little wary, says, "Are you all right, Alden?"

"Never better." After breakfast, she announces she is going for a walk.

She sees the two of them look at each other again but ignores them.

A walk is much better than Mass. The air is cold and the wind at her back urges her forward. No one has ever told Alden to do what she wants. Her life might have been different if someone had. What does she want? Is it too late to decide? She wants to work, and not just for boarders, although she has become good at keeping a boarding house. She could become good at anything. She's still good at numbers. No one else could have kept Patterson House going for as long as she has. She has balanced the accounts on a tightrope. She has kept every debtor just satisfied enough. That, too, is a skill.

She tries to think bigger, reminds herself she has no money, and then lets herself dream. Just for a minute. If money were no object, she would like to go somewhere. She has no interest in New York or even Paris or London. She has known a city all her life. She still hates crowds. She gazes out at the lake and wants to know what it is like to be in a boat on a vast body of water or to stand alone on a rolling prairie. What does wheat sound like blowing in the wind? Is it like the waves? She wants to look up at mountains, maybe even be on a mountaintop. What would that be like? She would love to see the ocean someday, experience the tides, understand how the waves of the ocean are different from the frothy whitecaps that dance around the shoreline of Lake Ontario on a windy day. She wants to be deep in a forest, an old forest. She has seen pictures of redwoods in California. That would be something. She wants to see bears—and not just in a zoo, trapped. What could be more depressing? She wants to see them doing what they are supposed to do, that is, what they want to do, whatever that is, in the places they are meant to be.

Is she meant to be at Patterson House? Or is it just where she is trapped?

There is something about the lake, the vastness of it, the wildness, that calms her. The vista frees the mind.

At Ashbridge's Bay, she realizes she might get frostbite on her cheeks if she doesn't turn back. She takes the whole journey again in the opposite direction and everything looks different. Approaching Balmy Beach, she wants to keep going, to climb the rocks and walk the shoreline all the way to the bluffs. She doesn't know if it's possible. She has never tried. She has lived here all her life and never tried to get to the bluffs. She has energy to burn. It is the energy of desire too long suppressed.

But the spectre of that man returning brings her back to her troubles. Even when he is not there, he dictates her choices. This cannot stand. The question she has asked herself a thousand times returns to her. "How could I have been such a fool?"

Back at Patterson House, everything is the same. He has not returned. She is still safe. She still has time. She goes into the kitchen to make herself tea and opens the window an inch to let in the fresh, cold air.

On Monday, the estate agent comes and takes most of the furniture from the blue parlour, including all the upholstered Jacques & Hay, the étagère, an oak console table with rosewood inlay that Constance polished to gleaming, and many of the china and ceramic display pieces. The last of the Orientalist work goes, as does the Germanic bisque. A bone china figurine of a woman holding an umbrella that Alden figured would fetch a few dollars is left behind. The agent points out a mended break that Alden did not know about. When did that happen? Constance asks if she can keep it, a request that could not have surprised Alden more. "Of course, you can," she said.

Several smaller landscape paintings scattered throughout the house capture the agent's attention, and Alden lets them go with the exception of the renderings of the lake path that show the land as it was. She also sells a third set of china from the dining room. As the sideboard is empty, she sells that too. The agent asks about the chandelier in the foyer. He would take it, but its absence would be another kind of dismantling, and she needs to think about it. He also offers to take the wolves and suggests a sum that Alden thinks is outrageously high, but again, Alden needs to think. It is not a one-time offer. Their absence would be so obvious. Even without the sale of the chandelier and the wolves, she can set Constance up in an apartment and will be fine through until March, maybe even April. She hides money again in the turnip bin downstairs. The Canadian Bank of Turnips, she laughs to herself. She has enough to pay Mrs. Schiffley back and is anxious to do so. She has kept one hundred and forty-two dollars to give to Mr. Grant and will pretend that this is what she received for the furniture, minus immediate bills that needed to be paid. She invents an accounting. He cannot possibly know the difference or the amount she owes everyone. She will not mention anything else that's been sold and hope that he doesn't notice. If he asks about one object or another, she'll say it has been put away until they have an opportunity to rearrange the furniture.

By the end of Monday, they are all exhausted. They stand in the nearly empty blue parlour, which now holds only the built-in bookcases and their books, a few worn area rugs, three unremarkable occasional tables, a small ladderback chair by the phone, and a few paintings on the walls, mostly of birds. Even the absence of William Patterson's portrait is not remarkable amid all the disruption. Or perhaps she is already used to it.

As they discuss how they will reconfigure the rest of the furniture, the sound of footsteps coming up the path puts them all on alert. Constance goes to the window in the foyer, looks through the lace, and says, "It's Father Moore."

Alden sighs deeply and curses under her breath, a little louder than she intended. Perhaps she will become a woman who curses. She will become like the mother of that girl in The Ward. She almost laughs.

John says, "Alden!"

"Don't answer it," she says.

Constance says. "He's already seen me." Father Moore knocks on the door. "You might as well get it over with."

"We'll stay with you," says John.

Alden sighs again, and says, "Constance, go make some tea, will you? Get the shortbread out."

Father Moore is an ancient mass of wrinkles with eyes and a collar. He walks with a cane and waves it to his carriage driver, who goes back to the street. Alden helps him unwrap layers of scarves and coats. Finally, they are down to his cassock and she leads him to the dining room, where there is still a table and chairs.

After the niceties are observed and they are sitting uncomfortably around the table with tea, Father Moore says, "I wonder if I could speak to you alone, my child."

"I've asked Mr. Hunt to stay," she says.

Constance takes her teacup and saucer into the kitchen and closes the pass-through door behind her, leaving them alone, but Alden assumes she is eavesdropping on the other side.

He doesn't waste any time. "You haven't been to Mass in two Sundays," he says.

"No, I haven't."

"Not since your marriage to Mr. Grant."

"That is correct."

"Father Henry told me you went to see him the next morning and asked for an annulment."

"Yes, I did."

The priest brings the palms of his hands together. They probably teach them to do that in the seminary.

"I would be happy to counsel you both."

"That won't be possible."

"Why not?"

She gestures around her and spreads her hands wide. "Because he is gone, Father."

"I beg your pardon?"

"After I saw Father Henry, when I got back to Patterson House, he was gone. He has not returned."

John interjects. "He took jewellery, things he could sell for cash. He is gone."

"I don't understand," says the priest.

You would think someone who deals with sin every day would be quicker.

"Father Moore, as I explained to Father Henry, he married me because he wanted my money. He learned on our wedding night that I have none."

"None?"

"Nothing. The house is mortgaged. Twice. I owe everyone money. The taxes are overdue."

"I see." His hands shake as he lays one over the other on the table.

"He did not want me, Father. There is nothing here for him. He is gone." She takes a sip of her tea and sets the cup back down in the saucer. Her eyes are clear and dry. If Father Moore expects emotion, he won't find it here.

John asks, "Is desertion grounds enough for annulment?"

"He may come back."

"I doubt it," says Alden. "How long must I wait?"

Father Henry closes his eyes and says, "There is no simple answer to that. Desertion alone is not grounds for annulment. If there are other circumstances, there may be a case."

"Have I not just laid out the circumstances?" Her voice has risen.

John taps his spoon against his teacup. A warning.

She lowers her voice. "I am assuming he will not return. In the meantime, I will take care of myself, as I always have. And not just myself. Mr. Hunt has returned to us from hospital."

"And Constance too, I see."

"Yes, Constance too."

"You need your faith now, my child."

Alden stands and extends her hand to him. "No, Father. What I need is an annulment. Thank you for coming, Father."

Alden is grateful when John stands too, a sure sign that the encounter is over. Father Moore's face registers confusion under the wrinkles, but he stands and blesses her nonetheless. A habit. Alden receives his blessing in silence.

After the priest leaves, Alden says, "That story will be everywhere by tomorrow."

Constance enters the foyer to join them. "You said yourself that you would rather not be the one to have to tell it over and over."

"Don't worry, Alden," says John. "Hold your head high. You have done nothing wrong."

She cannot meet his eyes. Mrs. Schiffley said the same thing in almost the same words. If only it were true. Only she knows how dark her heart is.

*

Just before noon on Christmas Eve, after Constance has left to do the last of the deliveries for Schiffley's, Alden and John are in the kitchen eating a light lunch. Cold chicken still on the bone and a few leftover vegetables with some bread and butter. It is a relief not to have to make a fuss. John is just pointing out the chickadees in the shrubbery outside the window, all knit-up, their feathers ruffled and puffed to protect them from the cold, when they hear someone try the front door. They both startle and look to each other. Carling Grant. A pounding knock rings through the house.

"It's him," says John, unnecessarily. Alden's heart pounds in her chest and she feels the same way she did when she was cowering in John's bedroom. She reminds herself that she will not be laid low by this wreck of a man.

"Let's go." They rise together and go to the front door.

As Alden opens the door, Mr. Grant is already talking, "What the devil?" When he sees John behind Alden, he is momentarily silenced.

"Ah, Mr. Grant. You're back," says Alden evenly. He is wearing a new suit. "As you can see, Mr. Hunt has returned to Patterson House as well." She is grateful that Constance is out at work and says nothing about her. The less he knows, the better.

"Hunt," he says, acknowledging him.

They are cagey with each other.

"I have some business to attend to," he says to Alden. "Afterwards, I will be leaving again."

"For how long?" Alden asks.

He does not answer but hangs his coat in the closet and goes toward the blue parlour, stops at the door, and explodes with anger. "What is going on here?" He smashes his fist against the door frame and Alden performs the monologue she has rehearsed so many times in her head.

"Mr. Grant. You left the day after our marriage without so much as a note. You know that Patterson House is out of funds. You made it clear to me that you have no money and that you will be unable to provide." Mr. Grant is not the slightest bit embarrassed by her announcement of the facts in front of Mr. Hunt. His attitude is one of impatience. "I did what I thought was best. I made decisions. I needed money. I sold some belongings. We all have to eat."

"How much did you get?" The crassness of the question does not surprise her.

Alden goes into the blue parlour and reaches into a small drawer in the built-in bookcases where she has kept the cash she set aside for him in an envelope, if he ever came back. She hands it to him. He looks inside and riffles through the bills. "That can't be all of it."

"There was more. I paid bills, paid the grocer, the milkman, the butcher. I gave enough to the bank to hold them off. Perhaps you would like an accounting." She goes back to the drawer and hands him another page. He appears to be calculating.

"I have not paid the taxes," she adds. She goes back in the drawer one last time and takes out the latest overdue notice and hands it to him in its open envelope.

"You did this without my approval."

"As I said, what else was I supposed to do? You were gone. I'll need money from that for housekeeping."

He is disgusted, folds the bills into his vest pocket and throws the tax envelope on the floor. He finally notices the blank spot over the fireplace and his eyes widen.

"An unfortunate accident," she says.

He looks at his watch, and as he does so, there is a knock at the door.

"I have no time for this now. My appointment is here. Answer the door."

They look at each other. Neither she nor John is interested in playing butler for Mr. Carling Grant. But John shrugs and pulls his balaclava out of his pocket, and Mr. Grant says, "Not you, for God's sake. Alden. You open the door." He closes the doors to the blue parlour, hiding its emptiness from his visitor. Alden does not move.

Mr. Grant must open the door himself, and when he does, his demeanour transforms to that of a charismatic and charming host. Alden watches him in fascination and, for a moment, forgives herself for being taken in by him. He could sell water to a drowning man. His hand is extended, and he smiles broadly.

Mr. Hunt, however, looks stricken. His hand goes to his forehead as though he has a headache.

"Hello, Mr. Martindale," says Mr. Grant. "This is my—wife," he says, tripping over the words as he gestures to Alden, "and I believe you know Mr. Hunt."

"Yes, indeed." The visitor steps forward to shake John's hand, genuinely enthused to see him. "I've come back for the Lozier."

Alden's sharp intake of breath is all that she gives away, but it is enough for Carling Grant to notice. He is gloating. He has won again.

"We'll do our business in the dining room," says Mr. Grant, ushering Mr. Martindale through the doors. To Alden, he says, "Bring us some tea." He stops for a split second, recognizing the absence of the sideboard.

Their visitor waves the suggestion off. "No time for that I'm afraid, but thank you, Mrs. Grant." Alden cringes. It is, she realizes, the very first time anyone has called her by that name. It will be the last too, she vows.

Mr. Grant closes the doors to the dining room behind him, but not before offering a glare that dares either of them to challenge him.

"Come," says John and motions her toward the kitchen.

In the kitchen, Alden leans against the work table. "How did I not imagine this?"

"Think," he says. "We don't have much time."

A low groan escapes her.

"All right. Let's try to talk some reason into him. Maybe we can get him to see his responsibilities."

"You saw how he pocketed all of that money even after I asked for some for housekeeping. I don't think so."

"Do you have a better idea? Get him to stay for lunch."

"You want me to serve that man lunch?"

"Please, Alden. If he leaves right after the sale, he will be gone and so will the money. I need time to think."

They listen as Mr. Grant and the buyer leave the dining room and make their way out the main doors and around Patterson House to the carriage house. John starts getting dishes down to set a place for him at the kitchen table. "Hurry. Set more lunch out. If the food is on the table, he won't walk away from it."

Truer words were never spoken.

Alden turns the oven on and makes up another plate. At best, the chicken will be lukewarm. "It's not much," she says, handing him a jar of pickles. "I don't know why you think he will listen to reason. He won't." She slices a few carrots to add to the pickle tray.

"Add some more bread. Is there any dessert?" he asks, trying to add more bait to the trap.

"Shortbread cookies. That's it. I have a Christmas pudding for tomorrow, but I refuse to let that man have it." A line must be drawn somewhere.

"Cookies are fine," he says, assessing the table. "Put them on the table, too."

By the time they hear the Lozier backfire in the garage, everything is ready. "I have an idea." He looks out the kitchen window and says, "Here he comes. Just go along with me."

John is seated at the table when Mr. Grant comes in, grinning smugly from ear to ear. You would think he had just negotiated the Treaty of Versailles. Alden says as casually as she is able, holding a plate of almost-warm chicken, "We were in the middle of lunch when you arrived. Would you like to join us?

He looks as self-satisfied as Judas. "Why yes, I think I will."

Plates are passed, and Alden says, "Father Moore was here last week. He will be pleased to know you have returned."

Mr. Grant takes in the information she has given him in silence. She wants him to know that his departure and his abdication of his role as provider is known by those outside Patterson House. If there are no secrets, there can be no blackmail.

John adjusts his napkin on his lap and says, "Since you are leaving after lunch, I'd like to settle a matter about the Lozier."

"And what would that be?" says Mr. Grant as though he is addressing a child.

"Alden and I made a deal. She offered me a percentage of the sale of the Lozier in return for fixing it up and finding the buyer."

John has a little larceny in him after all. She brings her napkin to her mouth to hide her smile.

"Yet it is I who have made the final arrangements, isn't it?" Mr. Grant says, dismissing John.

"Twenty percent," says John, unflinching.

"Was there a contract?"

"Of course not. Don't be ridiculous," says Alden. "Mr. Hunt and I have no need for contracts. He has dedicated considerable time to fixing the car and finding a buyer." Something else occurs to her. "I promised to pay for parts too, which he purchased out of his own pocket." She directs her next question to John. "You have kept a list of your expenses?"

"Yes, of course. It's upstairs. I'll get it."

Mr. Grant has already finished two slices of bread, thickly buttered, and is now gnawing on a breast and bit of wing. "It's a bit dry. Is there any sauce?"

Alden can hardly believe he has the nerve to complain. But she says nothing. There is some leftover mustard sauce in the back of the icebox from the fish the night before. That might do it.

He points to the jar of lily-of-the-valley salve still sitting on the counter. "How about some of that?"

Alden does not object. Instead, she gets the mason jar and spoons some of the salve into a small bowl. Her hands shake. Surely this is a sin. She can't do it. She hears John's voice in her head. "That's not who you are." She drops the dish on the floor and it breaks.

"Oh dear," she says.

Mr. Grant rolls his eyes. "Is any of it salvageable?"

Alden says, "I have something else," and takes out the leftover mustard sauce, puts it in a new dish, and serves it to him. She gathers the broken dish and wipes the salve from the floor and sets everything into the sink to take care of later.

He slathers the mustard sauce onto his chicken, nods, loads his fork, and stuffs a bite into his mouth. Then, he talks with his mouth full. "I'll pay Hunt for the parts. That is, *if* I find his bill reasonable. The rest we can sort out in trade. Consider it his rent for the next three months and we're even. I won't be here. It doesn't matter to me if he stays. You two can play house like you always have."

Alden is furious at the implication.

"But he will pay a proper rent once this is paid off." He looks at Alden. "To me. Not to you." He takes another bite and chews loudly.

Alden does not want John to hear her negotiate his presence in Patterson House. "Mr. Hunt has never paid rent at Patterson House. He is not a boarder. He is a family member."

"He's not my family." Mr. Grant slices a pickle, piles it on top of his chicken, and takes another enormous bite. His face reddens. He tries to speak but cannot. Coughing, he spews partially chewed food onto his shirt and jacket. There is mustard sauce on his tie. Alden shakes her head. The man is a heathen. He coughs more and a bit of chicken flies onto the table. Tears stream from his eyes. He grabs for a glass of water but knocks it over.

Alden says, "Good Lord. What now?"

Reaching for his throat, he tries to loosen his collar. Beads of sweat break out on his brow and his eyes are wild.

"He's choking," says John, rushing into the room. "Hit him on the back."

"No," yells Alden. "Don't touch him." She stands and blocks his way.

Carling Grant sputters and spits, his eyes panicked, accusing, looking from one to the other, hands clutching at his collar.

"But, Alden—" John tries to get past her.

"No!" she says again.

Mr. Grant rises and throws himself against the edge of the table, which shoots forward and everything on it spills.

Alden steps back to the kitchen threshold and crosses her arms over her chest.

"Alden!" pleads John.

Mr. Grant has failed to dislodge whatever is stuck in his throat. He throws himself against the table again, but it is no match for his weight and it overturns. Lunch scatters and dishes break.

When he falls to the floor on his hands and knees, John's voice is panicked. "Alden, we have to help him."

Alden goes to him on the floor and kicks him. John pulls her out of the way and drops to his knees, hitting Mr. Grant on the back with surprising force. It does no good. He rolls the man over, which is no small feat. Alden kicks him again and John cries out, "Stop!"

Mr. Grant's lips have the slightest tinge of blue. John reaches his stubby fingers into the man's mouth and removes food, flinging it to the floor. It does not help. He listens for breath, presses into the deep folds of his neck to feel for a pulse, and says, "He's so big. I just don't know." He repeats the whole exercise two more times and then sits on the floor beside him, defeated. "He's gone."

A small sound escapes from Alden. A little "hmph."

John looks up at her, quizzically.

What is she supposed to do? She makes the faintest shrug.

He rises and starts pacing. "Oh dear. We'll have to call someone."

"Yes, I guess we will," Alden says. "Just a minute." She stands over Carling Grant, goes to her knees, checks his pockets, finds the cash she gave him for the furniture and then the payment for the Lozier in his breast pocket. She counts it. Four hundred dollars. Thankfully, it is in cash and not a cheque. She rises, passes by John, and drops the money into the flour bin. "Check his other pockets, will you?"

"I will not!" He scans the disaster and sees the mason jar of salve in the sink with the broken dish. "Alden?"

Alden's face reddens. "Don't look at me like that, John. And no, I didn't. I thought about it, but I didn't. I didn't have to. He choked."

John puts his hands to his throat. "People choke to death every day," he says. "It's not uncommon. A man his size."

She tries to reassure him. "It's all right, John."

"People get run over by cars, drown in bathtubs, set themselves afire in the kitchen, trip and hit their heads. Fall off ladders. It was just an accident." He is creating the version of the story he can live with.

"Yes, it was. That is what happened, John. He choked. On the chicken."

"Probably a bone," he says.

"Yes, probably."

"I tried to save him."

"Yes, you did."

And I did nothing, she thinks.

He looks at her with one side of his forehead raised. "You kicked him," he says.

"Yes, I guess I did."

John leaves the kitchen and she hears him on the phone. Who will come? The police? The doctor? The hearse? It doesn't matter. She looks back and expects Mr. Carling Grant to rise and come after her, but he does not.

*

When Constance returns from Schiffley's, the neighbours are milling about on the sidewalk and the hearse is parked on the street. Her heartbeat quickens, and she runs the rest of the way. She hears someone say, "Oh Lord, here's Constance. Quiet down."

"What happened? Is Mr. Hunt all right?"

"Yes. He's fine. It's the other one. The fat one."

The fat one? Constance grabs onto someone's arm. "Mr. Grant?"

Mrs. Thatcher from two doors up nods her head. "That's him. And the two of them just barely married. A tragedy."

Constance runs around to the kitchen entrance just as the body is being carried out. It's him all right. She stands back, out of the way. His big, round belly sticks up under the shroud, and the two men on either end of the stretcher can barely carry him. They call out to the onlookers, "We need some help here."

She scoots behind them and into the house and finds Alden, who cautions her with a gesture and pursed lips and points at a policeman in the dining room speaking with Mr. Hunt.

"Don't say anything. He choked on a chicken bone."

Did he really? Or is Alden telling her what the story is?

The policeman comes back to the kitchen, sees Constance, and says, "This must be Constance Patterson."

Constance nods.

"Quite a shock. All very upsetting."

Constance says nothing, and Alden puts a reassuring arm around her shoulder.

"We have everything we need, Ma'am," he says to Alden. Someone will call about the arrangements.

"Thank you," she says. Mr. Hunt joins them and they follow the policeman to the front door where he departs, shaking his head. "The day before Christmas. Sad. Again, very sorry for your loss, Ma'am."

After they close the door behind the policeman, Alden goes to the stairs, holds the newel post, and is stationary for a moment before she sits down on the second step.

"What happened?" asks Constance. "When did he get here?"

Mr. Hunt begins. "At lunch. He came back to sell the Lozier. I guess the buyer called at some point and he must have answered it."

"Oh, and he was mad about the furniture. The state of the place." Alden points at the front door. "But his buyer came, and Mr. Hunt thought that we should try to talk to him over lunch, so we asked him to stay."

"And he choked," says Mr. Hunt, cutting the description short.

"On a chicken bone," adds Alden.

Constance slumps down on the floor in front of Alden. It is too much to take in. "He's gone," she says.

"He's gone," repeats Mr. Hunt.

Alden says almost to herself, "You know, I wanted him dead. Maybe it's my fault. I almost pushed him down the stairs the night we were married. I told you that, John. Remember? And I thought about giving him your salve to eat today, but I stopped myself." She looks at Mr. Hunt and repeats, "I stopped myself."

Constance says, "I once thought about putting borax in his dinner. Or bleach. I thought maybe I could poison him with the same stuff that was used on Mary Pickford's sister-in-law."

Mr. Hunt looks from one to the other in amazement.

Constance stands back up again and reaches out her hand to help Alden up. "I don't feel bad. I won't."

In the kitchen, they right the table and sweep up the broken dishes. Constance fills a bucket. Alden shifts the furniture out of Constance's path while she scrubs the floor. Mr. Hunt comes to the threshold and leaves without speaking three times before they hear his footsteps go upstairs.

Constance says, "Is he going to be all right?"

"Well, the man died after all. Right in front of us."

Constance remembers Alden the night she returned to Patterson House leaning against her bedroom door, admitting Mr. Grant had hurt her.

"I won't smile about it in public, but I'm not going to pretend to be sad. Not here. And I'm not wearing black."

"No, me neither."

"Surely Mr. Hunt can see this is for the best," says Constance. She wrings out the cloth and pours the water down the sink while Alden puts the table and chairs where they belong.

When she turns around, Alden hugs her. It is an act so rare and so surprising that Constance starts to weep. She doesn't even know why she's crying.

*

Christmas does not feel special. Constance resigns herself to a holiday that everyone would rather forget about. Mr. Hunt's silence is particularly disconcerting. When he came down in the morning for breakfast, he approached both her and Alden as though they were strangers.

Constance reminded him of the day and he said, "Oh, of course. I forgot," but added no "Merry Christmas" to his greeting.

Alden is in one of her better housedresses and wears an apron with a pattern of pine trees that she saves just for the holiday. She has made scones and surprised them with a jar of raspberry jam she had hidden away for the day. There are three oranges in the centre of the table.

Since they won't be going to Mass, there is no routine to anchor them. Missing Mass is one thing but missing the carol singing is quite another. Something is going to have to help them get through this day.

"Do you think we could visit Gwen this morning? Go wish her a Merry Christmas? And the other girls too?"

"Lovely idea," says Alden.

"There's no streetcar," says Mr. Hunt.

"We'll hire a car," says Alden. "Don't wear your Sunday best though," Alden suggests. "No need to make everyone self-conscious."

Mr. Hunt perks up a bit and says, "I tell you what. I'll bring some candy."

"Good idea," says Alden. "I'll pack up the rest of the shortbread and leftover scones. I should have made a double batch." She gestures to the three oranges and asks, "Would you mind?"

"She can have mine," says Constance.

"She's welcome to mine too," says Mr. Hunt.

"One more thing," says Alden. She goes upstairs and comes down with a delicately crocheted shawl. "We'll give her this. It is so cold every time we go there. It will see her through to the spring when she is due. Then she can use it for the baby. Eminently practical."

That is Alden. Eminently practical. Constance could not be more grateful for it.

*

After their visit, on the way home in the taxi, Alden asks, "Has Gwen thought about what she would like to do—afterwards?"

Constance hasn't shared any of the details of their plans. The future is a secret world they build together, and Constance is not ready to talk about it yet. She does not want to hear about all the flaws in her thinking. Not yet. But Alden is not like that anymore. She says, "We still plan on sharing an apartment."

"I mean about the baby."

"It's all decided. Babies born at Mercer get adopted."

Mr. Hunt asks, "And that's what she wants?"

"It doesn't matter. That's what happens."

"It does matter," Mr. Hunt sputters. "If she wants to keep it, she should be able to keep it."

"She doesn't want to keep it."

Alden nods. "Understandable."

Mr. Hunt appears confused. He is always a step behind them, but Constance doesn't mind.

It has occurred to Constance that her own mother could have felt the same. She will never know, of course. Gwen has made her see how the baby would be a constant reminder. It would be better off with someone else.

The line from *The Kid* returns to her over and over when she thinks of Gwen and when she thinks of her own mother. "The woman—whose sin was motherhood." She can't blame either of them for trying to put the situation behind them. Yet, there is something profoundly wrong. Why is it Gwen's sin? Why is it Gwen who bears the burden of the terrible thing Gerald Hughes did? And not just Gwen. The baby, too. No one knows better than she how the baby might feel as she grows up—that is, if she ever knows.

Mr. Hunt can't let it go. He says, "But—" and Constance interrupts. "It's what she wants."

Alden says, "Best to get past it."

Mr. Hunt's one eyebrow raises. "Get past it? It's a baby!"

Alden and Constance look at each other. Constance has never felt more grown up than she does at this moment. She and Alden share an understanding and she knows it. If Mr. Hunt weren't here, she might say, "Men," and Alden would nod. The cab driver looks back at them through the rear-view mirror. Their trips home from the Reformatory certainly provide a lot of fodder for taxi drivers.

Alden says, "A baby deserves a good home with people who want it. And Gwen shouldn't have to pay for this for the rest of her life. It's not her fault. The girl was raped." They all go quiet at the word. Mr. Hunt looks at his hands. It is the truth, and to hear it said out loud sends a chill through all of them. "A child should never be a punishment." Alden looks at Constance and smiles weakly.

"Besides, it's not our decision. It is Gwen's and she has made it. She has had enough decisions foisted on her already, don't you think?"

Mr. Hunt takes all of this in without comment.

They ride in silence the rest of the way.

When they are back at Patterson House, while they are removing boots and hanging up their coats, Alden says, "As for an apartment and where you want to move, if you haven't made any commitments yet, I wonder, now that Mr. Grant is," she hesitates, "no longer with us"—she hesitates again—"do you think you might stay at Patterson House, at least until Gwen can leave the Reformatory? It's your decision. You're not a child anymore. But I want you to know that I want you to stay. I would like it if you stayed."

Constance nods. "Yes, I can do that. I would like to do that." She feels relief. "But I thought you were going to sell?"

"That's nothing I have to do immediately now."

"Have you changed your mind?" asks Mr. Hunt. He looks relieved. It is obvious he would like to stay.

"Everything that was true before is still true now," says Constance. "The house is too expensive to keep up. And too much work. You'd be better off elsewhere."

Alden leads them toward the kitchen and puts on her apron. Christmas dinner will be duck and roasted potatoes with turnips and carrots and a pudding for dessert. "Let's get started with dinner," she says.

"Don't change the subject," says Constance. Mr. Hunt tries to shush her, but she says to him, "This is important."

Alden sighs and sits at the table. "It is important. But I have time to think about it, and I need to think about it more. There's no pressure. Not immediately, anyway. And I'd like to get you sorted out first. I was thinking, if you want, if you have changed your mind, you can even finish out your school year. You can still go back."

Constance feels too old to go back there. She cannot tolerate the thought of seeing that awful Mary Atkinson and the others again. She cannot face Sister Mary Agnes either. She simply cannot be treated like a child again. The Sisters of St. Joseph have nothing left to teach her.

"No, not back there. But I'd like to improve myself and learn enough to get a good job."

"Very sensible. There's a Baptist Ladies' College. We'll look into it."

Constance can hardly believe it. "You can afford that?"

"Yes."

"And we'll look into getting you out of Patterson House too," says Constance, refusing to let the issue drop.

*

The day after Christmas, Alden is called by the morgue to arrange for Mr. Grant's funeral. But despite Father Moore's repeated calls, she refuses to have a funeral or purchase a plot for him. "He is not grieved here," she says. She wants him buried in a potter's field, but he is not considered destitute, and neither is she, which makes her laugh.

She does the only thing she can think of doing. She has him cremated and resents every cent of the cost.

Father Moore is apoplectic. She does not care. "I'm not even sure he was Catholic, Father."

Weeks later, when she receives the urn with his ashes from the crematorium, they infuriate her. She cannot have them in the house and lugs the urn into the yard and looks around. She is not inclined to scatter them. She doesn't want to think of him everywhere. It would be like a plague upon the yard. Finally, she goes into the carriage house and comes out with a pickaxe. It feels good to slam the axe into the semi-frozen soil, ineffective though her efforts are. The action reverberates into her shoulders and a grunt escapes from her each time the axe hits the ground. Within minutes, she is sweating, frenzied. Her hair is shaken loose from its bun. She throws off her coat and keeps at it.

John and Constance watch through the kitchen window, and when John comes out to stop her, she doesn't break the pace of her swing. He goes to the carriage house and brings back a shovel, but she doesn't want his help. "No. Go back inside. I'll do this myself," she says. When she has dug deep enough, she dumps the ashes into the hole, pushes the displaced dirt back with her boots, and stomps it down.

It is not satisfying.

Her soul cries out for some sort of additional desecration. Perhaps she should have dumped him into a privy. Every part of her is taut with a malignant rage. She wants to scream. He is dead, and yet he still controls her. She cannot go inside and pretend to be calm in front of John and Constance. Instead, she puts her coat back on and walks toward the lake. She walks for hours, and when she is back, darkness has fallen. John and Constance are visible through the kitchen window in a pool of light, cleaning up from dinner. It is only then that the tension in her eases. That man has not taken them from her. He has not ruined her life.

She looks up into the beech trees and takes several deep breaths. Their bare branches reach to each other in the February wind, an almost black sky above them and Patterson House below. She closes her eyes and listens to the branches move.

Her grandfather planted these trees. Or did he? She knows only the myth of him, and realizes she knows nothing at all.

"He's all yours," she says over her shoulder to the grave of William Patterson and takes the empty urn to the alley before she goes in to wash up.

May 15, 1931

GWEN IS DEEP in the Mercer Reformatory, on a thin mattress set upon a table with those terrible stirrups. There is a faded flannel sheet over her legs. The shawl Constance gave her is around her shoulders, as it has been since Christmas. It is a reminder that she is loved, like a hug when she is alone and frightened.

They have called her mother, at least they said they did, but it feels like that was hours ago.

There are no windows in this room. She needs air. She begged them to call Mr. Hunt, but they won't.

Mr. Hunt is a dear. Why couldn't her mother have married him instead of that louse, Gerald. Well, he never asked, for one reason. That was some kind of childish fantasy she had. Constance is so lucky to have him.

Mr. Hunt will know what to do. He always does. He will go talk to her mother for her. He was just visiting yesterday. He said he was concerned that she didn't look well. She didn't feel well either. Indigestion or something. And she's been so puffed up. Her ankles are huge. Her skin feels like it is stretched to the limit, like it could break apart, it's so tight.

Constance has gone back to school and can only visit on weekends. She has been kind of mad at her ever since Constance saw Sister Mary Agnes leaving.

"You'll never guess who I saw on my way in," Constance had said.

"Who?"

"Sister Mary Agnes. From St. Joseph's. She's probably here recruiting. Like Christ needs any more brides."

Gwen's face gave her away. Gwen had told the nun everything. Sister Mary Agnes held her hand and listened. She was so easy to talk to.

"She was here for you?"

Gwen nodded.

"What did she want?"

"I asked her to come."

"What? You're not thinking of joining the convent, are you?"

It is a respectable way to get back to the world. She doesn't want to end up like that horrible Eleonore, in and out of here three times now, living

311

with men and doing *all that* because she needs a roof over her head. Eleonore had her baby two weeks ago and is gone. When she left, she said, "I'll be back," and laughed. Not Gwen. Gwen will never be back. If she becomes a nun, she will never have to worry about anything again. The Sisters of St. Joseph are teachers, but Sister Mary Agnes said that she could be something else if she wanted, even join a different order. She would be of service to others and to God. It all sounded so noble.

Constance dismissed her. "You're not Lillian Gish. Your life isn't a disaster, and this isn't *The White Sister*. I told you, I'll take care of you."

But how can Constance take care of her? She just turned fifteen. And Gwen doesn't want her to. Even though Gwen loves talking with Constance when she is full of her rambling thoughts about the future, what they can do together and where they might go, she knows none of it is real. It's like a novel. Or a movie. It gives her something else to think about, but it's not going to help her once she leaves this place.

A cramp convulses her and she gasps. Fluid oozes from her. Something big. Another baby? But the baby is already gone. Dead, they said. Born too early.

She never wanted it, and now it is gone. She has no right to feel sad, but she does. And she's so tired. Oh, the sweating. She's soaked to the skin. Shivering as if she were caught in the wind and rain by the lake. If only she could get washed. She would feel better.

The cramps. They're awful. They haven't stopped. She has been on this table forever and just wants to stand, get into a bath, and wash off all this sweat and blood. She makes the effort again but is too dizzy. So much blood. She had no idea that having a baby was such a bloody business.

There's Sister Mary Agnes at her bedside, reaching out for her, making the sign of the cross.

Maybe it is her fault that the baby died. Maybe it knew she hated it and it died.

Maybe now that she's not in the family way anymore, her mother will love her again.

Her teeth are chattering. What is happening now? There are a lot of girls around her, all looking at her, all shaking their heads with sadness. She doesn't know any of them, not a one. She doesn't understand. "Who are you?" she says. The head-shaking continues. A few of the girls cry.

There are more and more. The room is full. Where are they coming from? A chorus of girls crying. Hundreds of them. They get smaller and smaller as more and more join them. Hundreds, thousands of crying girls.

Oh, her mother. Here she is. They are on the ferry to the Island. They are like sisters. Everyone says so. Mum's hair blowing all around her in the sunlight, her mouth open, lipstick on, laughing. Her arms around her, squeezing her tight.

*

Alden has just gone to bed when there is a knock at the door. It's past ten. Another woman with a suitcase, or just a purse, or nothing at all. They arrived all winter and then through the spring and now it is almost summer, and they keep coming. All different. All the same.

It is hard to believe that just a few months ago that man (she refuses to say his name, even to herself) was lying dead on her kitchen floor. As John would say, it's best not to dwell on the bad things. And now it is May. Gwen is due in early June. Soon Constance will leave. She tells herself again that it is as it should be. It is right. The breeze shifts the drapes, and the scent of summer is in the air. And skunk. Oh dear. And Lake Ontario. Slightly fishy, but so familiar she must concentrate to smell it. Beneath the noise of a car going by and a few voices on the sidewalk are the waves, a deep breath in, a deep breath out.

The garden is planted. John is hoping for a bumper crop this year. He has thrown himself into the work and promises to have enough produce to put up jars and jars and jars for the winter. They won't have to worry about running out of food, he says. And he hopes they will have enough to send women off with a basket to keep them going. That is his dream.

Constance rushes down the stairs to get the door. She will show the new woman to the kitchen and give her something to eat and a cup of tea. The woman might want to talk, and if not, they'll go upstairs, and Constance will assign her to a bedroom. It might be the first room she has had to herself in her entire life.

How will she manage when Constance leaves? She has found a two-bedroom apartment on Avenue Road with hot water and gets it next month. It is all planned, even though she still hasn't talked Gwen out of joining the convent. Almost finished her term at the Baptist Ladies' College, she is already interviewing for work. A thoroughly modern girl, as Constance likes to say.

As for herself, it will be only a matter of time before she loses the house, and until then, she has decided to let it do as much good as possible.

The voices downstairs are quiet but urgent. Maybe this new woman will stay a few weeks or maybe only a night. Maybe she will wake in the morning and go back to her husband out of regret or shame or fear. If that is the case, nothing anyone can say will persuade her to stay. A woman must make up her own mind.

Sometimes the women pay and sometimes not. Cash is hard to come by in 1931. Sometimes, weeks after a woman leaves, Alden will receive a gift—preserves or a knitted blanket or some clean clothes to pass along to another woman. Every woman does what little she can.

There was a time when Alden would have wanted everyone to know about her charity. Not anymore. Now, all she wants is peace in her home.

Is she performing a penance? Maybe. She knows what her sins are. She sees that man sputtering and choking every time she closes her eyes. If only she could be free of him. Once and for all. Or worse, she feels his hands run along her back. She knows she used him, married him to save herself. She deserves worse than what she got.

Now she listens as women tell her their stories. Listens, nods, understands. She judges no one except herself.

John is a better person than she is. A truly good man. Even though he saw the evidence of her own murderous thoughts, the cravenness of her inaction, the way she took the money from the man's pockets before the authorities came, even though he saw how she tried to look as though she cared that her new husband lay dead on the kitchen floor when the police came, he blames her for nothing. He still treats her as though she is good.

She really should get up to help with the new arrival. There is a squeak and squawk of a little one. The new woman has a child with her. They have turned the blue parlour into a kind of nursery and playroom. It made sense since it was almost empty anyway. There are toys, a playpen, and a tricycle. The very idea of riding a tricycle in the house would have been unheard of when she was a child or when Constance was a child.

Now, it doesn't matter. The floors are ruined. It doesn't matter.

She puts on a robe and leaves her room and looks over the second-floor railing to the foyer. She still can't get used to the space left by the missing chandelier. Then she realizes who is at the door. It is Mrs. Hughes with Judith in her arms.

There is a suitcase on the floor beside her. Ah. She has seen the light.

Constance looks up to Alden. Her face is ashen. She grasps the wall and her knees buckle.

Alden runs down the stairs and takes Judith from Mrs. Hughes.

"What happened?"

Constance answers. "Gwen is dead."

March 2, 1937

JOHN HUNT DOZES in his bedroom. It is stuffed full of all the things he loves. Daffodils are peeking out from a pot by his bed. Spring again. Constance brought them to him. How did he get so lucky?

Frances's daughter, Judith, is playing downstairs. Frances, although she moved back into her own little house after Gerald died, comes over and helps Alden every morning. She lived at Patterson House for three years and, in that time, shared the housework. They became quite a team.

Out the window, there are buds on the trees, although the last of the snow is still melting on the north side of the yard. The asparagus will be sprouting any day now. He can't wait to see that lovely first green, the first green of spring, a green that is gold and full of possibility.

He listens to the birdsong.

Something falls downstairs and Judith starts crying. Just for a minute. If only he had the strength to get down the stairs to soothe her. He could read her a story or take her out in the garden and show her the buds on the trees. Maybe they will think to bring her up to visit. It would be lovely if she were sitting on the end of his bed, chatting away to him.

He has never had his own children, but he has been blessed with children in his life. When he arrived at Patterson House, Constance pulled off his balaclava, patted his face, and laughed. He had been afraid he would spend the rest of his life an object of fear, but Constance was never frightened of him.

Who would have thought that he, John Hunt, would have any girls to love him? And he has had more than one. He's been lucky. So lucky.

Constance brings him plants and flowers and seed catalogues. They look through them together, make notes about what might work where. Constance is smashing in her trousers and jackets and cropped hair. She brought a friend with her a few weeks ago. When she introduced them, she said, "This is Mr. Hunt. He has always been a father to me." Her friend took his hand and held it in hers for a minute and said, "I feel as though I already know you." Her best friend. Her only friend since Gwen. What was her name again? He saw the way Constance looked at her. He knows. And he is glad.

He hears footsteps on the stairs. Alden and Frances. Judith is with them too. His heart is full of gratitude.

The branches outside his window begin to leaf out, as though days pass in only a few seconds. The flowers bud and then, without any time passing at all, they blossom, slowly at first, into a beautiful pink. That's odd. It's a beech tree, not a cherry tree. But there they are, cherry blossoms, right outside his window, a riot of pink against the blue sky. There will be so many cherries this year. Alden will be pleased.

His door opens and William Patterson walks through, sits at his bedside, and takes his hand. "It's time," he says.

"Is it? Can I not see one more season?"

"I'm afraid not."

He tries to raise his head. "What will happen? Where will I go?"

"I cannot say. I do not know."

"Can I stay here? Like you?"

"No, I don't think so. You were always a better man than I."

September 17, 1947

ALDEN IS TOO TIRED. "I should probably see a doctor," she says casually to one of the newest women, Annie, who is helping her in the kitchen this evening. She has lost count of how many women have stayed at Patterson House over the years. She likes Annie, who is efficient and quiet. Her grandmother was a slave. Because of that, she doesn't like the idea of Annie working in the kitchen. It feels wrong. But Annie insists. Alden never needs to tell her what to do. After less than a week, she is quickly becoming indispensable, and Alden will be sad when she goes. But go she will. She must. Like the rest of them. They come. They go.

Constance. Frances too, after Gerald died, and she could finally go home. Alden tried to be happy for her. It wasn't as though she lost Frances forever. She moved only a few houses away. But Alden was bereft. She had never had a friend like Frances before, a woman friend, someone who really understood.

And they did understand each other, bound as they were by guilt and grief. When Gerald died, Alden whispered, "It's all right to feel relieved, Frances," and they clung to each other.

She drops a knife on the floor and it clatters. Annie picks it up and rewashes it, a look of concern on her face.

At least John didn't live to see the start of the war. As if the first one weren't enough. Another generation gone. It simply would have been too much for him to bear.

There are footsteps overhead. The house is full today. Even the third-floor rooms are in use. Children giggle and run down the back stairs, along the second-floor hallway, and down the main stairs to the parlour, which isn't blue anymore. After the war, they took down the decaying blue silk, patched the plaster underneath, and painted the room a sunny yellow. Everyone helped. It was quite a party. Constance still refers to it as the one and only day Alden ever wore pants.

Constance is "Aunt Constance" to Judith and to all the little ones in the house. Constance takes Judith to the amusement park or the movies. At the end of every summer, they go to the Exhibition. When Constance visits, she brings treats for any children who are in Patterson House, hard candies and licorice allsorts and humbugs like John used to keep. Then she has a cup of tea in the kitchen with Alden, just the two of them. Their private time. The women leave them alone to talk. Constance will urge Alden to get out of this place, as she always does. She'll say, "It's falling down around you." Alden will nod and say, "Don't worry, they'll take it from me any day now."

Her arm has been sore all day. She rolls her shoulder, takes her apron off, and says to Annie, "Do you mind if I go lie down?"

"I'll finish up, Miss Patterson." Half the women call her Miss Patterson and the other half call her Alden.

"Alden, please. Call me Alden."

"Yes." She tries it again. "Alden, do you want me to bring a cup of tea up?" Annie reaches for the kettle.

"No, thank you." Alden has everything she needs.

*

I lean on the slipper chair in Alden's room and watch over her while she sleeps. Alden's heart races and she is perspiring. She wakes, tries to rise, sees me, and her brow furrows.

"What are you doing here?"

"I'm not sure."

"Have you always been here?"

I nod.

And then she clutches her chest and is gone.

I expect something to happen. I watch, listen, wait. Nothing. Maybe she's not really dead.

"Alden?" There is no response.

There is so much I wanted to say to her.

The last Patterson is dead. My line is over.

I wait with her. What else is there to do?

In the morning, Annie taps on the door. When there is no answer, she says, "Alden?" and then with a little more concern, she knocks more firmly and says, "Miss Patterson?"

Reluctantly, she opens the door a crack, and then wider, walks to the bed and gasps.

October 15, 1954

"THIS IS WHERE you grew up? It's huge!"

Constance takes Corkie's hand and pulls her through the gate.

"Wait. It says, 'No trespassing.'"

"Who's going to do anything?" Honestly, sometimes Corkie's lack of spirit drives Constance crazy. "Do you think the police are waiting inside?"

The first floor is boarded up, but around the back, Constance pries loose the sheet of plywood covering the kitchen door and they slip into the darkness through the opening. The kitchen is a mess.

"Wow. Look at this place." Corkie tiptoes around the kitchen, leaving half-footprints in the dust. "Look at that fireplace! Did you actually use it for cooking?"

"No. By the time I was here, it was already sealed up."

In the foyer, Constance sees that there are stairs missing. The whole staircase looks poised to collapse. She tests the first stair.

"No way. You're not going up that. It's too dangerous," Corkie says.

They look up together. Constance sings, "*Old Man Patterson hangs from a rafter. Run by fast or he'll chase after.*"

"What?"

Constance laughs. "It's what the kids used to say about the house. About us."

"Huh," says Corkie. She looks at Constance, looks around again and says, "So you were rich." This is a joke between them. Corkie knows everything. But it has taken Constance this long to bring her to the Beach. To Patterson House.

Constance laughs. "Yes, that's me. Moneybags." Corkie wanders into what was the blue parlour and looks at the fireplace. "There used to be a portrait of William Patterson here. Alden threw a candlestick through it." Constance runs her hands along the edges of the shelves and wipes the dust off her hands.

It's not that Corkie looks bored, but she's not interested. "Let's get going." They are headed to a dance at Casa Loma tonight. The band is supposed to be cookin' as Corkie would say. Corkie loves to dance. They'll meet the boys at the entrance and arrive as couples. That's what they do. It's easy for two girls to dance together. Everyone knows Con and Corkie are practically inseparable. There's a joke that any man who wants to marry one of them will have to marry both. They share an apartment. Everyone thinks of them as old spinsters, finally giving up on the idea of marriage and saving by living together. They can think whatever they want.

"Come with me. I want to show you something in the garden."

Corkie complains, "In the rain?"

"It will just take a minute." Constance leads her through the kitchen door again, pops open their umbrella, and takes her into the garden. She clears some leaves off a stone with her foot. "His grave."

"Morbid," laughs Corkie.

"The portrait of him is in the garage. Do you want to see it?"

Corkie squeezes Constance's arm. "What is all this nostalgia? Come on. My hair is going to be ruined."

Constance reaches over and tucks a blonde curl behind her ear. "Not possible," she says.

*

A blue-black starling on the top branch of the tallest beech tree observes the two women in the garden, flits from branch to branch, and assesses the wind. As the sky darkens, it rises in flight. The rest of the flock rises with it, black against almost black, as though they are of one mind. They swirl, their murmuration carried on the wind.

It's not safe here. Everyone thinks the storm will fizzle out long before it crosses Lake Ontario. They could not be more wrong. Even the starlings know. How strange to realize how much I will miss it all, even them.

Constance came by earlier. She does that. Looks around. She comes into the house, always breaking in by the kitchen door. I'm not sure what she wants. Sometimes she speaks. Not to me. To herself. A sigh. "Oh, Alden," she'll say. Tonight she brought a friend. Showed her my grave. I wanted to tell her I'm not in there, show myself, speak to her. But no. Afterwards, they stood arm in arm on the sidewalk for a long time. She pointed at her old third-floor window. At me.

No one sighs for me.

Everyone goes on about their business, walking up and down the street, getting in and out of their noisy cars, and they make no preparations whatsoever for what is coming.

Soon enough, they will know.

The hurricane will destroy Patterson House and so much more. I wander from room to room and inspect my legacy for the last time. My portrait lies against a wall in the loft of the carriage house, forgotten, sideways and torn. The great William Patterson. Pfft. The truth was always right in front of anyone who cared to see. Look at how uncomfortable I am, how my shirt collar and tie chafe against my neck. Not a generation away from the farm, I was never at ease in society. The furrow between my brows reveals hesitation, not fearlessness. I was an imposter.

I called myself a self-made man, but a self-made man is merely a man who made himself up. My people are Irish, not English. They worked themselves to early deaths, day by day and season by season, portioning out the potatoes through the winter, eating only enough to survive and never enough to be full. They died in the Hunger, half-naked and filthy, and if I had not talked my way onto a ship in the place of another, I would have ended my days the same as my parents': wretched and starving.

I never said goodbye. Ma would have searched for me. I'm sure she thought I was dead. Lost in a peat bog, maybe. Why have I never thought about her again until now?

Boards cover broken windows on the first floor. Yet vagrants break in and find a corner to inhabit, start fires, are turned out by policemen, charged with trespassing and given fines they have no means to pay. Lawyers and bureaucrats argue over the disposition of my land while those with the real money sit back and salivate. There will be an apartment building, row houses, six smaller homes, something. A fortune will be made here. But there are delays. Busybodies from the historical society. Everyone wants a say in what happens to what I built.

I wouldn't have minded it going to the girl. She has always been steadfast. But the City took it for back taxes and the girl doesn't want it anyway. She knows it will weigh her down like it did Alden.

Meanwhile, bats hang in the attic, mice multiply in the walls, cockroaches skitter in the pipes. Water darkens the plaster ceilings, runs along joists, finds the fastest way to the lowest corner of the cellar and, from there, runs through the foundation to the swollen underground streams that flow to the lake.

In life, I told anyone who would listen that when a man's imagination is captured by land, he must act on it. Land can be a calling greater than politics or nation, and one more pure. With the right land, a man can be something.

Balderdash and blather.

What did I know? Nothing. Nothing at all.

In the end, we are all tenants. Eviction is inevitable.

The culverts are full to bursting. The temperature drops. Rain falls in sheets and bounces from the hard surface of the street not once, but twice. Puddles grow bigger. The marsh cannot be held back forever.

Patterson's Folly indeed. I created land where none had been before. But what I built was as temporary as my own life.

A crack of lightning brightens the sky over the lake and forks like branches of an upside-down oak.

In the Ottawa Valley, I cut white pine with trunks so wide that seven men with hands clasped could not get their arms around them. Every tree a cathedral—the work of centuries and felled in less than a day. There will never be others like them.

I remember the day I first saw this land, in the wind atop the bluffs, Lake Ontario shimmering beneath. Oh, if only I could reach down and pop a wild strawberry into my mouth or pinch a buttercup and drink the nectar. I would give anything.

The place teemed with life. Passenger pigeons migrated in flocks so great they eclipsed the sun. Millions of birds. Not one is left.

But still, there is this silvery ocean of freshwater. How I would love to cup my hands and drink from it.

Oh! The world is beautiful, and I was a fool.

A whole life—and afterlife—isn't that long after all. Not long enough to sort things out, not long enough to get a second chance.

I once stripped naked at the shore of the lake and dove into the cool water, escaping the mosquitos and the biting flies. I floated on my back until the blue of the water and sky were one. If only I could float like that again, everything a part of me and me a part of everything. A great egret, its long, graceful neck rising in the reeds by the shore, its white feathers bright against the foliage, took flight and I flew with him above the sumac and bulrushes and swooped over the slope where Patterson House now stands. That is how it all started. I wanted to live in that beauty forever. It had been that simple. I forgot.

The wind gusts higher, heavier, fuller. A canvas lawn chair flies in the wind, is carried upwards, and becomes entangled in the treetops. The beeches complain of the weight of their own branches. The fence tears from the border of the yard like a page from a child's exercise book. The pickets slam into the house. Glass breaks.

The saturated ground gives way and the house sinks on the south side, groaning with the strain. The streams burst the culverts and find their old paths. Patterson House is in the way. More shingles fly from the roof and one slices open the back leg of a panicked German shepherd running in the street, yelping in terror.

When the first beech tree falls on the house, it splits the roof open. I look up through the branches into the black sky and howl.

AUTHOR'S NOTE

Historical events and persons anchor *Patterson House* in time and place and, I hope, lend the story authenticity. However, my use of them crosses over into fiction. This means that *Patterson House*, while historical, is not an accurate historical record. Real people from history enter the narrative, but their lives and thoughts and actions are fictionalized. The Patterson family is entirely fictional, as is the house. Early readers of draft manuscripts have suggested they know where Patterson House is or was. No such house actually existed. It is based on many houses of the time, including but not limited to Spadina House in Toronto and 83 Beals Street, the birthplace of John F. Kennedy, in Brookline, Massachusetts. Both houses are open to the public, and I am grateful to the guides who patiently answered very specific questions about everything from clocks to wallpaper to gardens. In addition to knowledgeable tour guides, I am also indebted to the many librarians, curators, and archivists I have encountered during my research. Their work is so important and their salaries should be much higher and there should be a holiday that honours them, one that includes a parade. I am particularly grateful to John Clarke at CMHA in Toronto and Darlene Warren at the Military Museums of Calgary, Alberta.

My use of the Beach (singular) will irritate some Torontonians who will insist the correct usage is the Beaches. Usage has changed over time. My grandparents and parents lived in the Beach and always called it the Beach. I usually call it the Beach. A case can be made for calling it the Beach when referring to the past but the Beaches when referring to the present, as that is how it is generally known now. You can argue amongst yourselves.

ACKNOWLEDGEMENTS

In the almost twenty years since I first had ideas about this story, I have started over at least three times. Sometimes, I set the story aside for years. Each time I have picked it up again, it has been with the encouragement of excellent writers. Some of you I know personally, and others I know only through your work. Thank you for teaching me through your example.

Thank you to everyone who has helped in my recovery from a traumatic brain injury in 2016. At the time, I was almost finished this novel. Without your help, I could not have completed it.

My first writing group, organized by Inge Bremer-Trueman, kept me going as a writer. Thank you to the many members of that group. I have taken many writing courses and thank all of my teachers and fellow writing students. I have a special place in my heart for Joan Clark, who told me in no uncertain terms that I could write this novel. It was her voice I heard in my head when I doubted myself. I also wish to thank the students and mentors at the Solstice MFA in Creative Writing Program, now part of Lasell University, especially Sandra Scofield.

Many other people, too many to name, have read and offered feedback on the manuscript while it was in progress. Thank you to all of my readers, especially Julie Bain.

I also thank Elaine Morin, Rea Tarvydas, Shaun Hunter, Rona Altrows, Kim Suhr, and Sharon Butala for inspiration, encouragement, and writerly companionship over the years. Kimmy Beach and Karen Taylor made the manuscript better with their careful and expert editing. I am also grateful to everyone at Inanna, especially the late Luciana Ricciutelli.

My greatest thanks go to Rob and Kate, who have been with me through life, the book and everything. You really are the best.

Credit: R. Lunney

Jane Cawthorne writes about women in moments of crises and transformation. Her short stories and essays have appeared in newspapers, magazines, literary journals, scholarly journals, and anthologies. She has edited two anthologies with E.D. Morin, *Impact: Women Writing After Concussion* and *Writing Menopause*. Her first novel, *Patterson House*, is set in Toronto, her birthplace, and a city dear to her even when she lives elsewhere. Jane spent decades active in the pro-choice and reproductive justice movement and is a former Women's Studies instructor, as well as a former high school and middle school teacher. Her play *The Abortion Monologues* has been produced many times in Canada and the US and was once performed at the University of Texas/Brownsville as part of a Ford Foundation funded "Difficult Dialogues" initiative. She has an M.Ed. from OISE and an MFA in Creative Writing from the Solstice Program in Boston, MA. She lives in Victoria, BC. www.janecawthorne.com